NAMELESS

Praise for **TRACELESS**

"Skillfully managing a big cast, Webb keeps the suspense teasingly taut, dropping clues and red herrings one after another on her way to a chilling conclusion."

—*Publishers Weekly*

"*Traceless* is a riveting entanglement of intrigue, secrets, and passions that had me racing to its breathless end. I loved this book!"

—Karen Rose,
New York Times bestselling author of *Count to Ten*

"*Traceless* is a well-crafted and engrossing thriller. Debra Webb has crafted a fine, twisting thriller to be savored and enjoyed."

—Heather Graham,
New York Times bestselling author of *The Island*

Also by Debra Webb

TRACELESS

Available from St. Martin's Paperbacks

NAMELESS

Debra Webb

St. Martin's Paperbacks

This is a work of fiction. All of the characters, organizations and events portrayed in this novel are either products of the author's imagination or are used fictitiously.

NAMELESS

Copyright © 2008 by Debra Webb.
Excerpt from *Faceless* copyright © 2008 by Debra Webb.

Cover photo of woman © Herman Estevez.
Cover photo of city © Digital Vision/Getty Images.

ISBN: 0-312-94223-0
EAN: 978-0-312-94223-6

Printed in the United States of America

St. Martin's Paperbacks edition / February 2008

St. Martin's Paperbacks are published by St. Martin's Press, 175 Fifth Avenue, New York, NY 10010.

10 9 8 7 6 5 4 3 2 1

DEDICATION

Once in a great while, a young man comes along who epitomizes all that is right and good in this world. A young man whose compassion and love of others is given so freely that you are each day astounded that a mere human could be so caring and selfless. A young man who, despite his own imperfections, sees the good and beauty in all. A young man whose respect for others, whose enthusiasm for life, touched all who experienced the blessing of knowing him or simply meeting him. Jonathan Miles Christian was such a young man. In his short time on earth he touched more lives than most do in an entire lifetime. He is so very sorely missed. The impact he made, however, goes on. Jonathan, we love you and you will forever live in our hearts.

ACKNOWLEDGMENTS

The Federal Bureau of Investigation has one mission, only one: to protect. We often don't appreciate all that the FBI does to that end. Our only insight is what we see and hear in the media. Far too often we take for granted the sacrifice that the men and women in law enforcement and the military make. I wanted to take this opportunity to thank those men and women for protecting what we hold dear. Every single American is indebted to every single one of you for carrying out your mission every single day despite the personal cost.

There are people in my life who allow me the privilege of doing what I love: writing my stories. I would like to thank my family and friends for their endless support. I simply could not do this without all of you. In particular I need to thank Vicki Hinze for her amazing and twisted mind. Mike Cooper for being the coolest friend and attorney on the planet. Candice Thies for being a wonderful friend and a superwoman CPA. CJ Lyons and Kim Howe for their encouragement and friendship. I love all you guys!

Special thanks to all the folks at St. Martin's Press,

particularly Jennifer Weis, Matthew Shear, and Hilary Teeman, for their support and encouragement. Jennifer, Hilary, and my super fantastic agent, Stephanie Rostan, help me make these stories the best they can be. Thank you. This is what I love and I feel honored to work with all of you.

NAMELESS

CHAPTER ONE

Waking up dead would have been preferable to waking up with this screaming throb inside his skull.

Ryan McBride cracked open his eyes and blinked to focus. Morning light barged into his bedroom through the slits in the blinds. "Damn." He licked his lips and swallowed back the shitty taste in his mouth.

A few seconds passed before he dared to sit up, and still he regretted the move. He reached for his half-empty pack of Marlboros and parked a cigarette in one corner of his mouth then lit it. Gratefully inhaling the noxious chemicals necessary for tolerating his continued existence, he stifled a coughing jag.

Die, you son of a bitch. Cigarettes were doing their part. The irony was if he'd given one damn about living, he'd be dead by now.

He got up, waited for the room to stop spinning before taking a step. A muffled sigh drew his bleary gaze back to the bed. He scratched his bare chest. Who was the redhead tangled in his sheets? With effort he vaguely recalled picking her up at the club. Barbie or Becky. Something like that.

Maybe he'd think of her name later. Right now he had to

take a major piss. He ambled into the bathroom wishing he hadn't consumed enough alcohol to totally erase his memory, since he couldn't recall bringing anyone home—not even himself. Just one of the many bad habits he'd acquired since moving to the Keys. A hazard of the job. Mingling, blending in. Then again, if he drank enough he slept like the dead and he didn't have to worry about dreaming.

Even the thought of the dreams that haunted his sober nights made his gut clench. His hand shook as he took another drag from his cigarette. Blocking the nightmares required the drinking that resulted in mornings like this.

Considering his downward spiral during the three years since his career at the Bureau abruptly ended, he had decided that, in his case, FBI stood for Fucking Bad Idea. It was a shame it had taken him ten years of active duty to realize that. Just in time to be fired by the biggest prick carrying a badge.

There were some things a man just couldn't get past.

Ryan McBride, this is your life.

What a monumental waste of air space.

More of that damned battering at his skull had him closing his eyes and trying hard to calm the assault between his temples.

Wait a minute.

He struggled to focus enough brainpower to isolate a source.

The pounding wasn't in his head . . . it was at his front door.

He tossed the butt of his cigarette into the toilet then flushed it. Moving slowly to maintain his equilibrium, he followed the trail of abandoned clothing across the bedroom and along the length of the hall. He gave up on finding his boxers but managed to locate his jeans just in time for more of that confounded banging. Dragging them on, he stumbled toward the door, wrenched it open, and glared at the person waiting on the other side.

Female.

Her perfume's subtle fragrance resuscitated his sluggish senses. The tailored navy suit, buttoned-to-the-throat white blouse, and rigid posture told him two things right off the bat: professional and uptight.

"Ryan McBride?"

She knew his name. That couldn't be good.

He sagged against the doorjamb, exhausted from the effort of surviving a category IV drunk, and measured his visitor with an assessing look. Dark brown hair cinched in a French twist. Oh yeah, definitely uptight. Wide brown eyes lacking any sign of weariness or cynicism and devoid of the slightest hint of crow's-feet. Young, early twenties maybe. Despite the inexperience her age gave away, her determined bearing told him she'd come prepared for battle. The idea stirred his curiosity even as he reminded himself that her appearance at his door had to mean trouble.

"Are you Ryan McBride?" she repeated firmly, drawing his full interest to her mouth.

Nice lips. Voluptuous, pillowy. Made him think of hot, raunchy sex.

"Depends on who's asking." He'd spent all that time checking her out and she hadn't once allowed her attention to stray from his eyes. Talk about discipline. Uptight *and* a control freak.

As if she'd read his mind, she squared her shoulders and drew in an impatient breath. The movement accentuated the slight bulge beneath her jacket he hadn't noticed before. On the left of her torso just above her waist.

Well, well. The lady was a cop.

What the hell else did he *not* remember about last night?

"I'm Special Agent Vivian Grace. I need to speak with you on an urgent matter. May I come inside?"

A fed. Perfect. Before he could come up with some profound statement that would clarify his position on what the

Bureau could do with their need to talk or anything else, a sultry, feminine voice called out from behind him, "Who's at the door, baby?"

The redhead he'd left in his bed, dressed in slut-tight jeans and a hoochie-mama blouse, appeared next to him. She smiled for the agent, whose disapproval was written all over her lovely, prim face.

"I can come back in half an hour," Agent Grace offered crisply.

"Don't trouble yourself, honey." The redhead leaned in and kissed his stubbled jaw. "I gotta go anyway." She dragged her French-manicured fingers down his bare chest as she backed out the door, forcing the agent to step aside. "Call me, baby."

He watched her strut off toward the yellow Mustang parked next to his aging Land Rover, purse and strappy sandals dangling from her hands. The wicked sway of her hips jogged his memory as to why he'd picked her out of the crowd last night.

Bonnie? Betty? He didn't have a clue.

McBride straightened away from the jamb. "I need a smoke." He left Grace standing at the door and went in search of his cigarettes. For about three seconds he contemplated calling Quantico and asking what the hell they meant sending some baby agent-in-training down here to harass him.

Vivian Grace couldn't be more than twenty-four, twenty-five tops. Probably hadn't even finished her in-service probationary period. He flicked his lighter, sucked hard, and held the smoke deep in his lungs, mulling over what she'd said. What the hell urgent matter could the Bureau need to discuss with him? Had one of his old cases gone active again? That was doubtful. Every damned case he'd worked was closed with the perp or perps serving time or dead and the victim recovered safely.

Except one.

Pushing the memory aside, he decided there was only one way to find out why she was here. He wandered back to where he'd left her. She hadn't moved. The good little agent doing her sworn duty, braced and ready for battle.

If this was going to be complicated, he needed a little bracing of his own. "I won't be any good to either of us until I've had coffee," he warned.

She didn't object so he headed for the kitchen. If she wanted to continue with whatever she had to say she would follow. The front door creaked closed and her heels clacked on the hardwood.

Persistent, he liked that in a woman.

He scooped the grounds into the basket, added the water and flipped the switch. The smell of fresh-brewed coffee instantly began to fill the air, signaling relief was on the way.

After a final drag, he smashed the cigarette into an ashtray and returned his attention to his uninvited guest, who lingered the entire expanse of tiled floor away. "What do they want?"

"A six-year-old girl is missing and—"

"Welcome to the real world, Agent," he cut her off, an abrupt blast of fury churning his gut. What the hell kind of con was the Bureau running on him? "Kids go missing every hour of every day. Your esteemed employer has an entire unit dedicated to finding them. Unless you have reason to suspect I had something to do with the abduction, I can't fathom what you want from me."

The bastards fired him, then they had the balls to come running when they hit a case that confounded their elite unit? *Three freaking years later?* And he's supposed to help them out? No. Fucking. Way.

He didn't owe the FBI squat.

Though his reaction clearly startled her, his visitor wasn't ready to give up. Her chin tilted in challenge, she ventured two steps farther into the room, in his direction. The movement momentarily lured his gaze to the shapely calves revealed by her knee-length skirt. Great legs. Probably ran five at the crack of dawn every morning. Well, she could just turn her sweet little ass right around and run back to where she'd come from. He wasn't in the mood to play whatever the hell kind of game the Bureau had in mind.

"I know your story, McBride. There isn't an agent alive who hasn't heard about the legendary Ryan McBride. That's why I've come to you."

Oh yeah, the *legend*. Another memory he'd drowned with booze.

"I hate to be the one to tell you, but that legend died three years ago, Agent Grace." He reached for a cup, looked to her for any indication she was interested. She shook her head so he filled his own and kicked back a couple slugs of the hot brew. With enough caffeine tainting his veins, he might just reach the point of caring whether or not he survived the day.

"We need your help." Outright desperation flashed in her dark eyes. "You were the best the Bureau has ever had. It's going to take you to save this little girl."

Now there was a seriously *unoriginal* line of bull. He refused to think about the child. This wasn't his case, wasn't his problem. And yet he felt the tension rising, the coiling of emotions he couldn't hope to contain threatening to strangle him. He plunked his cup down on the counter. He didn't need this shit.

"Maybe you didn't pay attention to the last chapter of my story, Agent Grace," he countered, his voice taut with a bitterness he'd tried long and hard, and evidently unsuccessfully, to bury. "They fired me. It got ugly. There's no going back."

"I read the file on your last case," she confirmed. "I'm certain you made the only decision you could based on the facts available to you. Sometimes failure is unavoidable and someone dies. That's the flip side to what we do."

He had to laugh at that. "Deep, Agent," he said, patronizing her. "Do you think that matters? Dead is dead."

"Maybe not to you, but to those of us who admire what you accomplished during your career, it matters."

"Tell that to the kid's father." He turned his back to her, braced against the counter and squeezed his eyes shut in a futile attempt to block the images tumbling one over the other through his head. He couldn't do *this*.

"We don't have the luxury of time, McBride." Apparently bolstered by a blast of latent courage, she moved in right beside him as she spoke. As hard as he tried not to react, he tensed. "We have less than twenty-three hours. If we don't find her before then, Alyssa Byrne will die."

Alyssa. The name reverberated through him. He banished it. Couldn't help her. He'd given the Bureau everything he had for ten years. He'd maintained a perfect record. Never failed. Except that once. And the mistake hadn't been his. When the proverbial shit had hit the fan, the Bureau had refused to take the heat. They had needed a scapegoat and he'd been it. A decade of hard work hadn't made a difference any more than his so-called legendary status. Case in point. For nearly a year afterward, he'd actually expected someone to show up and beg him to return to duty.

No one had shown up. No one had even called.

So he had found other ways to spend his time and fill the void left by the part of his life ripped away from him. He blamed the booze on his current on-again-off-again occupation, but that was just an excuse. The ugly truth was that every time an Amber Alert had been issued he had turned to the one consistent thing within reach to help him forget that he wouldn't be there—distraction. With enough distraction, he could forget that he no longer made a difference.

That part of his life was over. There wasn't any going back . . . not for Agent Vivian Grace and all her hero worship . . . not for Alyssa Byrne and the people who loved her.

Truth was, even if he wanted to go back, he wasn't that man anymore. The pressure of working that kind of case was immeasurable. If he lost his focus, fucked up, someone died. If he wasn't fast enough, smart enough, someone died. He no longer had that kind of nerve, the edge it took to get the job done. The hero he used to be was long gone. Pretending otherwise would be a mistake. The kind he didn't want to make twice in one lifetime.

Nowadays he was just your plain old garden-variety coward.

Before he sent the agent on her way, there was one thing he had to know. "Why now?" He couldn't keep the resentment out of his tone; didn't really try. "In three years the Bureau hasn't once acknowledged that I still exist. What makes this case different?"

She searched his eyes, her own still hopeful that he would change his mind. *Not going to happen.*

"The kidnapper," she explained, her voice somber, "asked for you by name. He claims he'll provide clues to facilitate the search for the girl."

That damned headache started bearing down on him again, hammering at his temples. "What kind of clues?"

"Don't know. No you, no clues." She swallowed hard, the effort visible along the length of her slender neck. "No clues, McBride, and the little girl dies."

CHAPTER TWO

She had one shot. She couldn't screw it up.

Vivian Grace held McBride's icy blue stare without flinching. If he said no, she had failed. She couldn't go back to Birmingham without him. Too much was riding on his cooperation. For starters, a child's life. Getting the bastard, officially designated as the unknown subject or unsub, who had done this ranked a close second.

"How did the unsub communicate?" McBride asked grudgingly.

Relief trickled inside her. At least she had his attention now. That was a step in the right direction. She reminded herself to breathe.

"There was an e-mail at six last evening. Alyssa had been missing for ten hours at that point. Since she never made it to her classroom yesterday morning, we have to assume he picked her up somewhere at school immediately after her mother dropped her off. The e-mail informed us that she was in his custody and that she was safe. He gave us the time constraint and one instruction: that he would only deal with you."

At this point, there were details she couldn't share with

McBride. Her supervisor, Special Agent-in-Charge, SAC, Randall Worth, had instructed her to provide the minimum amount of information possible to get McBride on board. Not that they had that much. They didn't. Irrespective of that less-than-optimal situation, until McBride could be completely ruled out as a potential suspect, he had to be handled as one.

But Worth was wrong. McBride wasn't involved. If she'd had any doubts, finding him in bed with a friend at this hour of the day and obviously hungover had discredited most of those reservations. The flicker of pain and the surprise in his eyes on hearing about the child and the promised clues diminished the rest.

Then there was the matter of his overall appearance. McBride basically looked like hell. Nothing like the man depicted in the legendary stories of the Hunter, the last of the true bloodhounds, she had heard whispered about at the academy. The theory that he had plotted a kidnapping to draw attention to himself or to get back at the Bureau was hogwash. The man she was looking at right now was pretty much a disaster that had already happened. He wasn't planning anything except his next smoke, drink, and twist in the sheets.

"He provided proof of life?"

McBride's question interrupted her from her ruminations. Allowing her attention to drift like that was a strategic error she couldn't risk repeating in his presence. As far down skid row as it appeared he had gone, she had a feeling that beneath that hangover and I-don't-give-a-shit attitude, he was still damned sharp at drawing conclusions.

"Yes," she told him. "The e-mail included a photo."

He moved around her to help himself to another cup of coffee as if they had all the time in the world.

Anxiety and anticipation tightened her chest, making every beat of her heart an unnatural effort. Each second seemed an eternity. Each minute that got away from her was one she couldn't get back, one that might prove pivotal as this case played out. Standing around here wasting those precious moments had her tension mounting at breakneck speed.

To make matters worse, standing this close to McBride, she found it impossible not to inhale his scent—a mixture of man, heat, and his many vices. He seemed taller than the six one his personnel file had listed. Definitely leaner than the one ninety he'd weighed according to those stats. The instant he opened the door, he had put her off balance. Scarcely dressed . . . all that naked skin culminating in the fuck-me vee exposed by his unfastened jeans.

She had arrived prepared for his bitterness and underlying anger. Like he said, the way his career ended had been ugly, and very public. But none of her preparation had readied her for his blatant sexuality. He had been handsome before, but this edgy, primitive version of that man had her scrambling to regain her usual poise.

The angles of his face were more distinct than in the photos she'd seen, as if time and living a life of debauchery since leaving the Bureau had chiseled them so. A couple of days' beard growth accentuated those distracting changes. The whole package was very disconcerting.

"No luck tracing the IP?" he asked when he had made some headway on his second cup of coffee.

"None," she admitted. That was one of the few things they did know already, the unsub was smart. "This one knows how to erase his cyber footprints better than most."

"Sounds like you don't have much considering you're beyond the twenty-four-hour mark." He turned his head, stared directly at her. "That's bad, Agent."

"That's why I'm here." She held his gaze, understanding on some level that he used this probing intimacy as an intimidation technique rather than as the crude invitation he would have her believe. "We need you."

He set his cup aside. His hand shook and he immediately fisted it to halt the visible reaction to his apparent overindulgence in self-abuse. According to his psych evaluation, he hadn't been a drinker or a smoker during his time with the Bureau. This raw, uncut demeanor gave the definite impression that the crash of his career had taken a significant toll. His brown hair was longer, shaggier, as if he hadn't visited a barber in quite some time and didn't care. The Florida sun had streaked it with gold. His current occupation, when he bothered to show up, was acting as a spotter at a local nightspot. He mingled in the crowd, watched for trouble, giving security a heads-up as necessary. From the look of things, he mingled a little too much.

Whatever McBride's demons and addictions, the only thing she cared about was obtaining his cooperation. This was her first opportunity to play a principal part in a high-profile case. The only way she was going to get Worth's respect, or that of any of her colleagues, was to prove herself in the field. She had to make this happen. They needed to know she could do it. *She* needed to know she could do it.

Challenging Worth's decision on not bringing in McBride was a step in that direction even if it risked her career. Call it instinct, woman's intuition, whatever, but she had a feeling that McBride was the only one who had a snowball's chance in hell of stopping this unsub even if they did finagle the clues out of him.

Now if she could only get McBride to comprehend the urgency. Time was running out for Alyssa Byrne.

When he'd downed the last of his coffee, he lit a cigarette, blew out a lungful of smoke, and finally broke his silence. "Since I was personally invited to this soiree, did anyone take a look at who might have a hard-on for putting a bullet in my brain?"

The scent of seared tobacco invaded her senses, the knowledge that it had come from his lips irrationally disturbing. She resisted the urge to squirm.

"We understand that's a possibility. As you know, at the moment, our primary focus is rescuing the child." The theory that the unsub was attempting to lure McBride out of exile was still under consideration, along with the idea that the legend himself was somehow behind the kidnapping. She was not authorized to share that part with him at this point. "Of course we'll do all within our power to ensure you're protected."

McBride tossed her a look that said exactly how much stock he had in that promise, then he started to pace. He forked the fingers of his free hand through his sleep-tousled hair; let the cigarette dangle from the other. "If . . ." He stopped abruptly, trapped her in the crosshairs of his full attention. "*If* I agree to do this, I'll be lead on the case. I won't be taking any orders from your SAC or any-damned-body else, including you. Is that clear?"

That authority wasn't hers to give . . . but she couldn't afford to let him see her hesitate. "I'm certain that can be arranged."

He walked toward her, those blue eyes cutting straight through her like the laser-driven scope of a high-powered rifle. "You don't have the authority to make that guarantee, do you?" He didn't stop until he stood toe-to-toe with her. *"Do you?"*

"I'm certain," she reiterated, not about to let him see her sweat, "that every effort will be made to accommodate you. Your cooperation isn't optional; the unsub requires it." Somehow she managed to hold that intimidating gaze. "I must stress again how little time we have. The sooner we get started, the better our chance of success."

"Make the call." He tossed the butt of his cigarette into the sink without shifting his piercing glare one centimeter. "Confirm that condition and I'll consider your request."

At least he hadn't said no. She reached for the cell phone clipped to the waistband of her skirt. That he'd crowded into her personal space, pinned her against the counter, had jolted her pulse rate into a faster rhythm. As much as she needed his cooperation, she wasn't standing for his physical intimidation tactics any longer. If she didn't get some boundaries in place soon, this situation was only going to fly further out of control. That was a risk she couldn't take. "You're crowding me, McBride."

For a couple of seconds, then ten, she was certain he wouldn't back off. To her immense relief he relented, if only one step, giving her room to breathe.

She put through the call. Worth had been waiting to hear from her. He let her know that up front. She bit her tongue to hold back the argument that she wouldn't even be here were it not for Alyssa Byrne's father. When more than eighteen hours had passed without any measurable progress, Byrne had insisted on McBride's inclusion on the case. Worth had balked, just as he had earlier when Vivian suggested the same, and Byrne had reached out to his political allies, overriding any possible excuse the special agent-in-charge could hope to toss out.

"He needs an assurance that he'll be in charge of the case," she told the SAC without preamble. She barely managed not to flinch at his bellowed answer.

"Tell him that condition is nonnegotiable," McBride interjected as if he'd heard every single word of the response. The way Worth had yelled, it was possible he had.

"This condition is nonnegotiable," she passed along before endeavoring to moisten her dry lips. Didn't work, considering her throat was as parched as an Alabama creek bed in August. Worth gave her all the reasons that McBride's proposal was completely out of the question then he told her what she needed to hear. *Promise him whatever you have to, but get his butt up here.*

"Thank you, sir." She severed the connection and tucked the phone back into its holster. "You'll be in charge."

McBride's eyes tapered with suspicion. "That easy, huh?"

She refused to allow him to bully her. "You have my word."

He laughed, one of those soft sounds that lacked any glimmer of amusement and reeked of arrogance. "I hate to tell you this, Agent Grace, but I find that less than reassuring. You see, I know a rookie when I meet one." He reclaimed that step he had surrendered, leaned close enough to plant his hands on the counter on either side of her. "*You* can't guarantee me shit."

She fought the trepidation tugging at her composure. No more beating around the bush. "We're wasting time. You're either going or you aren't. If you want to help that little girl, then I would suggest that you get dressed so we can get this done. Otherwise," she added, her temper temporarily overriding her good sense, "get out of my way. I don't have time for the macho methods you evidently consider charming."

He didn't move. The fear that she had pushed too hard—that she couldn't handle this man—welled . . . clawed at her, but she kicked it back, refused to submit to it. She wasn't about to let him see that he could get to her so effortlessly. If she gave him that inch, he would take a mile she didn't have to spare. She might lack his experience, but she was the one with the badge. And the gun.

His haughty gaze dropped to her mouth. "I gotta tell you, Grace, you got some great lips."

Enough. She flattened her right hand against his chest, pulled her lapel aside with her left, leaving her weapon in plain sight. "Back off."

One corner of his mouth tilted shamelessly, but he straightened away from her, his hands lifted in mock surrender. "No need to get testy." He dropped his arms back to his sides and all signs of any amusement or smugness vanished. "What kind of transportation do we have?"

The sudden turnabout had her grappling. She reached for calm, couldn't find it handy, so she settled for quietly furious. "Private plane. It's waiting at the airport in Marathon."

Surprise lifted his brows. "Well, that's traveling in style."

"Mr. Byrne insisted, considering the time crunch. The Learjet belongs to him not to the Bureau."

McBride considered her a moment, stretching her patience to the limit, then said, "I'll need to shower first."

He was going.

The overwhelming sense of relief was almost more than she could hold inside. She shored up her professional deportment by hanging on to a little of that fury he'd ignited. "Make it fast. Our time is limited."

He acknowledged her order with a nod and walked away.

She wanted to kick herself for watching. For admiring the way his jeans gloved his lean hips. That he got to her on that level was not only infuriating but startling. No one ever got to her that way.

As if he had felt her gaze on him, he hesitated, turned back once more. "Just so you know, Grace, I'm doing this for the kid. Not for you. And definitely not for the Bureau."

He swaggered off, leaving Vivian struggling with emotions she couldn't begin to label—she was grateful for that small mercy. It was better not to know.

Keeping former Special Agent Ryan McBride under control wasn't going to be an easy task. The man he had become was far more than a loose cannon.

He was dangerous.

CHAPTER THREE

Three floors. Bulletproof, sound-insulated tinted windows. Without a doubt, state-of-the-art security. Metal detectors, X-ray machines, maybe even facial and retinal scans. Gaining entrance to the building was more complicated than getting past the most stringent security measures at any of the nation's international airports. Accessing the damned parking lot wasn't even permitted without authorization.

Welcome to today's FBI.

McBride moved his head slowly from side to side. What the hell was he doing here?

Temporary insanity.

No more tequila for him. Better to stick with the devil he knew.

As Agent Grace's silver Explorer came to a necessary stop at the gate, he scanned the block. An iron fence contained the entire area, including the guard station. Though downtown, the location was somewhat isolated, giving the impression of a small upscale prison. He imagined some

of the agents inside felt that way from time to time whether
or not they said so.

So this was where Vivian Grace worked. During his decade with Quantico he'd never had the occasion to consult
with any of the Alabama offices. He turned his attention
to her as she flashed her credentials for the guard, who
promptly opened the gate allowing her to enter the sacred
compound. Even in profile those lips were something special. Seemed wasted on such an uptight chick.

A strand of glossy brown hair had slipped loose and
draped against her cheek. His fingers twitched at the idea
of touching that smooth skin. Grace had the kind of pale
complexion that would age well, with those high cheek-
bones a woman either had to be born with or envied her
whole life. Too bad she was one of *them.*

She jammed on the brake hard enough to engage the
lock on his safety belt. "Do you have a question,
McBride?" The glare she aimed at him provided a major
clue to just how pissed off she was.

Busted.

"Just one." He met that furious glower with unrestrained curiosity. "Do you have a problem with men in
general, or is it just me?"

She pointed her fury forward, rolled into a parking slot,
and shoved the gear shift into park without so much as a
kiss-my-ass. He would take that as a "no comment."

The lady had a hang-up about her looks or about men
looking at her; the question was, why? Was she really an ice
princess or was the attitude a defense mechanism? Maybe
the boys in the office gave her a hard time. He could definitely see her working more diligently than the rest to gar-
ner the respect she deserved. Hey, maybe that was the
reason she'd ended up with this low-man-on-the-totem-
pole transport job. Her SAC probably figured that sending
her versus one of the guys would prove a better incentive
for cooperation.

McBride couldn't deny he was curious about the lady, but like he had told her, he was here for one reason. To help the kid. Admiring Grace's numerous physical assets and giving her a hard time was just something to pass the time.

He opened the door and climbed out of the SUV. The hellacious headache was gone thanks to Grace, who had insisted on hitting a fast food drive-through before going to the airfield in Marathon. At the time he could have cared less about eating, but now he was glad he had. Between the food, a handful of aspirin, and a nap on the plane he felt remotely human. But the tension contorting deep in his gut right now wasn't going to be relieved so easily.

What he really needed was a drink, but that wasn't happening for the next nineteen or twenty hours. A smoke would have to do.

He pulled out the pack, tamped loose a Marlboro, then dipped two fingers into the pocket of his jeans and fished out his Zippo. Lighting up, he inhaled the comforting nicotine, instantly relaxing a fraction. The dozen or so vehicles he counted in the lot told him that most of the staff was still on duty. A field office this size wouldn't likely employ any more than that.

"Looks like your colleagues are all on hand for your big coup." He felt a little like the trophy African buffalo at the end of a safari. What was the prize, he wondered, for bringing in the beast? *Respect or sympathy?*

Grace stepped out of the smoke's path, her nose wrinkled with distaste. "As certain as I am that everyone here is anxious to have your assistance and will be honored by your presence, no one's going home until Alyssa Byrne is found. Standard procedure. I'm sure you haven't forgotten how things are done."

She just doesn't know how far I've fallen. He stared at the entrance, his tension spiraling out of control way too fast. From day one of his Bureau career he had been assigned to the Child Abduction Unit at Quantico. He'd been damned good. The best, as Grace said. But that was a long time ago. He had forgotten more about this business than most people ever hoped to know. And why wouldn't he forget? He had stopped expecting to get called in on a case two years ago.

If he closed his eyes and concentrated, he could still see the face of each child for every Amber Alert issued that first year following his termination. After that he had stopped watching or listening to the news. Eventually, when he had learned just how much Jack Daniel's was required to get the job done, he'd passed the point of caring.

Yet, here he was. *Definitely a case of temporary insanity.* A trip over the edge that he was sure to regret.

He was here for the kid, he reminded that cynical voice nagging at him. One final drag from his cigarette, then he flicked away the fire and shoved the snuffed-out butt into his pocket. "Before we go in, I need one thing from you, Grace."

Even though there had been time on the plane, they hadn't discussed the logistics of how this would work. He had taken a seat and had promptly closed his eyes for some much needed sleep. When he had awakened, Grace had been dead to the world. Probably the first shut-eye she'd had in more than twenty-four hours. He remembered how it was.

"What's that?" The grim set of that gorgeous mouth warned that she was suspicious of anything he might ask.

"Whatever goes down . . . no matter what your SAC says, or what you think of me, you back me up. If I can't count on at least your cooperation, I'm outta here. Do we have an understanding?"

The slight flare of those wide brown eyes told him he had hit a nerve, saddled her with a heart thumper. Going up against her SAC wouldn't look good on a performance evaluation, but he wasn't backing off on this one. This was every man for himself and he wasn't going in there without at least one ally.

"We have an agreement," she conceded, "as long as backing you up doesn't jeopardize rescuing Alyssa."

That was a condition he could live with. He indulged in one last, lingering survey of his new partner. "Good," he said just as anger, motivated by his flagrant ogling, sparked in her eyes. "Let's do this thing."

She led the way into the lobby.

Sprawled across the marble floor was the FBI emblem found in all Bureau offices. The same emblem that had once inspired great pride in him. Now on seeing it the only thing he felt was animosity.

"Afternoon, Agent Grace." The security guard, Charles Williams according to his nametag, set two plastic containers on the counter. "You know the drill." The guard's welcoming smile dimmed a little when he turned to McBride. "I'll need to see some ID, sir, so I can check you into the visitor's log. Please empty your pockets before moving through the scanner."

McBride dug out his driver's license and passed it to the guard. He emptied his pockets, dropped his wallet, a few coins, his lighter, and an unopened condom into one of the provided containers.

Grace shot him a look. "Always prepared, I see."

"Just like a Boy Scout." He might not have any respect left for himself, but he didn't take chances with anyone else's life.

He followed Grace through the archway scanner then reclaimed his belongings, along with a visitor's badge bearing his name. Once Grace had retrieved her purse and weapon, she thanked Williams and headed for the elevator. If she dropped her purse and the contents spilled across the floor, what would he learn about the woman beneath the badge? Did she use a Datafax or PDA? Did she like sucking on an Altoid or chewing Dentyne? What flavor lip gloss did she use on those sexy lips?

Finding out those answers was about as likely as winning the lottery.

The elevator doors parted and Grace stepped inside and selected floor three. She lingered as close to the control panel as possible to wait out the ride. Keeping her distance, was she? Was that because she was afraid of him? Or was she afraid of herself *with him*? Interesting thought.

McBride leaned against the rear wall and took advantage of the opportunity to study her ass. She didn't have to know that his fascination with her kept him from obsessing on the idea that he was here, in a federal justice building, about to try resurrecting a past he had worked extra hard to kill.

He shifted his gaze to what he could see of her profile as the elevator bumped into motion. "I had you pegged for a stair climber, Agent." Judging by her toned calves and that nicely rounded behind the lady did some serious working out.

She kept her stare steady on the display where the digital one became a two. "I took the elevator for you."

Touché. He moved up behind her, appreciated again that subtle feminine scent she wore, just as a ding announced their arrival on three. She braced to make a run for it the instant the doors opened. "I appreciate your thoughtfulness, Grace," he murmured. She shivered. As hard as she tried to hide the reaction, he saw it, relished it—one of the few pleasures in life he still enjoyed. "I prefer saving my energy for other, more satisfying forms of physical activity."

The doors opened and she burst into the lobby like a racehorse charging out of its chute. Taking his time, he followed her.

The third-floor lobby boasted another of the widely recognized FBI emblems, this one a part of the royal-blue carpet. As they passed, a secretary glanced up from her desk. Her gaze stabbed into his back until he moved out of her visual range. *Nothing like being the traveling freak show.*

The corridor Grace chose was flanked by closed doors but the double doors at the far end stood open, waiting.

The conference room.

An invisible wall jumped up in front of him . . . bringing him to a jarring halt.

Reality check.

"Hang on, Grace."

She stopped, reluctantly swung her attention to him. "What now, McBride?"

For nearly three years he hadn't cared what anyone thought of him. Not one damned little bit. Even as he reminded himself that he still didn't give a damn what she or anyone else in this place thought, he found himself searching for something besides the too plentiful disapproval and impatience in her eyes.

He was a fool. But even fools had their moments.

"They're waiting," she reminded, that impatience multiplying like an unchecked virus even as he watched.

"I'm going to need coffee." He hesitated, not sure he should trust her with this admission. The people waiting in that conference room were going to be watching him, anticipating even his most minute misstep. Consciously or unconsciously, all of them would seek confirmation that the Bureau had been right to oust him. No way was he giving them the pleasure of watching him stumble. "Lots of coffee. To do this right."

Her unforgiving stare told him she wasn't going to just disregard the hard time he had given her, but the disapproval dwindled just a little. "No problem." She took the badge he had been issued from his hand and clipped it on his shirt pocket.

They entered the conference room together. He was braced for the expected scrutiny but armed with the knowledge that even if she had her doubts about him, she would back him up to keep him here.

An immediate hush fell over the room and all eyes shifted first to Agent Grace and then to him.

"Mr. McBride." Special Agent-in-Charge Randall Worth stood and crossed the room to meet him. His elegant dress and sophisticated comportment announced who was in charge before his badge got the chance.

Mid-fifties. Receding hairline and most likely burdened by a Napoleon complex considering his small stature. A yes-man of the highest order. McBride knew the type and wasn't impressed.

Worth extended his hand. "We appreciate your willingness to help us find this little girl."

McBride's attention bypassed the SAC's offered hand and zoomed straight across the room to the timeline the task force had created. "What've you got so far?"

"I'll walk you through it." Worth indicated that McBride should precede him, with the same hand he'd failed to shake.

A picture of six-year-old Alyssa Byrne and the time she was last seen was the first entry on the board. Four hours later the school was searched, every teacher questioned, and the parents were interviewed. Two hours after that the Bureau was contacted. Worth explained that the father, Allen Byrne, owned the two largest construction companies in the state of Alabama, and Fiona, the mother, was a stay-at-home mom and volunteer who worked with various fund-raising organizations.

"By the time the e-mail came in," Worth summed up, "the Byrnes' entire extended family and network of friends and business associates had been identified and prioritized for questioning. That process is ongoing."

"The e-mail?" McBride looked from the timeline to Worth, who snapped his fingers, and a hard copy of the e-mail was promptly provided by the nearest agent. Worth passed the document to McBride, then planted his hands on his hips and looked away as if expecting an unpleasant reaction.

Dear FBI,

This e-mail is to inform you that Alyssa Byrne is safe and in my custody. You have forty-one hours to find her or I will have no choice but to do the worst.

To level the playing field I will provide clues to assist you in finding her. However, not just any agent will do. I will only give my clues to Ryan McBride.

Reinstate him so that he may save this child. Forty-one hours . . . not a second more. Starting now.

A Devoted Fan

McBride reread the signature line, a charge of anger pulsing inside him like a ticking bomb. He pivoted to align his gaze with Grace's. "You didn't feel it was relevant to mention the 'Devoted Fan' part?"

Grace glanced at Worth.

Oh, hell no. Outrage tore through McBride. He got it. Three years out of the loop had made him a little slow on the uptake, but he was there now.

Worth cleared his throat and explained, "Agent Grace wasn't authorized to reveal certain contents of the e-mail. We didn't want that information to leave this room."

"You sent your rookie agent to get a status on me," McBride accused, his fingers clenched into fists, crushing the e-mail. "Whether or not I came back with her was never the point, was it? I'm a suspect."

He hadn't been just a fool, he'd been a fucking idiot.

"You're wrong about that, McBride," Worth insisted with a quick survey of the room as if gathering support. "We need you. You read the e-mail. The unsub will only give the clues to you."

"I need a smoke." McBride tossed the wadded e-mail

onto the conference table and strode out of the room. He didn't slow down until he had reached the elevator.

"McBride! Wait!"

The elevator doors opened and he stepped inside.

Grace dashed in just before they closed. "You have to look at this like an agent," she urged him. The elevator lurched into motion, making her sway.

Like hell he did. He'd been relieved of that grade three years ago. The Bureau wouldn't even be talking to him now if he weren't a suspect. He wanted out of here. The only thing on his mind was getting on a plane headed south.

More irony. His career had gone south and then he'd done the same. Had been doing it ever since. And the joke was on him.

"It's the logical process," she said, trying a different angle. "You were named in the e-mail. You separated from the Bureau under less than desirable circumstances. We had to be sure. We haven't been able to pinpoint anyone related to any of your old cases as a person of interest. That only leaves you."

The doors glided open and he burst out, stormed across the lobby and then out the door with the security guard calling after him—something about him signing out.

He had the Marlboro in his mouth and lit before the door whooshed closed behind him.

"McBride! Dammit! Think about that little girl."

He wheeled around and glared at Grace. "I am thinking about that little girl. You're the one who's not thinking. You set me up." He had to keep moving. He was too damned mad to hold still. He walked all the way to the fence and was still steamed. But because he couldn't go any farther, he stopped.

"You're right." She joined him, stared out at the same nothing he did. "I promised to back you up knowing I'd kept this from you. I was wrong." A pause allowed him to absorb the impact of those three words. "I know how that feels and I'm the last person who should've been caught doing it."

Yeah, right. She was too damned young to have a clue what he was feeling. "That's a nice sentiment, Grace, but I doubt we're talking about the same thing."

She stared at him a moment, her desperation building. He didn't have to look. He could feel the tension radiating off her in waves of uncertainty and agitation. Wasn't his problem. He wasn't going through this again.

They had people for finding the kid, they didn't need him.

"Someone I trusted a lot more than you could possibly trust me in the few hours we've known each other let me down." She drew in a deep, shuddering breath, then let it go. "I made the mistake of letting him see my one weakness and he used it to send me here instead of the assignment I had earned. He set my career back at last two years. I'm not sure I'll ever forgive him, but I've got a job to do. I figure showing him he made a mistake will be the best revenge. So can we please save the theatrics for after we find the kid?"

The kid. All this bullshit and the kid was the one who was going to lose.

There wasn't a reason in the world he should believe Agent Vivian Grace. Not one. But she was right about the kid. And about the revenge. Getting the job done would be the best kind. He flung his cigarette to the pavement and ground it out with his shoe. "Is there anything else I haven't been told?" He would stay, but he wouldn't be letting his guard down again. Not to her or anyone else whose title was "agent."

"That's everything." She held up her right hand. "I swear."

Maybe he was an idiot for putting himself on the line like this, especially considering he knew for sure that the Bureau still had the same shitty attitude about him. But he wasn't about to let that little girl die just because their attitude and his life sucked.

The guard didn't try to stop him or Grace as they reentered the building. McBride bypassed the elevator and headed for the stairs. He needed to work off some of this rage before he went back into that conference room. Otherwise, he would wipe the floor with Worth, which he was damned tempted to do anyway.

Grace kept pace with him and entered the conference room at his side. He went directly to the timeline board without a word to anyone. No one dared to question him. Not even Worth.

"There's no indication that anyone in the family, in the network of friends or business associates, might be involved?" This, he asked—demanded—of Worth.

"Not so far," Worth said with a questioning look at Grace. "The Byrnes have a lot of friends and business associates. Birmingham PD is helping run the names and interviews." He shrugged. "Could be a waste of manpower considering the e-mail and the connection to you."

McBride didn't like Worth. Mainly because of the whole making-him-a-suspect thing, but partly because he still held a grudge against the "in-charge" faction. There was always the possibility that the guy wasn't really the asshole McBride figured him for, but he wouldn't be hanging around long enough to find out.

He turned to Grace. "Let's give this 'Devoted Fan' what he wants."

"We've set up direct access for you," Worth explained, gesturing to one of a number of computer stations posted along the far wall. "We're prepared for a trace, for all the good it'll do." He cut Grace another of those speculative glances. "I assume Agent Grace warned you that this guy knows his stuff on the World Wide Web."

McBride nodded. "She mentioned it."

Worth shrugged as if he felt this whole exercise was pointless. "When you're ready to open up communication with the unsub, so are we."

McBride hesitated. "We'll need proof."

Devoted Fan would no doubt want some assurance he

was dealing with McBride and not someone pretending to be him.

"A photo," Grace suggested, then looked around the conference room. "Over there." She indicated the first entry on the timeline, the eight-by-ten photo of Alyssa Byrne.

McBride couldn't remember the last time his picture had been taken. By the media three years ago or maybe when he'd gotten his Florida driver's license. It wasn't something he cared to do now, but he didn't see any way around it. Grace snapped a shot of him using her cell phone camera. A couple minutes later she'd downloaded the image to an open e-mail. With her already seated at the keyboard, he dictated the brief note.

> Devoted Fan
>   You have my undivided attention.
>
>   McBride

A single click and it was done.

"I guess now we wait," Worth noted aloud for the rest of the room, most of whom were still eyeing McBride suspiciously.

Grace had no sooner pushed back her chair than the "new mail" warning sounded. As she opened the mailbox, McBride leaned closer. Had the bastard been standing by, waiting for that e-mail to arrive? How could he have been that sure that McBride would even come?

One click and he had his answer.

It was *him*.

> Welcome back, Agent McBride. Alyssa and I have been waiting.

"Print it," Worth ordered before McBride had even finished reading the first paragraph. "I want a hard copy."

Grace stabbed the command key for sending the image

on the screen to the printer. McBride crouched down next to her chair to get a better view of the screen, instinct taking over with the need to know what this son of a bitch had to say.

> Here, my old friend, is your clue:
>   Alyssa Byrne is interred in the dark on a hillside where hundreds of those who issue a form of assurance to the elderly can see. Her father would not know this place well since he often fails to pay proper homage. His mistake has cost much, but to pay with his daughter's innocent life is perhaps a stiff price. I have decided to show him mercy.
>   Find her, McBride. She has less than 18 hours before her fate is sealed.
>
>   Happy hunting,
>   Devoted Fan

"Agent Talley," Worth called out, "get Alyssa Byrne's father in my office now." His gaze met McBride's as he added with a little less enthusiasm, "The rest of you, do what McBride tells you." With that final order, the SAC promptly exited the conference room.

McBride felt the floor beneath his feet shake with that gauntlet hitting the ground. Worth had just dumped the entirety of this mess in his lap. Nice to see the guy was living up to McBride's expectations. Then again, he had insisted on being in charge, hadn't he?

His jaw clenched, McBride focused his attention back on the monitor and reread the words on the screen. "We need maps on the locations of every cemetery in this city," he told Grace. "Maps that include all surrounding buildings. And print me a copy of that e-mail, would ya?"

She hit the necessary key and pushed back her chair. "Done. You can pick it up on the printer. I'll need to access another system for those maps."

"Give me what you can as it becomes available. Hard

copies preferably." McBride stood and walked to the laser printer to retrieve the e-mail. There was something about the construction of the sentences in Devoted Fan's notes that seemed familiar. He studied the phrasing. Couldn't quite place it. But he'd read something written by this guy before.

"Excuse me, sir."

McBride glanced at the agent's badge. *Harold Pratt.* Tall, thin, not much older than Grace, with a mug only a mother could love. "Yeah?"

"Your coffee." He presented a steaming cup.

McBride didn't know when she'd had the time, but Grace had done just what she said, he'd give her that. "Thanks, Pratt." He accepted the cup as he considered the agents conversing among themselves on the other side of the room. While he had this guy's attention, he asked, "How about giving me names to go with those faces." He gestured with his cup to the trio who were likely laying odds on whether or not he could hack the pressure Worth had just piled on.

"The one with the purple tie is Boyd Davis," Pratt said with a nod to the man who looked to be in his late thirties and who wore his blond hair high and tight.

"Ex-military," McBride suggested.

"That's right," Pratt said. "And Dan Arnold is the big black guy who looks like he should be a linebacker for the Falcons." He leaned closer to McBride. "You don't want him mad at you. The older man"—Pratt arrowed a look at the agent with the full head of gray hair—"is Ken Aldridge. He's counting the days until retirement."

Aldridge glanced their way as if he'd sensed the mention of his name. Since he was senior, McBride opted to start with him. "Aldridge," he barked, "I need you to start running the contents of the e-mails through the system. See if you get a hit on the phrasing." He looked to the man built like a refrigerator. "Arnold, find out if there's anything on that IP trace yet."

Simultaneous "yes sirs" punctuated the agents' departure to do his bidding. Now that was more like it. His self-confidence boosted just enough to be above basement level.

"I could cross-reference the significant terms used by the unsub with the names of buildings," Davis offered, running a hand down his flamboyant tie, evidently worried he might be left out. "And see what I can come up with."

"Good thinking, Davis." McBride turned to the agent next to him. "Pratt, you work with Davis on that. Run down the names and purposes of all buildings located in the vicinity of each cemetery Grace isolates, then do the cross-referencing."

"Yes, sir."

The agents plunged into an organized chaos that McBride recognized all too well despite the passage of time and the distance he had put between himself and this world. People moved in and out of the room, talked at once, worked around each other, but there was a rhythm to the seemingly disconnected dance. A hum of productivity that meant things were happening, were coming together.

McBride downed a couple of badly needed cups of coffee and searched his mind, sifting through old cases for a possible link to this guy, but found none. Though he attempted to slam the door on the subject, his thoughts shifted to Worth. There was something there that he couldn't see . . . yet. Worth despised him, that was certain. But then, he'd expected that. It was the way he had looked at Grace that nagged at McBride. As if Worth were worried that she'd screwed up somehow. Whatever differences the SAC had with Grace were none of his business. The only thing he needed to do was find this kid.

Not a damned thing more.

Grace returned with her initial findings. "We've narrowed the search parameters but we're still left with more than twenty cemeteries." She spread the first five printouts on the conference table. "If you want to start with these, we'll keep moving forward."

She waited as if she expected him to instruct her further or to dismiss her. He didn't do either. She executed a sharp about-face and went back to her task.

The only other female agent among the group bellied up to the table next to him. "Kim Schaffer," she said as she surveyed the maps. "You can call me Schaffer. I've highlighted the maps with the hilly terrain. How do you want to do this?"

Now this agent McBride could get along with. Straight to the point, no crap. Schaffer wore her tell-it-like-it-is attitude right up front for all to see. The lack of makeup and short, no-fuss hair said she didn't waste time with frivolities.

McBride set his cup aside and picked up the first map. "Well, Schaffer. We're looking for a cemetery close to a nursing home or medical resource for the elderly. Some kind of facility that provides assurance. Could even be a bank or a security company that supplies home monitoring." He gave her a look that said she knew as much as he did. "Could be just about anything."

She nodded her understanding and grabbed a couple of maps. As she strode to an empty chair her hot-pink cowboy boots snagged his attention. The charcoal suit was classic, the boots a definite challenge to the establishment. She probably kept these guys walking the line.

Before diving into the maps, he asked the room at large, "Where's Worth?" He needed an update on whatever the man was able to get from Alyssa Byrne's father. That information could impact what they were looking for.

All present glanced up but Grace was the one to answer. "Worth is in his office preparing to question Alyssa Byrne's father. He'll brief us as soon as he has anything. ASAC Talley is coordinating the backup we may require with Birmingham PD's liaison."

Assistant Special Agent-in-Charge Talley was the only one Worth hadn't left with McBride. The boss had to have someone to order around.

"Good," McBride said though Grace had already returned to her map search. That left him wondering what to do next. He kept waiting for those old instincts to kick in but they just kept holding back.

For several lingering moments, he watched the interaction in the conference-room-turned-command-center. One thing quickly became clear; the guys gave Grace a wide berth as if they didn't want to risk crossing her. He would have to catch her in a weak moment and ask her why. He had her tagged as an ice princess but the jury was still out on that one. Maybe she just didn't know how to do the team thing. That was a personality defect with which he was intimately acquainted. Maybe they had something in common after all.

Right now he needed to lose himself to the process . . . and find that little girl.

An hour passed like a minute with the shuffling of maps and the tossing back and forth of building names and purposes.

"Wait." McBride hesitated on one map in particular. "What's this?" He tapped the image of a tall building that stood across the street from a downtown cemetery.

Schaffer moved in to get a better look. "Oak Hill Cemetery. First cemetery in the city. And that"—she pointed to the building in question—"I believe, is the Social Security Administration."

"That's correct," Davis chimed in, his fingers running over the computer keys. "Employs three hundred fifty people."

"Oak Hill Cemetery is an historic landmark only a couple of blocks from here," Grace said, leaning past McBride to get a better look at the map he and Schaffer were viewing.

McBride's long-slumbering instincts suddenly roused. Would the unsub have the balls to use a cemetery *that close* to the very authorities he was baiting? Judging by his actions thus far, that was an affirmative.

If the location was even a cemetery. For now that was a hunch, the only one they had. *He* could be wrong. The term "stiff" as used in the e-mail might not carry a double meaning as many of the other phrases obviously did.

"Cemetery's on a hillside?" he confirmed with Schaffer as he traced the highlighted area on the map.

She nodded. "It certainly is."

It all fell into place as if the answer had been typed in big bold letters in that e-mail. McBride tapped the map again. "That's it."

Grace chewed on her bottom lip a second, distracting him when he shouldn't have been distractible.

"How can you be so certain?" she countered. "This seems too easy. Sure, the Social Security Administration provides a form of assurance to the elderly and maybe Alyssa Byrne's father isn't paying as he should, but we can't be certain."

"Don't forget," Pratt piped up, "our unsub said 'where hundreds can see.' The SSA employs hundreds."

Grace exchanged a look with Pratt as if she didn't appreciate that he had challenged her assessment.

"You said Byrne owns a construction company," McBride said to her, his certainty solidifying in spite of her questions.

"Two of them," Grace confirmed, still seeming unconvinced.

"It wouldn't hurt to look into how many illegal aliens he employs," Schaffer offered, looking from Grace to McBride.

Taking that ball and running with it, McBride pressed, "Does he pay Social Security on every employee?" When Grace still looked skeptical, he tacked on, "This is the best lead we have based on the clues we were given. Unless we get something else, that's where we go."

Grace turned to Schaffer. "Can you nudge Worth to question Byrne about his hiring practices?"

"ASAP." Schaffer strode off to get it done, her boot heels tapping against the floor.

McBride glanced at the clock on the wall. The hours were counting off way too fast. The urge to make a move was palpable. "I don't want to wait," he said to Grace. "Let's go. Pratt, Davis, and Aldridge can rendezvous with the Birmingham PD team and meet us there."

"What if this turns out to be a wild-goose chase, McBride?" Grace asked, caution and inexperience making her hesitate. "Is there a backup plan?"

He picked up the map for Oak Hill Cemetery. "Then we'll do whatever we have to. That's our backup plan."

"I have to give Worth a heads-up."

"Do it."

Maybe this was too easy. Maybe he did have it all wrong. But there was only one way to find out.

CHAPTER FOUR

Oak Hill Cemetery
7:00 P.M.
16 hours remaining . . .

This felt wrong.

Vivian guided her Explorer onto the narrow road that led through the gate and onto cemetery property. Before the vehicle came to a complete stop, McBride hopped out. He walked a few feet then turned all the way around to take in the foreign setting that was so familiar to her. City streets flanked the property on all sides, creating an island of the dead surrounded by a sea of asphalt and commuters. Traffic provided a dull drone of background music underscored by the occasional incoming commercial airliner that heralded the airport's proximity.

No peace for the dead here.

As a kid, Vivian had come to this cemetery dozens of times for the walking tours. Her parents usually ended up searching the cemetery for her. She would sneak off to play in her favorite spot and then fall asleep. Her gaze landed on the Zinszer Mausoleum. She had dosed off in there once or twice.

She emerged from the SUV and glanced back at the only entrance, from Nineteenth Street, where a towering arch of wrought iron welcomed visitors. Several official vehicles arrived, along with Agents Pratt, Davis, and Aldridge.

From the entrance, the narrow serpentine drive flowed around and across cemetery property where magnolia and oak trees shaded the weathered headstones. Crape myrtles provided splashes of color, accenting the gray and green landscape. A small chapellike structure, the Pioneer Memorial Building, housed the administrative office and stood like a sanctuary amid the dead interred here. On the Seventeenth Street side of the cemetery was the old caretaker's cottage that now accommodated the Oak Hill Memorial Association office. Nothing had changed since she was a kid.

She looked to her right and in the distance the Social Security Administration Building loomed, its soaring, contemporary façade blocking the view of the mountains.

"*. . . where hundreds of those who issue a form of assurance to the elderly can see . . .*"

Why here? Why this close to the Bureau's office . . . out in the open, where anyone passing on the street could have seen him doing his dirty business? Had he buried the girl here? Vivian shuddered at the thought. Reminded herself to think like a trained agent, not a woman.

And why this easy? The clues were a joke. She could have figured this much out hours ago. Why drag a seasoned veteran like McBride into the case? What was the connection between Devoted Fan and McBride? He'd referred to McBride as his "old friend." What did any of that have to do with Alyssa Byrne?

Bottom line, could Vivian be absolutely certain that McBride hadn't set this up somehow, as Worth suspected?

Maybe not . . . but she was willing to do whatever it took to find that child.

She had a bad feeling that nothing about this case or this unsub was going to be what it seemed. Her gaze landed on McBride. Like him. She had seen that flicker of vulnerability in him when he had mentioned his need for lots of coffee. The pain and disappointment he hadn't camouflaged quickly enough with his fury when he'd learned she had betrayed him.

The man still had feelings, it seemed.

Maybe even a conscience.

But that didn't make him the hero that part of her wanted to believe in. At the academy, the legends about him had been romanticized. But this was real . . . somebody could die *for real*.

Vivian focused on the agents and uniformed officers gathered around McBride for their orders. As she slowly walked that way, the group dispersed, spreading out across the hillside to commence the grid search McBride had discussed with her en route. The sound of another vehicle arriving drew her attention to the truck with the K-9s and their handlers.

If Alyssa Byrne was here, they would soon know it.

Nearing McBride's position, she called out his name. When he turned to her, she pointed beyond him to the man exiting the memorial building with Agent Schaffer. "That's Lester Holcomb, the caretaker."

Vivian remembered him well. He'd worked here since she was a kid. His advanced age along with his stooped posture most likely prevented him from doing the heavy work around here anymore, but he was one of those who had every intention of staying on as long as he had a breath in him.

"Does he live on the grounds?" McBride wanted to know as she moved up alongside him.

"No. The locked gate is the only security at night."

When Schaffer was within conversational range, with Holcomb in tow, she made the necessary introductions. "He'll open the mausoleums for us since they keep them locked now." To McBride, she said, "I've called Bob Greene, Holcomb's helper. He's on his way in."

McBride considered the information before replying, "Have Davis or Pratt question him as soon as he arrives."

"Yes, sir." Schaffer immediately put through a call to pass along the instruction.

"Do the police perform any hourly drive-throughs at night?" McBride asked the caretaker as they walked to the nearest mausoleum.

"No, sir," Holcomb said, riffling through the big ring of keys in his hand. "When we finish for the day we lock the gate and go on home. Maybe you didn't notice the signs but the city made it illegal to be in the cemetery after dark."

Vivian and McBride exchanged a brief glance; undoubtedly he was thinking the same thing she was. Since when did a posted sign stop a determined lawbreaker? Since never.

"Have you had any trouble in the past?" McBride said, going on with his questioning.

Holcomb paused at their first stop. His gnarled hands shook as he poked the key into the lock. "Not in a good long while. But we did have a little vandalism a year or so back. Couple knocked-over headstones and some graffiti. Had to put locks on all of 'em after that." He gestured to the mausoleum and wagged his head sadly. "Damned teenagers got too much time on their hands. Gives the old Devil plenty to work with."

Once the rusty iron door was opened, McBride stepped inside. Vivian stayed close behind him. The musty smell invaded her nostrils with the first intake of breath. Dust and cobwebs held dominion over the interior, where a single tomb served as the focal point. McBride held out his hand and she slapped a steel Maglite into his palm, then sneezed.

"Bless you," the caretaker offered.

"Thank you." Her allergies always flared up in the fall. This dust wouldn't help. The dull ache that had started behind her forehead had her wondering about McBride's headache. She had watched him devour half a bottle of aspirin before he had fallen asleep on the plane. She had drifted off herself. The first sleep she'd had since before Alyssa Byrne was reported missing. Later, when she had awakened, McBride had been watching her.

Even now, his way of looking so deep inside her flustered her. The man had that whole intimidation thing down to a science. Not to mention he filtered every damned thing between them through an erotic lens. She had to get a grip on how to handle that aspect of his persona.

Zoning back in on the here and now, she followed the flashlight's beam over the limestone walls and floors, landing lastly on the tomb.

"Are the seals on all the tombs intact?" McBride asked their guide.

A shudder went through her and she braced against it. The unsub had said Alyssa's fate would be sealed. That possibility made Vivian feel ill. *Just let us find her.* As much as she had loved this cemetery as a kid, something about being here under these circumstances amplified the desperation and her awareness of time passing so swiftly.

Holcomb nodded. "Yes, sir. Resealing all the tombs is part of the master preseveration plan. This cemetery's on the National Historic Registry, you know. Every last one of the tombs had to be resealed to ensure the remains are protected. They started the process a couple months ago."

McBride's posture changed, signaling that he had just experienced the same epiphany as she. The sealing of the tombs couldn't be coincidence.

"Does the process require opening the tombs?" McBride pressed for specificity.

"No, sir." Holcomb touched the ledge where the top rested against the walls of the casket-sized tomb. "There's a couple ways of doing it, but these folks didn't want 'em opened. So the sealing is done right around this ledge with the lids sitting in place. That way there's no risk to the remains. Air ain't kind to 'em, you know? And there's always the fear that some no-account will steal something. Even some of the ones in the business of restoring can't be trusted. I had to be right with 'em as they done each one."

"So," McBride restated, "they've all been done? No chance one was skipped?"

Jesus, he was thinking the same thing Vivian was. Her body literally vibrated with the need to pry open every damned one of the tombs. But the timing was off. Holcomb had said the process had started two months ago, well before Alyssa went missing. That would eliminate the possibility of her being sealed up inside one of them.

Holcomb pushed his cap up his forehead and scratched the bald spot there. "There's—"

A burst of frantic barking had Vivian moving out of the mausoleum since she was closest to the door. The shouting that abruptly accompanied the barking sent adrenaline blazing through her veins.

Her cell phone shook in its holster. She reached for it, her gaze searching the grounds, attempting to locate the activity generating the ruckus. "Grace." Pratt was on the line; needed them at his location ASAP. One of the dogs had latched on to something. "We're on our way."

Vivian looked to McBride as she put her phone away. "Pratt may have found something."

"The girl?"

"Don't know." Her pulse was tripping at the idea that the handlers had been provided with the pajamas Alyssa had slept in the night before she disappeared, which meant the animals could be on to her scent.

As they started across the cemetery, McBride called back to the caretaker, "Double-check your records on the sealing of the tombs. We'll get back to that."

Holcomb looked a little flustered or perplexed but Vivian didn't have time to analyze his problem since McBride had taken hold of her arm and was tugging her along with him. She had to practically run to keep up with his long strides.

He jerked his head toward the street. "Looks like word's out that we're here."

Vivian glanced in that direction. The news vans and reporters had gathered in force. Birmingham PD was keeping them outside the cemetery gate, but that wouldn't stop their intruding zoom lenses. She understood that the media was part of this business but she didn't have to like it. The call letters of one station in particular, WKRT, caught her eye, which meant that Nadine Goodman was on the scene already. There wasn't an agent or a cop in Birmingham who liked the lady. She had earned her reputation of cutthroat reporting by stepping on and over anyone necessary.

She and McBride pushed through the crowd of cops when they reached Pratt's location.

"In here," Pratt said. He gestured to the open mausoleum.

"Was it unlocked when you got here?" McBride assessed the rusty iron door that stood partially open.

Pratt nodded. "The dog nudged the door open a little farther but it was already unlocked and ajar. The handler had to restrain the animal."

The dog had settled down but he was still visibly agitated.

"We'll check it out," McBride told him. "You and the handler stay put, but get the rest of these folks back to the search. It's getting dark fast."

Vivian looked up at the sky; he was right about that. She reached into her jacket pocket and passed McBride a pair of gloves and shoe covers. When she'd tugged her own into place, she unholstered her weapon and followed him into the mausoleum.

She grimaced at the pungent odor. *Blood . . . decomp.* The deeper they moved inside, the more the foul smell worsened. This mausoleum was larger than the last. Two tombs stood on raised stone platforms. The floor was clean, as if someone had swept it. The cobwebs and dust on the walls and every other surface indicated the floor shouldn't have been so clean. Their unsub wasn't leaving anything to chance, not even his shoeprints in the dust.

"He's been here," McBride muttered.

With no immediate threat visible, she reholstered her weapon. "Looks that way." As convinced as she had been that this was too easy . . . that there had to be a mistake, looking around now she admitted that McBride was right . . . *he* had been here.

"Oh God." She pointed to the corner on her right. She had to lean slightly in that direction to see it, but there was no mistaking what it was. "A burlap bag," she said aloud. Pain snarled deep in her chest. "Possibly bloodstained."

McBride eased between the two tombs, headed for that corner. She took care to follow his exact path to avoid disturbing any evidence that might be invisible to the naked eye on the cleanly swept floor.

"Should we get a forensics team in here first?" All the rules of procedure she had learned were suddenly missing from her readily accessible gray matter. God Almighty, she couldn't bear the thought of what that bag might contain. Damn it! Why did it have to turn out this way?

McBride looked from her to the bag. "If the kid's already dead, we need to know it now." He shook his head slowly, his face grim. "I hate these motherfuckers."

She couldn't agree more.

As he crouched down to inspect the bloody bag, images of what might be inside flared in vivid color before her retinas. Vivian told herself to move. To get over there and do what she could to assist him . . . but she couldn't prompt her body into action. Something she couldn't brand as fear but couldn't rule out as exactly that had paralyzed her.

And then, as if some mental door had suddenly swung open, the memories came.

Flashes of darkness . . . whispered words seared through her brain. And she was suddenly back there . . . in the dark . . . with *him* whispering in her ear . . . her every instinct warning that she was going to die.

A gasp drew dank, dusty air into her lungs.

"Agent Grace?"

McBride was staring at her.

Vivian blinked, wrestled for composure. "I'm . . ." She licked her lips, forced her legs to move. "I'm okay." She crouched down next to him. "Let's get it over with."

Focus, damn it! Analyze the details. Do your job! "The bag isn't large enough to hold a six-year-old girl unless . . ." She gulped back the bile rising in her throat. More of those flashes from the past bombarded her senses. Body parts . . . missing pieces . . . half-eaten flesh.

"Unless she's been dismembered," McBride finished for her, his expression questioning. "Not enough blood for that, Grace. Excluding the possibility," he qualified, his tone cool and analytical, "the dismembering took place at a different location."

Don't look at the past! Pay attention. This wasn't easy on McBride either. As collected as he sounded, he reached for the tie of the bag and his hands shook.

Details, Grace. Look at the details. Twine. Carefully knotted. A minute-plus was required for him to get the knots undone. Every second aged her a decade. Had the rage inside her building toward an eruption. *Please don't let this be that little girl. Please. Please. Please.*

When the bag was open, she leaned forward just as he did. Peered inside. *Shit!* She jerked back. Her butt slammed onto the floor.

"Is that . . . ?" She dragged in a bumpy gulp of air, looked to McBride for confirmation.

"Rats," he muttered as he stared into the bag. "A whole fucking bag full of rats."

Not the child . . . not the child.

Thank God.

Grabbing back her courage, she levered up from the floor.

"Hold this," he ordered.

Easy for him to say. Her hands shaking, her legs a little rubbery, Vivian crouched next to him once more and held the bag open. He used the Maglite to get a better look.

Why the hell would this creep kill all those rats? As much as she disliked the rodents, torturing any living creature was just sick.

"What do we have here?" McBride lifted a rat from the pile. What appeared to be a toe tag hung from its hind leg.

Vivian shuddered, felt her traitorous stomach do another of those warning flip-flops.

"UAB Medical Research Center," McBride read off. His profile hardened. "Andrew Quinn."

Vivian tilted her head to read the name written on the toe tag. "Isn't that your old supervisor?"

McBride heaved a mighty breath. "The one and only."

"Wait." She leaned closer, nudged one corner of the tag with a gloved finger. "There's something written on the back."

No more rats.

A muscle flexed in McBride's jaw. He carefully placed the tagged rat back in the bag. "We've got a whole tribe of rats in here, but nothing human as far as I can tell." His eyes locked with hers. "He's playing with us, Grace. He knew we'd use the K-9s. He must have had the bag in contact with the girl at some point to lock in her scent."

Vivian couldn't see a connection. And if there was no connection, why the hell was this bastard wasting the time he had given them? The theory that this was some kind of revenge McBride had plotted for being terminated by the Bureau kept rearing its ugly head. "What would any of this have to do with Alyssa Byrne?" she asked, trying not to sound openly suspicious. She was determined to give him the benefit of the doubt until he no longer deserved it . . . or until they found the child.

"Nothing," McBride admitted, "this is about *me*." He studied the way the bag sat against the wall. Picked up the twine and considered how it had been tied. "Whatever his game, this whackjob wants to draw out the anticipation. He probably gets off on the risk of playing in the shadow of authority." He turned his face to hers. "And you know what? He's not afraid of us or of getting caught. Not the least bit."

She hoped he wasn't right about that last part. Fear was what kept most people in line—and what made most criminals screw up. They needed for this nutcase to screw up—fast.

"What now?" Vivian wanted to scream in frustration. If the child wasn't at this cemetery . . . where did that leave them? Time was running out and they had nothing. Her stomach roiled. The putrid smell was getting to her. She kept seeing flashes of the movie *Willard,* the images twisting with the pictures she had seen of Alyssa Byrne . . . and with mental snapshots from the past she had thought was behind her once and for all.

McBride tossed the twine aside and stood. She rose, her legs liquid. This wasn't the time to allow the past to catch up with her and throw her off balance. She'd completely overreacted to this scene. That kind of behavior did nothing but work against her determination to be the best agent possible.

With one last look around the mausoleum, McBride said, "We'll need to find out if those rats came from the research center listed on the toe tag." He considered the bag a moment longer. "Were they stolen before or after being euthanized? Maybe we'll get lucky and our guy got in a hurry and left some DNA behind."

Vivian nodded. Wished she hadn't. The movement had her gag reflex kicking in. "I need some air." She couldn't get out of there fast enough.

Outside she gasped for a breath that didn't reek of rotting rodents.

McBride came out behind her, peeled off the gloves and the shoe covers. "If you need to puke don't hold back on my account," he encouraged. "Just find a spot away from the crime scene."

And here she'd begun to think the man had feelings. "I'm good," she snapped.

McBride quickly surveyed the cemetery before turning his next question on Pratt. "Where's our caretaker?"

Pratt pointed to the memorial building. "He's waiting inside with Schaffer."

"I want to know why the lock was missing and no one had noticed." McBride shifted his attention back to the mausoleum and then to her. "How long will it take forensics to get here?"

"Aldridge made the call en route." Vivian took another deep cleansing breath, wiped a loose strand of hair from her face. "They should be here soon."

"I don't want anyone going back in there until the techs have gone over it from top to bottom."

"That's the way we do things, McBride." She shot him an irritated look. "Believe it or not, we've done this before." Technically, she hadn't, but Aldridge and Davis and the others had—plenty of times.

"I'll be waiting here for the techs," Pratt assured him.

McBride didn't bother with a comeback to her smart-aleck remark, which was just as well. She wasn't in the mood. She led the way to the memorial building. The search of the grounds continued but nightfall would significantly hinder their efforts. If Alyssa wasn't at this cemetery, what were the chances they would narrow down her location before time ran out?

Not good. And that just wasn't acceptable.

Her gaze landed on McBride. He had to figure this out. He was all they had. *She* was counting on him.

Inside the memorial building Schaffer immediately brought them up to speed. "Holcomb double-checked the records. All tombs have been resealed except for the two in one mausoleum."

Anticipation nudged Vivian's faltering hope. "Which one?"

"The Wellborne mausoleum." Holcomb indicated a place on the cemetery map that hung on the wall. "It's the largest one. Sits next to Potter's Field."

McBride restrained Vivian with a hand on her arm when she would have headed for the door. "Why hasn't that one been resealed yet?"

"The family put up a fuss. There was a big write-up in the newspaper about three weeks back. They finally reached an agreement just last week. The final two are scheduled to be resealed tomorrow."

Another adrenaline surge blasted Vivian. The impression of a smile claimed McBride's mouth.

"What time tomorrow?" he asked.

Holcomb checked the calendar on the desk. "Eleven A.M. sharp."

A knowing look passed between Vivian and McBride.

"Take us there," McBride ordered the caretaker.

"It ain't far," Holcomb assured. "It was the first mausoleum built on Oak Hill."

Vivian knew the one. "Follow me," she said to McBride, moving toward the door. This time he was ready to go.

She put in a call to Aldridge to inform the others as they rushed toward Potter's Field.

The Wellborne mausoleum didn't look nearly so grand

as the others. Big and plain, its walls cracked and crumbling. She remembered she had never liked that one as a child, too creepy. It sat alone on the edge of the line that marked off the stretch of ground where paupers had been buried. The few forlorn headstones in that section leaned with the fatigue of time and the elements. The story had made her feel sad for the indigent and unknown folks buried away from the wealthier magnates who had made Birmingham a steel city during the late eighteen-hundreds.

The handlers and K-9s joined the progression toward the mausoleum but the animals showed no reaction. Half a dozen yards from the entrance McBride stopped.

"No one goes past this point until I've had a look."

Vivian wanted to argue but she didn't. Schaffer provided the necessary gloves since Vivian had already used those in her pocket and her purse was back in the Explorer.

Still no reaction from the K-9s. And yet, she felt charged. Psyched. This had to be it . . . Alyssa had to be here.

McBride tugged on the gloves and started forward. When Vivian didn't follow he glanced back. "You coming?"

Surprised that he hadn't included her in his edict, she quickly pulled on her gloves and hustled to catch up to him.

The door was closed, the lock secured.

"Holcomb!" McBride motioned for the caretaker to join them.

The man hurried forward with the ring of keys.

McBride held up a hand for him to stop a few feet away. "Toss me your keys."

Holcomb readily obliged. "Won't do you no good though." He pointed to the door. "That ain't one of our locks."

"Goddammit," McBride growled. "Somebody get me a bolt cutter!"

Agent Schaffer double-timed it back to the memorial building with the caretaker. Minutes ticked by, each second exploding in Vivian's chest like a blast of supercharged adrenaline.

Even McBride looked rattled now. Did he need more aspirin or maybe coffee? He'd probably tell her what he really needed was a good stiff drink. If he found Alyssa Byrne before it was too late, she would take McBride out and buy him anything to drink he wanted.

By the time the bolt cutters were in McBride's hand, Vivian felt certain her heart would rupture. He snapped the lock and tossed the tool aside.

Holding her breath, she watched him push the door inward then stop.

"I need shoe covers," he said to no one in particular.

Jesus. Even Vivian had forgotten. Agent Davis rushed forward to provide the necessary protective measures.

Fully prepared now, Vivian followed McBride into the mausoleum, her hand on the butt of her weapon. The first thing that grabbed her attention was the smell. Unlike before, no blood or decomp. This odor was unmistakable. Skunk. Her stomach seized. She covered her nose with the back of her hand and wished she had some Vicks salve.

Like the other mausoleum the floor had been swept clean, and the two tombs sat atop their platforms seemingly undisturbed.

Nothing appeared out of place. No burlap bag. Just a skunk carcass stinking up the place.

"Is this more of his games?" Vivian asked as she scanned the gloomy interior a second time and still found nothing.

"The skunk scent kept the dogs from picking up on anything else."

Damn. He was right. She should have thought of that.

McBride walked over to the first tomb and ran his fingers along the edge where the lid sat atop the sidewalls. Vivian did the same. No gap. If Alyssa was inside there . . . Vivian forced the thought away . . . didn't want to think like that yet.

Then he moved on to the next tomb. She reached for that same edge, traced the seam. The gap between the top and the walls that held it up made her pulse jump. That much of a crevice shouldn't be there.

McBride crouched down and examined the gap more closely. "See this?"

She eased down next to him to check out what he had found. Small metal objects had been evenly placed all the way around between the lid and the walls. The gap provided just enough space to ensure a reasonable inflow of air . . . maybe enough for survival.

"Grab the other end of this lid," he ordered.

She took up a position at the foot of the tomb.

"We're not trying to pick it up," he clarified. "We just want to slide it down your way."

He pushed. She pulled. The lid moved. A couple of the spacers popped out. McBride jerked his hands back in the nick of time.

"Close," he muttered, then put his hands back into place. "A little more."

The slow, cautious push-pull started again. Wasn't happening nearly fast enough.

"Let's swing it around," Vivian suggested. Going that direction couldn't possibly be any harder than doing it this way and would give them faster access to more of the interior. Dragging anyone else in here for assistance would only further contaminate the scene.

McBride nodded and started the tedious process of twisting the lid perpendicular to the tomb. More spacers popped loose.

When they had moved it far enough, they looked inside the gaping tomb together.

Six-year-old Alyssa Byrne, a white towel beneath her, lay atop the bones of a Wellborne ancestor. Her eyes were closed, her hands bound behind her back. Silver duct tape stretched across her mouth. The word INNOCENT had been written in black marker across her forehead.

Vivian's hand trembled as she reached inside and touched the child's carotid artery to check for a pulse.

Her breath caught and her gaze connected with McBride's. "She's alive."

CHAPTER FIVE

Night had fully invaded the cemetery.

McBride sat on the steps leading into the Pioneer Memorial Building. He lit a Marlboro as he watched the paramedics loading the gurney into the wagon. The Byrnes climbed in with their daughter, neither prepared to let their only child out of their sight again. Probably wouldn't until the kid was at least twenty-five.

The girl appeared a little dehydrated but there were no visible physical injuries. Her stats were good, but since she was unconscious she'd been put on a monitor to watch her blood pressure and oxygen level, then C-collared and backboarded for transport. Additional tests and close observation would give the full story.

Between the cops, the febbies, and the press, there was a regular circus going on around the cemetery entrance, complete with spotlights scattered about. Forensics techs had arrived and were going through the steps in both mausoleums as best they could with their spotlights. A second sweep would be conducted tomorrow to ensure nothing was missed. Yellow tape decorated the two known locations where the unsub had been. Holcomb and the other caretaker, Greene, were being questioned by Birmingham PD and Aldridge.

SAC Worth had arrived and taken over once the child was located. Fine by McBride. He had done what he'd come to do. He was ready to get the hell out of here. He refused to consider the significance of the tagged rat or his former superior's name being listed there. That was the Bureau's problem, not his.

He scanned the crowd for Grace. Located her off to the side of the media/cop cluster fuck. Judging by their body language, SAC Worth was reading her the riot act and she was taking it like a good little soldier. Worth's movements looked strangely disconnected with the backlighting barrage of blue lights and spotlights.

Annoyance furrowed McBride's brow, which reminded him a headache was brewing from lack of caffeine. He couldn't figure out the deal with Grace. She had come to Key West all fired up to get him here. His first impression had been that she was tough and determined. But there was a hypersensitive spot when it came to her sexuality or men or both. An ice princess, he'd thought. Considering the facts, her sensitivity to being female was not so surprising. For the most part the Bureau was still a major boys' club. Having that body and those lips likely hadn't helped her in the respect department with her male peers.

Then there was Worth. He either had a thing for the lady or for some reason he felt overprotective of her. Maybe because he disliked McBride so much and didn't want his newest agent being corrupted by him. He watched her like a hawk.

Too complicated.

McBride took another drag from his smoke. He could do without complicated. Waking up every morning and getting through the day was problematic enough.

He'd found the kid. It was time to go.

"There you are."

McBride looked from the hot-pink boots to the smiling agent. "What's up, Schaffer?"

"Everyone's been a little busy." She glanced over at where Worth was still chewing out Grace. "I just wanted to make sure someone mentioned what a good job you did here today."

"Thanks, Schaffer." He tried to work up the enthusiasm for a smile but it didn't happen.

She gave him a thumbs-up and headed back into the fray.

A good job. Yeah, right. One of the actors from CSI could have figured out this one.

The idea that there was something way, way off with this whole Devoted Fan scenario tugged at him. The clues for finding the kid had been a freaking joke. He'd expected someone to jump out of the bushes any second with a camera and the punch line from some new twisted reality show.

Fake . . . not real. That was how it felt, even now.

But the missing child had been real. The possibility of her being sealed off from life-giving oxygen and dying had been real. If she had awakened and made sounds someone could have heard her before the tomb was sealed, that was true. But she'd been heavily sedated so the risk had definitely been valid.

Why kidnap a child from a wealthy family, secure her in a public place with all the risks to exposure involved, then give her back with scarcely a contest? Why no ransom? If playing the game got this guy off, why not make it more challenging? Draw it out?

"Your Devoted Fan." Didn't add up. Except for the rat with Quinn's name on it.

If McBride had any sense he'd forget the whole damned thing.

"You ready to make a run for it?"

He glanced up as Grace approached. Even in the meager light that reached this far, she looked as exhausted as he felt.

"Past ready." He tamped out his cigarette on the step and stuffed the butt into his pocket as he stood up. "You have a plan?" The circus act around the gate had barely parted to allow the ambulance passage. Birmingham PD was having a hell of a time keeping the media behind the temporary barricade. Going out that way was the express lane for making front-page news. If anyone recognized him or if one of Grace's colleagues leaked his participation, it would be three years ago all over again.

No, thanks.

Grace pushed a smile into place that he couldn't say looked genuine, but the opportunity to watch those lips in action made him glad she did.

"There's a car waiting for us on Seventeenth. We're going over the wall behind the caretaker's cottage."

"Over the wall?"

"This way," she said, heading into the darkness without further explanation.

Following her wouldn't really be a chore, but he figured if he wanted that ride out of here he'd better keep that comment to himself. So he fell into step with her without any more questions. She led the way across the dark cemetery, rarely bothering with the flashlight.

"Looks like you know your way around this place," he said just to break the silence. He wasn't big on conversation himself but this was a little too quiet. He was used to all the noise on the beach outside his windows.

"I came here a lot as a kid," she said as they passed the caretaker's cottage. "I used to lie on the graves and pretend I was dead." She went mute as if she'd just realized that she had actually made the statement out loud.

"I guess that makes me a little strange," she noted, her tone a degree or two chillier.

"No, Grace, that makes you *a lot* strange." His lips twitched with a smile, something they didn't do often. "But a lot of people are strange so I wouldn't worry about it."

McBride's mind conjured the image of Grace as a child skipping around the bleak headstones. Certainly didn't fit with the uptight federal agent she had grown into.

At the Seventeenth Street wall, they made their way across the lowest point in the brick wall to a waiting taxi.

"The paparazzi won't be expecting a member of the investigating team to load into a taxi," she explained as he opened the door.

"Brilliant strategy," he allowed, figuring it was her idea and that she felt in need of a pat on the back.

Grace hesitated before ducking into the back seat. "Worth wanted me to tell you how much the Bureau and the Byrnes appreciate what you did."

McBride waited until she'd gotten in and he'd scooted into the seat next to her before saying, "I'm sure Worth was ecstatic." He understood that his presence was something the man in charge would have preferred to avoid.

"The Tutwiler," Grace instructed the driver.

At McBride's look of confusion, she explained, "We'll have you on a plane headed home tomorrow. Tonight you're to relax and enjoy, compliments of the Byrnes and the Bureau."

Getting on a plane tonight wasn't exactly at the top of his list of things he couldn't live without. But staying was somewhat out of his comfort zone. He had to wonder if the Bureau had a hidden agenda. He didn't trust any of them, not even the pretty lady doing the babysitting.

She was way outside his comfort zone.

That knowledge didn't stop him from going stupid. "As long as you'll keep me company, that'll work."

The city lights filtering into the back seat allowed him to see that guard she wielded whenever he crossed into personal territory go into lockdown. She set him straight posthaste. "Dinner I can do."

"You drive a hard bargain, Grace." He let it go at that.

Probably the smartest move he had made all day . . . with the exception of finding the kid.

Vivian wasn't sure dinner with McBride was a smart move. Being alone with him was like feeling her way through a maze. She never knew what would be around the next turn or when she was going to run into an impenetrable wall. And just when she thought she knew how to avoid getting caught in his traps, she found herself already in one. That unorthodox charm was getting under her skin and that was a mistake. Trusting this man in any capacity would be a major error in judgment.

The driver pulled beneath the canopy at the historic Tutwiler and Vivian paid the fare. An attendant opened the door and she emerged, glad to be away from the media frenzy at the cemetery. Alyssa Byrne was safe and that was all any good agent could ask for. Vivian should be relieved and grateful. But she couldn't quite reach that nirvana. Too many questions were nagging at her.

As she and McBride made their way to the entrance of the grand old hotel she implemented a conscious effort to relax. The man intrigued her even as he tripped her every internal alarm. There wasn't an agent in her graduating class who wouldn't give her or his firstborn to have this chance to learn more about the legendary Hunter—no matter the circumstances that had brought them together.

Her thirst for wisdom was unquenchable. She wanted to reach that same kind of zenith in her career. She just didn't want to fall the way he had. Even if her curiosity weren't going a hundred miles per hour, making sure he was settled for the night was her job. Worth had given her strict instructions.

All she had to do was make sure McBride didn't breach her personal boundaries and there wouldn't be a problem.

Her mind kept wandering back to this afternoon's events. She felt confused at best about the way the rescue had gone down. Success was the end result, but she had all those damned questions. One being, what was the significance of the word written on the child's forehead? That and many other questions she would like very much to direct at the man next to her, but Worth had specifically instructed her to move on. He would handle the final loose ends on this case, including a call to Quantico with the information regarding Andrew Quinn's name having come up. Her job was to entertain McBride, and when the approval was given, see that he got on the plane. For her, it was case closed.

If she could just accept that, life would be a hell of a lot easier.

Unfortunately easy had never been her style.

Inside the glorious Tutwiler lobby with its marble floors and crystal chandeliers, she approached the desk and pushed a polite smile into place for the clerk. "I'd like a room with a balcony and a nice view." Might as well make McBride's night in Birmingham as pleasant as possible.

Fearing that he would suddenly disappear on her, ultimately smearing her hard-earned record, she checked to see that he still waited near the French doors on the other side of the reception lobby. For a moment she allowed her gaze to linger on the man. He pretended not to care about anything, yet she had witnessed firsthand just how much he cared. Finding that little girl had meant as much to him as it had to Vivian. There was far more of the former special agent left in this guy than he wanted her to see . . . maybe even more than he knew.

But that didn't change the fact that the Bureau was still suspicious of his part in this odd case.

Strong-arming her attention away from him, she surveyed the luxurious lobby. Her parents had given her a lavish going-away party in the ballroom just before she had left for college. She would never forget that night. Surrounded by her friends and only months away from hitting that eighteen mark. Her world had been perfect and full of dreams for the future.

A scant month later her life had forever changed, sending her on a whole different journey than the one she had expected to take.

The clerk's voice snatched her out of the past. "I'm sorry," she confessed, "I was lost in thought."

"Your credit card, ma'am," he repeated.

Vivian shook off the haunting memories and searched her wallet for the American Express the Bureau had issued her. When the card had been swiped, the room number and key provided, she thanked the clerk and rejoined McBride.

"Do you need some time to freshen up or would you like to go directly to dinner?"

Despite having spent the past eight or so hours with the man, when he looked at her, she was not prepared for the impact of those penetrating blue eyes. Standing here, in this setting, just the two of them, with the key to his room in her hand, was suddenly a big deal. She was tired, not at her best.

"If you're giving me the option, I'll go with the one that includes the drink first."

The way he had performed this afternoon, she had almost forgotten about that bad habit. "The Pub it is then."

He allowed her to lead, one would surmise because she was familiar with the hotel, but she knew better. He just liked watching her from behind. She would bet her favorite Miles Davis collector's album that he used those lewd glances and remarks to keep her at a distance. He probably did that with a lot of people. Then again, she could be giving him too much credit, like Worth said.

Vivian selected a table on the farthest side of the room, in a dark corner. If McBride was half as spent as she, and she felt confident he was, they didn't need any outside stimulation.

Not that any other stimulation was required with him around.

She dropped her purse in a chair. "I need to make a call. If the waiter shows up, order me a club sandwich, which I highly recommend, and a glass of white wine." She didn't pause long enough for McBride to ask any questions. Weaving through the tables headed for the restroom, she could feel his gaze on her. Looking back would only make her hesitate. No hesitating.

In the ladies' room she stood in front of the sink and stared at her reflection. None of this was right. She had known something was wrong, off, whatever, as soon as she had read the first e-mail from Devoted Fan. Worth had played off her concerns. At the cemetery, she had told him again how she felt about the way this one had played out. It didn't add up.

Nothing she said had convinced him to look at this logically—logically from *her* perspective, at any rate. In her opinion, the kidnapping hadn't been about Alyssa Byrne or her father. The clues had been elementary. The location practically right around the corner from the field office. No ransom. No physical injuries to the child. When she had brought up all those details, Worth wouldn't talk about it. He was too smart not to recognize the same inconsistencies she did. Schaffer, Davis, Pratt, they all saw the same things whether they said so or not.

And all of it pointed in one direction—to McBride. Vivian was certain. Oh, Worth agreed that the elements of the case pointed to McBride, but he leaned toward the theory that McBride had somehow set up the whole thing. He wanted McBride in town for the next twelve to eighteen hours to give him time to explore that avenue more thoroughly. And for Andrew Quinn, now retired, to be advised of the situation.

Vivian was the one who was supposed to keep McBride

entertained. In other words, set him up a second time. Worth was on a witch hunt.

"God." She closed her eyes, shook her head at the short-sightedness of the man she generally respected. How could he not see how wrong he was? Was it possible that someone higher up was putting the pressure on for him to investigate McBride? McBride's connection to Quantico and the ugly ending to his career would logically point in that direction.

Unquestionably, she was prepared to do whatever necessary to get to the truth. If selling McBride out several times over was necessary to get the bad guy in the end, then so be it. But this was off . . . way off.

"Pull it together, Grace." She took a breath. Stared sternly at her reflection. "Get through this. Don't overanalyze. Do the job." She couldn't screw up her career over a burned-out legend. Like Worth said, her instincts could be wrong. The only thing standing between her and getting the job done was her own inflexibility.

When she returned to the table, the drinks had arrived.

"Did you make your call?"

The question startled her then she remembered the excuse she had given. "Oh. Yes." She settled into her chair and savored a healthy swallow of her wine. If she were lucky, he wouldn't ask her any questions she couldn't answer. After the events of the past thirty or so hours, she had to consider that maybe McBride had the right idea. *If you couldn't change it, just drink it out of your head.*

He lifted the tumbler to his lips, took a long drink of his whiskey, watching her as if he suspected she was keeping something from him.

"You ordered the food?" she asked in an effort to make conversation. She hoped so. Having not eaten in hours, she surely didn't need the wine going straight to her head, as tempting as that might be.

"Two club sandwiches, fries, and another round of drinks."

She quelled a shiver. That he had that effect on her made her want to kick herself. Giving herself a break, she admitted that there was something about the man's voice. Deep, sexy in a blatant, I-know-I-could-make-you-scream-my-name way. Any woman alive would react to the sensuality of it. But that was the thing. She didn't usually react like other women. Maybe it was the mystique related to the legend that got to her. The whole "idol" thing. Every agent wanted to be able to accomplish what McBride had—before that fall anyway.

Whatever it was, she wasn't going there.

Shifting her attention elsewhere, she surveyed the pub. "Quiet tonight. I guess we beat the crowd." There were seven or eight couples spread around the dining area that was usually filled to capacity.

If he just wouldn't stare at her that way, through hooded eyes that reached right inside her. If her own mutinous gaze didn't keep straying to his lips, damp from the whiskey, or to those ridiculously sexy whiskers darkening his jaw. Then she might be able to pretend that he couldn't in a million years get to her that way.

But all of the above prevented her from pretending.

"What is it you're not telling me, Grace?"

The waiter arrived with their sandwiches. Vivian smiled and thanked him, more for the interruption than the food. She consciously relaxed her posture. "I don't know what you mean."

He dragged a cigarette from his pack and planted it in one corner of his mouth then lit it. As much as she disliked smoking, she observed each action with utter fascination.

"What's the deal with Worth?"

Oh damn.

As if God had suddenly taken pity on her, her cell phone buzzed against her stomach. "Excuse me." The relief in her voice came out way too obvious. She checked the display. Worth. So much for a welcome interruption. "Grace," she said in greeting. Worth cut straight to the chase, his words souring the wine in her stomach. "I understand," she assured him. She closed the phone and slid it back into its holster, a chill invading her bones.

Steeling herself as much against what Worth's call meant as the questions McBride would no doubt have, she looked directly into those piercing blue eyes. "We have to go back to the office."

The glass he had lifted for another sip froze halfway to his mouth. "Any particular reason?"

He asked the question as if he could care less but she didn't miss the trace of curiosity and maybe the slightest hint of uncertainty in his tone.

"There's been another e-mail."

CHAPTER SIX

"I want to know who he is." Nadine Goodman watched the seemingly quiet conversation between Special Agent Vivian Grace and the unidentified man dining with her at a table across the pub. Nadine knew all the agents employed by the Birmingham field office. But this man . . . she studied him more closely beyond her companion's shoulder . . . was a wild card.

"He could be from another office," Thomas Jacobs, one of Nadine's few confidants, suggested. "Montgomery or Huntsville, perhaps."

Nadine moved her head side to side. "No. He's not a fed. He isn't nearly polished enough." She sipped her wine and considered the roguishly handsome man. "I suppose it's possible the Byrnes hired a private investigator or one of those freelance negotiators."

"Possibly," Thomas agreed, "but then that theory begs the question, why would he be having a drink with a rookie? Why not with Worth or one of the more seasoned agents?"

"True." Her friend's point was definitely a valid one, adding another layer of mystery to the man in question.

Nadine hadn't dealt directly with Agent Vivian Grace, but from what she had seen, the agent wasn't exactly the sort to kiss and tell. This cozy dinner seemed quite out of character.

Though Nadine had not been formally introduced to Grace, she, like any other person representing law enforcement in Jefferson County, would know Nadine. Having come directly from the cemetery after covering Alyssa Byrne's rescue for WKRT, Nadine had improvised a disguise by pulling her long, trademark black hair into a clip and wrapping a colorful scarf around her neck to drape over the shoulders of her gold jacket. Being recognized by Agent Grace would not be a pleasant encounter. As an added precaution, Nadine had called for backup from her friend Thomas. He lived in a downtown loft and had managed to arrive before Grace had finished procuring a room for her friend.

Another of Nadine's contacts, one who worked as a dispatcher for Magic City Cabs, had tipped her off to the pickup on Seventeenth Street. She had gotten all she was going to at the cemetery so she had followed Grace and the gentleman. Nadine's lips lifted into a wry smile when she considered that she was definitely using the term "gentleman" loosely. He looked more rogue than gentleman.

She definitely needed to know who this man was. While this story was still hot, preferably. She looked directly at her partner in crime. "I need you to find out for me, Thomas."

Thomas sighed. "Oh dear. I should have seen that one coming."

Nadine settled her stemmed glass on the table and placed a hand over his. "You know I rarely ask a favor of you like this. But there's something going on here. I can feel it. This isn't over . . ." She searched for a reasonable explanation of what she sensed but couldn't quite pinpoint it. "Yes, the child was rescued, from all reports unharmed, but there's more." She considered the stranger again. "A lot more."

"What makes you think I have any contacts at the Bureau?" Thomas countered, but his eyes gave him away.

The man might have a penis but his mind was as feminine and intuitive as Nadine's. The wheels were already turning inside that pretty blond head.

Before Nadine could pursue the exchange, Grace received a call on her cell, prompting her and her guest to leave, drinks unfinished and food untouched. Nadine considered following them but she needn't worry. If anything big were going down, her contact at Birmingham PD would let her know. And she was just about to land a possible contact at the Bureau. Her former contact there had retired to New England a couple of months ago. It was time to cultivate a new one.

"You have that . . ." Nadine pursed her lips and tried to recall the name. "That nice-looking gentleman I saw you out with that night." She didn't have to mention the name of the club. It was the sort of place one didn't forget. Sodom and Gomorrah some called it. "I'm certain you remember, Thomas."

His lips twitched with the impulse to divulge explicit details. Nadine knew how he loved to go on about his conquests, but he loved the feeling of power . . . of making her beg so much more.

"I can try," he allowed. "I make no promises but I will try. He and I . . . well, we haven't run into each other since that night."

Nadine glanced at the time on her cell phone. She had done the segment at the cemetery live, breaking into the regular broadcasting. As a follow-up, she would do another short segment for the ten o'clock news. For that she would need to get to the station soon. But she could push it another fifteen minutes or so, long enough to finish her wine and seal this deal with Thomas.

She leaned forward, her more cutthroat instincts pushing good manners aside. "Remind him what the two of you shared that time. I'm certain he'll tell you anything to keep that quiet." It didn't take a lot of imagination to guess what went down that night after the intense making out she had interrupted. Thomas had a voracious sexual appetite. He loved a man who still had one foot in the heterosexual world. He devoured them like Godiva chocolates.

A wicked gleam flashed in Thomas's eyes. "Perhaps it won't come to that, but I'll talk to him." He swirled the wine in his glass. "I might be able to sweet-talk a little something out of him."

Nadine picked up her glass once more. "I know you have your ways. I'll trust you to make it happen." She took a swallow and savored the merlot. "This is going to be big, Thomas. I can feel it."

CHAPTER SEVEN

He should have had a double while he had the chance.

McBride hated to wait. Worth had called and demanded their presence then kept them waiting in his office for fifteen minutes.

There's another e-mail.

This thing wasn't going to go quietly away. Murphy's Law McBride style: Nothing was ever easy. This was supposed to be a one-shot deal. Come, do what he could to save the kid, and then leave.

He regarded Grace from the corner of his eye rather than looking directly at her. Eye contact would prompt conversation and just now he had no desire to talk. He was relatively certain she didn't know any more about what was going on than he did. She sat perched on the edge of the other designed-for-discomfort chair stationed in front of the SAC's desk, looking as miserable as he felt. But that wasn't possible. You had to have hit a place so low that it didn't even register on most people's rock-bottom radar in order to feel *this*. It took skill to fall this far.

The door burst open and Worth rushed in, his posture as rigid as any general's. "I apologize for keeping the two of you waiting." He rounded his wide mahogany desk, placed a folder atop its gleaming surface, and rested his hands there as if bracing for war. "I've just come from a tele-conference with Quantico."

That he focused on McBride as he made the statement was an added indication that this wasn't going to be good for him. The idea of having some hotshot agent he'd once mentored or supervised show up to tell him what to do ranked on about the same level as pissing broken glass.

"Since we don't yet have a second victim," Worth went on in that authoritative tone he'd refined to a monotonous roar, "and we're still waiting on the forensics folks to get back to us with any evidence found at the scene, there isn't a lot Quantico can do to assist us with developing a profile."

Typical. "That all sounds just dandy," McBride interrupted when Worth would have launched into the next segment of his monologue, "but you called us here about an e-mail." He inclined his head in question. "Is there an e-mail we need to see? You're cutting into my personal time with a friend." In this instance, his friend was Jack Daniel's. No offense to the lovely Vivian Grace. He doubted she would be caught dead spending any more time with him than necessary. If he was smart, he would adopt the same attitude.

Next to him, she shifted in her chair, a clear signal that his high-handedness with Worth was making her nervous.

She'd just have to get over it.

"Yes, McBride," Worth said, his tone reluctant, as if what he was about to say were a last resort. "There is another e-mail from the unsub who refers to himself as Devoted Fan."

Worth opened the folder he'd placed on his desk and removed a single sheet of white printer paper. He passed it across his desk. "Read it for yourself."

McBride read the words, each one adding another layer of suffocating tension.

McBride,

    Bravo! You saved Alyssa Byrne. I am sure you recognized the simplicity of this challenge. I wanted to give you a practice run in case you were a little rusty. Now, we shall remind them just how good you really are. The next one will not be so simple. Get a good night's sleep. I will e-mail your new challenge tomorrow. Soon they will see!

                                    Honored,
                                    Your Devoted Fan

McBride passed the page to Grace without meeting her eyes.

Who the hell was this guy?

He scrubbed his hand over his face. What the hell did the bastard want from him?

Finding the Byrne child had been a piece of cake. Like the e-mail suggested, the clues had been simple, the time-line ridiculously ample.

That was where the good part ended.

Didn't this nutjob get it? He *was* rusty. The "special agent" in him was over, a has-been. There was no going back to the *legend* he used to be. Not now, not tomorrow.

Determined not to entertain Worth, McBride grasped the arms of the chair to prevent his hands from shaking. Maybe if he e-mailed this Devoted Fan and told him straight up that he wasn't that hero anymore, the guy would go away.

Yeah, right. And immediately afterward he would e-mail his Christmas list to Santa. One of those plans was about as realistic as the other.

"This is far from over," Worth said when Grace lifted her attention from the page. "For now, whoever this Devoted Fan is, we have to assume that he's serious about this plan to . . . ah"—his gaze settled on McBride—"make you a hero again."

That he said the last with a distinct element of derision didn't really bother McBride. He'd been insulted by more important pricks than this one.

"Looks that way," McBride agreed. No point in denying the obvious. "So, do you and Quantico have a plan?" That was the usual strategy in situations like these. Even if Quantico wasn't sending a profiler or team in to assist, they generally had advice.

"We have no choice but to react." Worth lowered himself into his chair and gave the impression of relaxing but McBride didn't miss the tightening along his jawline, around his mouth. "I'll assign three of my best agents, Talley, Aldridge, and Davis to work with you until this is done. Once we have a clearer picture of where this is going, Quantico will provide whatever else we need. At this point we don't have a pattern or any usable evidence. We don't have anything." Worth kept his attention steady on McBride, didn't spare Grace so much as a glance. "We'll, of course, accommodate you at the Tutwiler as long as necessary. Since you didn't come prepared for a prolonged stay, Agent Davis will see that you have any personal items you require."

Worth had been a busy little bee.

"As much as I appreciate your attention to detail, especially the personal ones," McBride admitted without his standard sarcasm, "nothing about that careful plan you just laid out addresses the fact that I have an employer to answer to or that I haven't agreed to stay." He forced his fingers to unclench, his posture to relax. He might not have a lot of choices in his current circumstances but there were at least two he intended to make whether or not Worth or Quantico liked his decisions.

"We can't make you stay, that's true," Worth allowed, the tension McBride had already noted ratcheting up visibly. "We're all assuming, of course, that you'll want to do the right thing."

Oh yeah, the *right thing*. "You mean the way the Bureau did three years ago when I got the boot?"

Worth nodded, his expression smug. "You see, that's

the thing that gives us pause, McBride." He tapped the folder on his desk. "No one has anything to gain by proving what a hero you are or that the Bureau made a mistake three years ago. No one, except *you*. Don't you find that ironic?"

Yeah, that term just kept popping up lately. Apparently, Fate had a hell of a sense of humor.

Time to cut the crap.

"Here's the deal, Worth." McBride nailed him with a look that warned there would be no negotiations. "This unsub hasn't left me a choice, so I'll do whatever I have to. Your boys can be on standby to provide whatever backup I need, but the only agent I'll work with is Grace. That's *my* deal, take it or leave it."

The stare-off lasted all of five seconds.

Worth leaned forward. "Let me just get this out of the way," he said, his tone seething, "I don't like you, McBride. You're all about flash and dazzle and breaking the rules. Well, I'm real happy that worked for you for a while, but the fact of the matter is, that's exactly why you're where you are now and I'm where I'm at."

He reclined into his chair once more and released a big breath. "That aside, we'll play this your way for a little while. Agent Grace will provide support for you until further notice. But don't think you're going to go all Dirty Harry on me. I'm still in charge. You will report to me. The decisions made on this case will be a team effort, no exceptions."

McBride leaned forward this time, stared straight into his eyes with cold, unflinching conviction. "But the final vote will be mine. Since," he added mockingly, "we're playing this my way for a while."

Worth didn't cave immediately, at least he didn't say the words. But McBride knew he'd won. He knew exactly how the Bureau felt about him before Worth had given his little speech. There wasn't an agent on active duty, including Grace, that McBride could trust. But she was a rookie, and a woman; he would take his chances with her. He might be rusty, but he wasn't a fool. He understood where his strengths lay.

"The final vote is yours," Worth agreed.

Vivian had had enough. "Don't I have a say in this?"

The attention of both men swiveled her way. Until that moment she had felt as if she weren't even in the room.

"Do you have a question about your orders, Agent Grace?" Worth leveled a look on her that said she should not try playing hardball with him.

She hesitated, but didn't back down. "Yes, I do. What voice do I have in this? I'm supposed to do whatever McBride says?" She glanced at him, didn't dare linger. Putting up with him for the day was one thing, but if she was going to be working with him for an unknown period of time, she wanted clear boundaries. The man had absolutely no respect for the concept, and bottom line, he scared the hell out of her. There was absolutely no way to gauge what his reactions were going to be in a given situation. Kidding herself would be stupid.

Before Worth could respond to that part of her question, she went on, "It's been three years since McBride was on active duty. A lot has changed. I need clearance to ensure that current procedures and protocols are followed." That he was staring at her made her want to fidget, but she defied the impulse. She wasn't backing down. Not on this.

"That goes without saying, Grace," Worth said, his tone subtly reprimanding. "Both of you"—he looked from her to McBride and back—"will be expected to follow the rules. These circumstances aren't an excuse to do otherwise. Until we get this guy, we have a somewhat unique situation, but that situation does not"—he sent a pointed look at McBride—"I repeat, does not, give either of you carte blanche for ignoring authority."

McBride got up, sent another glance in Vivian's direction that she couldn't ignore. "I'll be outside."

Startled that he would just walk out, she prepared to follow him. Dammit. Every time she pushed back, he made her afraid she had gone too far. With this unsub threatening more challenges—victims, in other words—McBride's cooperation could become even more essential.

How did she keep him in line while staying on his good side? She was reasonably sure of the option he would prefer but he could forget about it. She wasn't putting her career on the line for him. Going up against Worth initially had been for Alyssa Byrne, not for Ryan McBride.

A thin, jagged line—one she would just have to find a way to walk.

"We need a minute, Grace," Worth said, waylaying her. "Close the door."

A new kind of tension shuffled through her. She closed the door and returned to stand in front of the SAC's desk. Sitting was out of the question. It was all she could do to prevent her foot from tapping impatiently. She needed to get out there and smooth things over with McBride. But first, she was apparently going to have to hear about questioning Worth's orders in McBride's presence. Unfortunately, this wasn't the first time she had stepped on his toes in the six months she had been assigned to the Birmingham office. Not exactly the best way to further her career. She knew this, but her determination and ambition always got in the way of her humility and, oftentimes, her good sense.

A less than stellar performance evaluation wouldn't look good when she came up for reassignment or promotion.

"Yes, sir?" That he had let her stand there and stew had her nerves jangling.

"First, just so you know, Alyssa Byrne is fine. The doctors found no indication of harm or abuse. She was sedated, but the drug utilized was safe for pediatric use. So far, she doesn't remember anything after getting out of the car at school."

"Could that be from the drug?" Memory loss was a common occurrence after prolonged sedation, like during surgery. They might never have a description of her abductor—even if the child had gotten a look at the unsub.

"That's a possibility." He released a long, beleaguered sigh, signaling that he was ready to move on to the real reason he had asked her to stay. "I'm going to let your disrespect in questioning my orders slide this time considering what you're dealing with."

She experienced some amount of relief, yet at the same time she felt just a tad guilty for condoning with her silence what sounded like a cut-down of McBride. He had come to Birmingham with her and helped rescue that little girl. But, neither guilt nor appreciation could get in the way of doing this right. If he got out of control and things went wrong, it would be her career on the line. She wasn't going to let that happen. The Bureau was her life. She wasn't risking all she had worked for. Requesting clear boundaries had been necessary.

"Thank you, sir. I honestly meant no disrespect, it's just that—"

He held up his hands for her to wait. "Never mind about that." He propped his hands on his desk and clasped them as if he felt the urge to pray. "Quantico is still concerned that McBride might somehow be behind this."

McBride was on the edge, she would go along with that for sure. His reliability and reasoning were in doubt without question. But this concept of him being the bad guy simply wasn't realistic. "Sir, I can't see how that's possible."

"As much as I hate to admit it," Worth said, surprising her, "I'm inclined to agree with you."

Her impatience giving way to curiosity, she wilted into the chair she had abandoned and searched his face for some clue as to what he knew that perhaps he hadn't divulged so far. "It feels like McBride is a pawn in this, the same as we are."

Worth nodded in agreement, perhaps somewhat grudgingly. "I said basically the same thing to Quantico. That mess three years ago set the Bureau on its ear. No one wants this situation following that same path."

Vivian remembered McBride's last case. The media had focused on it for weeks. But it was reading the final reports McBride had written that had driven all the ugly details home. Kevin Braden had been abducted by his godfather, a man trusted and loved by the family. McBride had tracked him down and the child was still alive. He had gotten close enough to reach out and touch the boy when his superior, Special Agent-in-Charge Andrew Quinn, had insisted on a change in strategy. Quinn had claimed McBride was too close to the edge, a loose cannon. Things had gone to hell in a hurry and Kevin Braden had ended up murdered by his abductor who then killed himself. The autopsy report indicated that the boy had been sexually molested by his beloved godfather.

McBride had taken the fall.

"Our control over how this plays out is limited," Worth said, dragging her from those awful thoughts, "but we absolutely have to keep McBride under control. That order came straight from the director."

Worth would get no argument from her there. "I agree," she confessed, "it would be in everyone's best interest for McBride to have some close supervision."

"This isn't going to be easy, Vivian," Worth warned. "This is your first major case and, frankly, I'm worried. McBride's hanging on by a thread. From all reports, he's a drunk. You could be biting off more than you can chew."

Evidently he was worried. Worth never, ever called any of his agents by their first names.

"I can handle it, sir." She had to make him see that she was capable of dealing with this kind of pressure. The past she had worked so hard to overcome proved a constant hurdle even now. Like the few other people who knew her history, Worth felt it necessary to be cautious, protective. And dammit, she was tired of it. She had plans and goals—like landing a spot on one of Quantico's elite specialized units. The past was not going to hold her back. "My performance at the academy and my work ethic since coming to Birmingham have given you no reason to question my ability. Don't do it now."

"As long as you keep your objectivity we won't have a problem," he insisted. "If you suspect for a second that you're losing control over the situation, let me know. Don't hotdog, Grace. We can't afford to let McBride go—"

"Dirty Harry on us," she supplied. "You can count on me, sir." Her pulse rate reacted to an adrenaline dump. This case was hers. Officially. 'Bout time.

Worth pointed a finger at her. "Just watch him. Don't let him charm you into trusting him. Despite your assessment, we still can't completely rule out his involvement."

"I understand, sir." She stood. "I won't let you down."

"One more thing."

Again she hesitated, waited for him to say whatever else was on his mind.

"Agent Pierce called."

Anger flared too fast to prevent it from showing. "Was the call relevant to me?"

Worth made an impatient face. "You know it was."

Somehow she had thought that she'd made it clear to her former friend and mentor that he was to keep his nose out of her career. Special Agent Collin Pierce was the reason she was stuck back in her hometown when a highly sought after Baltimore assignment had been hers. Graduating at the top of her class had come with a perk or two, but Pierce had screwed her out of what was rightfully hers. All because of that damned past.

"If he somehow influences anything relative to my

career," she warned, "that borders on harassment. I won't stand for it, sir." She had said it before and she meant it. As dear as Agent Pierce had once been to her, still was on some level, she would not tolerate his interference any longer.

"He heard about this business with McBride and he wanted to see how things were going." Worth searched her face too long before he said, "He's worried about you, Grace. Should he be?"

There were a number of things she started to tell Worth he could pass on to Pierce for her, but she kept them to herself. "Tell him I'm fine. Is there anything else, sir?"

Worth shook his head and she walked out. Headed for the stairs. Taking them hard and fast would help her work off some of this steam. Pierce had no right checking up on her. She could do the job. This was *her* case. Finally. And she wasn't going to let Pierce undermine Worth's confidence in her.

In the lobby, she hesitated and considered the real facts here. As much as she would like to believe the end decision for giving her this case was based on her ability, she knew better. Especially considering the call Worth had gotten.

She was on this case because McBride had insisted.

For that, she owed him some amount of allegiance.

He waited in the parking lot by her SUV, the ever-present Marlboro tucked between his lips. That her gaze lingered there as she approached was not a good sign. Objectivity was essential. She couldn't let him get to her on any level.

"I think you should program my number into your cell," she suggested, reaching into her purse for her keys. She hit the remote to unlock the vehicle's doors. If they were going to be working together they might as well act like partners. "And I want you to know I appreciate your vote of confidence. That you trust me enough to work closely with me, is . . ."—she shrugged, going for nonchalance—"flattering."

Oh God. Did that sound as stupid as she thought?

McBride took one last drag from his cigarette before putting it out and finally meeting her gaze across the hood of her Explorer.

"I wouldn't exactly call it trust, Grace," he corrected in that arrogant way that he somehow managed to pull off as sexy. "My options were limited and you seemed like the safest bet. Let's just hope we can get through this without regretting it."

There was something about the way he said the words, the blatant uncertainty coming from the man whose reputation as the best had been unparalleled, unmarred by failure—except that once—that triggered her own insecurity.

For the first time in her career she wondered if she really had what it took to do this. What if everyone else was right and the past had damaged her somehow that doomed her to failure?

Only one way to find out.

CHAPTER EIGHT

Wal-Mart Supercenter
Hackworth Road
11:00 P.M.

Almost time.

Martin's fingers tightened on the steering wheel. He had planned for so long. Waited and waited. Finally the time had come.

Nothing could stop him from succeeding with this mission.

At first the most difficult part of this challenge had been how to avoid the surveillance cameras. Every Wal-Mart was outfitted with equipment for continuous monitoring of both the interior and exterior of the building, including the parking lot. The idea made a person wonder about the clientele of a business that found such all-encompassing surveillance necessary.

But Martin knew it wasn't entirely Wal-Mart's fault or the everyday ordinary shopper's for that matter. Unfortunately, as Wal-Mart should have learned, there were ways to get around even the tightest security. It was such a shame there weren't more heroes like Special Agent Ryan McBride around to protect the innocent.

Rage lashed through Martin at the idea that those FBI fools had set McBride aside as if he were unimportant.

They had used him for their own purposes then tossed him away as if he no longer mattered. Martin knew this for a fact. He and Deirdre, his beloved wife, had watched McBride's career from the first time they had seen him on the news.

"Idiots," he grumbled. Most of those FBI fools were nothing more than rats trapped in their humdrum offices, running around in circles and bumping into dead ends at every turn. None of them were as good as McBride. All put together they could not hope to fill his shoes.

Solving crime was Martin's passion. He and Deirdre watched all the good crime and investigation programs on television. Not the make-believe ones like *Law & Order* or *CSI*. The docudramas that exposed the true story behind real-life events. They followed cases in the news religiously until their resolution. Nothing was more frustrating than having a case go unresolved, like the one involving young Natalie Holloway from right here in Alabama who had been abducted on her high school class trip to Aruba. McBride should have been on her case.

Foolish, foolish FBI.

Martin would show them. Wal-Mart's cameras wouldn't stop him. He was well out of range and his plan was foolproof. Utterly and completely foolproof. He had studied the behavior of one employee in particular for a very long time. Some part of him had always known that his connection to her would play some pivotal role one day.

Now, that day had come. A few minutes from now, the next stage of his strategy would be set in motion.

She would have been first but then he had read in the newspaper about the sealing of tombs at the cemetery. The concept hadn't been part of his original strategy but his dear, sweet wife, his beloved Deirdre, had found it inspiring and urged him to use the opportunity. He could never let her down.

Whatever she wanted, she would have.

But now he was back on schedule with the oblivious Mrs. Katherine Jones.

Five nights per week Katherine left her second-shift job at Wal-Mart and drove home to her empty house. Her husband had been killed in an automobile accident two years ago and she had chosen not to remarry. Martin understood that kind of loss. There was no way to replace a lost loved one.

There was only vengeance, atonement, and mercy. Before he was finished those FBI rats would know all three intimately.

For Katherine Jones life had been so sad for so long that she wondered at times why she bothered. Approaching forty now with no children and no prospect of romance, she had decided that nothing would change this monotony of sadness. She had said so in the journal she kept on her bedside table. She had also written about her one mistake . . . that long-ago blip in time for which she had never forgiven herself. She remembered that evening, not as vividly as he, of course, but she had not forgotten.

She would never forget.

Katherine Jones needn't worry that her life was over. Her time had finally come. Tonight was her night. Her life was about to change, to become a part of something much bigger. This was her chance to redeem herself, to make up for that one momentary lapse that had cost so very much.

Martin smiled as he watched her exit the grocery side of the store's front entrance. She chatted with two of her coworkers as she crossed the parking lot to her decade-old Buick. The four-door sedan wasn't much to look at but it was paid for and it allowed Katherine to support herself with reasonable comfort on her paltry salary.

Katherine said good-bye to her friends and scooted behind the wheel of her car. She drove to the nearest exit and merged out onto Hackworth Road. At that same time, across the street, Martin pulled away from the parking lot of a gas station. He adjusted his speed, switched lanes so that he was right behind Katherine's Buick, and settled in for the drive.

It wasn't far. Only a few miles and that one weekly stop. That was what made Thursday nights special. Each and every Thursday night, Katherine stopped at the minimarket on her way home. One would think that was an odd thing to do since she had only just left the Wal-Mart where she worked and prices were certainly lowest. But Katherine had her reasons. She didn't want her coworkers to know about the wine she purchased each Thursday night. Friday and Sunday were her days off. Sundays she had church, but on Fridays she slept in. A whole bottle of wine made sure her Thursday nights were restful ones. She didn't dream about the husband she had lost or the lack of opportunity in her life. Or about that one mistake that would haunt her until the day she died.

She stopped at the minimarket and Martin drove on past, went directly to her small ranch-style home and parked across the street, keeping a careful distance from the one working streetlight on the block.

A few minutes later Katherine arrived and parked in her garage. Moments later the lights came on in the living room.

Her bottle of wine, he knew from watching her before, would be cloaked in a nice brown bag so no one could see it. She was so very careful. It was a shame she didn't take such pains in her home security. No dead bolts, no alarm system. Nothing at all to deter the unexpected. Which told him more than anything else that she thought she had become invisible, that the world had forgotten her. Or perhaps she wanted to be forgotten, so she, in turn, could forget.

In a couple of hours she would be sound asleep and a new, exciting episode in her life would begin.

Katherine Jones would be terrified. He regretted that

part but it was necessary. The fear would wash away her one sin. But she had no cause for alarm. Special Agent Ryan McBride never failed. He was a true hero. He would save her.

Martin knew the truth about what happened three years ago. He would make them all see how wrong they had been and they would finally understand the gravity of their mistake. The *rats*.

McBride would take his rightful place once more and Martin's beloved Deirdre would be so proud. She had been devastated by the way the FBI had treated McBride. Martin would make this right . . . and she would finally be happy once more.

One day when he and his hero had the opportunity to meet, perhaps McBride would thank Martin. Pride welled in his chest. Yes, that would please him very much.

Martin lived for that day.

Soon. Very soon.

CHAPTER NINE

Friday, September 8, 8:45 A.M.
Tutwiler Hotel

Vivian clutched the shopping bag in one hand and rapped on the door to McBride's hotel room with the other. She squared her shoulders and braced for facing him.

When a reasonable length of time had passed she knocked again. She hoped he hadn't stayed in the bar until it closed last night. If he was still in bed and hungover, Worth would count it as *her* failure.

It wasn't like she could watch the man twenty-four/seven without sleeping with him. Unbidden and damned unwelcome, hot shivery sensations raced over her skin. That he could get to her on that level in spite of her determination not to allow it made her mad enough to spit.

Between worrying about him and fighting the nightmares, she had scarcely slept at all last night. McBride or the rats or the cemetery or a combination of all three had ruined her night . . . made her vulnerable.

She hadn't had one of those godforsaken dreams in over five years. The memory of it . . . of the whispered voices . . . the darkness . . . made her shudder.

Sedatives usually efficiently blocked the nightmares, but going that route right now was out of the question.

And, unlike McBride, she refused to try drinking her demons away.

As she lifted her fist to pound a third time, the door opened. And there he stood, filling the doorway, half naked and to her surprise half shaven.

"Come on in," he invited, that smoke-and-whiskey-roughened voice rumbling from deep within his bare chest.

The sound brushed against her senses, instantly disturbing her equilibrium. Mentally scrambling to recover, she remembered the bag and thrust it at him. "I stopped at Target and picked up some clothes for you. I hope I got the sizes right." She considered the shaving cream on his jaw. "Toiletries too."

He waved the razor. "Room service," he explained. "It's amazing what they're willing to provide." He took the bag with his free hand. "You coming in?"

Vivian managed a stilted nod as she crossed the threshold into his room. She would die before she would ask exactly what room service had provided in addition to shaving implements. The scent of soap permeated the air, but it was the tousled sheets that immediately captured her attention.

The door closed behind her and she jumped. *Don't start off this way.* She had dreaded this moment all morning. Her reactions to his masculinity were foolish. Davis or Pratt or Aldridge wouldn't have this problem. That thought propped up her determination, giving her the courage to face the man. Just like yesterday, he had dragged on his jeans, leaving them unfastened as if he were prepping for an Abercrombie ad campaign. Physically he looked damned good for a guy who drank too much, smoked no matter that it was no longer PC, and was closer to forty than thirty—all the more reason to utilize extreme caution in his presence.

"I'll finish up," he offered, then headed into the bathroom.

She relaxed and took stock of the room. A room service tray sat on the table. Curious, she picked up the silver coffee server. It was empty. So he'd had coffee. Good. She didn't see any indication that he had eaten. She would have to remedy that. Wandering closer to the bed, she picked up the pad of paper on the bedside table. He had written several names there and eventually crossed out most. Suspects? A number forty-one had been written and circled beneath the names. She would have to ask him about that. The only connection to the number she could call immediately to mind was the time limitation Devoted Fan had used with Alyssa.

The notion that McBride had worked last night, even if he had visited the bar or had had drinks delivered to his room, was a good sign. *Let's just hope we can get through this without regretting it.*

Something else she had worried about last night. But her new temporary partner seemed chipper and raring to go this morning. Maybe this wasn't going to be as difficult as she had imagined.

Expect the best, prepare for the worst, her father always said. Seemed good advice just now.

"You did good, Grace."

McBride strode into the room dressed in the jeans and the navy button-down shirt she had purchased. Both appeared a perfect fit. Finding a customer at the store who looked about the same size as McBride had proven a useful strategy.

He made a sound of approval, drawing her too avid interest to that taunting mouth and his smooth jaw. The man cleaned up surprisingly well. If she was completely honest with herself, she would admit that he looked a little too good in most any state. The wicked half grin he wore should have clued her in that trouble was coming, but she missed it . . . too caught up with inventorying the details of this slightly more gussied-up version of the fallen legend.

"Just one question." He walked right up to her, so close she could smell the sport-scented Right Guard she had purchased for him, and lifted the writing pad from her fingers. "How did you know I wasn't a briefs man?"

That was when she made her first real mistake of the day: she looked directly into those devilish eyes. The mischief twinkling there was far too intriguing, way too appealing. Where did those flashes of genuine charm come from? Certainly not from the raw, barbaric man she had met yesterday.

"I saw a pair of boxers on the floor at your place." That her voice held a distinct breathless quality only added to the theory that she was not herself when alone with this man.

"Very observant of you." He tossed the pad on the bed and walked over to the chair where he had left his shoes.

That small distance allowed her to breathe again. He tugged on the well-worn sneakers without bothering to untie them, then stood up. "We ready?"

She adjusted her purse strap and met his expectant expression, mentally bracing for any sneak attack on her composure he might have planned. "Ready."

He walked past her, opened the door like the perfect gentleman she knew firsthand he was not.

"Worth called." She cleared her throat, but the effort did nothing for the persistent tightness prompted by the uneasiness associated with the unexpected. "The toe tag wasn't the only item from UAB's research center; the rats were too."

McBride followed her into the corridor; let the door close behind him. "Already euthanized?"

"According to the log, they had been euthanized and were scheduled for incineration." She followed the corridor toward the bank of elevators. "The tech who noticed them missing filed a discrepancy report with his supervisor yesterday."

"Black looks good on you, Grace."

The rhythm of her step altered clumsily and just like that he had her unsteady again. At the elevators, she stabbed the call button. How did he do it? More importantly, why did she let it get to her?

"Thank you," she returned with enough of a chill in her tone for him to get frostbite. Turning around wasn't required for her to know that he was having a good, long look at her butt.

The ding announced the elevator's arrival a couple of seconds before the doors slid apart. She stepped into the car, pressed the button for the lobby, and waited anxiously for it to start moving again. McBride assumed his usual position against the rear wall. Keeping her attention on the changing floor numbers prevented her from staring at his image reflected in the shiny metal doors.

They had almost reached their destination when he did that thing that made her want to hit something—usually him. He moved up close behind her as the elevator slowed for the lobby level. That her traitorous body reacted to his nearness made her want to join a convent.

"Do me a favor, Grace." His hot breath heated the skin on her neck.

"What?" She didn't look back at him. Didn't dare move with him practically on top of her.

And still he leaned nearer . . . near enough to whisper in her ear. "When we have sex, wear those shoes."

The elevator bumped to a stop and the doors slid open. She hesitated before stepping out of the car, uncertain her legs would hold her upright. During that pause she turned her face to his. Her respiration hitched. She hated that she couldn't contain the response, but she was only human. All the more reason to get this over with. "Don't hold your breath, McBride."

With that out of the way, she strode across the lobby

and out the front door to where her Explorer waited beneath the valet canopy.

Time to go to work and catch the *other* bad guy.

1000 Eighteenth Street
9:30 A.M.

"Devoted Fan thoroughly erased his cyberspace footprints again," Worth said to those present in the conference room. "Quantico can't give us a profile on the unsub until we can give them something to work with. We're still pretty much left in the 'react' mode."

Worth had insisted on daily briefings that included Aldridge, Pratt, Schaffer, and Davis, though Schaffer was missing in action. The briefings were a good idea. These agents were his and Grace's backup, he didn't expect them to be left in the dark. The goal was to keep as tight a lid on this operation as possible, using local law enforcement when necessary. The Bureau didn't like airing its dirty laundry in public, most especially when it involved an ex-agent whose departure from service had already caused a considerable scandal.

McBride's interest slid across the table to Grace. The silver blouse she wore beneath that black jacket sported a scooped neck that *almost* gave a hint of cleavage. When she'd unbuttoned her jacket and taken a seat across the table from him, he had been pleasantly surprised. Her hair was restrained in a shiny silver clasp that held it ponytail-style at the nape of her slender neck. Maybe the lady really wasn't the ice princess he had first labeled her.

Or maybe he'd succeeded in setting her thermostat to thaw.

"Davis, where are we on that list of names?" Worth asked.

McBride's focus snapped back to the head of the table. This was the first he had heard about a list of names. He shouldn't be surprised. What the hell had he expected? He wasn't going to be treated like an equal. There wasn't any-one in this room who wanted him here. His participation was a necessary evil.

Davis shuffled the pages in front of him. "We've come up with more than five thousand hits."

Worth rolled his eyes. "Why don't you brief everyone about this list and we'll do a little brainstorming to see if we can come up with some criteria for narrowing it down."

Davis glanced at McBride as if he dreaded explaining himself. "SAC had me come in at five this morning and start pulling together a list of names in the Bureau's incoming-mail database." Davis tugged at his collar as if he needed to make room for spitting out what came next. "Letters and e-mails either addressed to McBride or with a subject line that related to him or one of his cases."

Grace leaned forward to look past Aldridge. "And there were over five *thousand*?"

Guess the lady hadn't realized just how popular he had been.

Davis nodded. "And I only got it down to five thousand after I narrowed the search parameters to work-related e-mails. There were a lot more asking for dates and . . . offering marriage." Davis tapped the stack of pages and smirked. "You had yourself a regular fan club, McBride. Just like a rock star."

That explanation didn't appear to sit too well with Grace. She leaned back in her chair, her face impassive, as if she could care less. "Shall we differentiate the sexes?" she suggested to Worth, not sparing McBride a glance. "Are we operating under the assumption that our unsub is male or female?"

"Considering the rats," McBride said, waiting for her to

meet his gaze. She refused. "I'd lean toward male, but that's just me. Maybe I prefer to believe my female fans wouldn't be quite so hard-core."

She looked at him then, her dark eyes flashing with disdain. "I've met one of your female fans, McBride. I wouldn't rule out that possibility."

Obviously she was still ticked off about the shoe comment. He angled his head in a gesture of touché and she redirected her attention to the SAC.

"It just so happens," Davis piped up, "that I did that. Eighty percent are female." He looked at McBride now with something that resembled admiration.

Clearly not impressed and certainly not in awe of McBride, Worth asked him, "Any other parameters you'd recommend for narrowing down the list?"

"Go backward," McBride suggested.

Worth looked skeptical. "Backward?"

To Davis, McBride explained, "Look for repeat offenders. Whoever Devoted Fan is, male or female, this unsub has followed my career for some time, not just one case."

"And how do you know that?" Worth challenged. "Other than that one line where he referred to you as his 'old friend,' what else is there?"

"Forty-one," Grace said, with an I-got-this-one look at McBride. "That's the number of high-profile cases you solved during your career."

There had been a lot more than forty-one cases, but she was right, there was exactly that number that had captured the media's as well as the nation's attention, spanning from year one all the way until the curtain call. Tragedy TV. There were those who couldn't resist watching . . . like passing a car wreck.

"I thought it was strange," McBride said, his gaze lingering on her then looking from her to Worth, "that the unsub would select forty-one hours as the allotment of time for rescuing Alyssa Byrne. Most of these scumbags are rather anal. They work with nice round numbers, like twenty-four or forty-eight. Forty-one was a clue. We just didn't see it right away." By "we" he meant Worth, but no need to piss the guy off this early in the day.

"Secondly," McBride continued, addressing Davis with this part, "look for mail with northern Alabama, southern Tennessee, eastern Mississippi zip codes. Our unsub isn't far away."

"That may be a waste of time," Grace countered, "if the unsub has moved in the past three years."

"True," McBride agreed, "but it's a usable parameter that could be advantageous."

"What about relatives or close friends?" Aldridge spoke up. "Is there anyone you can think of who would want some sort of revenge for the Bureau's decision three years ago?"

One corner of McBride's mouth twitched. "You mean, besides me?"

Aldridge exchanged a look with Worth.

"I'm aware that you're going to consider me a suspect until you have someone else to blame," McBride said, letting both men off the hook. "Just don't let that aspect of your investigative work keep you from looking for the real suspect."

"We know how to conduct an investigation," Worth said. "We've got folks at Quantico reviewing your old cases, checking on any possible family connections to perps you've eliminated or put behind bars who might bear a grudge. You made a few enemies in your time, McBride."

He couldn't deny that charge. McBride was just glad to hear that at least some effort was being directed toward any theory at all that didn't include him as a suspect.

"Excuse me, sir." Agent Schaffer strode into the room.

McBride had wondered where she'd gotten off to. Today she wore shiny red cowboy boots. The lady did like her boots.

Worth looked up as Schaffer approached his end of the conference table. "Yes, Agent Schaffer?"

She glanced at McBride then said, "We have a new communication from Devoted Fan."

Everyone in the room prepared to move into action, but McBride was the one to go to the computer to view the newest communication. He felt Grace move up behind him as he clicked the necessary keys to open the document.

Good morning, McBride,
    I trust you slept well in your grand accommodations.

"He knows where you're staying," Grace said, her voice thin.

McBride cleared his mind of both distractions, Grace and the idea that this scumbag knew where he'd stayed last night, and read the rest of the e-mail.

Here is your next challenge:
    This city was built on blood, sweat, and determination. Even now, mightiest to weakest, hard work is what makes it thrive . . . is what forged the path from atop Red Mountain.
    A Jones is a hard worker, but there was a time when she was oblivious. She is remorseful of that mistake and its consequences. But remorse is not always enough and is inevitably too late.
    Her life is in danger, McBride, you must find her before she drowns in her regret. Death can be so cold; she need not die to find her atonement. Her preservation is in plain sight. You have twenty-four hours . . . don't be late.
                                        I remain . . .
                                        Your Devoted Fan

McBride reread the last two lines. Only twenty-four hours this time. The wording and details given were much more obscure . . . not as definitive as before. Uncertainty snaked around his chest and squeezed. First, he should . . . his mind scrambled for the proper protocol.

"Who is A. Jones?" Grace called out to the others. "We need to know the answer to that question ASAP!"

"I'm on it," Pratt tossed back.

Okay. McBride knew how to do this. *No fear.* No self-doubt. *Focus.*

He printed a copy of the e-mail and pushed away from the computer. *What next?* "Davis . . . you . . . you stay on narrowing down those fan mail lists. Aldridge, you and Schaffer work on what Devoted Fan has given us this time. See if you get any matches on possible locations in the city using this verbiage."

"The first thing that comes to mind is steel," Grace said as she retrieved the hard copy of the e-mail from the printer. "This city was built by the steel magnates." She studied the e-mail. "He uses the word 'forged.' "

"Iron Man," Schaffer suggested, taking Grace's theory and running with it.

"Atop Red Mountain," Grace concurred. "Schaffer's right. Vulcan Park, home to the Iron Man atop Red Mountain. And he's definitely in plain sight." Grace looked to McBride. "That would be a good place to start, maybe even before we identify the victim. We could get a search team over there to have a look around. Park security could assist."

"See if Birmingham PD will authorize a small search team to get started," McBride agreed. "Any head start is better than none." The *A* before Jones worried him. Was the *A* an initial or an article referring to Jones? That one missing piece of punctuation would cost them precious time . . . but then that was likely the point.

Worth held up his hands and moved them back and forth as if erasing the suggestion Grace had made and McBride had approved. "We don't even have a line on the victim yet. What she looks like, how old she is, nothing.

We need to know who we're looking for prior to launching a search."

"But there *is* a victim," McBride argued. "We just don't know the specifics."

As valid as Worth's point was, this wasn't about him. It wasn't even about the victim.

This was about McBride's ability to meet the challenge.

And he only had twenty-four hours.

CHAPTER TEN

"The K-9s have been over every inch of this park." Vivian mentally cringed as she reported her status to Worth. There's nothing here, sir."

Six hours, ten acres. And nothing. *Dammit.*

Worth had been right.

McBride had sent her here to head the search while he focused on identifying and tracking down anything he could find on the victim. And she had gotten nowhere. She had wasted time and resources.

A reporter, Nadine Goodman, and a cameraman from WKRT had shown up and attempted to question Vivian. Park security had sent them on their way. Fortunately, that one news crew was all that had bothered. Leave it to Nadine Goodman to sniff out the scent of a story ahead of the pack.

The hoopla at the cemetery had been about Alyssa Byrne, the daughter of one of the city's prominent families. If the media had gotten wind of McBride's participation, there was no indication. Vivian hoped their luck held out. Still, it seemed odd that a high-profile reporter like Goodman would show up for a missing persons search without a socially elite name attached. Goodman was the one to worry about. She was ruthless. If she got wind of McBride's participation, this case would ignite in the media.

Worth ordered Vivian back to Eighteenth Street. That lone command proved more devastating than if he had raked her over the coals.

She shoved her phone back into its holster and considered the official vehicles scattered around the parking area. All of it a major waste of time.

McBride, Pratt, and Davis were still working on identifying the latest victim and narrowing down the list of fans that had followed McBride's career. Finding the victim was like looking for that single four-leafed mutation in a field of clover. There were hundreds of Joneses in the Birmingham area; more than a third had first-name initials that began with the letter *A*—if the letter was even intended as an initial.

Basically, they had nothing.

How did you look for a missing person when you didn't even know who you were looking for? Coming to Vulcan Park had been a shot in the dark at best.

What Vivian needed was a Coke. She had barked so many orders and walked so many miles over the park grounds, she was exhausted. The high sugar content would do her good. Lunch had come and gone with no time to care. After giving Birmingham PD's team leader the final word to head home, she made a stop in the gift shop.

"Dollar fifty-nine," the clerk said after ringing up the soft drink.

Vivian handed her two one-dollar bills and reached for her Coke. A long line of brochures advertising local attractions filled display racks on the counter next to the register. The first couple snagged her attention. Shelby Ironworks and Sloss Furnaces. Both historic landmarks, the latter was now a huge open-air museum. Vivian had visited the Sloss Furnaces on a sixth-grade field trip. She reached for the brochure, some distant memory vying for her attention. She definitely needed that sugar; her brain was going to sludge.

She and McBride had considered Sloss Furnaces and Tannehill Ironworks as well as Shelby Ironworks as secondary search locations, but none of those were located atop Red Mountain like Vulcan Park. That one factor had advanced the park to the top of the priority list.

But they had been wrong . . . *she* had been wrong.

"Now there's a neat place to visit," the clerk said with a knowing nod. "I take my kids there every year for the haunted house they put on. Scares 'em to death."

Maybe it was the low blood sugar level or the gut-wrenching frustration, but Vivian opened up the multi-folded brochure for a look. Anything to take her mind away even for a second. "It's been a while since I was there," she remarked, more to herself than to the woman behind the counter.

"Oh, you definitely need to go back," she urged. "Why, that old place is something to see. Towering smoke stacks and furnaces." She cackled. "Old pipes snaking around in every direction like steel ghosts peeking around corners."

Vivian smiled, allowing the woman's enthusiasm to put a chink in her tension. "Sounds like fun." She twisted the top off the drink bottle and downed a long, much needed swallow.

"Good educational experience too," the clerk went on as she passed Vivian her change. "Been here over a hundred years. Those blast furnaces melted all that ore dug outta this very mountain and turned it into steel. That's what made this city. Birmingham wouldn't be nothing but a fuel stop between Huntsville's Rocket City and the capitol in Montgomery if it hadn't been for places like Sloss." She gave a resolute nod. "Don't let those rusty old boilers and water tanks fool you, they're an important part of our history."

Vivian almost asked her if she got a commission for her sales pitch, but then that final remark the lady had made cut through all the fatigue and frustration and kindled a spark of relevancy—rusty old boilers and water tanks.

Water tanks.

"*. . . you must find her before she drowns in her regret . . .*"

"May I take this?" Vivian quickly refolded the brochure.

"Take a handful. We got loads of 'em."

"Thanks." Vivian hurried out the door, her renewed enthusiasm morphing into heart-pounding anticipation as she punched in the speed dial number for McBride. She had programmed him in at some point last night. She had almost programmed him right back out after his smart-ass comment in the elevator this morning. They would be talking about boundaries again very soon.

As soon as McBride answered his cell, she blurted, "I think we started with the wrong place. Can you meet me at . . ."—she paused at the driver's side door of her Explorer and glanced at the front of the brochure—"Sloss Furnaces on Thirty-second Street?"

McBride had news of his own. He had ID'd the victim. He would provide details when they rendezvoused at Thirty-second Street. She opened the vehicle door, tossed her phone onto the seat, and jumped behind the wheel. Maybe things were starting to come together. 'Bout time.

En route she put in a call to the leader of the search team provided by Birmingham PD and requested support at the Sloss Furnaces location. The team leader didn't sound too thrilled, it was Friday and his team was ready to call it a day, but he agreed to meet her there. This could be another dead end, but waiting was out of the question. They had to try.

Calling Worth would be a last step, right before they launched the search on-site. If she were lucky McBride would brief him and save her the angst. The SAC wouldn't appreciate her sidestepping him but she couldn't afford to waste the time and McBride was supposed to be calling the shots anyway.

At every traffic light that caught her, she glanced over the history of the old steel mill to refresh her memory.

Sloss Furnaces and the production of steel from the iron ore of Red Mountain had been pivotal to the rapid growth of Birmingham "... *forged the path from atop Red Mountain* ..."

Hundreds of men had died there, most burned to death, but the work never ceased "... *built on blood, sweat, and determination* ..."

Jesus, they should have been looking at that e-mail from a much broader scope. She had wasted all those hours.

Get a grip. This sudden charge of inspiration could turn out to be nothing more than wishful thinking. But with nothing else to go on, this was the next logical step. All she could do was make decisions based on the facts she had available.

The same way McBride had three years ago.

For the first time since she started her career in the Bureau, she understood how easy it would be to fail. The realization made her respect McBride's incredible record all the more. The dedication and determination required to even begin to set that kind of precedent boggled the mind. Maybe that was the reason he had done a full one-eighty after leaving the Bureau. Just maybe he didn't know how to be anything else, so he didn't even try.

She pushed the troubling thoughts aside. Now wasn't the time to be distracted. And his personal problems were not her concern. Going down that path would only lead to places she did not need to go.

Considering they only had about two hours of daylight left, she put in another call to the search team leader and suggested he send two smaller teams to Shelby Iron Works and Tannehill Iron Works. Neither of those locations

was as high profile in Birmingham's history as Sloss Furnaces but why ignore any possibility? The hours were
ticking down. She was banking on the idea that the unsub
would go with the higher profile location just as he had
when selecting a cemetery . . . but then there had been ex-
tenuating circumstances at Oak Hill with the resealing of
the tombs.

Damn, every time she believed she had a valid point,
something else bobbed to the surface of her tumultuous
thoughts to negate it.

She had made the decision to go with Sloss . . . now she
had to face the possibility of having made the wrong one.

7:00 P.M.
Sloss Furnaces
20 Thirty-second Street
15 hours remaining . . .

McBride and Pratt were waiting when she arrived at the
parking area under the First Avenue viaduct. Aldridge
was briefing Birmingham PD's search team. The Coke had
prompted Vivian's second wind. She was ready to solve
this puzzle.

The steady thump-thump of cars passing on the viaduct
overhead resonated in the air like a heartbeat. A train's
lonesome croon somewhere in the distance underscored
that repetitive thud.

When she reached the gate where McBride waited, he
showed her a four-by-six photo of a blond woman.

"A Jones?" she asked.

He shot her a look that said, if only it had been that
easy. "A Jones turned out to be Katherine Jones. Thirty-
nine. Widowed. No children. She's employed by the Wal-
Mart on Hackworth Road. She got off work at eleven last
night and no one has seen her since. We might never have

gotten to her name in time using the telephone directory if her sister hadn't reported her missing."

"How did her sister know she was missing?" Those who lived alone sometimes went for days before anyone noticed they were missing.

"They were supposed to meet for lunch today. The sister's been worried about Katherine's depression. So she went to her house when several hours passed with no word. The back door had been opened by force and there were signs of a struggle." He lit a cigarette, took a deep drag. "Looked staged. But, however he got her out of the house, she was gone. Forensics is there now."

"Neighbors?" Vivian asked as they entered the Sloss property.

"No one saw a thing." He gestured to the K-9s and their handlers. "Aldridge has the blue vest Katherine Jones wore to work last night. Hopefully that will put the dogs on her scent. Worth and Talley are questioning her family. The vic's husband was killed in an automobile accident two years ago. According to her sister, she hasn't been herself since."

"... *her regret* ..." Mrs. Jones had lost her husband. Had to still be grieving. Fury roared through Vivian. What was this scumbag doing? First a child, then a woman who had already lost her husband. What harm could either of these victims ever have done to the unsub? That was the one thing Vivian looked forward to in all this, putting him behind bars.

"Where do you want to start?" She refolded the brochure so that the map faced out, then surveyed the sprawling industrial complex that had the look of being trapped in time. The goliath restored furnace she remembered vividly from that elementary-school field trip. The towering blast stoves and enormous smokestacks too. She had felt like a tiny speck surrounded by the massive metal giants that had somehow dragged her back a full century. Felt that way now.

"I take it you've been here before."

She glanced up at McBride, some foolish part of her mind noting the five o'clock shadow that darkened his jaw despite his having shaved that morning. "Sixth-grade field trip."

He considered her a moment, for once not staring at her lips. "You know, maybe this is about you as much as it is about me."

The statement gave her pause, made her frown for a second or two. That wasn't possible. No one knew about her past . . . she had no career reputation yet to encourage that kind of attention.

"That was a joke, Grace."

Her frown turned into a glower. "It wasn't funny." She turned back to the rusting graveyard and repeated her question. "Where do you want to start?"

McBride took a moment to evaluate the situation. "I've already instructed the team to conduct the usual grid search." He glanced at her. "You and I will start with anything that holds water."

"*. . . before she drowns . . .*"

If Katherine Jones was here and the danger to her was paralleled by the clues in the e-mail, as had been the case with Alyssa Byrne, then she would be at risk for drowning. Some place in plain sight.

In other words—Vivian looked around once more—just about anywhere.

As they passed through the shadow of the cold, quiet blast furnace and threaded their way between the sky-high smokestacks, she had to wonder what around here *wouldn't* hold water. Valves, pressure gauges, and pipes that ran in every direction with vines climbing along and around the rusty metal surfaces. Steam vents and shaft openings gave the impression of a landlocked submarine.

Night was coming way too fast. Even with flashlights the iron grate paths along the main walkways were damned gloomy. Somehow in the last century trees had pushed their way up through the sandy earth and stood like alien beings in this metal wasteland. The wind rustled through their leaves, adding another layer to the creep factor.

The search team would scour the dilapidated brick buildings, including the supposedly haunted blowing-engine rooms. A site manager had arrived to assist the search team through the maze of metal.

The gates of hell. That was what one of her classmates had called this place. He had heard his daddy talk about the hundreds of workers who had died here during the factory's century of operation. The sound of footsteps on the catwalk high overhead jerked her attention there even as she knew a dozen or more team members and two dogs had fanned out in every direction.

Shake it off, Grace. You aren't twelve anymore. And you don't believe in ghosts. Between the numerous reported ghost sightings and the fact that Sloss Furnaces had been labeled as one of the most haunted places on earth, she wasn't exactly looking forward to the next few hours. Her freak-o-meter was set to hypersensitive.

Deep down she knew it wasn't really this place . . . it was the coming darkness and the unknown that had her rattled.

Would they be able to find Katherine Jones in time?

Applying her undivided attention where it belonged, back on what she had come here to do, she pointed to a doorway up ahead. "That leads down to the tunnel. It comes out on the other side of the mill. I don't think there are any side tunnels or cubbyholes for hiding, just a straight path. The team may have already swept through there."

"I'd like to check it out anyway," McBride said, setting a course for that destination.

Vivian glanced toward a pair of uniforms up on the nearest section of catwalk then took the plunge and descended those stairs into the tunnel. She remembered this

part all too well. Nothing had changed. Long, pitch-dark,
spooky tunnel. No place to go but forward or backward,
just like she had said. The sounds of their breathing . . . of
each trickle of water . . . echoed in the tunnel as if time
stood still and the sound stretched to compensate. Ankle-
deep water splashed around her feet, soaked her shoes and
chilled her feet.

When they finally reached the other end, she was more
than ready to leave it behind.

"Over there." McBride indicated a row of large tanks in
the distance.

Vivian glanced at her map. "Boilers," she pointed out.

Decrepit and rusty, they seemed pretty much past holding water, but the need to be sure wouldn't be abated by
conjecture. Making certain was necessary.

A woman's life depended on it.

Dusk had settled and Vivian desperately wished that the
dogs would lock on to a scent. *If it was even possible.* That
reality hit like a ton of bricks. If Katherine Jones was in
water, the dogs might not be able to pick up her scent.

There was always a slim chance that moving her to her
destination would have left a scent trail the dogs could
latch on to but no guarantee.

Vivian checked the time on her cell phone. They still
had twelve hours but most of those would be night hours
and not nearly as productive.

One by one, they checked the ten gigantic boilers, every
cubbyhole in the walls or in the ground, under- and above-
ground rooms, any pipes large enough to accommodate a
body, furnaces, stoves—they examined every damned thing
they encountered that would hold water and/or a body. And
burned up more time—that precious commodity—without
yielding the desired results.

"Where the hell is she?" McBride muttered.

Vivian understood his frustration. Neither the dogs nor
the team had spotted a single piece of evidence that might

give hope. About every ten or fifteen minutes the "clear" signal echoed across the deathly quiet industrial yard and, each time, her hope sank a little lower.

"Maybe she isn't here." Vivian hated to say the words out loud but someone had to. As sure as she had wanted to be about this location, she had to face the looming reality that she was, apparently, wrong.

"She's here," McBride argued.

When had he decided that with such certainty? What gave him that kind of confidence? Ten years in the field doing exactly this? Or had he been born with an innate sense of finding the lost? His former reputation would certainly seem to indicate so.

As he stood in the spotlight of one of the few lights around the property, McBride's gaze met hers and she knew instantly that he was on to something.

"We've spent all this time looking in every imaginable hiding place," he said with a final survey around him. "She has to be someplace easy to access *and* in plain sight."

Vivian had considered the whole "public" complex as being in *plain sight*. Time to reduce that focus. "You mean, like someplace more specific or . . . obvious?"

"Exactly." He took another look at the map. "To pull this off"—he hesitated as if considering a theory—"he would need running water, not standing water like we've seen in a lot of these old boilers and containers."

His renewed optimism was contagious, so was his theory. "He would need to control the flow of water into wherever he's holding her—to facilitate the timing?"

"Yeah." McBride nodded. "And it's someplace right under our noses. 'Plain sight.'"

He was right. Adrenaline bumped up her pulse rate. "Let's find that site manager." Vivian put through a call to Pratt.

The entire search team rendezvoused in front of the massive flywheel in the main blowing engine room.

McBride made eye contact with every member of the group. "We need quiet. Wherever she's hidden, the water will be running." He turned to the site manager. "Can you narrow down the locations where there's running water access?"

He nodded and quickly pinpointed the spots on his map. McBride deferred to the search team leader for directing his people to the targeted areas. Then, he and Vivian methodically scanned each location, looking for anything the others might miss. Still they found nothing. Heard nothing but each other scrambling around in the dirt and gravel.

The odds for success looked bleak at best, but McBride refused to give up. Vivian had to admire that because she damned sure felt her optimism waning.

If Katherine Jones was here . . . somewhere . . . she would be terrified and she, too, would be losing hope.

3:00 a.m.
Seven hours remaining . . .

Vivian looked at the digital display on her cell phone. They were no closer than they had been two or four or even five hours ago.

McBride had ordered everyone back to his or her vehicle except her. They stood in the darkness on the ladle car tracks listening. She was pretty sure that she was the only one who still held out any hope for finding the woman at this location. On the other hand, with each minute that passed, McBride grew more certain that she was here.

For some totally irrational reason, Vivian couldn't give up on *him*.

Slowly, painstakingly, he began a meticulous repeat search of a fifty-by-fifty perimeter around each accessible water source on the property. Vivian stopped when he stopped, and started when he started, mimicking his movements with a second look.

They had gone over their current location two or three times and still she noticed something new she had missed before. The darkness . . . the fatigue . . . both were playing tricks on her eyes.

This go-round, that something new was a narrow strip of disturbed earth. It was a miracle she had noticed it at all. Whoever had done the digging had smoothed it back over especially well. She crouched down and touched it. Loose dirt. Rock. Just beneath a shallow layer of those elements, something cool and smooth brushed against her fingertips. Aiming the flashlight for a closer inspection, she studied it, followed the path of the furrow for several inches . . . a water hose?

A water hose!

"McBride!"

Before she could even look up, he was crouched next to her. She held the light on the strip of hose she had uncovered. He pushed to his feet, followed the barely noticeable trail all the way to a small window in the old powerhouse.

But they had searched that area two or three times.

What had they missed?

Her heart pounding, Vivian hurried inside right behind him. They located the spot where the hose entered the room.

A dead end.

Dammit.

The hose hung limply down the wall, its ringed end going nowhere.

"Son of a bitch!" McBride snarled. He whipped out his pack of cigarettes and planted one in his mouth, then lit it.

Vivian hadn't seen him smoke all night. The stress was getting to him. She felt the final remnants of hope draining out of her. Yet, *something* nagged at her, wouldn't permit her to let it go completely.

Outside the water hose had felt cool. With the temps in the eighties and nineties by day and the sixties and seventies by night, there was no reason for the hose to be cool unless water was flowing through it.

Her gaze landed on the limp section of hose dangling from the window. She crossed back to it, touched it, room temperature, not cool like the other—no water running through it. She went back outside to where she had located the trench and knelt down to scan the area on either side with her flashlight.

And then she found what she was looking for.

Old fuel and oil cans had been arranged in a haphazard pile to camouflage a secondary path that branched off from the first. The first path had been a decoy. The unsub had counted on the idea that once they found that section of hose entering the window and going nowhere they would assume that was it and move on. Since their search had been focused on areas where water could be contained, a pile of leftover rust-eaten cans and crates wasn't of interest.

"Over here, McBride!"

Together, she and McBride moved the cans and other junk aside to see where the path led. They had been in and around this building a dozen times. The site manager had said that mostly "junk" was kept in the old powerhouse. It had only taken a quick glance to know there was nothing of the size necessary for storing a body, but they had checked all the same. That there was no water source had eliminated the building's potential altogether as the search had continued.

But their unsub was a smart guy; he had provided his own supply.

Vivian stalled, got a glimpse of a hose draped along the back of an old Reddy Ice freezer. Anticipation jolted her. "I think this is it."

McBride moved around to where she stood on one end of the commercial container.

"It goes through there." She pointed to the back of the freezer, up near the top. This had to be it. These old Reddy Ice freezers weren't designed to *make* ice, only to keep it frozen. There wouldn't be any need for a water supply.

A single metal door in the front was the only access. Jesus. If she had only been looking rather than visually eliminating possibilities, she would have recognized this thing's potential all the times she had walked past before.

Plain sight.

She moved to the front of the container and pulled on the door handle. It didn't budge. As she trailed the flashlight's beam around the door, she could see no apparent reason for it to be that difficult to open.

McBride came around to the front. "The motor isn't running, but the side is cool to the touch."

Like the water hose.

"I tried pulling the hose out. He must have attached a nozzle from the inside and it's too big to come through the hole." He pulled at the door the way Vivian had. "Call Pratt," he said as he pulled even harder. "Tell him we need a couple of pry bars and some more muscle over here. Maybe a saw that can cut through this thing."

Stunned at the idea that it could have been this simple, Vivian made the call, reholstered her phone, then tucked her flashlight under her arm. Her heart thudding, she wrapped the fingers of both hands around the handle and pulled in unison with McBride. It still didn't budge. "It's . . ."—their eyes met—"like it's sealed." Her chest constricted. "Can she be getting any air in there?"

McBride roved his light over the front and sides of the dirty white container. Found nothing other than the occasional rusty spot in the paint. Knots formed in Vivian's stomach. No holes . . . no air.

He shoved a bucket off the top of the old freezer, leaned against the front to get a closer look. Vivian's throat went dry as she watched the flashlight's beam go back and forth over that surface.

The beam suddenly stopped, then moved more slowly. Her heart did the same.

"Air holes have been drilled into the top," McBride said over his shoulder, "all the way across the back." Relief weighed heavy in his voice. "We have to get this damned thing open." He inspected the gasket around the door, then pitched his flashlight to the ground and grabbed the handle with both hands.

A new rush of fear poured through Vivian, sending her pulse back into a frantic rhythm. If Katherine Jones was in there, was she still alive?

Instinct, or maybe desperation, taking over, Vivian pounded on the side of the freezer while McBride pulled at the door. "Mrs. Jones, can you hear me?"

"I don't know what kind of glue he used," McBride said as he put his whole body weight behind the pull, "but it's not coming loose."

"Mrs. Jones," Vivian shouted as she pounded some more, "answer me if you can!"

Vivian stilled, listened. She'd heard something. *Had it come from inside the freezer?*

Holding her breath, Vivian flattened her ear against the side and listened. Another sound reached out to her—soft like a moan, barely audible. Adrenaline ignited, rushing along her limbs and making her tremble. "We're going to get you out of there," Vivian shouted, hoping the sound would carry through the insulated wall. *Don't worry.* She wasn't sure if she had said that last part out loud. "She's in there, McBride! I can hear her."

They had found her.

They had found her!

How deep would the water be now?

"We have to hurry!"

Where was Pratt? Davis? Anyone?

She rejoined McBride's efforts but the door just wouldn't give.

Pratt, Davis, and the site manager arrived with the pry bars.

Thank God.

Pratt and McBride pried at the door.

Finally it gave way.

Vivian directed the flashlight's beam inside.

The interior space was empty save for Katherine Jones and the slowly building water that had reached her shoulders. Bound and gagged, the woman sat, knees to chest. She lifted her gaze to Vivian's and moaned pitifully. Her mouth was duct-taped closed. One word was written in black marker across her forehead: OBLIVIOUS.

"Let's get an ambulance out here," Vivian said, with a glance back at Pratt.

"On its way," he assured her.

McBride ushered Vivian aside. "I'm going to try and pull her out of there." He reached inside, lifted and tugged at the woman's shoulders until her head and upper torso were out the door. Vivian pulled the cold, wet woman into her arms as McBride threaded her lower body free.

Too weak to stand, Katherine Jones crumpled to the ground, taking Vivian with her. McBride knelt down to get a better look at her condition. He slowly peeled the tape away from her mouth.

Vivian wanted to cry. She was so damned tired and relieved. Katherine Jones was alive!

"Don't worry, Mrs. Jones," she urged, "you're going to be fine now."

Mrs. Jones sobbed as McBride unbound her hands and feet. Vivian scrambled up onto her knees, peeled off her jacket and draped it around the poor woman's trembling shoulders.

Vivian's phone vibrated so she stepped aside to answer it. The drain of adrenaline had her sagging against the freezer for support. As she drew her phone from its holster, black lettering on the interior of the open door reached out and grabbed her attention. She peered at the letters, some of which were written very small while others were much larger.

T . . . w . . . o. Two. d . . . O . . . w . . . n. Down.
H . . . O . . . w. How. M . . . a . . . n . . . Y. Many.
T . . . O. To. g . . . o. Go.

Two down . . . how many to go?

The world stopped for a moment, leaving Vivian's mind reeling with disbelief.

He wasn't nearly finished. Resignation dragged at her muscles . . . made her legs go rubbery again.

She turned slowly, her gaze landing on McBride where he sat on the ground speaking softly to Katherine Jones.

They had saved two . . . but would their luck hold out as the challenge intensified?

Vivian peered back at the innocuous words that added up to the promise of danger.

It only took one mistake . . . one failure . . . for someone to die.

CHAPTER ELEVEN

Saturday, September 9, 8:15 A.M.
University of Alabama Birmingham (UAB) Hospital
Sixth Avenue

"I'm sorry." Katherine Jones's voice was a raw, raspy croak. "I just don't know."

"You focus on recovering, Mrs. Jones," SAC Worth promised, "we'll find the person responsible for this."

Worth, Grace alongside him, paused at the foot of the patient's bed to speak with the doctor.

McBride watched from the position he had taken next to the door. He wasn't wasting his time, or the victim's, with questions. The unsub they were dealing with was far too smart to have allowed her to see his face.

Considering what she had been through Mrs. Jones had been in damned good shape when they pulled her out of that freezer. Other than scared half to death and dehydrated, despite sitting shoulder deep in water, her stay in the hospital was for observation only. Feeling the water rise and knowing you couldn't get away would shake anyone to the core, sedated or not. Poor woman. When she'd first heard Grace and McBride talking she had thought she was dreaming.

The best part of the whole ugly episode was that she had lived to tell about it.

Worth cut McBride one of those "this is your fault" looks as he exited the room.

Grace hesitated at the door, didn't follow her boss. "You coming or did you have additional questions?" She craned her neck to see if Worth was out of hearing range.

He shook his head and pushed away from the wall. "Let's go."

In the sterile, endless corridor outside the room, he had to remind himself which way to go for the elevators. He was beat. He'd survived solely on coffee for the past twenty or so hours. Caffeine could only go so far.

Worth hadn't waited, which suited McBride just fine. The SAC had already given his thoughts on the latest search-and-rescue endeavor. This whole charade was out of control, in his opinion. To his way of thinking, no former agent should have thousands of fan letters and some stalker fan kidnapping and terrorizing innocent people. Someone was going to end up dead and the Bureau would be blamed. Bottom line: McBride was an albatross. This whole mess was his fault.

What's new? He hadn't expected Worth to feel any other way. Frankly, McBride didn't give one shit how Worth felt. But he wholeheartedly agreed with the theory that if this nutcase Devoted Fan kept at it—*two down, how many to go?*—someone was going to die.

And that would be McBride's fault.

Grace pushed the call button for the elevators. "You okay?"

Hell no, he wasn't okay.

He rubbed at his eyes with his thumb and forefinger, attempted to block out the spots floating in front of his retinas. Bad sign. He knew the symptoms. Lack of sleep, alcohol, and nicotine. And a kind of fear he hadn't felt in a long-ass-time bullying its way into the mix.

His hand shook as he lowered it back to his side.

He needed downtime.

No . . . What he needed was to get out of here before someone died on his watch.

The elevator doors slid open and he couldn't move. Couldn't walk into that cramped space.

Grace stepped into the waiting car and prepared to make the necessary floor selection. "You coming?"

"I'll . . . ah . . . take the stairs."

He didn't explain, just headed for the end of the corridor with her shouting to him to watch out for the paparazzi in the lobby. The stairwell was empty so he took a moment to try and derail what he knew was coming. Deep breaths. *Let them out slow.* He wasn't going down this road. *No way.* Couldn't.

He shouldn't have come here at all. Rescuing that kid had been so simple . . . but this last time hadn't been quite so easy. If Grace hadn't been there to back him up, he might have failed. What the hell would he do next time?

And there would be a next time.

What if he couldn't fix it? Those old instincts might fail him entirely . . . and because of him someone would die.

Taking the stairs quickly, he kept one hand on the railing since the world seemed determined to tilt on him. Get outside. Get some air. *Don't slow down.*

Sweat popped out on his skin. His gut clenched.

McBride ascended to the first floor in a near run and emerged into the lobby. Crews from dozens of news channels were hanging around, hoping to catch a break on whatever the hell was going on. He moved wide around where they had gathered near the elevators. The visiting hours crowd had filtered in, making forward movement a challenge. Ignoring the glares and remarks of the people he bumped into in his haste, he plowed through. Had to get outside. A half-ton weight had settled on his chest. He couldn't breathe . . . couldn't think. Damned sure couldn't risk running into a reporter.

He hit the sidewalk. Air flooded his lungs.

Breathe.

Deep.

That was it. More deep gulps. *Hold it. Release.* The weight on his chest lessened. Finally, the knot in his gut relaxed.

He was not going to let anyone die—not this time.

He could still do this . . . *he hoped.*

"McBride?"

He closed his eyes, chased away the demons, and grabbed that fuck-you attitude that worked so well for him . . . most of the time. "What?"

Grace flinched at his growl. "You okay?"

He ignored her question, dredged up the control he'd allowed to slip. "How'd you avoid the reporters?" She had taken the elevator and the hordes of reporters had been waiting there like buzzards after roadkill. That was the thing about ambulances. Anytime one was called to a scene, the media was bound to show up.

"Worth has them distracted with a statement he decided to issue."

McBride didn't bother asking what Worth planned to say in his statement. He didn't give a damn.

"Let's get out of here." Grace started walking toward the parking garage where she had left her Explorer. "You want Waffle House or IHOP?" she asked as he fell into step next to her.

"You're kidding, right?" The last thing he wanted to do was eat. He paused, fished a Marlboro from the pack and lit up, the rush of nicotine instantly calming.

"You need to eat, McBride."

This conversation sounded familiar. "Look." He glanced at her breasts then at her lips; she tensed and outrage immediately flashed in her eyes. "You're not my mother or my nurse. I'll eat when I eat." He inhaled another lungful of smoke. "Let's see how Davis is doing on that list. We need to see if Schaffer can connect these two victims in any way."

Glaring at him a ball-busting moment or two, Grace didn't say a word. Eventually, she pivoted on her heel and continued toward the garage. She gave him the silent treatment from that point forward but that was fine by him.

If they talked she would only bring up his little episode back there and then ask questions he would refuse to answer. Talking about his past was something he didn't do.

Ever.

1000 Eighteenth Street
2:30 P.M.

Davis had the list narrowed down to just under one thousand. More than half of those hailed from good old Dixie, which resulted in around six hundred names. McBride had joined him at the conference table where two laptops had been set up for their use. Schaffer was looking for any connection between Alyssa Byrne and Katherine Jones.

Across the room, the timeline had been updated. The photo of Alyssa Byrne remained along with comments regarding the resolution of her abduction. Next to that was a photo of Katherine Jones with the same information. A separate section had been created for known facts about the unsub. There were only two: he, assuming he was male, was a fan of McBride and lived somewhere within a hundred-mile radius of Birmingham.

The MO was curiously different in each incident and the victims were totally unalike. Not one damned thing usable for putting together a decent profile. Which, McBride surmised, was the point.

Grace arrived, a folder in one hand and a steaming cup of coffee in the other. She placed the cup in front of McBride, then sat down at the table.

Never one to turn down a fresh cup of coffee, even
when it came from a potential enemy, he took a welcome
swig. "Thanks."

"Are you ready for an update?"

This was the first time she had spoken to him since they
left the hospital. She had taken the initiative and followed
up on the evidence found at the various crime scenes,
which, he imagined, would net them nothing useful.

He lowered the laptop screen and turned his full attention on her. "Shoot."

Her speculative glance told him he shouldn't tempt her;
after all, she did carry a weapon.

"The sedative used on Alyssa Byrne and Katherine
Jones was a dead end. Nothing reported missing; at least,
nothing in the system. It's possible the unsub ordered
something on the Internet from Canada or Mexico. For the
most part, those sales are untraceable. So we can't get a
lead on him via that route."

McBride downed another slug of coffee and waited for
the rest. There would be more. The lady was thorough. She
wouldn't come to him with nothing. Grace was a good
agent—as agents went. He wasn't shaving any points for
her freezing up at the cemetery. Newbies often balked at
the sight of death or suspected death the first few times.
Still, instinct told him that hers was a deeper reaction, to
something beyond this case.

Not his problem. He had to remember that.

He wasn't here to play amateur psychologist or to give
career advice. Anyone who sought career advice from him
was not operating on all cylinders.

"Forensics found nothing in the way of evidence in
either mausoleum," she went on. "The floors were swept
with a broom the caretakers use on the property. No hair,
no trace evidence whatsoever."

Hearing her reiterate what he had already guessed made

him feel ill. Every time an agent walked through those doors he tensed, worried that another e-mail had arrived.

A more demanding challenge. *One I might not be able to meet . . .* even with Grace's help.

It was only a matter of time before another communication came; manipulating names on a list or rehashing what they already knew wasn't going to stop this guy. The reality abruptly hit like a punch to the gut.

"Damn it!" He plopped his empty cup down on the table.

Grace blinked, her own frustration visibly restrained.

On the other side of him, Davis scooted back from the table. "Let me refill that for you." Davis reached for the disposable cup.

McBride exhaled some of the tension and turned the cup over to the agent. "Thanks."

"As you know," Grace carried on, as if he hadn't just shown how close he was to coming undone, "Katherine Jones didn't see our unsub. She stopped at a convenience store and picked up a bottle of wine. The last thing she remembers is emptying the bottle. When she woke up she was in that Reddy Ice container with water up to her waist."

He motioned for Grace to get to the part he didn't know. Listening to that summation was like going for a repeat root canal. It hadn't been fun the first time.

"We may have gotten lucky at the Jones residence."

Now that got his attention. "How lucky?"

"There were prints but we're still ruling out family members. Hair and other fibers appear to be connected to the victim."

"Grace," he said with a pointed look, "I'm waiting for the lucky part."

She met his annoyed look with one of her own. "I'm getting there." She paused for effect or to irritate him further before continuing. "A neighbor came forward."

"Wait a minute." He sat up a little straighter. "I was under the impression all the neighbors had been questioned and that no one saw anything."

"None of them did." She tried to suppress a smile but that wasn't happening and he wanted to shake her. "A neighbor's beau saw something."

McBride frowned. "Beau?"

Grace nodded. "Mrs. Roberta Norris. She's seventy and a widow. Horace Jackson is her boyfriend. When she called him this morning to tell him about the police questioning her, he told her what he'd witnessed. At the time he wasn't aware it meant anything."

"It being . . ." McBride prompted, seriously out of patience now.

"The night Mrs. Jones disappeared, Mr. Jackson stepped out back to smoke. Evidently Mrs. Norris doesn't permit smoking inside."

McBride could do without the asides, but he understood that Grace was yanking his chain. He supposed, if one took into account the tactics he used on her every chance he got, he deserved it. What could he say? He was only human. Finding a way to make life bearable without the aid of his usual tactics was a challenge all its own. He hadn't found a solution yet.

"Mr. Jackson heard Mrs. Jones's garage door open and since it was after midnight he was curious. He took a peek around the corner of the house and saw her car leave the driveway. A man wearing corrective glasses was behind the wheel."

Anticipation zinged McBride. "Did he give us hair color, approximate age? Anything else?"

"Nothing that specific. He's only sure the driver was male and he wore glasses . . . the old horn-rimmed style. Hair might have been dark but he wasn't sure about that."

"I'll be damned," McBride said, an epiphany dawning.

"*He* used her car." Drove to the scene and then back to retrieve his own vehicle. That took some major balls. This completely changed the way the vehicle was viewed. The Buick had been dusted for prints and checked for trace evidence on-site, but this required additional analysis.

McBride turned to Grace. "Forensics will need to—"

"Already taken care of. The vehicle is on its way to the lab as we speak."

Twenty, thirty minutes. That was how long it took to drive from the residence of Katherine Jones to the Sloss Furnaces. The return trip would be the one. After unloading the woman from the car, getting in through the gate, and securing her in that abandoned freezer, he would be sweaty. Sweaty, maybe with an abrasion or a cut, if he had done the air-hole drilling during that same time as well. That would have made him much more likely to leave behind DNA.

Davis returned with the coffee refill.

"We have some additional criteria for you, Davis," McBride said with the most enthusiasm he had been able to muster all day.

Davis set his own coffee cup on the table and readied his laptop. "Let's hear it."

"Male, over forty, and with a very high IQ."

Grace looked surprised by that last part. "Smarter than the average repeat offender," she said, "probably, but higher-than-average IQ, how did you come to that conclusion?"

"Think about it," McBride said. "He knew exactly how long it would take that box to fill with water. He timed it exactly for us to rescue her, the same as we did Alyssa Byrne."

"That's speculation," Grace countered.

"We found her shortly after three with about seven hours to go, or roughly thirty percent of the time we'd been given. She was sitting on her butt against the bottom of the appliance, with water reaching her shoulders. Do the math, Grace. Any way you look at it, this guy knew exactly how much time we needed."

She considered his explanation, her expression thoughtful. "You're right. He knew the time the tomb Alyssa was in would be resealed. Katherine Jones said Thursday night was the only night she deviated from her routine of going straight home. He planned it all that carefully. Down to the minute." Her face grew more animated with each deduction.

"Leaves no prints or trace evidence," Davis said, joining the summation, "and he knows the Internet. Can't catch him by any of the usual means."

Worth strode into the room, drawing all eyes to him. "Heads up, people. We have a new communication."

Tension rippled through McBride, setting his already raw nerves further on edge.

Worth, Davis, Pratt, and Schaffer gathered at the workstation for McBride to open the e-mail, as if they feared some plague would be released among them if they dared do it themselves.

McBride dropped into the chair and made the necessary clicks. Sure enough, there it was.

Bravo, bravo, McBride!
    Another marvelous success! I knew you would show them. I am very pleased! Ah, and your new partner suits you.

McBride glanced at Grace. The unsub had definitely been watching. Bastard.

I'm certain you are anxious to learn the clues for your next challenge, but tomorrow is the Lord's day and you should rest. I will contact you on Monday.

Do not worry, my friend. When this is done and you
have surpassed each challenge they will know the truth and
the prize will be yours.

Ever faithful,
Devoted Fan

Fury boiled up inside him and McBride clicked the
mouse to open a reply box.

"What're you doing, McBride?" Worth demanded.

"What I should have done already." He wasn't letting
the son of a bitch continue to manipulate him. This had
gone far enough!

"Wait," Grace urged, "this could backfire. If this guy is
some demented freak, he could be hanging on by a thread.
The truth could cause him to crack."

"Let's hope so," McBride growled from between
clenched teeth. "Maybe he'll do the world a favor and off
himself."

"Damn it, McBride," Worth warned. "You can't—"

"My way," he cut him off, "remember?"

McBride typed the few, straightforward words.

"What if he already has the next victim?" Grace argued.
"This could cause him to—"

Clicking the send tab derailed whatever else she had intended to say.

McBride was finished. This guy needed to understand
that his plan wasn't going to change the facts. McBride's
FBI career was over. End of story.

Devoted Fan,
    I don't work for the FBI anymore. Let's leave it at that.
McBride

Before anyone could snap out of their shocked silence
the alert that he had new mail sounded.

Sending the unsub a kiss-off e-mail suddenly didn't feel

like the right thing to do . . . but it was too late to regret it now.

"Open it," Worth ordered. "Let's see how badly you screwed this one up."

McBride's hands balled into fists on either side of the keyboard. The urge to pound this dickhead expanded, a palpable force inside him.

Grace placed her hand on his arm. He flinched at the touch. Wished he could trust what felt like a sign that she was on his side.

"Open it," she urged quietly.

Ordering his fingers to relax, he went through the necessary steps. The box opened, revealing the new mail.

Special Agent McBride,

I sincerely regret any difficulty my actions are putting you through. But please understand that this is for your own good. The world needs you. I need you.

Respectfully,
Devoted Fan

P.S. I am aware that they assuredly made you say such a thing. The rats.

McBride pushed the chair back and stood. "I need a smoke."

Silence swelled in the room, crowding out the door behind him.

He had a respite . . . before it started again.

And again after that . . .

Between now and the next time, he had to find a way to end this before Devoted Fan discovered just how wrong he was.

CHAPTER TWELVE

4:30 P.M.

"I know I've never visited your fair city before, Grace," McBride said with a leisurely look around at the passing landscape, "but I'm reasonably sure this isn't the way to my hotel."

Definitely not the way to his hotel. Vivian reminded herself that the job sometimes required going above and beyond the call of duty. *This* fell precisely there.

"You need some serious sleep, McBride. Worth is arranging security for you since we know Devoted Fan has been monitoring your hotel. Until then you're staying with me." Even as she said the words, Vivian's fingers clenched on the steering wheel and a twisting sensation pulled at her stomach. *Mistake! Mistake!* Her internal alarm screamed at her but she mentally slammed the snooze button. Couldn't worry about that right now. Like Worth said, she was the only one McBride even halfway trusted.

After Worth had issued the order, she had rushed outside to find McBride waiting by her SUV. Part of her had been afraid he had left . . . though that would have been difficult since he didn't have any transportation. But she had known how angry he was, as much at himself as at Devoted Fan or Worth.

It was her job to see that he cooled off and got some sleep. *Big mistake*. She turned onto Valley Avenue, headed over to Ashland.

"Well, damn, Grace." McBride turned those assessing blue eyes in her direction. "All this time I thought you were going to take the prize for being the most uptight hot chick I've ever had the pleasure of meeting and then you go and take me home with you."

She was certain there was a compliment in there somewhere. "This is only for a few hours, McBride. I'm going to make sure you eat and sleep, in that order." With another pointed look in his direction, she added, "Maybe a shower first."

"You're the boss," he said with a truckload of innuendo.

They had both gotten pretty grungy during the rescue. Her suit might just be beyond saving. The dry cleaner would likely take one look and shake his head. She couldn't wait to get it off. The more she thought about the sweat and filth, the more she itched. With Devoted Fan's latest communication there was time for the essentials like food, a bath, and some sleep. Trying to push forward without rest was a recipe for disaster. Pratt, Aldridge, Schaffer, and Davis would rotate nine-hour shifts for the next thirty-six. Unless Forensics came up with something from Katherine Jones's car, the fan letter list and a meager description of the unsub were all they had and someone had to stay on it.

As much as Vivian hated to think this way, sometimes another victim was the only way to gain new evidence like additional factors for attempting to connect the victims or to ascertain an MO.

And Devoted Fan was going to strike again. There was no way to stop it. Worth had released minimal information to the public without mentioning McBride's name. Holding out as regards the potential threat wasn't an option any longer. Male, forty or older, eyeglasses, random abductions. That was basically all they had to release . . . all they had, period. But if releasing the information would put folks on guard maybe Devoted Fan's job would be a little more difficult.

The knowing it was going to happen and that there was nothing they could do but wait was almost worse than chasing clues after the fact.

Vivian waved to the guard on duty at the gate leading to her secure neighborhood and drove on through. A minute later she pulled over to the curb in front of her town house. There was a garage entrance in back but since she would leave again in a few hours she didn't bother. "This is it."

Grabbing her purse, she climbed out of the Explorer and rounded the hood. McBride got out and shoved the passenger side door shut then took his time assessing the place she called home. She hit the clicker to secure the vehicle and strode up the walk, ignoring his blatant appraisal.

The neighbor's dog had knocked over a pot of geraniums again; she paused long enough to right it. She didn't have time for pets but she did have flowers. Filling the pots each season was her therapy, according to her mother. Vivian just liked the idea of cultivating something.

At the door, she shoved her key into the lock. She loved the pink brick and white columns that set the front façade of her place apart from the neighbors'. It was hers. Her safe haven. She had barely gotten settled, but it felt like home already. That part had come as a surprise, considering she didn't want to be here.

Inside, she tossed her purse and keys onto the table by the door and took a deep breath, letting go of a big chunk of stress. She was glad to see this day end.

"I'll call Steak-Out," she offered, "the beef tips are great. How do you like yours cooked?"

"Medium."

She grabbed the cordless phone and entered the number

she had memorized. As she placed the order, she removed her weapon and shoulder holster and went into her bedroom to put both in the bedside table drawer the way she did every night. Vivian thanked the voice on the phone that assured her the order would arrive within forty-five minutes. She would have to prowl around in the fridge for a snack to tide her over; she was starved.

"The food's going to be—" McBride sat on her sofa thumbing through a photo album. That privacy invasion sent her guard up. "Forty-five minutes."

He closed the album, set it aside, and sank back in the cushions, the navy of his shirt a stark contrast to the white slipcover of her sofa . . . to the white of the wall behind it. She hadn't realized until that moment how bland and white her space was. Everything about him seemed to stand out, left all else in obscurity. The darkness of his clothes . . . the shadow of a day's beard growth. His tanned skin. And that probing gaze that locked in on her as if she were a target.

She wasn't letting him do that to her . . . not here . . . not now with them alone. Bringing him home had been a risk, but like Worth said, the unsub was watching him. Leaving him alone in that hotel room was a bigger risk. And McBride wouldn't have agreed to go with anyone else.

"I know what you're thinking, Grace." He draped his arms across the back of her sofa as if inviting her to join him.

Oh, no he didn't. If he did, he would be arguing that a big tough guy like him could definitely take care of himself. And he could, she had no doubt. But this freak, Devoted Fan, was smart, just like McBride said. He planned his every move down to the last detail. No mistakes were made in the carrying out of those plans, which indicated there wasn't a high level of excitement or passion involved in the execution. Determination, satisfaction maybe, but nothing so undisciplined as any of the more thrilling emotions. With this latest victim and the vague description they had from the witness, Quantico was attempting to put together a profile.

But she already knew what it would say. Obsessed. Relentless. He wasn't going to stop until he got what he wanted. The scary part was, did he really know what he wanted? A man as brilliant as he surely had to know he couldn't manipulate the Federal Bureau of Investigation.

That on the table, what was his ultimate goal?

"You're thinking," McBride picked up where he'd left off, "that you need to protect me."

She could only imagine where he was going with this. "I know, I know. You're big and strong." She strode across the room, picked up the photo album, and tucked it back on the shelf where it belonged. "You don't need protecting."

He rose from that white background in one fluid motion and took a step toward her. "But I do."

Without a single pause he moved directly into her personal space. Incredibly, she let him.

"I need you to protect me from myself, Vivian Grace." He studied her face as if he had just one shot to memorize every tiny detail. Lastly, he homed in on her lips, licked his own. "You have the most—"

"Amazing lips," she finished, her outrage going from mild to mighty in just one downward sweep of his inordinately thick lashes as his undivided attention zeroed in on her lips. "I've heard it before, McBride."

His gaze linked with hers and the wicked satisfaction twinkling there incited her competitive streak.

"You've been bucking for a reaction from me since the moment you opened your front door and found me waiting on the other side," she accused. "You're not going to get what you want. You might as well give up now."

He reached out and she stiffened, those long fingers of his twined in and trailed the length of a wisp of hair that had fallen loose from its clasp. "You should wear your hair down."

As angry as she was, that surly, sexy voice of his still managed to make her tremble inside.

"Fine. Let's get this over with, McBride."

His gaze flew back to hers as she grabbed him by the shoulders and, in that instant before she pulled his mouth down to hers, she saw two things . . . surprise and hesitation. His reaction spurred her courage. She kissed him hard on the lips, lingered a moment to ensure he got a good taste of hers. That was what he'd harped on . . . obsessed about . . . driven her crazy over—her lips.

Just as abruptly, she pushed him away and backed up a step. "Now that we've gotten that out of our systems, take a shower. The food'll be here soon. And I don't know about you, but I want some sleep."

As she walked away, she called over her shoulder, "Leave your clothes outside the guest room door and I'll throw them in the wash."

She closed her bedroom door behind her and sagged against it. Had she just done that?

Her trembling fingers touched her lips. She'd had a point to make, that was all. Then why did she feel all shaky and warm inside? That wasn't supposed to happen. She had been aiming to back him off . . .

Somehow she had missed the mark, by about a mile.

10:30 P.M.

"Be still."

Vivian froze . . . didn't even breathe. The wet fabric of the tank top clung to her skin, molded to her unrestrained breasts. If she moved . . . if she dared to drag the dank air into her lungs he would notice.

A finger flicked across one pebbled nipple.

Her gasp was involuntary. Be still! Don't move. Don't breathe.

He smiled, the expression a stark, mocking contrast to the bejeweled mask covering the entirety of his face above that sneering mouth. "You like that, don't you?"

Bile churned in her stomach. "Yes," she lied, careful to keep her voice submissive, her eyes lowered. She would never forget those demonic eyes. Never.

The tip of that same finger trailed down her rib cage, over her belly to stop at the edge of her panties. It took every ounce of resistance she possessed not to shudder in disgust.

"On your knees," he demanded, his voice cruel, his eyes glowing like amber coals straight from hell.

She lowered to the cold, damp stone floor. Inside, she screamed. Please make him stop. Somebody please help me. But outside, where he could see, she remained composed, obedient. His servant.

She stared at his crotch through slitted eyes; the bulge there made her jaw tighten. She struggled to loosen those clenched muscles. Had to relax. Don't let him see the tension.

Please, please, don't let him do this. Not again.

"Suck me."

The savagely whispered order sent dread creeping over her flesh, sinking into her bones. Her fingers went directly to the fly of his trousers. She knew better than to hesitate. If she hesitated, even a single second, she would die. Like the others.

She opened his trousers and cautiously worked him free of his form-fitting briefs. He groaned. Her body operated on autopilot . . . her mind took her someplace else. Far away. So she wouldn't have to see . . . so she wouldn't have to feel.

He gripped her chin ruthlessly, tilted her face upward. The pad of his thumb smeared across her lips. There was no physical or mental response to his touch. She felt nothing now . . . nothing . . . not even the fear. She was in that *place he couldn't reach. It was her only escape. Her heart knew the truth, and now her mind accepted it. No one was coming to save her.*

"Such a lovely mouth." He forced her lips apart and dipped his thumb inside. "Make me happy, Number Thirteen. Make me happy, and I'll let you live another day."

A scream wrenched from her throat.

Vivian bolted upward, her arms flailing. She had to get away. Had to run!

"Grace!"

Fingers clamped around her arms, shook her. *Fight him!* Don't let him win!

"Grace! Wake up!"

Vivian froze. The breath was trapped in her lungs as her eyes flew open.

The lamp on her bedside table allowed her to see that it was McBride who sat on the bed next to her, his fingers biting into her arms.

"You okay?"

For five, then ten, seconds she didn't know how to respond.

McBride. Her bedroom. Devoted Fan.

The trapped air rushed out of her lungs.

The nightmare. She'd had the nightmare. *Again.*

Brain synapses fired once more. "God." She pushed her hair out of her face, became aware of the perspiration dampening her skin and of the sheets twisted around her legs. "Sorry. I . . . I had a nightmare."

"No shit." He released her, exhaled a big breath. "You scared the hell out of me."

She glanced at the alarm clock, half past ten. Why hadn't Worth called by now?

"I don't know about you," McBride said as he stood, "but after that I need a drink." He offered his hand.

In nearly five years not a single nightmare. Her first big case, her first opportunity to move to a new level in her career, and it had to start *again*.

Losing what was left of her battered mind or just plain old suffering from a moment of utter weakness, she put her hand in McBride's, kicked free of the sheets, and clambered out of bed.

He led her through the dark house as if he had already committed to memory the layout of her home. In the kitchen, he flipped a switch that turned on the light over her sink.

"What have you got around here, Grace? Wine? Beer? Anything?" He released her and went to the fridge to have a look.

The Styrofoam containers from Steak-Out sat on the counter stinking up the room. She should have taken care of those before collapsing.

"I think there's a bottle of wine under the sink," she said when McBride emerged from his perusal of the refrigerator.

He was half dressed as usual, jeans riding low on his hips. At least they were partially zipped this time. Thankfully she had pulled on a pair of lounge pants and a camisole after her shower. Jesus, she hadn't expected to sleep straight through to this hour of the night. She had counted on having McBride back at his hotel by dark. Mostly she had hoped to have some much-needed distance. Things were shifting into dicey territory between them and she had to stop that plummet toward disaster.

"White merlot." He made a strange face at the bottle he had discovered, then shrugged. "That'll work."

When he started prowling through drawers for an opener, she said, "The one next to the dishwasher."

He located the corkscrew, deftly opened the bottle, and snagged two glasses.

Watching those movements, knowing what they would lead to, her good sense abruptly kicked in. She opened her mouth to put a stop to his plan here and now but he hesitated right in front of her as if he had known exactly what she was going to do. "Come with me," he ordered.

It was in that moment with him standing only inches away that the haze of the haunting dream and the confusion he made her feel cleared enough for her to remember . . .

She had kissed him.

Oh, dear God.

He strode to the sliding door across the adjoining living room and stepped out onto the deck.

The way he moved held her captive until another realization poked its way through her bewilderment.

He had left her door unlocked. Open. Was he crazy?

No, he wasn't crazy. *She was.* Bringing him here was crazy. Kissing him was just plain dumb. Shaking her head, she took the same path he had only with wholly different intentions. If they were going to be working together for an unspecified time, she had to get some kind of boundaries back into place. Somehow, her plan to get the whole meeting-of-the-lips thing over with hadn't exactly accomplished the goal she'd had in mind.

Her deck was awash in moonlight, which she appreciated. The lower the light, the less likely he could assess her every expression and gesture. Oh, but he would try.

She climbed into her favorite wicker rocker and curled her legs beneath her. Might as well get comfortable. Until Worth called, she had no choice about keeping him here. McBride's lighter flashed and the fiery glow from the lit cigarette glittered as he took a long, leisurely drag.

"Tell me about the nightmare."

No way. "That's personal, McBride." Where was her cell phone? "I need my phone. Worth'll call and—"

"Don't move. I'll get it." He left his cigarette in the ashtray and went inside.

She could've argued with him but it wouldn't have done any good. Frankly, she wasn't sure it was possible to set any boundaries with him. The man didn't play by the usual rules and that left her grappling for balance and structure.

The breeze was chilly or maybe it was only because her skin was still damp from sweating out her private demons. That McBride had been in her room, was in there now, touching her phone and anything else he damn well pleased, made her shiver.

Idiot. God, she had kissed him. She was a complete, utter idiot.

She had hoped to diminish that tension building between them with that hasty gesture. Unfortunately her attempt appeared to have flopped big-time.

McBride returned, placed her cell as well as his own on the table next to the ashtray.

He settled back into the chair and took a drag from his Marlboro. "Where were we? Oh yeah, you were going to tell me about the nightmare."

Did he honestly think she would share something that private with him? He had to be mental.

When he continued to sit there, waiting, she reiterated, "I'm not telling you anything, McBride."

He smashed out his cigarette in the ashtray. "You share your war story, I'll share mine. I know all about night-mares, Grace."

That gave her pause. She was tempted. Like every other new recruit, she had heard all the speculation about what happened to the great Hunter. No one knew for sure. When this assignment came up, she had read the report he had submitted on his final case, but it had been edited, declas-sified. Big black lines blocked out a good portion of the in-formation. That told her there was far more to the story than the top brass wanted anyone to know.

"Sorry," she tossed back. "No can do."

He poured the wine, passed her a glass.

"Don't think you'll ply me with drink." She laughed, the sound more brittle than she would have liked. Damned dream. She hated the way it left her feeling. Shaken and afraid. She hated being afraid.

"Let me take a shot at it," he offered.

The hand holding the glass trembled. He couldn't possibly know. No one did, except Worth and Pierce.

"Forget it." She gulped the merlot, needing some form of relief that didn't include . . . *him.* She blocked the images trying to burst through the thin barrier she used to protect herself from the past. Under normal circumstances she was very good at that.

"This incident involved a man."

That cruel voice . . . the vile whispers in the dark . . . she had tried so hard to forget echoed in her head. "Give it up, McBride," she tossed back, playing off his suggestion. She couldn't let him hear the reaction in her tone, that would only egg him on.

"Took place at or during college."

She stilled. How could he know that?

"Ah-ha. I'm right."

"You're guessing," she countered, her voice way, way fragile. A dead giveaway.

"Didn't have to guess." He sipped his wine. "Your photo album told me."

She bit her lips together to prevent asking how the hell her photo album had told him anything.

"Lots of snapshots during high school, a few before that, and then nothing until the academy photos. That's a sizable lump of time. Important time. College days."

Her throat tightened and her stomach rebelled at even the idea of more of the wine. Her heart rate had kicked back up to postnightmare pounding. She should call Worth. Find out what the holdup was.

"Tell me, Grace," McBride whispered through the darkness, his voice soft and cajoling. "It's just you and me. *Partners.* You can't possibly have any demons uglier than mine."

Her lips quivered and before she could stop herself she said it. *"Nameless."*

The word resonated through her, making her insides writhe with equal measures of fear and disgust.

The initial silence told her he hadn't expected that.

"You were the final victim . . . ?"

Oh yeah. Surprise. Shock. Horror. Worth's reaction had been the same. She hadn't wanted to tell him, either, but Pierce had insisted. Either she told Worth or he would.

Damn Pierce. She had trusted him and he had let her down.

"But . . ." McBride hesitated, that too discerning mind no doubt analyzing every tiny detail he had learned about her to date. *"Grace.* That's not your real name."

"It's my mother's maiden name." She had been born Vivian Taylor. Changing her name, changing colleges, it had been the only way to endure what came after survival. *Living with it.*

McBride stood. She tensed. He moved to the edge of the deck and braced his hands on the railing, seemingly peering out at the darkness.

A minute or two elapsed, long enough for her to squirm. She shouldn't have told him. Major mistake.

He turned, leaned against the railing. "What the hell are you doing with the Bureau?"

"My job," she snapped. "And in case you haven't noticed, I'm damned good at it."

"When you don't freeze up."

That was a low blow. She held back her first reaction to his statement, then she hugged her arms around her knees and told him the truth. "My past has nothing to do with the present. The Bureau is my life now. I'm not looking back, McBride. It isn't healthy." As you should well know, she considered tacking on but didn't.

"How many years of therapy did it take for you to get this deep in denial?"

That was it. She dropped her feet to the deck and stood. "I'm calling Worth."

McBride pushed off the railing, took a step toward her. "I was deep into an abduction case of my own at the time you went missing, but I heard some of the details. He kept you two weeks, didn't he?"

When she didn't answer he took another step toward her. She refused to be intimidated. She was finished with that. This conversation wasn't happening.

"How many times did he rape you?" He went on with his heartless interrogation.

The rage she had thought she could hold back erupted inside her. How dare he ask her that? "Shut up, McBride. Just *shut up*."

"Every day?" he pushed ruthlessly. "Twice a day? More?"

Fury overrode her common sense and she took the final step, got into his personal space for a change. "That's right, if you must know. Every damned day. I lost count of the times." She laughed, a dry, nasty sound. "And I killed him. Just once," she qualified, "but that was all it took."

More of that deafening silence. They stood so close she could feel the tension running through his body, could smell the sweet wine on his breath.

"You were what," he murmured, the sound harsh, "number twelve or thirteen?"

Number Thirteen. She shook with the words shuddering through her. "Thirteen victims in five years. I guess I was his unlucky number."

The voices and images tried to intrude. The blood all over her . . . the taste in her mouth. She shuddered and fury twisted her lips, made her want to scream. But she held it back . . . she had learned how to do that with the fear too. Only once in a while did she screw up and let those old emotions get the better of her. Like freezing up in front of McBride. If Worth found out . . . her career would stall and she would never get a chance at reaching her full potential. Damaged agents weren't reliable in the Bureau's opinion. She was looking at a prime example.

Hell yeah, she spent a hell of a lot of time pretending the past hadn't happened. And she wasn't changing that strategy now.

"Did you ask for this assignment? To come back home and prove you could live only a couple of hours away from where it happened?"

Answering that question would just give him another avenue to explore. She was not going there.

"You were attending college in Nashville, right?"

He just kept right on digging . . . forcing the issue.

Damn him.

"Or was it Memphis?" he prodded.

"Lipscomb," she admitted, knowing he wouldn't stop until she did. "I was barely half a quarter into my freshman year, a month shy of my eighteenth birthday." The memories howled inside her like an imprisoned beast. She wrapped her arms around her middle to hold herself steady. Nameless, Satan himself, had stolen her out of her warm, happy life. He had taken over her whole world.

He. He or *them*? She still couldn't put the idea out of her head that there had been two of them. The whispered voice had *felt* different at times . . . as if there were two different men taunting her. But when the police had discovered her and the body, there was only one. All DNA and trace evidence had pointed to him. There was absolutely no evidence of a second unsub . . . just the confusing voices in her head. But her shrink had insisted that the creation of the second persona could have been an attempt by her mind to escape the evil . . . to pretend she'd had an ally or to excuse her inability to escape her captor sooner.

So, she'd spent seven years pretending not to hear the voices . . . pretending she wasn't that person anymore. Pretending made it go away.

Eventually she had changed her name and transferred to Boston College, to escape all of it—even her overprotective parents. She had cut ties with the friends she'd had her entire life and never once looked back. Six months back in Birmingham and she hadn't called a single one. Took pains to ensure that if she ran into anyone she used to know she looked away or hurried in the other direction. Her parents didn't fully understand her decision but they honored her wishes. Unlike this Neanderthal.

"Is that why you came back here?" he persisted.

"I asked for Baltimore." She closed her eyes a second and concentrated on banishing the images and voices. "But I got Birmingham." She knew who to blame for that. Her mentor and friend, Special Agent Collin Pierce. Maybe one of these days she would actually forgive him.

"Couldn't be coincidence," McBride guessed. "Sounds like someone wanted you to deal with the past. Does Worth know?"

That was all he was getting.

"Your turn," she demanded. She couldn't talk about this anymore. She had told him too much already.

"Fair is fair," he confessed. "Hit me."

Her cell phone trembled against the tabletop, the drone cutting through the tension.

She considered not answering it. McBride damn sure wasn't getting off this easy. Transporting him to his hotel could wait. If Worth had the security detail in place, he could leave her a voice mail.

Ring number two.

"You have to answer it," McBride suggested.

"We had a deal, McBride. It's your turn."

"It may have to wait."

That he looked so smug and that he was inarguably right only made the statement more infuriating.

A third ring.

Dammit.

She snatched up the phone and flipped it open. "Grace."

It was Worth all right. The information he barked into her ear sent a cold chill deep into her bones. "Yes, sir. We'll be right there."

Closing the phone, she faced McBride, dread mounting at warp speed. "We have to go to the office."

"Tell me there isn't a new e-mail."

"There isn't a new e-mail." Her fingers felt limp around the phone. He was not going to take this news well.

"What the hell is it, Grace?"

His usual cocky tone had gone cold and impatient.

"At five-thirty this evening WKRT aired a story about you that was picked up by all the networks. Worth found out a couple of hours ago; he's been running damage control with Quantico since. He'll brief us both when we—"

"What kind of story?" McBride demanded. "I don't want to hear it from Worth. I want to hear it from you."

Vivian braced for his reaction. "An anonymous source provided details as to why you were right in the Braden case and your superior, Andrew Quinn, was wrong. Some of the details in the story were straight out of your final report, McBride. The original version, not the declassified one." She swallowed back the bitter taste that rose in her throat. "An hour ago, Derrick Braden went to Quinn's home and shot him once in the head, then shot himself."

Silence.

Standing so close, she could not miss, even in the meager moonlight, the disbelief and shock that played out on his face.

Vivian could only imagine how many times Braden had replayed those final days before his son's murder. How many times had he asked himself what he should have done differently? What the Bureau should have done differently? Now the world knew some of the answers to that last question . . . and Derrick Braden hadn't been able to live with it.

McBride shook his head, denial etched in the planes of his face. "Braden couldn't have—"

"He did."

"But—"

"We have to get dressed and go in." She turned away, her movements stilted. This couldn't be happening.

"Wait." He clutched her arm, hindered her escape. "What else did Worth say?"

Telling him the rest would only add insult to injury. She would rather he hear it from Worth.

"What?" he demanded.

"Director Stone called." She didn't have to explain that Stone was currently *the* director of the Federal Bureau of Investigation. McBride would know that. Anyone who watched Fox News or CNN would know that.

"And?"

"He wants you disassociated with the Bureau and *off* this case."

CHAPTER THIRTEEN

This was very distressing.

Very, very distressing.

Martin changed the channel to another twenty-four-hour news station. This could not be correct. And yet, on every channel, the breaking news was the same.

After three years, a distraught father carries out his vengeance for an inept investigation.

No, no, no, no. This wasn't supposed to happen.

There was no room in Martin's careful plan for that kind of distraction. Death was not his goal. He was not a murderer, which was far more than he could say for some he had chosen to take part in his plans.

But that was not the worst of it. He had also learned that Tuesday's scheduled event had been moved up to Monday. This simply would not do. Timing was everything.

Martin moved restlessly about the room. He picked up the newspaper, folded it neatly, and placed it on the table next to his recliner, then straightened the doilies his wife had made for the arms.

He had planned each challenge very carefully. There was absolutely no margin for error where emotions were concerned. Precise calculations of each move and estimations of the possible repercussions were essential. He had studied criminal investigations in-depth . . . he knew all the essential steps. Had followed hundreds of cases on television news and in the newspapers. *FBI Files* and *New Detectives* were among his favorite docudramas. He knew how this worked. His planning was too careful for such a deviation!

The news flashed Quinn's and Braden's pictures.

How could this be?

Three years! If the poor man hadn't sought his vengeance in three years, why now? Martin had watched interviews with Derrick Braden that first year after his son's death. The man hadn't been a fool. He had surely known that there was a possibility the Bureau had failed in some way. Martin could have told him that. The Bureau failed far too often.

The second year after his son's death, in honor of his memory, Braden had started a Web site to instruct parents in how to spot the signs of an abusive family member or friend. Martin had admired that effort.

Calm down, Martin.

"What?" Martin turned a bit too sharply to face his beloved wife. "How can I calm down?"

She smiled at him patiently. *You must carry on.*

But he knew she was right. He couldn't fall to pieces over this unexpected and unfortunate turn of events. His mission was far too important. He must carry on.

Still, the timing was essential. Deirdre wasn't math inclined so she didn't quite understand just how serious this other glitch in the schedule could prove. The business on the news was one thing, but the schedule change quite another.

He had to stop replaying the news report over and over in

his mind. That was not his doing . . . not part of his plan. Focus was necessary to his success. He had spent twenty-five years paying attention to the most insignificant details in his work. Distractions could not be tolerated, then or now.

The question of "why now?" persisted, making him anxious.

Three years ago, every single thing about the Braden case had played out in the media. Special Agent McBride had been crucified! Braden hadn't gone after him or his superior then—not in all this time. Why this sudden violence over a mere news report that finally told some semblance of truth that the man could have deduced on his own?

Martin could not reconcile this behavior.

McBride was a saint . . . a hero that came along only once.

It's time the world knew.

Deirdre was right. She always was.

As unfortunate as this tragic news was, sacrifice was at times necessary for justice to be realized. If this was one of those times, then so be it.

He would move forward with his plans and put this other sad business aside.

"Of course, you're always right, dear," he said to her. "This is not an insurmountable setback. And the news about Braden and Quinn is simply none of my concern." He lifted his shoulders ever so slightly. "Though I must say, Quinn surely deserved no better."

Deirdre didn't say as much, but he saw the agreement in her eyes. She had realized this mission to exonerate McBride had to happen before he had. She always saw things more clearly and more quickly than Martin. That was her gift. This was the least he could do for her.

Martin turned back to the news on the television and faced this newest challenge with the knowledge that his goal was far too important to allow an unexpected encumbrance to alter his course.

To the contrary, he would do exactly as Deirdre suggested. Not only would he proceed, he would move his next objective forward to accommodate the schedule glitch.

He would triumph.

The world now knew a great deal more of the truth.

That left only the Federal Bureau of Investigation thrashing in denial.

Time to make those shortsighted fools face the music.

No one was as good as Special Agent Ryan McBride.

Once he was officially reinstated, Martin's work would be done.

Then he would be a hero in Deirdre's eyes too.

CHAPTER FOURTEEN

Sunday, September 10, 12:01 A.M.
1000 Eighteenth Street

McBride watched the final moments of the news segment on the wall-mounted plasma in Worth's office. Ms. Nadine Goodman certainly had all her ducks in a row, including a few to which she shouldn't have had access.

No one knew better than McBride what Derrick Braden had gone through. There were no words to adequately articulate that kind of pain. McBride would have given anything to go back and fix that moment in time. To save that boy and make his family whole again. But he couldn't. Quinn had made the ultimate decision and the boy had died. McBride had spent three years blaming him when the truth was . . . he couldn't be sure if anything he could have done would have made a difference either.

There was no way to know and that was what he had to live with. Evidently Braden had decided that he could no longer live with the not knowing and had opted to take the man he deemed responsible for his unhappiness with him.

Worth clicked the remote and the recorded broadcast vanished. He shifted his attention to McBride. "Strange that you're in town barely forty-eight hours and our top-ranked investigative reporter suddenly has all the facts on a three-year-old case." His gaze turned openly accusing. "More of that irony, huh, McBride?"

McBride shouldn't waste his time debating, this prick was going to believe what he wanted to, but for the sake of self-satisfaction he would set the record straight. And make one minor point. "I don't even know the woman. When would I have had a chance to collaborate with her? Thursday night I never left the hotel, last night and tonight I was with Agent Grace." Now for his point. "You have a leak."

Outrage turned Worth's face an unpleasant hue of purple. "This office *does not* have a leak."

McBride turned his palms up. "Then your investigative reporter is psychic. Believe it or not, Worth, suspect interrogations actually work. Have you questioned Ms. Goodman regarding her source?"

The purple faded to more of a reddish-blue color. "She's not talking. We're holding her as a person of interest for a few hours to see if she'll budge."

"There are certain details," Grace said, drawing McBride's attention to her, "that no one at this field office could have given Goodman."

"That's right," Worth said. "The copy of the case file that we received electronically had been declassified."

Didn't change McBride's opinion. "Then the information had to come from someone at Quantico."

Worth snorted. "We both know that isn't the case." He did that little forward-lean intimidation maneuver that wouldn't have worked had he been standing up. "You and Quinn were the key players in that saga and Quinn is dead. That leaves you."

"Your powers of deduction are astounding, Worth." McBride shook his head. "I'm sure the Bureau is very proud."

Grace shot him a warning look.

"I actually went up against Quantico for you on this

whole Devoted Fan fiasco," Worth said, his tone incredibly level for a man who clearly wanted to rip off McBride's head and piss down his throat. "I believed you were a pawn in this case, but that may have been a mistake on my part."

McBride'd had about enough of this bullshit.

"If we find out you're Goodman's source," Worth warned, "or that you manipulated these events somehow or had any contact whatsoever with Derrick Braden, I will nail your ass to the cross so help me God."

McBride stood. "I assume we're finished here." He had stayed this long out of consideration for Grace. He didn't want his actions coming back on her after he was gone.

Worth rose, postured himself with that authoritative panache guys like him utilized to distract from their lack of personality. Like the thousand-dollar charcoal suit and crisply starched white shirt accented with a red power tie. He was in charge and he didn't plan to let anyone forget it.

"Agent Grace will escort you back to the Tutwiler," he announced. "She and Agent Pratt will be your personal security until you're on an eight A.M. flight to Miami. A representative from the Miami office will pick you up and escort you back to your residence in Key West." Worth took a breath. "If you divulge to the press anything you've seen or heard during your stay here, formal charges will be forthcoming. Your attitude, your appearance, your whole life is a disgrace to the hundreds of agents who work hard and play by the rules."

This whole affair had stopped being McBride's problem when Director Stone ordered him off the case. He should have walked out when this bastard paused to catch his breath.

But he hadn't and now it was too late for that.

McBride leaned forward, flattened his palms on that glossy desktop, and put himself at eye level with Worth. "I want you to remember this moment when you come begging

for my help again. So that when I turn you down cold you'll
know that whatever happens is on your head."

Worth backed off first. He shifted his gaze to Grace.
"Don't let him out of your sight until he's on that plane
headed the hell out of here."

"Yes, sir." Grace tugged at McBride's sleeve. "Let's go."

McBride held Worth's gaze for two beats more before
walking away. Fury roared deep in his gut. He had come
here to do the right thing. Just went to show that doing the
right thing was vastly overrated.

At the stairwell door, Agent Pratt's voice interrupted
their exit. "Wait up, Grace!" He hustled over to where they
stood. "SAC said I was supposed to go with you."

"I want a drink," McBride announced to the two of
them. His bullshit index had hit maximum.

"That's not going to be easy at this hour," Grace
warned.

Pratt reached for the stairwell door. "I know a place
that's open all night."

Things were looking up. McBride clapped Pratt on the
back. "Good. You can drive."

On the landing inside the stairwell, Grace paused and
said, "This whole thing is a mistake, McBride." She
searched his face and eyes as if she hoped to see some hint
of agreement or sense of indignation.

"If you're referring to the drink, you can give it up. If
it's that load of crap Worth just dished out, don't waste the
energy, Grace."

"Look," she argued, "I have my issues with you,
but I'm pretty sure you don't care for reporters any
more than I do. This *is* crap. The director's decision was
unfair."

McBride had stopped expecting life to be fair about
three years ago. Who knew? Maybe he had started to get
a little cynical even before that. After what she had been
through, Grace should understand that feeling. Or maybe

she was still looking through the rose-colored glasses of youth.

Whatever, his excursion into the worst of his past was over. "Let's get the hell outta here."

1:15 a.m.

Pratt's source turned out to be a friend who operated a liquor store and who was willing to provide on the house a bottle of Jack Daniel's Tennessee sipping whiskey.

Grace was annoyed with McBride as well as her colleague, but right now the demons were grumbling and McBride needed some peace. The images and voices in his head just wouldn't shut up. Mixed in with his own personal demons were some of Grace's. He had heard more than enough about the ravaged bodies left behind by the serial rapist-murderer referred to as Nameless to have a reasonable handle on how that horror went down for her.

That she had survived that sick son of a bitch and had put her life together so well was an outright miracle.

But the bastard had left his mark.

McBride studied her from the corner of his eye as they exited the elevator on the seventh floor of the Tutwiler. That was why she had balked those two times. Why she had a problem with comments about her body.

Goddamn, he had been an asshole.

He hadn't taken into consideration that she might have suffered in her life the same as he had. But then, she was so damned young, who would expect such a horrific past? She'd only been seventeen when that twisted fiend took her.

She had every right to be hypersensitive about her body and he had unknowingly capitalized on that.

Outside the door to his room, rather than stick the key-card into the lock, Grace faced him. "Don't you dare look at me that way, McBride." Her eyes warned that she knew exactly what he had been thinking.

McBride kept in mind that Pratt was right behind him. "Sorry, Grace. I was just admiring your . . . shoes."

Pratt chuckled.

Grace took it well enough. She arched one eyebrow and suggested, "Shove it, McBride." She glanced past him. "You too, Pratt."

She unlocked the door and completed a walk-through of the room and adjoining bath while McBride pulled JD from the brown bag wrapper. He reached for a tumbler. "I don't suppose either of you would care to join me."

"You know how it is," Pratt said with a halfhearted shrug.

Grace tossed her purse onto a chair. "Are you going to drink that straight or do you need a Coke?"

He picked up a glass from the silver tray on the table and poured a hefty serving. "Obviously you don't know your whiskeys, Grace." He indulged in a slow, soothing swallow, then turned to the lady glaring at him. "Otherwise you wouldn't ask."

"I'll take the first watch," Pratt offered.

He grabbed one of the chairs at the table and headed for the door.

McBride looked around the room. No way was he talking openly in here where any number of bugs could have been planted by his friends at the Bureau. But he had things to say to Grace. He opened the French doors and walked out onto the balcony, balanced his drink on the banister, and lit a smoke. He stared out at the city where Grace had grown up and wondered if she recognized that her need to escape to that bigger assignment was more about running away than proving herself. If she stayed clear of the past she didn't have to own it. Didn't even have to acknowledge it unless someone, like him, forced her to.

It wouldn't do anything but fester. And one of these days,

when she least expected it, she would wake up and discover that the infection had spread, consuming her entire existence.

Then she'd be just like him . . . nothing.

Eventually she strolled out to join him, as he had known she would. As much as she wanted to pretend she was on *their* side, she wasn't. She was on his. That was another one of those things she hadn't owned yet.

He kept his attention on the city lights and the way the skyscrapers thrust toward the night sky with the brooding mountains in the background. Nice view. Out there and next to him. He didn't have to rest his eyes on her to appreciate the way she looked tonight. Deep emerald skirt and matching jacket that made the green flecks in those dark brown eyes stand out. Black blouse beneath, vee-neck showing just enough cleavage to whet the appetite. And those sexy black shoes he'd already admired.

But the real attention-grabber was her hair. She had worn it down. Maybe because there hadn't been time to do otherwise. They had been on her deck with a glass of wine in hand talking about her past one minute and the next they had been rushing to get to Eighteenth Street.

He'd almost succeeded in erasing that hurry-up-and-wait Bureau mentality from his head. Jump higher, rush faster. Play by the rules. Make sure the Bureau never looks bad. No risks. No gray area. Just black and white. *Do as you're told.*

Grace leaned against the railing, asked nonchalantly, "You have any idea who could have leaked those details?"

As casually as she issued the question, he recognized the tension in her posture. He had won her over to some degree and now she wanted to be able to explain away the possibility that he had done anything wrong.

"Not a clue." He sipped his drink. *Not a fucking clue.*

She turned to study his profile. "After I left you here that first night, you didn't hang out at the bar?"

He looked her in the eyes. "Yes, as a matter of fact I did.

But I didn't talk to anyone. Ask the bartender if you feel the need. He'll tell you that I repeated a single word several times. *Another*."

She looked away. "I had to ask."

"Sure." He knew the way it was done. "We all do what we have to."

"You didn't bring anything written with you that someone could have taken from your room?"

He had to laugh at that. "Well, Agent, you were there. You saw what I brought with me. The clothes on my back. Not even a toothbrush." He patted his back pocket. "And I don't carry a copy of old case reports in my wallet."

She exhaled a big exasperated breath. "There has to be an explanation. If it didn't come from Quantico and it didn't come from you . . ."

As least she sounded like she believed him.

"Lots of people knew what went down," he offered for lack of anything else to say.

"But not word-for-word details," she countered.

She was right about that. "Other than the notes I kept in my office at Quantico and the official file, there was no place to get verbatim information except from a live source."

A frown tugged at her pretty face. "What happened to your working notes?"

He shrugged. "Who knows? I walked out with nothing." A memory bobbed to the surface of the cesspool of negativity in his brain. "They shipped my personal stuff to me later. Maybe the notes were in there. I suppose they could have opted to retain the work-related memos and notes."

"What'd you do with the stuff they sent?"

"Never opened it." He knocked back the last of the JD in his glass. "Still packed up in boxes at my place in the Keys."

She reached for her phone. "Worth needs to know that there may have been work notes at your residence. There could've been a break-in since you've been away."

"Forget it, Grace. It doesn't matter. Worth—the

Bureau—wants me out of this. Don't you get it? No matter what you prove, nothing is going to change. They don't want the world to know what happened three years ago. As long as I'm guilty, they're innocent." He laughed. "The truly ridiculous part is that none of it matters. The boy died. Proving who was responsible won't bring him back. Won't change the fact that his daddy blew his brains out. Or that he killed an agent.

"It's done. Over. Let it go."

"And what happens when Devoted Fan e-mails us on Monday?" she countered.

"Worth will deal with it." Tension he tried hard to ignore negated the relaxing effects of the one drink he'd consumed.

"What about the victim? Considering we don't have a trace of evidence and there's no pattern to his work, the victim could be anybody. He could be stalking that person right now. Are you just going to let the next one die?"

He turned his face back to hers. "You can do this, Grace. You were the one who figured out Jones was at the steel mill, not me."

"That's not true," she argued. "I just juggled the priority list, that's all. You were the one who ID'd her so we would even know who we were looking for."

"The point is, you've got Pratt and Schaffer and all those other guys. Work with them. Let them in. If you keep pushing all your colleagues away, you're never going to make it. This business takes teamwork."

"You're pretending this is all going to go away," she argued, "and you're wrong. He's planned this very carefully. Whatever he has in mind for the next round, saving the victim will be about you . . . not me, or any of the others. He wants to prove how invaluable you are. Each round will be harder, more personalized. Mark my word, without you, we'll lose and someone will die. That's assuming we can even fool him into believing you're still on the case."

"I need another drink, Grace."

He went back into the room, reached for the only comfort he trusted.

As much as he'd love to leave Grace feeling warm and fuzzy about the hero she had thought him to be, this wasn't his problem anymore.

CHAPTER FIFTEEN

3:00 A.M.

The door of the hotel room opened and Vivian snapped to attention. She tugged at her skirt and righted her jacket. Her bottom was numb from sitting in this damned chair.

McBride stepped into the corridor, let the door close behind him. "How you holding up?"

"Well, let's see, I've counted the stripes in the wallpaper five times. What does that tell you?"

He crouched down to her level. "I think you can come back into the room. I'm pretty sure no one's going to try breaking down the door. Birmingham PD and hotel security are making sure the media doesn't ambush us. There's no need for you to sit out here like this."

She produced a smile, mostly at the idea of McBride trying to be sweet. In a totally unsettling way she found this charming. "Thanks, but I'd better follow orders." Worth had been specific. No one was to come near McBride's room.

That he was still awake surprised her. She had halfway expected him to drink himself into unconsciousness. Maybe he wasn't the drunk he wanted people to believe he was. His don't-care attitude kept everyone at a distance.

She had already decided that he used intimacy as a tactic to ward her off. That whole cocky, swaggering attitude was more for show than anything else, she would wager.

The problem was, it didn't exactly work. The last time she had been this physically attracted to a guy she had been seventeen and graduating high school. No one since. All the dates and one-night stands added up to nada.

"I wanted to finish the discussion we started last night," McBride ventured as if he had read her thoughts.

"Oh no." She waved off that idea. "I did all the talking last night and you got off with just listening."

He already knew too much about her.

"I shouldn't have made all those cracks about—"

"Don't you dare," she snapped. She'd seen that look in his eyes when they had first returned to the hotel. The sympathy. She hated that! "I'm over the past."

"You're over Nameless?"

She shuddered inwardly, did all in her power to prevent him from seeing the reaction. "Yes."

"Then say it."

This was ridiculous. "Go back in the room, McBride."

"Say it."

Fury tightened her lips. "Nameless." Hot bile rose in her throat. She glared at him. "Are you satisfied now?"

"You've had sex since then?"

Was he kidding? It was a damned good thing there weren't any guests in the rooms on this end of the corridor. Having a balcony put him in a corner room and this wasn't exactly prime tourist season.

"My sex life is none of your business." She crossed her arms over her chest and rolled her eyes. The man was unbelievable.

"Just answer the question, Grace. It's a yes or no response. Simple."

He was nuts. But one look at his face told her he wasn't

going to shut up until he had his answer. "Okay. Yes. Of course." She added in a whisper, "I've had sex. Lots of times."

"Lots of times, eh?"

"Go away, McBride." There was a crazed fan out there kidnapping people to make him look like a hero and he was asking her about her sex life? Talk about a trip into the Twilight Zone . . . they were there and checking out T-shirts.

"Did you feel it?"

"Okay." She shot to her feet. "That's enough." She paced, mostly in circles, but it seemed the thing to do. Anger sparked, making her want to kick something.

"I'm not talking necessarily about an orgasm, Grace." He pushed to his feet, propped against the doorframe. "I'm talking about *feeling it*. Here." He patted the center of his chest. "Or do you disappear during sex the way you must have when Nameless made you . . . do those things."

She stopped, pointed a furious look at him. "There's nothing wrong with me, McBride. I'm fine. I can do my job. I can lead a normal life. I'm not the disappearing girl."

Her circle expanded, became more of an oval shape. She had to keep moving or risk hitting him.

She had heard all those questions before. *You need more therapy, Vivian. How can you expect to experience true intimacy if you remain in denial?* Each new voice echoing in her brain made her more furious. She hadn't done anything wrong. She had survived. That was all. Yes, she'd had to do . . . *things* . . . she never wanted to think about again. But she was alive!

There were twelve other women lying dead in the ground because of that twisted piece of shit! She had lived to tell about it and that was what counted.

She refused to think about *him* or that time. That part of her life was over. She had a career. Building that career was her focus now. A deeper relationship would come later. She had barely turned twenty-five. There was time, dammit.

McBride waited for his answer. Damn him.

"Go back into the room," she snapped.

He shook his head. "Not until you tell me the truth." That husky, rich voice slid over her skin, making her shiver despite the fury lashing through her. "Do you remember the truth? How to really feel? To let go and enjoy the moment? How to savor the pleasure . . . to allow your partner all the way inside?"

"I suppose you know all about the pleasure and getting all the way inside," she mocked. He was such a hypocrite! Here he was telling her how she should lead her life and he was hiding behind booze and *sex*!

"I might be running away from who I used to be, but I know who I am now, Grace. I feel it more than I want to. I don't always like it, but I'm damned sure not afraid of it."

She strode up to him, stared at that face with all its too intriguing angles and lines. Peered into those assessing blue eyes. "I'm not afraid, McBride. Remember, I kissed you."

He licked his lips as if he had just remembered that too. "That's when I knew you did that little vanishing act. I felt you disappear."

"You don't know anything about what I feel!" How dare he be so damned arrogant! "If, as you claim, I disappeared during that kiss it was because my mind wandered. Maybe that was about you, not me."

He straightened away from the doorframe, put his body close enough to hers that she could feel his heat . . . close enough that he could have kissed her with the tiniest shift of his head.

"When I kiss you, Grace, you'll feel me."

Her body humming with the need to let him prove his point, she retreated a step. "Go back into the room." She took her seat and aimed her attention straight ahead. One more hour. All she had to do was get through one more hour.

6:00 A.M.
Birmingham International Airport

"We're inside." Vivian scanned the line at the ticket counter. "He's at the counter now," she told Pratt. "We'll wait for you at the food court."

She put her phone away and met McBride as he left the counter. "Pratt's coming from short-term parking. We'll meet him in the food court."

Operating on less than an hour of sleep was going to make for a long day. She had relieved Pratt at two-thirty. At four-thirty they had prepared for the trip to the airport.

Most of that time in between she had either been arguing with McBride or walking off the fury he had ignited with his psychoanalyzing. The part that infuriated her most was that a whole lot of what he had kindled hadn't been fury.

Her first high-profile case and she couldn't keep her head screwed on straight.

Maybe she did need more therapy.

As they followed the signs to the food court she tried to recall the last time she'd had sex. Last month? July?

Sad. Really sad.

When you had to work that hard to remember, it couldn't have been memorable.

But she knew where the fault lay. That McBride had nailed exactly how she *disappeared* made her want to fuck his brains out just to prove him wrong.

She grabbed on to the tiny slither of calm that tried valiantly to recover from her frequent and explosive emotional outbursts. If this was any indication of how she handled pressure, she was in trouble.

Everything about this case was wrong, including his leaving, but some part of her would be relieved when McBride was on that plane headed back to the Keys. He disturbed her . . . shook up her carefully controlled world. Somehow she was defenseless against him. Unlike with Nameless, when the main crux of the battle had been physical, this was completely emotional.

"How about we sit here?" She indicated a table in sight of the main thoroughfare so Pratt could locate them easily.

"Looks the same as all the rest." He pulled out a chair but waited for her to settle in before taking his seat.

She considered that he had selected the same pair of distressed jeans he had worn on the trip up here, and the same khaki shirt; it made her wonder if that was symbolic . . . him going back to the way things were before she intruded in his life.

Probably just the first thing he grabbed when he rolled out of bed.

"Would you like breakfast?" She hated to put him on the plane hungry. "Coffee?"

"Sure."

One-word answers. He'd certainly had plenty to say a few hours ago.

"So, what're we eating?" Pratt asked as he sauntered up.

Grace pushed out of her chair. "You guys decide. I'll be right back."

She left her purse on the table and walked to the ladies' room. It wasn't far. Glancing back, she could still see the table and both men. Front and center, she ordered her gaze. This was not the time for distraction. Besides, what was she worried about? Pratt had the same orders she did. He could handle babysitting McBride for a few minutes.

The airport was fairly deserted this early on Sunday morning so there was no line for a stall. The janitorial staff had apparently just cleaned since the place looked spotless and smelled freshly sanitized.

Vivian took care of business, washed up, and checked her hair. She hadn't taken time to put it up and now she wished she had. After a quick finger-combing, she headed for the table. She could use a biscuit with egg. And a massive cup of coffee.

For a moment she was certain her eyes had played a trick on her. "Where's McBride?"

Pratt pointed back the direction from which she had come. "Men's room. I'm surprised you didn't pass him."

"Damn, Pratt. We're not supposed to let him out of our sight!"

Pratt held up his hands. "I have his cell phone. The man just went to the toilet, Grace. It's not a big deal."

But he wasn't the one who would have to answer to Worth if he was wrong.

She did an about-face and stamped back toward the bathrooms.

"Grace!"

She held a hand up in a stop gesture and kept on going. Jesus. Was everybody around her so incompetent or was she making a mountain out of a molehill? Maybe McBride was right and she didn't know how to let anyone close . . . even her coworkers. *Stop it, Vivian Grace.* She wasn't buying into his anti-Bureau theories.

Back ramrod straight, she strode right into the men's room. Flashed a fake smile for the gentleman she encountered drying his hands. Staring at her, he wandered out, obviously confused or startled.

She scanned the stalls. No feet. Her anxiety level pumped up a few more degrees. A toilet flushed. There. She marched up to the door on the other side of the expansive restroom where his sneakered feet and jean-clad legs were visible. She banged on it hard enough to rattle the hinges.

"McBride!"

He yanked the door inward, glared at her. "Is the building on fire?"

She blinked. "No."

"Then what the hell are you doing in the men's room? It's not like I'm going anywhere."

That was it. She went toe-to-toe with him, caused him to stagger back a step. "You have pushed me around for the last time." She poked him in the chest. "I've put up with your lewd comments and your inquisitions and I've had it!"

"Don't hold back, Grace," he murmured, those blue eyes glittering with something like mischief.

And then reality sank in.

She glanced down. That step she had forced McBride back had him straddling the toilet.

The toilet.

Oh hell.

Her horrified gaze met his.

He grinned.

"Now that's feeling it, Grace." He reached over her head and pushed the door shut behind her. "You get so lost in the moment, in the passion, that you forget about everything else."

And then he kissed her.

Not some slow, tender sweet kiss. His fingers dove into her hair, held her head still while his mouth covered hers. He kissed her hard. Invaded her with his tongue. Fire roared through her. Her fingers clenched in his shirt.

She wanted more.

Her arms went around his neck. She wanted to kiss him back the way he was kissing her. Openmouthed . . . lips bruising lips . . . tongues battling.

His right hand slid along the length of her throat, reached beneath her jacket and closed over her breast. She groaned. No tiny, feminine sound . . . a throaty roar. Her hands roved over his chest, felt the contours she had already admired, crinkling the pack of cigarettes in his shirt pocket. She wanted to touch all of him! Now!

His hands moved downward, over her bottom, pulled

her hips against his pelvis. The needy sounds she made were swallowed up in his kiss. She tugged at his shirt buttons, wiggled her hands beneath the fabric to touch his skin. More! She snaked her arms upward, threaded her fingers into his hair. It felt exactly as she had known it would. Soft, silky.

He worked her skirt up her thighs . . . lifted her. Her legs instinctively curled around his waist. She threw her head back, arched her hips . . . God, she wanted him inside her. He kissed his way down her neck. She wanted to tear her blouse off so that he could access her breasts. Sensing her needs, he pulled the vee of her blouse aside and lathed his tongue beneath the lace of her bra.

"Oh . . . God!" She bucked, bit back a scream. Her cell phone clattered to the tile floor.

He pressed her back against the side wall, used the fingers of one hand to push the damp silk panel covering her out of the way and one finger slid inside. Her muscles clamped around him and he groaned in satisfaction.

"Hot," he murmured. "Wet." He slid that finger in and out a couple of times, smiled as if he had found just what he wanted, then he pressed . . . probed and pressed some more . . . until he did this thing at just the right spot that sent her over an edge she hadn't even come close to . . . in *years*. Or maybe ever.

He put his mouth over hers to muffle the sounds of her orgasm, his lips smiling.

She rode out the incredible climax . . . but she wanted more. She had to have *him*. Now!

Her heavy lids opened just enough for her to peer into those sexy blue eyes. "No more playing. Do it!"

He kept one hand under her bottom and fished in his pocket with the other. He tucked the unopened condom between his teeth and then, one at a time, braced a stiletto-clad foot against the metal wall behind him. Then he reached for his fly. She used her back and feet to maintain her position, as he ripped the condom open with his teeth and fingers and then slid it into place. That intent gaze never left hers, the promise there driving her crazy.

Then he did that thing again, thrust one finger inside and found that spot that sent her instantly into orgasm. This time she bit her lips together to hold back the cries and watched him watching her. Her entire body undulated with the waves of pleasure.

He nudged her with the head of his penis and she lost her breath. One slow, solid inch, then two filled her, teasing as he took his sweet time.

"Feel that?"

"Shut up." She couldn't talk . . . couldn't think. She could only *feel*.

Then he pushed all the way inside, burrowed fully between her thighs and kissed her until she could no longer hold her breath.

She arched her hips, he moved in deeper still.

A hard poke in her ribs had her gasping, "Wait!" She struggled to speak. "Gun!"

He drew back slightly, his breath as ragged as her own. She wrestled the weapon out of its holster. Couldn't drop it, so she held on to it, wrapped that arm around his neck and kept the door from swaying inward with the other.

The harder he pounded, the harder her stilettos scrambled for purchase on that slick surface. His movements grew frantic, his breathing more jagged. Finally—oh God!—he was losing it the way she had twice already.

He stopped mid-stroke. She wanted to scream. Her body throbbed for more.

He nibbled at her lips. "I do love those lips, Grace."

"Move," she ordered, shifting her hips, contracting those inner muscles with all her might.

He shuddered. "In a moment. But first." He teased her lips with his own. "Just one more for the road."

Confusion reigned for about two seconds, and then he caressed her where his penis already had her stretched so tight. Massaged and pressed until she felt herself coming all over again. Then he moved once more, in and out, slowly, making her breath catch, making her body convulse all the harder.

He started to come. Closed his eyes and worked it out, one measured stroke at a time.

He leaned into her, kissed her lips tenderly as if he hadn't just made her come three times.

He braced her weight against him until her feet were steady on the floor, then he withdrew. The sensation made her gasp, made her ache at the loss.

Stunned, bewildered, tingly, out of breath . . . she felt all those things.

He pushed her skirt down her thighs, took the weapon from her hand and tucked it back into its holster. "You'd better go, Agent Grace."

She nodded, uncertain of her voice.

Vivian slipped out the door, glanced around the room. The sight of the urinals hanging on the wall drove reality home. She had just had sex in a men's bathroom. In a stall!

With McBride.

She strode out the door, thank God without encountering another man, and darted into the ladies' room.

Her eyes rounded at the image in the mirror. Her hair was a mess. Her blouse was twisted.

"So, so dumb."

She righted her clothes. Washed her hands. And smoothed her hair.

Pull it together. She couldn't go back out there and face him if she didn't.

Deep breath. It was just sex. No big deal. In an hour or so he would be gone and it wouldn't matter anyway.

Except that it did matter.

He was leaving and this case wasn't right.

There would be another e-mail from Devoted Fan. And without McBride . . .

She touched the holster at her waist. Where was her phone? The sound of metal bouncing on tile echoed in her head.

"Shit." She had left it in the men's room. Holding back the urge to run, she walked to the door.

McBride leaned against the wall between the two restrooms.

He held up her cell phone. "Looking for this?"

She snatched it from his hand. "Thanks."

The phone vibrated against her palm. She jumped.

"I'll catch up with Pratt." McBride pushed off the wall and sauntered back to the table.

Vivian watched him walk away, the long fluid strides making her throat dry.

Pratt looked up, came to attention as if he had been dozing as McBride joined him.

Vivian's phone vibrated again.

She cleared her throat and answered it. "Grace."

Worth.

One sentence.

Don't let McBride get on that plane.

CHAPTER SIXTEEN

1000 Eighteenth Street
9:00 A.M.

There wasn't a lot happening in downtown Birmingham as nine o'clock rolled around on a Sunday morning. The city looked deserted. McBride figured most of the good folks in this Southern town were probably having breakfast or getting ready for church. But every damned reporter from Huntsville to Montgomery had joined in the vigil outside the Bureau gates.

If it bleeds it leads. And this one was bleeding Bureau blue. Andrew Quinn had moved up the hierarchy during his service, all the way to the executive level before retiring. But the bigger headline was the man wielding the gun, Derrick Braden—grieving father and child advocate.

Just like three years ago all over again. McBride could have done without that particular trip down memory lane.

Birmingham PD forced the mob back as Grace turned her Explorer onto the block. Once they were inside the gate, the camera flashes and shouted questions accompanied their trip from the vehicle to the main entrance of the building. With no guard on duty inside just yet, a slide of Grace's ID card got them through the door and out of reach.

Just another circus act. This bizarre story and its connection to a high-profile federal case of the past would boost ratings and everyone wanted center ring.

Judging by the number of bodies rushing around inside, McBride decided that all agents assigned to Birmingham's field office and maybe some borrowed ones from a neighboring office were on hand. Though he didn't recognize some of the faces, he was certain they were all feds. He could spot a federal agent a mile off. Ever-present formal bearing, shoes always shined, and sleek business uniforms ready for inspection. Could shoot 'em and bury 'em in the same suit.

McBride, on the other hand, wore his comfortably tattered jeans, his favorite khaki shirt that was now missing two buttons, and the earthy feminine scent of Special Agent Vivian Grace.

He should be ashamed of himself for having sex with her in a bathroom stall, but he wasn't.

If he got the chance, he'd do it again.

As soon as they reached the third floor, ASAC Talley invited McBride to wait in the conference room then diverted Grace to Worth's office. Gathered around the long table were a couple of the usual suspects, Agents Pratt and Davis. Schaffer and Aldridge were conspicuously missing.

Then the expected waiting game began.

McBride loathed waiting. The Bureau utilized the tactic for building and manipulating three things: discomfort, frustration, and fear. Even when they said please and thank you, offered coffee and promised to be right with you, the maneuver was designed for promoting one of those three elements. He should know, he had utilized that very method on enough suspects.

On cue, the instant McBride lowered his empty cup to the table, Pratt jumped to the task of going for a coffee refill. There was always the chance that the agent had taken this particular task on as his personal quest to support the effort of keeping McBride functioning. But, more likely, he had been instructed to make sure McBride didn't get antsy.

Across the room, the timeline related to the ongoing investigation into Devoted Fan remained intact. Pictures and notes regarding Braden and Quinn had been posted, along with a sidebar related to investigative reporter Nadine Goodman's breaking news. Interestingly, two additional computers had been set up on one side of the room, along with a second plasma monitor. A complete command post.

McBride doubted that he had been dragged back here and left with Pratt and Davis to stare at each other if another e-mail had been received. Wasting the allotted time would be a major infraction of procedure. Worth was too anal for that. Whatever was going down, Worth was prepping for how to approach McBride on the situation. The additional search and monitor systems set up in here indicated the same. Something was definitely brewing around here besides the local supermarket's store brand of coffee.

There was always the chance that they had come up with some aspect of this investigation to blame on him. But McBride wasn't worried. What could they possibly do to him that they hadn't already done?

Couldn't destroy his career since he didn't have one and, oh yeah, they had done that already anyway. Couldn't take away his life . . . he didn't have one of those either.

All present at the table sat in silence, suggesting that orders not to discuss whatever had occurred since late last night had been issued or that the agents were as in the dark as McBride. Just something else he loathed, the tendency of the managerial level to hold back as much knowledge for as long as possible in order to ensure they wielded all the power.

They could have it; he wanted no part of it.

There would be another flight to Miami sometime today. As long as he wasn't taken into custody and didn't go completely stupid, he still had a chance of getting out of here.

As if some Fate had it in for him more so than usual, Grace entered the room and McBride's attention riveted to her. The jade suit fit her shape in a way that had him remembering every single curve and mound he'd explored. An unfamiliar and annoying tightening sensation in his chest made him want to stretch it out or walk it off.

Talley and Worth appeared, preempting any opportunity to ask Grace what the hell was up now. Or to drag her to the nearest closet and go for an encore. He doubted she would allow that to happen again in this lifetime.

If she hadn't been so pissed off at him and frustrated with Worth and the case, McBride felt reasonably certain that walk on the wild side at the airport wouldn't have happened at all.

Grace was far too controlled under normal circumstances.

One thing he could say for certain, she damned sure hadn't disappeared for even a second while they were bumping and grinding.

Worth assumed a position at the head of the table, placed a file folder there, then pushed his lapels aside and rested his hands on his hips. His expression was unreadable and that nudged at McBride's suspicions. Since he'd basically slept about half an hour last night, he wasn't going to waste any energy worrying about whatever this guy had on his mind. Good, bad, or indifferent, McBride was halfway out of here already.

"McBride," Worth announced, glancing around the table as if what he was about to say was of particular importance to all present. "I, and the Bureau, owe you an apology."

Now there was a revelation he hadn't seen coming. McBride folded his arms over his chest and studied the man with avid curiosity. He felt Grace looking at him but he was enjoying watching Worth sweat too much to meet her eyes.

"You were correct," Worth went on, "when you suggested

that the leak was in this office." He surveyed those seated around the table for a moment before continuing. "Agent Aldridge inadvertently mentioned your participation in this case to an acquaintance who then tipped off his friend Nadine Goodman. Agent Aldridge realized the mistake was his late last night. He will remain on administrative leave until the case is resolved."

McBride kept the "told you so" to himself. The open apology was more than he had expected. Maybe Worth wasn't all asshole.

"According to Ms. Goodman," Worth explained, "she sent an associate she refused to identify down to Key West to get some current background on you. The overly enthusiastic associate broke into your home and discovered some old work files you evidently have in your possession. He found a copy of the final report you had written on the Braden case and passed certain key details to Goodman who used the information in her expose."

At least now McBride knew for sure what was in those boxes. "The Bureau shipped four boxes to me. I never opened them," he clarified just to ensure there was no misunderstanding this time.

"Agent Grace explained that," Worth acknowledged. "As a precautionary measure, Agent Schaffer is en route to Key West to go through those boxes to see if there is anything else that might prove relevant to this case. Though Goodman insisted that her associate didn't physically remove anything from your home or pass along any other information not yet released, we want to verify that for our own edification. There's no word yet whether charges will be pressed against Goodman." Worth's expression remained closed, his tone businesslike. "Since a crime was committed at your residence we didn't need your permission to have a look."

No big deal. McBride didn't have anything to hide. "Get to the point, Worth." He didn't see any reason to beat around the bush either. There would be a point. The apology was to set the stage, maybe earn a few points before going for the real target. "Why am I still here?"

Worth stared at the table a moment before leveling his attention back on McBride. "Director Stone has asked that, in addition to passing along his sincerest apologies, I implore you, on his behalf, to give your continued cooperation in stopping this madman."

McBride took a beat to absorb and truly appreciate the confession. Three years ago they had taken *everything* from him, hung him out to dry in the worst way. If they expected him to be grateful now, they were going to be seriously disappointed.

"Don't you just hate when that happens?" McBride lifted one shoulder in a negligible shrug. "If I hadn't been right, you wouldn't have to beg like this. Must be humiliating."

"McBride," Grace cautioned.

Worth held up his hand to silence Grace. "McBride and I are going to need a moment."

Grace and the others stood and filed out of the room. She shot McBride one final warning look as she made her exit.

When the door closed, Worth tried valiantly to hang on to his professional tone but he failed. "That's the difference between us, McBride." That firm grip on his Bureau-perfect demeanor was gone; outrage had scratched its way to the surface and seized control. "I don't think for one second that I know everything or that I'm always right. I fully understand that I'm only human and that mistakes are inevitable.

"Unlike you," he went on, disdain oozing from every pore, "I don't assume that no one else can do the job the way I can. Isn't that what happened three years ago?" he goaded. "You thought you were the only agent in your unit who could do the job right. You worked day and night, the way I heard it. Rarely slept, hardly even went home. Your termination report said you tried to solve all the cases personally. Had done so for years. A real team player."

Worth shook his head slowly in unconcealed pity. "Let me see if I can get this right. The wording was"—he gestured vaguely—"a perfect definition of your character. 'Agent McBride repeatedly and brazenly spread himself too thin. He showed no regard for authority or procedure. Crash and burn was inevitable.'"

There it was. The whole Ryan McBride story in a nutshell. *Crash and burn.* Ten years of service and that was the summation. Yeah, he had spread himself too thin. Hell yeah, he'd ignored the rules and done things his way. But, by God, he'd gotten the job done.

McBride held that condescending gaze. "And yet, here we are. In the same place."

"Trust me," Worth guaranteed him, "if there was any other way to do this, you would be out of my town so fast that enormous ego of yours would have to be FedExed to the Keys to catch up."

All that charm and a sense of humor too. "Is all this foreplay leading someplace, Worth? Because, to tell you the truth, I'm not feeling it."

A quiet fury, hampered by a distinct resignation, settled over the SAC's face. "We don't know where this is going." He shrugged. "Devoted Fan has abducted and drugged two innocent victims. He's facing several felony counts already. And from the looks of things, he isn't finished yet. That doesn't even take into account that the fallout has indirectly cost two lives. We need to find this son of a bitch before this thing takes any more unexpected turns."

Worth let go a mighty breath. "That said, we received another e-mail."

What the hell? The guy goes through all that bullshit before getting to this? "You couldn't have mentioned that first?"

Worth held up both hands in a hold-on gesture. "No victim, just an e-mail."

Relief deflated some of McBride's surliness. "Let's see it."

Worth reached into the file and removed a sheet of paper and passed it to McBride.

The e-mail got straight to the point.

Dear Foolish FBI,
    If McBride gets on that plane there will be no clues for the next victim. Are you prepared to take responsibility for that, Agent Worth?
    The mistake is yours to make. As it is, you have made far too many.

                                            Devoted Fan

"I don't know how," Worth said, the fury kindling once more, "but this guy is watching us. Watching you. We can't afford to trivialize his threat."

McBride tossed the e-mail on the table. "We need to focus on finding a connection between the two victims. Devoted Fan talked about Katherine Jones and atonement, 'oblivious' was written on her forehead. He mentioned Byrne's mistake and a stiff price to pay. His daughter was marked with the word 'innocent.' There has to be a link here that we're missing."

"Agent Schaffer was working on that," he said, reminding McBride that Schaffer was headed to Florida. "I'll put Talley on it in her stead."

McBride shook his head. "We need Aldridge." He pushed on when Worth would have tried to argue. "He made a mistake, you can deal with that later. Right now I need experience on this, and from what I've seen, he's the most experienced agent you've got. This isn't about leadership skills; this is about instinct. We need him."

With some reluctance, Worth said, "All right." He

reached back into his file folder for another document, then slid the page down the table to McBride. "Also, the director has authorized me to temporarily reinstate you for the purpose of sorting out this case. If all goes well, you may be looking at *permanent* reinstatement. Second chances don't come along every day, McBride. Don't blow it off."

McBride stared at the directive that transformed him from a civilian to a federal employee again—with one stroke of the director's pen. For a year after the termination McBride had waited for exactly this. For the Bureau to recognize the mistake they had made. For the opportunity to have his old life back.

Now he had it.

The expected euphoria didn't materialize.

Because it was too late.

He wasn't that man anymore. There was no going back.

That he had succeeded in finding the first two victims in this case was only because the time allotted had been inordinately generous and the clues provided practically a dead giveaway. And because he'd had Grace backing him up. If this got more complicated, he would be useless. Setting himself up for that kind of fall would truly be a major step toward going stupid. Something he had promised himself before walking in here that he wouldn't allow to happen. Bottom line: he was a coward. The idea of putting himself on the line like this scared the hell out of him.

Yet, refusing would make him far worse than a coward.

If he tried and failed, that was bad. If he refused to try at all and someone died, that was unpardonable no matter how low he had fallen or how stupid it appeared to make him.

As much as he wanted to walk out of here and pretend this had nothing to do with him . . . he couldn't. Some honorable gene he hadn't succeeded in completely corrupting with alcohol evidently still functioned.

And all this time he had been certain he had succeeded in eliminating all traits belonging to the man he used to be.

"Can we count on you, Agent McBride, to see this through?"

Agent McBride.

"I need a smoke."

McBride left the directive he would have given most anything to have been offered two years ago lying on the conference table and walked out. He passed the others waiting in the corridor. Grace started to speak to him but he just kept moving. She didn't attempt to follow him as he headed for the stairwell. He needed a few minutes alone outside the confining walls of this place.

By the time he hit the lobby he had the Marlboro between his lips and was ready to push out the front entrance and fire it up.

"I don't think you want to go out there, sir," the guard called after him.

And he was right.

The media clowns were still out there. McBride had forgotten about the dozens of reporters, the news vans with their satellites . . . the cameras. All poised to get a shot or a sound bite for their networks.

Nope, he definitely couldn't go out there.

He turned back to the guard. "Is there a men's room on this floor?"

The guard nodded, pointed to a side corridor near the stairwell door. "But you can't light up in there either." He made a face as if he didn't like the rule himself. "Smoke detectors are too sensitive."

McBride muttered a thanks and stalked off to find the men's room. He pushed through the door, let it close and slumped against it. His fingers traced the outline of the Zippo in his pocket as every cell in his body screamed for nicotine.

What the hell was he doing?

Sweat dampened his skin and in the blink of an eye, a tenth of a second, his body reacted to the chemical triggers that seriously fucked with his head. Heart pounded. Chest constricted. He straightened away from the door, flung the useless cigarette into the trash bin, and started to pace.

How the hell could he believe for one damned minute that he could play this game? His hands shook, answering the question.

He hadn't fired a weapon in three years. No one's life had depended upon him in the same. Counting Alyssa Byrnes and Katherine Jones would be a joke. Finding Jones had been slightly more difficult, but Grace and the others hadn't actually needed him for the job. Other than trading e-mails with this psycho fan, McBride understood that he was just a fifth wheel in the whole effort.

Hell, he had spent most of the time playing head games and doctor with Grace.

The next victim could present a real challenge. Like the ones he used to face on a daily basis.

McBride paused to stare at his reflection in the mirror.

Who was he kidding?

He was a drunk. A nobody. A has-been.

His initial reaction to this when Grace first showed up at his door had been right. He had known then that there was no going back. Two *Sesame Street*–level rescues did not a hero make.

The hero was gone. How many times had he told himself that in the past three years?

Flattening his palms on the counter, he leaned nearer the mirror, looked closely into the face staring back at him.

"You can't do this."

But he wanted to.

God damn it.

He wanted to.

That was the truly fucked-up part. He wanted to be that hero again . . . just for a little while. Just for Grace.

He didn't want to disappoint her.

"Stupid, McBride. First-class stupid."

After splashing some cold water on his face, he grabbed a paper towel and scrubbed it away. He took a minute to focus on his breathing. Slow, deep breaths, pushing out the center of his chest and then tightening his belly as he released in a destressing technique that occasionally worked.

It was true. He was a drunk now. Smoked a pack a day. Used sex for a distraction rather than for true physical intimacy. His life was a train wreck with carnage lying all over the place.

But he still wasn't going to walk away and let some scumbag wreak havoc in his name. Hell no. He would get this piece of shit. And then he could go back to being the coward who didn't give a damn if he lived or died.

Sounded fair enough.

If he screwed up and somebody died maybe Worth would just shoot him and put him out of his misery.

McBride hesitated once more before going back to the conference room, took one last look at the fear in his eyes.

Someone *could* die.

Even with Grace's help, he might not be able to save the next victim. But in this screwed-up scenario, if he didn't try, the victim didn't have a chance.

"Fuck it."

He walked away from the fear in the mirror and took the stairs to the third floor. When he reached the conference room he still felt breathless. He didn't let that stop him, he barged in and assessed his audience. Worth had taken a seat and all, including the SAC, looked at McBride expectantly.

"Grace"—he allowed his gaze to linger on hers a moment before he went on—"touch base with Schaffer and tell her to look for any files marked 'random.' That's where I stored my personal notes on various cases. Also . . ."—he crossed the room to study the timeline board—"ask her to look for any fan mail I received. There's something familiar to me about the way this guy words these e-mails. I noticed it in that first e-mail." He shrugged. "The sentence structure or phrasing. Something."

Grace reached for her cell phone. "I'll text her now. I should also remind her of the search parameters we're using on the fan mail list, yes?"

"Yeah, that'll help her narrow things down." Next McBride turned his attention first to the photo of Alyssa Byrne, then the one of Katherine Jones. Totally different, not a single thing about their lives corresponded. "Pratt, find me a place where the lives of these two"—he pointed to Alyssa then Katherine—"intersect. There has to be something. This guy is too intelligent and meticulous to simply be choosing random victims. There will be a connection. Find it."

"Yes, sir," Pratt said as he made notes in his PDA.

"Davis." McBride turned to face the table once more. "Stay on the fan mail list." He shifted his attention to Worth. "When Aldridge gets in, have him start looking at the crime scenes again. From the point of abduction to the point of rescue and everything in between. Is there any relevancy between, say, the cemetery and Wal-Mart or Sloss Furnaces? Have we considered every possibility on the evidence collected?" That was a dead end, he was certain, but it needed to be looked at again.

"ASAC Talley and I are at your disposal as well," Worth reminded him with a sincerity that couldn't be faked even if the man wanted to bother.

"Talley," McBride said, addressing the assistant special agent-in-charge, "visit that neighbor's boyfriend, Horace Jackson, again." McBride pointed to the notation on the timeline regarding Jackson's statement. "Press him. Maybe he'll remember something else."

"I'll get right on it," Talley guaranteed.

Lastly his full attention settled on Worth. "Put together

a major press conference. Use our buddy Goodman."
McBride saw the skepticism in Worth's eyes but, to the
man's credit, he didn't argue. "Let's send Devoted Fan a
big, public message about how the director himself has reinstated me."

Worth pushed out of his chair. "Sounds like a good
move. I'll run your suggestion by the director. If he's agree-
able, I'll set it up."

McBride gave him some ammunition. "Devoted Fan's
goal appears to be making sure the Bureau knows what a
mistake was made three years ago, to see that I'm reinstated, yada-yada-yada. Let's see if he's being honest with
us . . . or even with himself," McBride added as an afterthought.

Grace was the first to pick up on where he was going
with that theory. "You think he's using you as a ruse? That
there's a bigger plan in motion?"

Now he would have to explain the impression and it had
only just occurred to him. "Either that or we're looking for
an unsub with a previous medical condition or, hell, an
incarceration that slowed him down. I was canned three
years ago. Why wait so long to show his support?"

McBride looked directly at Grace as he spoke, couldn't
help thinking about the way she'd come three times for
him. Maybe they shared more than one wave length. "Why
Birmingham? Why these particular victims? Why Oak Hill
Cemetery or Sloss Furnaces? What is Devoted Fan trying
to tell us? Maybe he really believes this is about me when,
in reality, it's about him."

McBride's instincts sharpened; that old familiar release
of galvanizing adrenaline took hold. "Whatever he's up to,
it isn't just about me. This guy has a story to tell. We just
have to be able to see the words."

CHAPTER SEVENTEEN

Renowned heart surgeon Dr. Kurt Trenton savored his Sunday afternoon tee times. No appointments, no surgery schedule—selecting patients and dates for surgery was among the perks of having reached prominence in one's chosen field. Sunday mornings were spent in church with the wife and children, but Sunday afternoons were his alone.

Sculpted from the peaks and valleys of the Appalachians, Oxmoor Valley offered picturesque forests, countless creeks, and rigorous elevation changes for the truly dedicated golfer. The Valley Course provided beautiful rolling fairways with a dramatic finish at the eighteenth hole, a 441-yard par-4 fondly dubbed "the Assassin."

Sheer ecstasy for Kurt Trenton.

When on the green with his favorite driver in hand, he let go the stress of life-and-death situations. Valve repairs and heart transplants were far from his thoughts.

But Martin thought of those things often.

Very often.

He and Deirdre had discussed every article written about the great Dr. Trenton and his astounding medical feats. Even on Sunday afternoons while he watched

Dr. Kurt Trenton prepare for his one o'clock tee time, Martin thought of those miracles. And he pondered the hazards of the journey.

UNOS, United Network for Organ Sharing, was not as fair as it could be when it came to doling out those life-saving organs. It wasn't supposed to be so, but there were ways to get your name higher up on the list. All it took was money and the right connection. Part of the problem was that the number of needed organs far exceeded the number of donors. A sad, sad fact. If a patient was fortunate enough to survive until his or her name came to the top of the list, then all hope shifted into the capable hands of the surgeon.

As with all else in life, one generally got what one paid for. Some surgeons were mediocre while others were quite good. And, once in a great while, a truly gifted surgeon like Kurt Trenton came along.

Martin had done his research, as he did in all things. Trenton was the absolute best, bar none, in the entire country. If a patient were lucky enough to have been granted that golden second chance with a call from UNOS, having Dr. Trenton perform the surgery was guaranteed success. A rescue from the very clutches of death.

As dedicated and esteemed as Trenton was he still had his faults. Along with his fame had come a kind of arrogance that had hardened his heart . . . perhaps rendering him in need of a new one. Martin often mulled over that notion as well.

At nine tomorrow morning the illustrious Dr. Trenton was scheduled to perform one of his miracles on the honorable Donald Shelby, one of Alabama's most beloved former governors. As Ronald Reagan had been to California, Donald Shelby was to Alabama. The whole state would be watching the news tomorrow for word on his condition. Prayers would be offered, but no one would really be worried about his survival. Dr. Kurt Trenton never lost a patient.

Before he left the elite clubhouse today Trenton would receive an unexpected call urging him to rush to the prestigious UAB Hospital where his wife hovered near death after a tragic car accident.

Trenton would, of course, dash to his Cadillac XLR-V, forgetting his beloved tee time.

He would arrive at the hospital and no one would have the foggiest idea what he was talking about. He would call his wife's cell phone and discover that she was fine, shopping with the children at the Summit Mall. Then, bewildered and angry, he would return to his car left where he always parked in the dimly lit basement garage. His emotions would prove far too distracting . . . he wouldn't see the danger until it was entirely too late.

Trenton had a date with destiny. As Martin's grandmother would have said, the good doctor was in sore need of a humbling experience. For as much as he would love to believe otherwise, he was not God. Yes, he made life-and-death decisions every day, except Sundays, but he most assuredly was not the Almighty. He needed to learn that . . . he needed a simple lesson in how it felt to be vulnerable and helpless. His fame and wealth had long ago relegated those two emotions to a place so distantly out of sight and mind that he had completely forgotten they existed.

Tonight he would remember both well.

His lesson would prove a truly newsworthy challenge for McBride. The timing was, as usual, perfect, though Martin had been forced to move things up one full day. Martin had simply worked around tee time. The world would be watching. Would McBride be able to save Trenton in time to perform that rare, life-saving surgical procedure on the beloved Donald Shelby? So much would be at stake. Those FBI rats would surely see just how badly they needed to have Agent McBride on their team once more.

The world needed heroes so very desperately.

Perhaps Martin and his dear Deirdre would have a special place in heaven when the time came, for proving what a great man McBride was.

For now, it was time for Martin to do his part.

Time to show them all.

CHAPTER EIGHTEEN

Vivian couldn't take it any longer. She had to go home and shower. Not that having McBride's scent indelibly imprinted on her was such a bad thing. But it had been immensely distracting all day, a constant reminder of the mistake she had allowed to happen. Diving right into work as if nothing had happened had been essential. Allowing Worth to pick up on even the slightest hint that she had crossed the line . . . would be a total and complete disaster.

Work had allowed her to forget for a while, but waking up from the twenty-minute power nap she had stolen at her desk around six had snatched her right back to those minutes she wanted to pretend hadn't happened. Her mind had first and foremost become aware of that subtle scent of his clinging to her skin and clothes.

Then and now heat flushed her face.

Rushing through her condo, she stripped off her jade suit and black blouse. By the time she reached her bedroom she was wriggling out of her felonious silk panties. She kicked them aside. And the shoes. She would never, ever be able to wear those shoes again without thinking of him . . . and sex.

After setting the water's temperature in her shower, she gathered a towel and pinned her hair up out of the way. There was no time for washing, drying, and styling that mane. This had to be a fast wash-away-McBride's-scent and, if she was lucky, the memory of his touch.

Worth wanted her back at the office as quickly as possible. She felt that urgency herself. Not only did she not want to miss anything, she didn't want to risk someone else taking her place. As selfish as that sounded, in her work world it was every man for himself—even though she was a woman.

She stepped beneath the hot spray of water and relished the relaxing feel of the heat. Her muscles instantly loosened. Rubbing the soap over her skin had her remembering the way McBride had touched her . . . and the place he had found that prompted an orgasm in under ten seconds. Unbelievable.

Orgasms had never come easy to her. Hadn't come at all in a really long time. She knew the ugliness with Nameless had left her damaged goods in the sex department. But she had worked diligently to overcome those awful memories. She'd had sex plenty of times since.

Not at first. Those initial two years afterward had been a situational trial and error. Lots of therapy and slow progress with physical intimacy. She had known that in order to get past the fear she would have to take it slow and get back into the game. Then she had gone a little overboard, mostly to prove she could do it. Lots of lovers her senior year in college. Despite the embarrassingly high number she had always practiced safe sex. Maybe a little too safe. Not only had she insisted on the use of condoms . . . she had stretched an invisible shield around her emotions.

Vivian's hands stilled, the soap clutched against her abdomen. McBride had been right about the whole disappearing act. That was exactly what she had done. She never allowed herself to feel any of it. The decision wasn't conscious . . . more instinct than anything. Self-preservation instincts.

This was the first time she had admitted that to herself. Having sex with McBride was the first time she had permitted herself to drop her guard and get so lost in the moment that she had come, over and over again.

All those other times she hadn't been fooling anyone but herself. No man had been able to give her the big "O" since before Nameless. The few she had experienced had been through focused masturbation, which didn't require the presence of a man, just a little patience and concentration. She had begun to think that she would never feel anything that intense with the opposite sex again.

The possibility that normal sex could still be a part of her life was a surprise and a tremendous relief.

If one could call what she and McBride had shared in that stall "normal."

Smoothing the soap over her skin, careful of the tender spots that hadn't been worked so thoroughly in so long, had her nipples standing at attention and her body heating unexpectedly. Or maybe it was the fact that she had allowed him into her head just now.

Going with it, she closed her eyes and moved her sudsy hands over those parts still hungry for human touch. Her breasts in particular needed lots of attention. She squeezed, massaged . . . then moved lower, to her labia. She shivered when she slid one finger along that channel and then dipped inside. Heat flared. She moaned softly.

She recalled the way he had touched her . . . kissed her, and then of him moving in and out of her. Her body aching for it now, she searched for that special spot where he had worked such satisfying magic.

There.

Oh yes.

Soon the waves of completion were flowing over her, inside her. She sagged against the tile wall and let it happen. But it wasn't the same without McBride to do the job right.

That was when she recognized just how much trouble she had gotten herself into.

Her eyes snapped open and she gave herself a good swift mental kick. This was more than just a mistake on a personal level, this was her career.

She had worked too hard to get here. Had big plans for her future.

No mistakes.

With a quick rinse, she hurried through the drying process and got dressed. When she returned to the office, she would do so with a new attitude. Back to business.

All business.

No more falling victim to his rugged charm.

No more sex, no matter how amazing.

9:30 P.M.
1000 Eighteenth Street

Vivian grabbed her notes from her desk and hurried to the conference room. Everyone else was already there. The shower had helped tremendously. She felt human again. And ready to focus.

"Let's talk about what we have," Worth suggested, his comment directed at McBride.

"I'd like to hear what Aldridge has come up with on the scenes." McBride rested his attention on the older man. "Anything new on that?"

"Possibly." Aldridge glanced over his handwritten notes. He was old school, no PDAs for him. "Oak Hill Cemetery," he said "is the final resting place of the steel magnates who put Birmingham on the map. It holds a prominent position in our city, right downtown."

McBride nodded. "So the cemetery represents the upper crust of Birmingham's society."

"Right," Aldridge agreed.

"What about Sloss?" Worth asked.

Vivian's attention swung to him. The SAC wasn't unaccustomed to sitting in the background. But he, along with everyone else in the Birmingham office, had been given strict orders by the director to work with McBride. To get this done fast.

"The working man . . . blue collar," Aldridge said about Sloss. "Hundreds of men died there, laborers, totally expendable."

"Katherine Jones worked at Wal-Mart," Vivian said, the idea seeming to go along with Aldridge's response. "Low salary base, serving the public in a manner of speaking. Just another clerk in a blue vest, easily replaced."

"The lower class, the invisible," McBride deduced.

Exactly. No specialized training required, just hard work.

"No connection between the vics yet," Pratt added during the lull that followed. "The Byrnes don't shop at the Wal-Mart on Hackworth Road, if they even shop at discount stores at all. Not related by blood or marriage, even distantly. Don't travel in the same circles, social or otherwise. No church or community connections. Nada."

"Nothing from Schaffer yet," Vivian said when McBride turned to her, before he could even ask. Just having those blue eyes linger on her had her nerves jangling. *Focus, Vivian.*

Lila Grimes, Worth's secretary, rushed in and whispered something in the SAC's ear. Vivian was thankful for the distraction. But the visible shift in Worth's posture cued her in that this was not a call from his wife to find out when he would be home.

This was bad news.

"We have another communication," Worth said, his gaze connecting with McBride's.

McBride pushed out of his chair and moved to the computer set up for tracing anything incoming. Vivian followed. There wasn't supposed to be another communication today. This was the Lord's day, Devoted Fan had said. They were supposed to have a few more hours.

McBride took a seat and opened the mailbox.

There it was, new mail.

It was him.

One click and the message box opened.

McBride, my friend,

Unfortunately, an unavoidable glitch has forced me to move forward ahead of schedule. You have my sincerest apologies, but this challenge will not wait. It will prove how right I have been all along.

Kurt Trenton worships his fame and his own arrogance. He holds life in his hands, giving it, likewise taking it away. For this reason he must be humbled. You see, Trenton needs to remember how it feels for his life to rest in the hands of another. He is not God. This he will learn quickly as he awaits death, just as the One he would pretend to be once suffered so selflessly. Oppression is evil.

Find him, McBride, before it is too late. Remind him that justice is everywhere and threatens injustice anywhere. You have twelve hours . . . starting now.

Your Devoted Fan

"Okay, folks," Worth shouted. "Who is Kurt Trenton? Has he been reported missing? Find everything you can on who he is and where he is. The name sounds familiar. This guy may be a regular in the media. Start there."

McBride read the e-mail's last paragraph once more, his tension compounding with each word. Twelve hours. The time was cut shorter again and the difficulty level had been escalated. As promised by Devoted Fan's previous communications. McBride's hands shook as he sent the e-mail to the printer.

He'd made his decision, he was in. There was no other option. Any hope of this thing having a happy ending had just vanished. At six this evening Worth had announced McBride's reinstatement on all local news channels and still the e-mail had come.

It was just as McBride had surmised. This was far bigger than him. Somehow he was the linchpin, the connecting thread, but he was certain each one of these victims was somehow involved . . . somehow a part of the story Devoted Fan wanted to tell.

Before getting up from the computer, McBride decided to try one last effort to end this before anyone else was put at risk. He opened a reply box and started to type.

One by one the agents in the room gathered behind him, including Worth.

Devoted Fan,
    You must have seen the news release. I have been
reinstated. There is no need to continue your valiant efforts.
I am back and I have you to thank.

                                    McBride

"Do you think that will accomplish anything?" Worth asked.

McBride glanced up at him. "Maybe, maybe not. Only one way to find out." He hit the send button.

Less than a minute passed before the announcement that he had mail sounded. McBride clicked the necessary tabs to open it.

McBride,
    Yes, I saw this on the news. It was very exciting. I feel
that you and I together have accomplished the first step. But

I fear that we have not yet shown them just how invaluable
you are. I am certain this ploy will not last if we do not
carry on with our mission. Rescue Trenton and you will be
very close to the end of your trials. With these final
challenges you will truly be exalted to the glorious position
you deserve.

                                                    Devoted Fan

"Davis, Aldridge"—McBride pushed away from the
computer and looked to the two agents—"see if you can
nail down the location these clues are alluding to. Run the
phrasing through the system, particularly the part about
justice and injustice. We're going to have to make every
second count on this one."

"If he follows the same MO," Grace offered, "the location will be highly visible."

McBride nodded. "That's right. Prioritize your findings
with high-profile locations at the top of the list." He walked
to the printer to retrieve the hard copy of the e-mail. "Pratt,
as soon as we know who this Trenton is, see if he ties in
with either of the other victims."

"Working on it," Pratt called out.

"I'll work with Pratt," Grace offered. "At least until I
have something from Schaffer."

McBride nodded, using the opportunity to take a long,
unhurried look at her even as she turned her back and
walked away. She'd gone home to shower and change. The
burgundy suit was different from the others, tighter, just a
tad shorter. More of those killer shoes, these a perfect match
to the suit. He followed the path of her toned legs from her
ankles to just above her knees.

His pulse reacted to the X-rated images of all the things
he would like to do to her.

Later . . . when he wasn't scared shitless that he would
let someone die.

He stared at the e-mail, read the puzzling lines once more.

"*. . . holds life in his hands . . . he is not God . . .*"

"This Trenton," McBride announced, "is a doctor." He looked from Pratt, to Grace. "A doctor with a major God complex."

Grace looked away first but not before he saw the glow of pride in her eyes. At first the idea baffled him, then he realized what it meant. She was proud of him. That unfamiliar feeling constricted his chest once more and he shook his head. The rookie had latched on to some unexpected real estate that he hadn't even realized was on the market.

The last time anyone had owned a piece of his heart, he'd been a kid.

He just hoped the lady understood the kind of shitty neighborhood she'd bought into.

Grace abruptly swiveled away from the computer where she worked next to Pratt. "I've got him." Her gaze homed in on McBride's. "Dr. Kurt Trenton, forty-eight years old, five eleven, one-sixty, gray eyes, salt-and-pepper hair. Cardiac surgeon."

"Not just any cardiac surgeon," Pratt added, twisting around to face McBride as he evidently landed the info as well. "This guy was one of the country's leading transplant surgeons. He's been on *Good Morning America.*"

"Is," Grace clarified with a glance at Pratt, "the leading transplant surgeon." Her attention fixed back on McBride then. "On Tuesday he's scheduled to perform a rare procedure, an autotransplant, on former Alabama Governor Donald Shelby. Only two people have survived the procedure. In both cases, Trenton was the surgeon."

"News flash," Pratt cut in, apparently determined to one-up his colleague, "the procedure got moved up. The surgery's scheduled for nine *tomorrow* morning."

A new load of pressure settled onto McBride's shoulders. Now there were two lives depending upon his ability to pull this off.

"Tell me about this autotransplant," he said, striding

toward where Grace and Pratt worked. "Why can't someone else do it. What's the big deal?"

Grace clicked a few keys. "Shelby has a tumor or mass
of some sort in a heart valve. The heart has to be stopped
with chemicals, removed from his chest, and placed in
a bucket of ice and water. The patient's life will be sus-
tained by a heart-lung machine while Trenton removes
the tumor and makes the necessary repair to the heart.
Then the organ is placed back in the chest and recon-
nected. Few surgeons would even attempt the procedure
and, as I said before, Trenton is the only one who has been
successful at it."

"If we don't find Trenton"—McBride dared to say the
words aloud—"then Shelby dies too."

Worth strode into the conference room. "I just received
calls from the chief of police as well as the mayor. Dr. Kurt
Trenton's wife reported him missing one hour ago. Birmingham PD discovered his car in the parking garage of
UAB Hospital."

"Your next call," McBride warned him, "will come
from the governor."

A frown drew Worth's brow into a pucker. "What do
you mean?"

Worth's secretary burst through the door. "Sir, I'm sorry
to interrupt but Governor Wiley is on the line for you."

Timing. It was all in the timing. Devoted Fan had a
statement to make. He had just moved from a side note in
local news to prime time.

Monday, September 11, 3:00 A.M.
Six hours remaining . . .

Davis rushed to where McBride sat reviewing schematics
of every hospital in the city. He'd already gotten a citywide
layout showing where every church was located. Hospitals

and churches: the two most likely places for a miracle to happen. And most larger hospitals had chapels.

Worth had been pacing like an expectant father. The pressure was on. If Trenton wasn't found, former Governor Shelby would most likely die. His condition was deteriorating by the minute.

"Sir . . . Agent McBride?"

McBride looked up, startled at being addressed that way. "Yeah, Davis, what have you got?"

"I may have something on that phrase 'justice is everywhere and threatens injustice anywhere.'" He shuffled the pages in his hand. "During his stay in a Birmingham jail, Martin Luther King wrote a letter using a variation on that phrase." Davis read from his notes, "'Injustice anywhere is a threat to justice everywhere.'"

Martin Luther King. Oppression. The fight to be equal. Lines from Devoted Fan's e-mails tumbled one over the other into McBride's head. *God. Worships his fame. He must be humbled.*

"I don't think he's alluding to a jail." McBride studied the wording of the e-mail again. "He talks about God and Trenton believing he is God, holding life in his hands . . . 'awaits death just as the One he would pretend to be once suffered so selflessly.'"

Aldridge joined the conversation, tapped the pad where he'd written his notes. "There's a monument, a statue of Martin Luther King in Kelly Ingram Park." Aldridge looked from McBride to Davis and back. "Should we search the park?"

"Wait." Grace pushed away from her station and stood. "The Sixteenth Street Baptist Church is there. You can't get any more high profile. The church is an historic landmark. It was the hub of the civil rights effort—part of Birmingham's history is written in the blood of four little girls who were killed in that church as part of the movement to oppress blacks."

"Oppression is evil."

But this oppression wasn't about race, it was about money. Financial means . . . security. Rich versus poor. Just like the Byrne girl at that high-society cemetery and the Jones woman at the blue-collar steel mill. The girl born with the silver spoon in her mouth; the woman who worked hard for every dollar.

Trenton was a renowned surgeon. It would take big money or the right kind of insurance to obtain treatment from a surgeon of such status.

"Okay . . ." McBride said slowly, "Trenton's class in a sense oppresses the poor by having the best of everything while the working man only gets what's left over." McBride scrubbed a hand over his stubbled chin. "Trenton has the God complex we talked about earlier. He, according to Devoted Fan, is in bad need of humbling."

"His arrogance is documented in a number of newspaper articles," Grace contributed.

"He holds life in his hands by selecting some patients and turning others away, probably based on their ability to pay," McBride considered aloud.

Worth butted in. "Those kinds of statements have to be kept in this room," he admonished. "We can't go around disparaging friends of the governor's."

McBride ignored Worth, locked gazes with Grace. "The church." He nodded as if he needed that physical acknowledgment to confirm the thought. "That has to be it. Where else would we find the One, capital *O* if you'll notice"—he tapped the e-mail—"Trenton pretends to be?"

"You're right," Grace agreed, then shook her head. "But not just any church, *the* church."

McBride tossed the e-mail aside, anticipation soaring. "Where the likeness of Mr. King still watches over from the park, reminding all that 'oppression is evil.' "

"Talley," Worth called out, "find out who the reverend at

Sixteenth Street Baptist is and wake him up. We don't have time or"—Worth's attention settled on McBride—"the necessary probable cause for a warrant. We need an invitation to take a look inside that church." Worth turned to Aldridge then. "Get Birmingham PD to rendezvous there ASAP."

To McBride Worth said, "You really think this is it? Time is fast running out on us, McBride. We have to find this guy. If we don't, we're going to be in a world of shit."

Birmingham PD was scouring the city one hospital, morgue, church, and neighborhood at a time. But the sweep was broad, not focused, because they didn't know exactly where to look. And, like Worth said, time was their enemy. The good doctor's survival depended upon McBride's conclusions. If he was wrong about the Sixteenth Street Baptist Church . . .

"This is the one," he told Worth with as much certainty as he could muster. "Grace and I aren't waiting, we're going now. We'll meet the reverend at the church entrance."

"Just don't go inside without him." Worth fixed Grace with a stern look. "Find Agent Arnold. Take him with you. He's a damned good agent and the fact that he's African-American will prevent the two of you from looking like a pair of white feds pushing your weight around."

"Yes, sir."

McBride had to remember that there was a history of racial problems here . . . one that appeared to be in the past, but no one wanted to risk going down that road. Least of all him.

"One other thing," McBride said, remembering the circus outside. "We're going to need Birmingham PD to hold those reporters back until we're out of here. I don't think you want any of them showing up at the church."

"I've already taken care of that. When you leave the parking lot, you'll get a five-minute head start before the road block is lifted."

Grace rounded up Arnold and the decision was made to take his sedan. It was a dark charcoal and far more nondescript than her silver Explorer. As promised, barricades had been put into place by Birmingham PD at each end of the block, preventing the reporters from following.

4:55 A.M.
Four hours, five minutes remaining . . .

When they arrived at the corner of Sixteenth Street and Sixth Avenue, the Reverend Simmons waited on the steps leading into the historic church.

McBride surveyed the area when he emerged from the car. Dark, quiet. But something in the air had his senses on alert. Those old instincts were humming. If they were all lucky, that was a good sign.

He leaned against the car, lit a Marlboro, and gestured to the reverend. "Explain what we need." He looked from Grace to Arnold. "I'll catch up."

Arnold hustled up the steps, Grace followed more slowly. She didn't have to say a word, McBride could read her surprise right there on her face in the glow of the street lamps. Time was balls-to-the-wall short, what the hell was he thinking taking a smoke break?

Because he needed it.

His hand shook as he lifted the cigarette to his lips and took another deep drag.

If he was wrong and Trenton wasn't in this church . . . there likely wouldn't be enough time to narrow down another location before time ran out. Trenton would die and so would Shelby.

McBride's inability to get the job done would prove Devoted Fan a fool and that the Bureau had been right to off-load him three years ago.

Sure, the big exposé that reporter had done revealed the

war that had gone down between Quinn and McBride, but any agent worth his salt would know that didn't prove a damned thing. McBride's retrieval plan could very well have gone wrong just as Quinn's route had. There was no way to ever be sure. Maybe the Bureau had been right . . . maybe he had been destined to crash and burn. And just maybe if he hadn't been, Quinn wouldn't have snatched control away at the last minute.

Any way you looked at it, McBride couldn't say it wasn't his fault. All the more reason he shouldn't be here doing this. People were counting on him and he wasn't sure he could live up to the expectations.

Unfortunately, there wasn't shit he could do about it.

One last pull from the smoke and he pushed away from the car. He dropped the butt on the sidewalk, ground it out, but then picked up the snuffed-out remains and shoved them into his pocket. This was a church, after all.

Sacred ground. Where four little girls had died in a bombing because some asshole had thought he was better than them.

". . . he must be humbled."

Confidence nudged at McBride. This had to be the place. Devoted Fan wanted this high profile. He wanted the world watching . . .

McBride rushed up the steps two at a time, reached the entrance just as Grace and Arnold followed Simmons inside.

The main sanctuary was filled with pews dressed in thick red cushions and that same brilliant red spilled across the floor in the form of carpet. A balcony circled the sanctuary, providing additional seating. Massive stained-glass windows, each telling a story, wrapped the room in biblical accountings.

The Reverend Simmons led the way through the sanctuary and to all rooms and halls on the upper floor. McBride's gut twisted as each area revealed nothing.

"What about the basement level?" he asked, when it was obvious that the sanctuary level was clear.

"This way." The reverend indicated the door to his right. "I was here until around seven last night," he explained as he led the way down the winding staircase. "And we had service this morning."

"To this day the church gets bomb threats," Arnold said to McBride. "Condoleezza Rice was here a couple years ago and the Bureau responded to a threat after her visit."

"Lord have mercy, Jesus." Simmons gasped.

McBride moved down the last step to stand next to the reverend, whose horrified gaze had fixated on the abomination erected in the center of the large basement's gathering place.

"Nobody move," McBride warned.

He weaved between the tables and chairs until he stood before the rudimentary cross where Dr. Kurt Trenton had been lashed crucifixion style. Using extreme caution, McBride reached up, touched Trenton's carotid artery. "He's alive," he called back to the others.

Alive and naked, save for the bomb on his chest. Trenton's eyes were closed. Written in black marker across his forehead was one word: GODLESS. His arms and legs had been bound in place with silver duct tape. His mouth was taped shut the same as the other vics had been. At least Devoted Fan was sticking with his tools of choice. Except . . . for the bomb. That was definitely a little more high tech.

"Is that . . ." Arnold asked without coming any closer, "what I think it is?"

"Looks like." McBride watched the digital timer count down from three hours forty-nine minutes then he considered the IED, improvised explosive device. The working parts were strung together against the doctor's chest with no casing or enclosure of any sort. Just the guts. As if the doctor's innards had been bared for the world to see. And they would be if this thing went off.

McBride turned to face the man of the cloth waiting with Grace and Arnold. "Reverend, I want you and Agent Arnold to go outside and start knocking on the doors of any houses or businesses close by where there might be people. Birmingham PD will assist when they arrive. If this thing goes off, I don't want anybody in the possible blast radius."

McBride's throat tightened. He swallowed. Didn't help. "Grace, go outside with the others. Call Worth and tell him to get me a bomb unit over here. *Now.*"

"I'll make the call and then I'll be back."

He'd expected that. No way was he allowing her to play hero. "Arnold, if she tries to come back in here, restrain her."

"Yes, sir."

Returning his attention to Trenton, McBride felt the daggers flying at his back. This was no time to argue. Grace could thank him later. *If* he didn't end up splattered all over the Magic City.

The digital clock was ticking right on down, but, barring any unexpected deviations from Devoted Fan's usual MO, there was plenty of time for the bomb unit to get here and take care of this.

McBride studied the assembly. The timer and battery were connected to a detonator, which led to a block of what looked like C-4. Defusing this thing shouldn't be a problem for a trained technician. He had defused one during his career but it had been a long-ass time and he had been in contact with an expert during the whole process. He hoped that wouldn't be necessary this morning. He'd hate like hell to get this fancy doctor killed . . . or be responsible for the loss of this historic landmark.

Unless . . . maybe he could get it off the victim's chest, lay it carefully on the floor, then get the victim out of here. That could work.

Careful not to touch anything, he leaned down and peered at the way the bomb was attached to Trenton's chest since there was no tape or strapping visible.

Not seeing a thing, McBride tried to work his finger between the timer and Trenton's chest, but his skin seemed attached to the device. Then McBride knew. Glue. Something powerful like . . . Super Glue. Maybe the same glue the unsub had used to trap Katherine Jones.

"Smart bastard," McBride griped under his breath. Why couldn't he have gotten a stupid unsub?

Trenton groaned. McBride straightened, reached up, and started to peel the tape from his mouth. Trenton's eyes snapped open. He tried to scream, jerked and bucked in a futile attempt to break free.

"Don't move, Dr. Trenton," McBride urged, drawing his hands away from the man in hopes of calming him. "Don't move!"

Trenton stilled but his eyes were huge with fear.

"My name is McBride and I'm with the FBI. Help is on the way. There's—" The readout on the digital timer jerked his attention there.

59:38

What the hell? A minute ago it had displayed more than three hours forty minutes to go. Now there was less than sixty minutes? McBride's tension shot to the next level.

Trenton started groaning and doing that wiggling-jerking motion again.

The timer went into fast-forward.

"Stop!" McBride glared at him. "Don't move! There's a goddamned bomb strapped to your chest. Every time you move the countdown speeds up."

The man froze except for the sobs muffled behind the tape still partially covering his mouth.

The timer displayed three minutes eleven seconds and ticking down.

Shit!

Desperation cutting off his air supply, McBride dug out his cell phone and called Grace. "What's the ETA on that bomb unit?" His heart thumped harder with each word.

Grace's words echoed in his ear like a death call. The bomb unit was more than three minutes out.

McBride lowered the phone, let it fall to the floor.

They were fucked.

As if he had said the words out loud, Trenton's sobs grew more frantic.

McBride met his gaze. The terror there twisted his gut.

This man, God complex or not, was going to die if McBride didn't do something. Being in a church wasn't going to make one damned bit of difference. They were on their own.

McBride wasn't going to give up without trying. He considered the design of the bomb again. C-4 required a detonating charge. Any detonation required a power source. No power source, no detonation of the igniting charge. No igniting charge, no boom.

Simple. All he had to do was stop the process.

He wished for a cigarette and a drink, but he'd just have to wait until he was through here. A tremor jerked his hand as he reached out to the battery. Each piece of this thing was glued to Trenton's chest, so there was no moving any one part. He had to defuse it by cutting the wires.

Too bad he didn't have a knife.

1:46

And all this time he'd thought he was prepared carrying a condom around.

Okay, what were his options?

He could try pulling the wires loose.

The wire to the timer first or to the detonator first? The way they were twisted around who could tell what went where?

To hell with it.

He'd just do them all.

Red went first.

1:12

Sweat beaded on his forehead as the seconds kept ticking off. *1:08 . . . 0:59 . . .*

Green wire next.

0:42

Black.

0:36

"Goddammit."

Blue.

0:22

How many damned wires did it take?

White.

0:14

"Son of a bitch!"

Only one more.

0:09

Yellow.

0:04

What the fuck?

There were no more wires!

Trenton groaned and bucked.

McBride's heart stopped stone-still.

0:00

5:18 A.M.

"What the hell is happening in there?" Vivian glared at Arnold. "I'm going in."

"Bomb unit's a minute out," Arnold argued. "We'll wait for them."

Four Birmingham PD cruisers had arrived and blocked off Sixteenth as well as Sixth Avenue, keeping curiosity seekers out of the blast radius.

"Dammit, Arnold, he's been down there over five minutes *alone*. I'm going in."

Arnold, his frame a mile wide, stepped in her path. "No

way, Grace. You heard what McBride said, we stay out here. You're not going in."

There was movement at the entrance of the church. Her breath stalled in the vicinity of her lungs. McBride rushed out with Trenton leaning heavily against him. The man's naked body had been draped with some sort of dark cloth.

What the hell had happened? Had McBride defused the bomb?

Vivian ran for the steps.

The bomb unit roared to a stop on the street.

"Are you all right?" she demanded of McBride as she reached his position in front of the church. She did a quick visual sweep of Trenton, who looked like hell but was definitely still breathing.

"Didn't hear a boom, did you?" McBride jerked his head toward Trenton. "I do owe the reverend a new pair of curtains."

Fury descended on Vivian with biblical proportions. He had forced her to leave him in there alone with a damned bomb and a victim. And now he comes storming out talking about freaking drapes. "You are the absolute, biggest, goddamned—"

"Hold on, Grace," McBride cut her off as he shifted Trenton's weight. Then he inclined his head in her direction and said softly, "You're practically in a church."

Booted feet charged toward them. She snapped her mouth shut.

Trenton was alive.

McBride had done it again.

Vivian couldn't decide if she wanted to hug him or kick his ass.

CHAPTER NINETEEN

"Zoom in on her face," Nadine Goodman ordered her cameraman.

Agent Vivian Grace, along with newly reinstated Special Agent Ryan McBride, stood aside as Dr. Kurt Trenton was hefted into a waiting ambulance. According to Nadine's source from Birmingham PD, the victim had had a bomb attached to his chest and the word GODLESS written across his forehead.

Nadine knew Dr. Trenton. His reputation in the medical world was unparalleled. His wife served on a dozen charitable committees. He had two brilliant children at the prestigious Altamont School.

Special Agent-in-Charge Randall Worth's unannounced press conference last evening hadn't mentioned anything about an ongoing case, only that Ryan McBride had been reinstated and temporarily assigned to the Birmingham field office. Obviously whatever case McBride had been brought here to solve was ongoing.

There was something going on that no one was talking about. In her eight years as an investigative reporter, Nadine had never encountered a case with a tighter lid. No one knew anything. She had spoken to Katherine Jones upon her release from the hospital and gotten nothing. The Byrnes refused to answer any questions regarding their daughter's abduction.

And now an elite surgeon is tossed into the mix?

Was the same perpetrator committing these abductions? All three had taken place at historic landmarks. Dozens of police officers were involved and yet no one knew a damned thing. If they did, Nadine would have gotten something from someone, and her sources were bone-dry.

She supposed it didn't help that charges related to the break-in at McBride's bungalo were pending.

She was very good at what she did. Some called her ruthless. She, on the other hand, called her methods survival of the fittest.

There were two consistent details in this puzzling investigation: Ryan McBride, whom she had already outed, and Agent Vivian Grace, a rookie and the newest agent at the Birmingham field office—besides McBride of course.

Why wasn't Aldridge or one of the other more senior agents partnered with McBride?

Just another aspect of this strange investigation that made no sense.

"Let's do the final segment with the departing ambulance in the background," Nadine instructed her cameraman.

She would get this out of the way, then hang around the hospital to see if she could get an interview with someone . . . anyone. Afterward, she was going on another digging expedition.

Before this day ended, she would know all there was to know about Agent Vivian Grace.

CHAPTER TWENTY

4:00 P.M.
1000 Eighteenth Street

McBride dragged out his Zippo and lit a Marlboro.

Seven hours ago, as scheduled, Dr. Kurt Trenton had pulled himself together, despite the objections of his friends and family, and performed the needed surgery on former governor Donald Shelby.

Trenton was a hero. A tragically wounded one, if only in the emotional sense.

He might not be God but an angel certainly sat on his Versace-clad shoulder. Maybe, just maybe, because he would put himself through the rigors of a life-saving surgical procedure after his terrifying night in a hell designed just for him, the good doctor was actually a humbler man. Time would tell.

McBride sat on the counter of the first-floor men's room and inhaled a deep drag from his cigarette. Worth had given up and authorized him to smoke there since the press whores were still camped outside. A technician had been brought in to temporarily override the smoke detector so the alarm wouldn't go off every time McBride lit up.

Worth was officially off McBride's asshole list. He still didn't like him much but that was because he was a prick.

Pricks were different from assholes. And Worth was definitely a prick.

Getting back to another prick, Trenton's high-powered attorney had reduced the doctor's official statement down to one sentence: "Dr. Trenton recalls returning to his car in the hospital's parking garage and sitting down behind the steering wheel." "That's all, gentlemen," his attorney had insisted. "He didn't see anyone or hear anything.

Trenton's pimped-up Caddy had been taken into custody by forensics. So far they hadn't found jack shit. Nothing in the hospital garage that couldn't have belonged to any one of several hundred other people. Nothing at the church.

Nothing. Nothing. Nothing.

The media was all over the story. McBride's past had been rehashed again. All sorts of speculation about the three victims and the possible perpetrator had hit the papers as well as the television and radio news.

Worth had issued a statement saying there was a possibility the abductions were connected and that the Bureau was investigating that avenue.

McBride closed his eyes and leaned back against the mirrored wall. The C-4 explosive glued to Trenton's chest had been fake—a substance similar to polymer modeling clay. The detonating charge had been a small homemade explosive configured from an illegal type of holiday fireworks commonly sold under the table. Basically a cardboard tube packed with explosive materials like a "quarter stick" or an M-80. Had Trenton not been found before detonation, that charge could have caused a serious enough injury to pose a threat to his life. The reverend had said that he generally started tours in the church by noon on weekdays. That would have been too late, lending credence to the possibility that before being discovered, Trenton could have bled to death.

And that was the thing . . . Devoted Fan didn't appear to

want anyone to die. Sure, this last challenge had been a little tougher, but not so much so that the likelihood of failure was greater than the likelihood of success.

McBride had concluded that the man wasn't a murderer . . . maybe, under ordinary circumstances, not even a criminal. Yet, something had triggered him to act, and he was trying to prove some point. Something beyond McBride's hero status. Something personal.

But what?

The door opened and Grace walked in, a folder in hand.

"Is Worth looking for me?" McBride took another drag. He felt like a brand-new freshman skipping class, hiding out in the men's restroom.

"Not yet." She scooted onto the counter on the other side of the sink. That burgundy skirt hiked up, revealing several inches of very nice thighs.

"You have a thing for men's rooms, Grace?" He turned on the water in the sink, wet the cigarette butt to ensure the fire was completely doused, then tossed it into the waste bin beneath the paper towel dispenser. Color darkened her cheeks. He smiled, couldn't help himself. He'd done that now and again since meeting her. More irony. This was the last situation that should make him smile.

"Let's talk," she suggested, opening the file she'd brought with her.

"Let's." She could talk all night and he would be content to watch her profile as those lips moved, forming each word. His brain instantly retrieved the imprinted memories of having those lips meshed with his own. So soft and yet so full. The image instantly morphed into other scenarios that included him and that lush mouth. He would be more than happy to repay in kind. He couldn't think of a thing he would enjoy more than having his mouth on every part of her.

She swiveled her face toward him, stared straight into his eyes. "Stop looking at me that way."

He ordered his pulse to slow. "Sorry." But he wasn't sorry. He was hard and horny and he wanted her again. And again after that. Right here would be fine, right now would be better than fine.

"I want to go over a couple of theories with you." She turned her attention back to the folder.

"Hit me."

She glanced at him again with that look that suggested he might want to rephrase.

"We," she said before settling her attention back on the pages in the file, "have three completely unrelated victims, two female, one male. Two adults, one child. Two rich, one poor. Three historic landmarks as crime scenes. And you." Those big dark eyes rested on him once more. "And that's it. No evidence, no prints, no witnesses other than Mr. Jackson, who didn't see enough to be useful."

That about summed it up. "How is Davis coming along with that fan list?"

"He has it narrowed down to less than two hundred and he's making phone calls. When he eliminates those who have moved away or died or whatever, he and Arnold are going door to door."

"Nothing from Schaffer?"

Grace shrugged. "Nothing significant. She did find your notes on that final report. So Goodman's associate told the truth about that part anyway."

"Speaking of Goodman," McBride ventured, recalling the pushy lady from last night outside the church, "what's the deal with her? Just another pushy newshound?"

Grace closed her file and clasped her hands atop it. "She's been around for a while. Came to Birmingham about five years ago from Pittsburgh. Most people consider her the voice of what's happening in this city. Divorced. No children. Totally dedicated to the job. A bitch."

McBride considered his temporary partner. "Sounds like you don't care for the lady."

"She hurts people to get what she wants. I have a problem with that. The Byrnes were ready to take out a restraining order to keep her away from their house after their daughter was rescued. I'm sure Katherine Jones has suffered the same treatment only she doesn't have a fancy lawyer. Hospital security will probably keep her off Trenton's back." Grace gave her head a little shake. "Look what she did to Mr. Braden and Agent Quinn. And you," she added, a flicker of some undefined emotion in her eyes.

Could she possibly give one shit about his feelings? "That exposé of Goodman's didn't hurt me, Grace. The man she targeted is gone, this one"—he patted his chest—"isn't that guy. He's just a bum who does what he has to and nothing more." When she would have argued, he went on, "What she wrote hurt Derrick Braden and Andrew Quinn . . . the two people left from that nightmare who still had something to lose."

That was the truth if he'd ever spoken it.

A knock on the door drew their attention there.

"Grace?" Pratt called through the door rather than coming on in.

Maybe he was afraid of what he would see. He hadn't asked any questions about the episode at the airport but the guy had to have noticed the tension between McBride and Grace after that.

Grace slid off the counter and strode to the door. McBride took the opportunity to admire those gorgeous legs. He'd gladly sell what was left of his soul to have them wrapped around him one more time.

She opened the door, the back of the hand holding the file propped on her hip. Her colleague peeked past her to see what McBride was up to. "What?" she demanded.

"Worth wants the two of you upstairs." He looked from Grace to McBride and back. "There's some guy from Quantico here."

McBride had wondered when the Q would get around

to sending somebody down for a look-see. Took them longer than he had expected.

Grace followed Pratt up the stairs and McBride followed her. He definitely got the better end of the deal. If he loitered a few steps behind he could see up her skirt just far enough to get a glimpse of smooth thighs.

Didn't take her long to figure that out. She stopped. Waited for him to catch up, then gave him the evil eye.

Like he said before, he was only human.

Worth waited in his office. The agent from Quantico sat in one of the chairs facing Worth's desk, his back to the door.

"Agents Grace and McBride," Worth said, "have a seat."

The visitor stood, turned to greet them and McBride stopped.

Collin Pierce.

"Agent Grace." Pierce extended his hand. "It's good to see you."

She accepted his hand, her action delayed just enough for McBride to notice.

"Agent Pierce," she acknowledged, drawing out the syllables as if surprised or reluctant.

During that instant, that fraction of a second, when Pierce held on to her hand before she pulled away, McBride observed something. Some infinitesimal impression that said these two shared a connection, past or present, which still simmered.

"McBride." Pierce turned to him next, thrust out the same hand. "It's been a while."

McBride gave his hand a quick, firm shake, more a challenge than a greeting. "Not nearly long enough."

Pierce smiled and made one of those noncommittal sounds that was supposed to be humorous or indulgent but mostly came out like a pissed-off grunt.

"Agent Pierce," Worth spoke up as he gestured for them to take their seats, "was in Montgomery speaking to a group of potential academy candidates and he dropped by to see how we were coming along on the Devoted Fan case."

Like hell.

Before McBride could say as much, Grace did.

"Your checking up on me is inappropriate, Agent Pierce."

Well, well, at least now McBride knew. There *was* something between these two. He liked it when Grace got spunky. She only did that when she was damned pissed off or pushed into a corner.

"Agent Grace," Pierce said in that patient, wiser-than-thou way he had of talking down to others, "I'm not here to check up on you. I'm here to offer assistance on the Devoted Fan investigation."

As if she'd just realized what she said and that she'd done it out loud, her lips pressed into a firm line and her smooth, porcelain skin flushed.

"I hate to think you've wasted your time," McBride said, deciding to take the heat off Grace, "but we've got things under control here, Pierce. There's not a lot you can offer."

"I was sorry to hear you'd been terminated, McBride." Pierce shifted his interest from Grace to McBride and allowed a lack of it to show. "At one time you were the best."

McBride laughed softly, the real thing, not one of those fake sounds. "I was sorry to hear you'd turned to teaching. But then, I guess when you can't cut it in the field, it's best to do what you can."

"Gentlemen," Worth interrupted, "we were going to review what we have on this case. Why don't you get us started, Agent Grace?"

5:02 P.M.

Vivian was ready to get the hell out of there.

She had never been so furious in her life.

Every particle of self-discipline she possessed had been required to remain seated during the past forty-nine minutes while Worth and Pierce and McBride went back and forth over this case. She had purposely kept her mouth shut after her opening remarks.

Pierce's visit had nothing to do with this case and she knew it.

He was here about her.

He was worried about her. Worth had told her that much already.

Dammit.

The one real surprise was that McBride and Pierce appeared to know each other. She should have realized that was a possibility since they were both at Quantico at the same time. Pierce wasn't anything like McBride. He was as tall as McBride but leaner. His hair was black, cut short and neat. His eyes were almost as dark as his hair and were ever watchful. There was no fooling Pierce, he never missed a thing.

McBride abruptly stood. "If we hear anything from Devoted Fan, let me know."

What the hell had happened while she'd been seething?

Vivian pushed to her feet, scrambling to catch up as McBride walked out. "Was there anything else, sir?" She faced Worth, careful to keep her attention fixed fully on him and off the other man who had suddenly stood.

"Stay a moment, Grace," Pierce said.

When she glared at him, he was busy sending Worth a not-so-subtle "give us some privacy" look.

"Excuse . . . me," Worth stuttered. "I have to check on . . ."

The way he was mumbling Vivian didn't catch the last of his excuse as he made his hasty exit and closed the door firmly behind him.

This was beyond ridiculous. She shook her head at the man watching her. "I considered you a friend. I trusted you." She hadn't spoken a word to him since the announcement that her assignment had been changed. She had avoided him at all costs, ignored his phone calls and his e-mails.

"Grace." He reached out, touched her arm. "I know you don't understand—"

"You're damned right I don't," she snapped. "Let's leave it at that." She had wanted that assignment in Baltimore so badly. Her whole reason for joining the Bureau had been to make a difference. An assignment like Baltimore would have given her that opportunity. What the hell was she supposed to do here? Even when a big case came up, Worth didn't put her on it. He wouldn't have this time if McBride hadn't insisted. How could she get the experience she needed for moving to the next level if she wasn't given the chance?

Pierce drew in a big breath, let it go. "We both know why you decided to make law enforcement your career."

What of it? Who wouldn't want to fight the bad guys after going through that kind of thing? She had needed to turn her fear and hatred and bitterness into something constructive.

"In case you haven't noticed," she said, her voice harsh and stilted, "I'm doing a good job. I don't need you looking over my shoulder." If she hadn't had that one episode at the academy none of this would be happening! But she had. She'd frozen up, just like she had with McBride at the cemetery, only worse. Her failure in that one training exercise had caused the deaths of two civilians and one agent, hypothetically of course.

She had been so upset, that she had come apart in Pierce's office and had admitted that she still had problems with what happened when she was seventeen. Big mistake. Hiding that entire history would have been impossible, the background investigation would have exposed it. But she had fooled the psych evaluations, had convinced everyone that she was past the whole Nameless incident.

And then she'd had to go and let her core instructor see her crack.

Now she was paying the price. He had suggested an assignment to a smaller field office until after her probation to ensure less stress. So here she was, back in her hometown trying to prove she could take the pressure.

"Grace, you survived your worst nightmare," he said, ignoring her assurance that she didn't need him minding her business. "You killed the man responsible. You were strong and it showed in your ability to survive."

Here came the but . . .

"But then you changed your name and ran away, pretended it never happened."

Fury bolted through her. "Do you really think I wanted to hang around and let the media hound me? To have people looking at me the way you are right now?"

Why couldn't the past just be over? She didn't want to look back. She wanted to move forward.

"If that were the only reason," he said, without the exasperation he surely felt at this point, "we wouldn't be having this conversation. You've been hiding for seven years. You have to face those demons and defeat them the same way you did the real thing. Otherwise you'll be dealing with them forever."

"Do we have anything else to talk about, Agent Pierce?" She stood at attention as if she were still one of his students. "If not, I'd like to go home. I've had a long day and I had a long night before that."

For several seconds he looked at her with that concerned, caring face that her father wore at moments like this . . . that Worth wore whenever he passed her up for a prime case . . . the same damned one McBride had worn this morning when he had ordered her out of that church.

Damn them all!

"I guess that's all I have to say."

Before she could escape, he added, "I'll be here for a few days. We could have dinner."

"Sure." She wrenched open the door and fled to the corridor. She wanted out of here. Away from the weakness Pierce wanted to shove down her throat. She wasn't weak. She was strong. The past didn't matter anymore. It was over. Why didn't he just let it go? How was she supposed to leave it alone if everyone else kept bringing it up?

"Grace."

Worth was striding toward her.

"Yes, sir?"

"You're needed in the conference room. McBride is already there. We have a new communication from Devoted Fan."

Her shoulders slumped with fatigue. Not another one. Hopefully there wouldn't be another victim already.

She followed her SAC and, as if he'd smelled the trouble, Pierce wasn't far behind her. Pratt, Davis, and Aldridge were there already, as was McBride. They gathered around the computer screen and read the latest e-mail from the unsub who was now officially a serial offender.

McBride,

You truly are the best. You and your fine partner, Agent Grace, did a spectacular job of solving my puzzling clues. I am astounded at your greatness. As you know by now, Dr. Trenton's illustrious patient is in recovery and doing well. His survival, as well as the good doctor's, is solely your doing. I daresay, Trenton will have a new attitude from this day forth, as well he should.

The time has come for me to inform you that, at last, the final challenge is at hand. I do, of course, realize that you have had little rest and I shall save the grand finale for tomorrow.

Rest well, my hero, for there is still one more lesson to
be taught—this one is a lesson I am sure you will
appreciate as much as I.

Humbled,
Devoted Fan

"McBride, Grace, and Pratt, I want each of you to take a
copy of this e-mail home with you and study it while you
get some rest. Be back here at four A.M. At that time Davis
and Arnold will take a few hours at home. Meanwhile"—
he directed his full attention to those two agents—"I want
every number on that list called, every potential suspect
visited before four A.M. If folks are asleep, wake 'em up."

Simultaneous yes-sirs echoed as the two agents moved
back to their stations.

"I'll be here until midnight," Worth said to everyone
gathered. "I sent Talley home for some shut-eye. He'll be
back before I go. If I have anything new, you'll hear from
me." He started to go but then added, "McBride, Birmingham PD will have a guard at your door for the duration of
your stay here . . . just in case."

McBride grabbed a copy of the e-mail. "Whatever."

Vivian picked up her copy and shot McBride a look for
the good it would do. What was up with him? Besides the
usual. She'd have to ask him about the history between
him and Pierce. Then again . . . if she did, that would open
the door for him to question her.

SAC surveyed the room as if he had suddenly remembered something relevant. "I want everyone to stay aware.
We don't know who the next victim will be. It could be
anyone, including one of us."

"Feel free to utilize my expertise," Pierce offered. He
said the words to Worth, but glanced at Vivian. "I'm prepared to jump in with both feet."

"I'm sure everyone here"—Worth sent a look at Vivian—
"is glad to have your experience and expertise available."

Maybe she hadn't made herself clear enough.

"Agent Grace," Worth said as she headed for the door, "Agent Pierce will also be staying at the Tutwiler. Why don't you let him follow the two of you there?"

She glanced at Pierce. "Of course."

Vivian didn't look at either man as she stormed down the stairs. No way was she getting trapped in an elevator with the two of them together. They would probably end up going for each other's jugulars.

At her Explorer, she hesitated. "Where are you parked?"

Pierce gestured to the black Chrysler 300. Luxury rental, probably flew first class too.

"Just follow me." She got into her SUV and slammed the door. What kind of car he drove or how he chose to fly shouldn't make her angrier, but it did. It was the whole arrogance thing. The "I'm older and know it all" thing. She was sick of being pampered . . . of being coddled.

McBride climbed in. "Why don't you just shoot him and get it over with?"

"Buckle up," she snapped. She wasn't in the mood for any of his arrogance either, no matter how freaking sexy he managed to make it.

She rocketed out of her spot in reverse, jarred to a stop, then jetted toward the gate, squealing tires.

McBride grabbed at the dash as if he feared for his safety.

The gate slid open and she lurched out onto the street. Despite the diminishing press crowd, Birmingham PD remained on duty to keep them at bay, allowing for an unencumbered exit.

She saw neither hide nor witch-black hair of Nadine Goodman. If Vivian never saw her again it would be too soon. As far as she was concerned the woman had stepped way over the line this time.

"He thinks I'm going to appreciate this next challenge."

Vivian glanced at McBride, thought about his statement.

"Are you concerned that the victim may be someone you know?"

"I'd say that's a safe bet."

She braked for a light and met that intense blue gaze. "Or maybe someone he knows you would despise?"

"Maybe."

Quiet crammed into the vehicle and she knew the question was coming.

"So what's the deal between you and Pierce?"

God, she hated that question. Even Worth had asked it. "He was my mentor at the academy. We *were* friends. I suppose we still are once you get beyond all his crap about me and my past."

"He doesn't act like just a friend, Grace."

Her teeth clenched to hold back the words that immediately raced to the tip of her tongue.

"I know Pierce," McBride went on. "He doesn't look at his students or his friends the way he looks at you."

"Why did you storm out of Worth's office?" she tossed back at him. "Looked to me as if you and Pierce have a history of your own."

"Pierce and I go back a ways," he confessed. "We weren't in the same academy class or in the same unit. We just don't like each other. Had something to do with that whole legend then. There were a lot of Qs who didn't like me because of that." McBride turned in his seat so he could study her. "But Pierce likes you."

She parked beneath the valet canopy in front of the hotel. "I don't want to hear it, McBride," she said with all the fury she could infuse into her tone. "You're not exactly in a position to judge me or anyone else."

If he hadn't been looking at her with those eyes . . . with that tiny, tiny glimmer of pain in his eyes, she might have been able to pretend that she hadn't hurt his feelings.

All this time he had been making a big deal out of how he didn't care about anything or anyone. Apparently, his indifference was wearing a little thin . . . all those other emotions he conscientiously denied were showing through.

Reminded her a little too much of herself.

To put it his way, this whole thing was truly fucked up.

McBride said nothing more, grabbed his bag, the one that contained the clothes and essentials she had bought for him the day after he'd gotten here, and entered the hotel right behind her. The clerk, who knew her on sight now, passed her the key for McBride's room the moment she approached the counter. Out of a sense of civility she should have disregarded, she waited while Pierce checked in. They parted ways on the fourth floor. Her job was to keep an eye on McBride. Pierce could take care of himself.

On the seventh floor she led the way to McBride's room . . . the same one they had checked out of about thirty-six hours prior. Worth's secretary had called and arranged for the room when McBride's travel plans changed.

Vivian handed him the key and he opened the door, tossed his bag inside and turned back to her.

"I don't suppose you'd be interested in keeping me company at the bar."

In one express trip her gaze took in the man, from those intense blue eyes, past the ludicrously sexy stubble on his jaw, to the missing buttons of his shirt, down those long jean-clad legs and back to his eyes. Right now, the way she was feeling it would be damned easy to say yes . . . or maybe to push him into the room and have her way with him. Enjoy those great orgasms he seemed to so easily mine from her.

But she wouldn't. Couldn't. "No, thanks," she told him before his eyes could change her mind. "The only thing I have on my mind right now is sleep," she lied.

She couldn't possibly stay and risk letting him too

close. That one time was all it took to know that this innately sexy man held the power to take anything he pleased from her.

"Use room service," she advised. "Less visible. Your guard should be here soon."

She didn't like the idea of leaving until Birmingham PD was in place, but staying presented those perils she was all too well aware of.

When she turned away, he reached out and took her hand to keep her from going. "You know if you walk out now, Pierce is only going to call you and invite you to dinner."

His fingers teased her hand as he said this, making her heart flutter foolishly.

"And I'll tell him the same thing I did you. No."

He held her gaze, unwilling to let her go. "Good night, Grace."

The vibration at her waist made her jump. She snatched her hand away from his as if she had been caught playing doctor with the boy next door. Pushing all those crazy notions aside, she squared her shoulders and answered the call. "Grace."

Worth.

"You want me to what?" She couldn't have heard right.

He repeated his instructions and she pushed past McBride to get into his room. "Which channel?" She sought and located the remote control for the television and selected WKRT, home of the wicked bitch of the South.

The rest of the world faded away, leaving her mind focused completely on the woman, Nadine Goodman, on her voice coming from the six o'clock news broadcast. McBride took the remote from her and pumped up the volume.

"Agent Vivian Grace, formerly Vivian Taylor of Bessemer, a community just outside Birmingham proper, was the thirteenth and final victim of the heinous serial rapist-murderer known only as Nameless. Even after seven years,

the twisted monster's real name is not known. He existed under a number of aliases, moved from city to city, raping and murdering at least twelve women in only five years. His victims were gruesomely dismembered. More after the commercial break . . ."

For three seconds, then five, Vivian told herself this had to be a mistake . . . it couldn't have happened. She had been so careful. No one was supposed to know . . .

Now everyone knew.

CHAPTER TWENTY-ONE

9:15 P.M.
Beale Street
Memphis, Tennessee

The alley was dirty and dark. His hunger, a beast roaring to be fed. The homeless shelter on the corner was filled to capacity . . . there was nowhere left to go for the desperate souls lurking in the night. They would be found here and beneath overpasses in cardboard condos and tents. Anywhere that offered protection from the wind and the rain.

Those who were smart stayed hidden . . . kept their eyes and ears closed.

He remained in the shadows and watched. Watching had always been his part . . . but it had been different then . . . when there had been two. His beloved would bring home the prize and when his pleasure was finished, he was allowed to take what he would. The love had made the watching and waiting complete. Had, as nothing since, fulfilled him.

Being alone was so very painful and he had been alone so, so long. There was no one to love him or protect him.

He watched the two men beating the third, taking shoes, clothes, and the precious wallet that perhaps contained enough money to sustain them for a few days. Their needs were too desperate for anything less than barbaric behavior.

The residents in those pretend condos and tattered tents trembled in fear, but not one dared to defend the helpless victim.

The scent of spilled blood reached him, exploded in his nostrils, filled him with need. What he would give for one taste . . .

He would have to wait until the other two were finished taking what they would. Then he would take what remained.

It was the only way to fill his needs . . . to be satisfied, if only by the tiniest fraction.

Nothing filled him completely . . . not since he had lost the other part of himself.

The pain howled through him. He groaned with the force of it. Wrestled it away.

The frantic struggles at the other end of the alley ceased. Those committing the violent acts turned their attention in his direction . . . searching for trouble.

He would need to leave now or risk exposing himself.

He could not be exposed at any time for any reason.

Never.

His true identity could not be known until he was dead. Then they would all know the truth.

But he was not ready to die tonight.

He scurried out of the dark alley and onto the well lit sidewalks of Beale Street and embedded himself within the crowd of tourists heading for their bus.

Hailing a taxi, he resigned himself to the fact that his needs would not be slaked tonight.

Tomorrow, perhaps.

As he settled into the back seat he provided the driver with his home address. If he had only caught himself in time to notice how small she was, he could have given another address, a remote one where they were sure to be alone. He could have taken the driver.

He was certain he could have handled her.

But then she could be carrying a weapon . . . or pepper spray.

No. It was best to do what he had been trained to do. To watch and take what remained.

Thirty minutes passed before they reached his quiet home on a cul-de-sac surrounded by small, attractive homes where mothers and fathers and children lived their lives as if all were right with the world. As if no harm could ever come their way.

He paid the fare, but no tip. The driver shouted vile names at his back as he strode up the sidewalk. She would never know that he had left her the most valuable tip of all—life.

As he unlocked his door he thought of the Stewarts to his right and the Barretts to his left. Both had small children. Little toddlers and even one still crawling around on the grass like a puppy. Many nights he had lain in his bed and considered stealing into one of those quiet homes and snatching the perfect snack. But his shelter, his work was here. Such an undisciplined act would only force him to relocate again. To change his name and start over.

He had done that far too many times already.

This time he would be extremely careful. The homeless, the elderly who lived alone, those would have to do. No one usually cared or put up much of a fuss over those victims. They were expendable.

Take one child and the whole fucking world was after you.

Inside, he locked the door behind him and went in search of food. If nothing else, he would gorge with chocolate. It wasn't nearly so good as soft, warm flesh, but it would have to do for tonight.

He clicked the remote to catch the news. He had been taught to always remain aware of the goings-on around him. Vigilance was essential.

The words and images on the screen captured his attention immediately, prompting him to unmute the sound.

". . . was identified as the final victim. The former Ms. Taylor is now a special agent with the Federal Bureau of Investigation. She changed her name seven years ago after surviving the most brutal serial rapist-murderer of the last century, Nameless."

He dropped the box of chocolates and walked across the room, didn't stop until his nose was no more than an inch from the screen.

"Agent Vivian Grace is assigned to the Birmingham, Alabama, field office and . . ."

The words died away as the image . . . long silky hair . . . huge brown eyes . . . and those lips . . . perfect, lush . . . appeared on the screen.

It was her . . .

Number Thirteen.

Hatred coiled inside him. She had killed the other part of him . . . his heart . . . his soul mate.

Had she been that close all along?

He touched the face on the screen . . . traced those unusual, puffy lips.

"I've been watching for you, Number Thirteen . . . and now I know exactly where you are."

CHAPTER TWENTY-TWO

10:20 P.M.
Birmingham, Alabama

"Isn't she lovely, Deirdre?"

Oh yes, very lovely.

Martin smiled at his beloved wife as she watched the final few minutes of the ten o'clock news. The part about Agent Grace was so hard to hear. Poor girl. The thought that all those years ago she had been mistreated so badly by that vile creature infuriated both of them. There was a special place in hell for such evil.

McBride should have been on her case. He would have stopped that horror long before twelve women were brutally murdered, their bodies ravaged. Martin shuddered. He would look into this Nameless business. The report said he was dead, but Martin's curiosity was stirred now. He would learn all there was to know. That was his way. It was Deirdre's way as well. Perhaps there would be something he could do for Agent Grace. He did so love helping those who helped others. Especially the heroes, and Agent Grace was swiftly joining those ranks.

"What's that, dear?"

McBride could have saved her.

Martin nodded. "You're so right. If Agent McBride had

been in charge of that case he would have stopped that nonsense before that sweet girl was harmed."

McBride likes her.

Martin chuckled. "I agree. I think he likes her too."

A good couple.

Martin patted his wife's hand. "Yes, that's true. McBride needs someone in his life." He smiled at the woman he had loved since high school, over forty years now. "The way we have each other."

Martin turned his attention back to the news. Usually, he and Deirdre watched Fox News, but at five and ten, they caught the local news on WHMG, never WKRT. They had no use for that woman—that Nadine Goodman. She was not a nice person.

Before the hour grew too late, Martin should clean up the kitchen. It was the least he could do after his wife had prepared such a delicious meal. He would see her to bed, tuck her in as he always did.

And then it would be time to set the final challenge in motion.

Soon the trials would be over for McBride.

And all those who needed atonement would have found it.

Then life would be just as it should. He patted Deirdre's hand. She would finally have peace. Their family had been torn for far too long. It was time for peace and happiness.

Finally.

CHAPTER TWENTY-THREE

Vivian's parents had called twice to make sure she was all right. She appreciated their concern but she didn't want to talk about this.

Pierce had tried her cell three times. The third time she had told him she didn't want to talk.

Not to him anyway.

She wasn't sure she would be ready to talk about anything personal with him again in this lifetime. Trust didn't come easily. Which made the fact that she had spilled her guts to McBride completely irrational. They had talked about her childhood, which couldn't have been more satisfying or complete. High school had been high school. She hadn't exactly been a nerd . . . but she hadn't been popular either.

Then college, and her life had turned upside down.

Until it happened to them, no one realized how much could change in a mere instant.

The night air was cool; the view from the balcony calming in a strange way. What lay all around her was home, though for years she had tried to deny it.

McBride had loosened her up with a miniature bottle of

Jim Beam whiskey. What could she say? She was a cheap drunk. One little bottle and she was ready to tell him anything he would sit still long enough to hear.

Or maybe she just needed to tell someone.

"After study group ended," he prodded, reminding her that she had stopped mid-story.

"I was on my way back to my dorm." She moistened her lips and forced her mind to look at that painful memory. "It was late. Dark. Past curfew. I knew if I was caught I'd be in trouble, so I stuck to the shadows. Stupid, huh?"

"Not stupid." He leaned against the banister, exhaled the drag he had taken. "Understandable. You were seventeen. You were more afraid of disappointing the dean and your parents than you were of the dark."

She made a derisive sound. "Boy, I learned that lesson in a hurry." Taking in a big breath, she continued. "I never saw or heard him. I woke up in a room later, hours, maybe minutes. Felt like a basement. I found out later it was. The bastard had a mansion in Brentwood, just outside Nashville. He was a doctor . . . or at least he pretended to be one. His license was phony. Dr. Lyle Solomon didn't exist beyond the two years he had been practicing medicine in Nashville."

McBride didn't ask any questions. He just let her talk.

"The first few days I was certain someone would come. Then I slowly began to realize that no one was coming." She remembered that moment, as if it had only been that morning. The realization had almost caused her to give up. Then, for some reason she would never understand, her determination kicked in. "From the beginning I did whatever he told me. I'd heard about a couple of his other victims. I knew what would happen if I didn't. Maybe it was the whole obedience mentality of growing up in a conservative Southern home. Whatever. I did exactly what he told me—no matter how sickening."

"Hey, you're alive. You were smart."

Or a coward. "I wasn't smart, McBride, I was desperate." She rubbed her hands up and down her arms, but the chill came from deep within. "I didn't have a weapon. He was bigger and stronger than me. I was helpless. Then he said something to me that made me think." She shuddered at the memory. "He touched my throat . . ."—she demonstrated—"at the pulse and reminded me how fragile life was. I thought about that and decided he was right. All I had to do was hit the right spot. I'd have only one chance. I'd either kill him or he'd kill me."

"Desperate can be good," McBride allowed. "You got the job done."

Yeah, she did. "I never saw his face until after he was dead. Just heard his voice . . ." She had always been certain that there were two men. That certainty nagged at her even now.

"You made sure he couldn't hurt anyone again," McBride said as he tamped out his cigarette. "That's something to be proud of, Grace."

"There were times . . ." Should she do this? The shrinks, the investigators, they had all told her that the second man's voice was her mind playing games on her. The fact that she had murdered a man, even such a sicko, in what could only be called a heinous manner, had caused her to invent the other voice. "I was certain there were two men. Two distinct, different voices. But the evidence indicated only one subject was involved and I killed him."

McBride considered her revelation a moment. "Are you afraid that the owner of that other voice is still out there? Do you look over your shoulder when you cross a dark parking lot?"

The answer was yes. She did. As hard as she tried to pretend she didn't, she did. "Yeah, I do." She took a deep breath. "I guess I'm still a little afraid when I let myself dwell on it. Maybe that's why anonymity felt safer."

He assessed her with those blue eyes that saw right into

her soul. "Then you're human, Vivian Grace. If you felt anything else, you wouldn't be."

He was right. For the first time in a really long time, she felt that someone understood.

"Thanks, McBride. You're not nearly as shallow as I originally thought."

"I'll take that as a compliment." He straightened away from the railing. "Have another whiskey, Grace." He sniffed his shirt. "I need a shower."

She watched him disappear into the room, the smile on her lips widening instead of slipping. Though she had known him four days, she had scarcely cracked the surface of the complex man beneath the indifferent veneer. What she had found underneath, she liked . . . a lot.

Maybe she would have another of those whiskeys. She could sleep like the dead for a couple of hours and then get back to the office. One thing was clear, she could not live her life hiding from the past any longer. It was time to face it head-on. If any of her colleagues gave her any grief, she would set them straight.

She had just twisted off the top of another miniature bottle when her phone vibrated. On the table next to the bed, McBride's phone trembled against the wooden surface.

She looked at her phone's display before taking the call. Agent Davis.

She flipped it open and then answered, "Grace."

Davis's first three words had ice forming in her veins. *Come in now.*

Vivian glanced at the alarm clock on the bedside table, her pulse reacting to the tension in Davis's voice. "It's only one-thirty." She and McBride weren't scheduled to go back in until four. "What's going on?"

Davis told her that he had tried to call Worth at home and had gotten his wife. Worth hadn't made it home and there was no answer on his cell. But the strangest part was that his car was parked in his driveway.

Devoted Fan's most recent e-mail scrolled past her mind's eye, pausing on one particular part: ". . . this one is a lesson I am sure you will appreciate as much as I."

How could Devoted Fan have known that Worth and McBride didn't particularly like each other? The bastard couldn't be watching them that closely.

"I'll call Pierce," she told Davis. "McBride and I will meet him and head that way."

Vivian closed her phone. Jesus. If this scumbag could get to Worth . . . no one was safe.

2:00 A.M.
1000 Eighteenth Street

McBride drove since Grace preferred not to after having had that single shot of whiskey. Pierce followed. If he knew any more than they did, he had said nothing.

As if the media had sensed trouble in the wind, the crowd outside the field office had multiplied to what it had been prior to Trenton's rescue.

The rush inside and up the stairs left no opportunity for chitchat. Suited McBride fine. He had nothing to say to Pierce. Neither did Grace it seemed.

"Let's have an update," Pierce ordered as soon as they entered the conference room that had served as a command center for the past few days.

"Talley and Aldridge are working with Birmingham PD on the scene at Worth's home," Pratt related. "Apparently he drove his Crown Victoria straight home after leaving the office. His wife and son were in bed asleep and didn't realize he had even arrived or that he hadn't come inside until Davis called. According to ADT Security Services, Worth didn't enter the home since the alarm was activated at 10:15 P.M. and that status remained so until Mrs. Worth got up to check on his whereabouts at 12:50 A.M."

McBride propped a hip on the edge of the conference table and studied the timeline board where new notations were in the works as Pratt spoke. Davis was scribbling away with a Dry Erase marker.

An agent McBride hadn't met, male, young, skinny guy, hurried into the room. "Agent Pierce," the new guy said, evidently knowing where the most power lay, "there's a new communication from Devoted Fan."

McBride shoved off the table and headed for the computer. Grace waited next to his chair. Pierce, Pratt, and Davis moved up behind him as he clicked the necessary tabs.

McBride,

As I am sure you know by now, Randall Worth is a part of your latest challenge. He has a lesson to learn, atonement to find, as did the others. Once more, survival depends upon you.

It is such a shame that when someone or something grows older, many times it is set aside for a newer model. Flesh and blood, brick and mortar, nothing is respected for its true value.

Unfortunately for Agent Worth, the tearing down of the old could destroy him as well. Amid a cloud of controversy the old sometimes falls, ending many, many stories. Perhaps the fall is inevitable. In the end, it is only the truth that really matters, not the story at all. Not even a century of stories.

This is the final test, Agent McBride. I trust you will not fail . . . Agent Worth is counting on you . . . he is hanging by a thread. This time I do have one minor condition: no one but you and Agent Grace are to enter the scene. I will be watching; any failure to adhere to that condition will result in great calamity. You have six hours . . . starting now.

Sincerely,
Devoted Fan

"Does any of the phrasing reach out to anyone?" Pierce asked.

Six hours.

That phrase reached out and grabbed McBride by the throat. *Fuck.*

"I'll run the phrasing against any historic landmarks in Birmingham," Pratt volunteered. "Brick and mortar ... stories." He shrugged. "Controversy."

"So far, historic landmarks appear to be his crime scene of choice," Grace explained to Pierce. "If Worth is at risk of falling as suggested by the e-mail, then we're looking for a location with more than one floor or an elevation of some sort."

Lila Grimes, Worth's secretary, appeared at the door, her eyes red and swollen. "I thought you might need my help," she offered. She cleared her throat. "Agent Worth's cell calls have been forwarded here. I'll take those calls until he ... he returns." She hesitated, seemed to gather her composure. "There was a call from Agent Schaffer. She's faxing a number of letters she found in Agent McBride's files."

Schaffer. The boot lady. "Thanks," McBride said to the distraught secretary as he pushed out of his chair. He strode over to the fax machine, which had already whirred to life.

Davis joined McBride. "Sir, I may have found a connection between a name on the fan list and Dr. Trenton."

McBride shifted his attention to Davis. "What kind of connection?"

"It may not be relevant," Davis qualified, "but—"

"Agent Davis," Pierce interrupted, "if you have an update, we'd all like to hear it."

Davis looked from McBride to Pierce. "Yes, sir." He pivoted and addressed the room. "Agent Arnold and I have been narrowing down a fan mail list." He gestured at McBride. "Fan mail for Agent McBride." Davis adjusted the tie he'd loosened sometime earlier in the night. "Anyway, we found a name, Martin Fincher. Fincher's wife was a transplant patient a couple of years ago. Dr. Trenton was the surgeon of record."

McBride felt that old familiar tension ripple through him. "There has to be a connection to the others as well," he urged. "One isn't enough. Look harder."

Davis nodded. "Yes, sir."

"Where's Agent Arnold?" Pierce wanted to know.

Davis seemed a little less nervous with the second question. "He's going door to door down the list of names. That was SAC's order. I was supposed to catch up with him but then the news about Agent Worth came in and . . ."

Pierce nodded. "I understand. You should locate Arnold now." Pierce surveyed the room. "I don't want anyone going anywhere alone. We work in pairs."

McBride mulled over the idea of Devoted Fan as Martin Fincher with a wife in ill health. If it was about something Trenton did or didn't do . . .

"Pratt," McBride said, "wake up someone on Trenton's staff. Find out how the surgery on Fincher's wife turned out."

"Will do."

Grace joined McBride at the fax machine. "What did Schaffer find?"

Remembering what he'd come to the fax machine for, McBride grabbed the stack of pages. Six in all. He read the note from Schaffer on the lead page. "Discovered one letter from this same guy in your fan mail file. Found five others, unopened, in the bottom of one of the boxes shipped to you. Whoever packed the boxes just tossed the letters in and then shoved your files on top of them. You just can't get organized help anymore."

McBride appreciated her cutting sense of humor. The part of his brain that wasn't in shock at the idea of having only six hours wondered what color boots Schaffer had on. Purple? Green? Pushing aside the distraction, he shuffled to the first letter, read it, then read the next and the next after that. The adrenaline searing through him turned to ice.

"Son of a bitch." He passed the letters to Grace, his gaze colliding with hers. "It's Fincher." That one letter he'd read from the man years ago was why the e-mails had felt familiar to him. The formal prose, the wide margins and excessive spacing. And damn, the man had even signed the last two "Martin Fincher, your devoted fan." Two of the letters had been sent after Fincher's son had been murdered. In both he had lamented that he was certain McBride could have saved his son . . . but the special agent-in-charge refused Fincher's request for McBride. Randall Worth had been the special agent-in-charge.

"Fincher probably blames Worth for the loss of his son," Grace said as she read the final letter McBride passed to her. "Oh, my God . . . this guy has been obsessed with you for years." Her gaze collided with McBride's. "And you were right . . . he does have a story to tell."

Davis rushed back into the room. "Got a call from Arnold as I was heading out. He says McBride needs to see what he's found."

"At Martin Fincher's residence." McBride guessed.

"You got it," Davis confirmed. "He's already ordered a forensics unit."

"Pratt, you keep working on this e-mail and any connections you can come up with," Pierce said. "Grace, McBride, we'll follow Davis."

McBride tossed the letters onto the conference table. If they were damned lucky, there would be some kind of clues at Fincher's house about where this latest challenge was going down.

Otherwise, Agent Worth was fucked.

And McBride would fail . . . again.

3:30 A.M.
Seven Oaks Drive, Vestavia Hills
Four hours, thirty minutes remaining . . .

The forensics van waited at the curb. McBride, Grace, and Pierce arrived, pulling in behind it.

Agent Arnold stood at the door of Martin Fincher's small cottage. "You gotta see this, man," he said to McBride. "I didn't want to let anyone else in until you'd taken a look."

"Good work, Arnold," McBride confirmed. Any change in the unsub's environment could alter an investigator's or profiler's overall assessment of what he was dealing with.

Once outfitted with gloves and shoe covers, they followed Arnold inside. The house was clean and neat; the decorating and furnishings older, but in immaculate condition. A picture of Fincher, his wife, and son sat on a table. Fincher wore dark, horn-rimmed glasses just like Horace Jackson said.

"First," Agent Arnold said, "you need to see his office."

Arnold led the way through the living room and down the narrow hall to the first door on the left. The office couldn't have been more than ten by twelve feet, but every inch of wall space, floor to ceiling, was covered in newspaper clippings. Most were about McBride.

"Here's something on Trenton." Arnold indicated one of the articles. "Katherine Jones." He pointed to another, then looked at McBride. "Here's a full-page spread on Byrne and the article mentions Worth."

Grace moved closer and started reading.

"Give me the *Reader's Digest* version," McBride said to Arnold. "I'm on a tight schedule here." The tension was expanding with each passing minute, making it harder and harder to stay calm and focused.

"Six years ago," Arnold began, "Martin Fincher's twelve-year-old son went missing. Agent Worth was in charge of the case. Four days later, the boy's body was found, along with another teenage boy who had gone missing in Jefferson County the week prior. The boys were found at a construction site."

"A *Byrne* construction site," McBride offered.

Arnold nodded. "That's right."

"How does Katherine Jones fit into this?" Grace asked, pausing from her reading.

"She was the clerk on duty in the electronics department at Wal-Mart the evening the Fincher boy went missing."

Grace's gaze met McBride's. "She didn't notice the abduction . . . making her guilty in Fincher's eyes. *Oblivious*."

McBride figured the same. "What about Trenton?" There were several headlines about him plastered on the wall.

"Oh yeah," Arnold said, "Pratt called while you were en route. Couldn't get through on your cell," he said to Grace. "He spoke with Trenton's office manager who checked the schedule. She didn't like it, said she had to pull up a whole different program to do it. Anyway, Trenton turned Mrs. Fincher's surgery over to one of his colleagues because Tipper Winfrey's name came up on the list for a heart that same day. The office manager reminded Pratt that the surgery had taken place two years ago, and that if there was a problem, the doctor's office never heard about it."

"State Senator Tipper Winfrey?" Grace asked for clarification.

Arnold gave her an affirming look. "The one and only."

"Where's Fincher's wife?" McBride knew where this was going.

"Now that," Arnold said, his big frame looking even larger with the cockiness that went hand in hand with knowing something no one else did, "is the really creepy part. Come this way."

He led the way to a bedroom farther down the hall and to the right. A woman wearing a flannel nightgown lay in bed. If she had slept through all this, then she was on heavy drugs.

McBride approached the bed slowly.

"Don't worry," Arnold called after him, "she's dead."

McBride studied the body. Damned good condition if she'd been dead two years. A dozen bottles of prescription medicine sat on the table next to her. Transplant patients required lots of drugs, immune depressors, blood thinners. He didn't know all the names, but he didn't have to. The picture was crystal clear.

"Mummified?" Grace asked as she moved to his side.

"Looks like she's been coated in plastic or some kind of clear varnish." McBride touched one smooth cheek. "At least now we know why Dr. Trenton's office didn't get a call back when things didn't go well. Fincher wanted to keep her at home."

Pierce joined the party. "Fincher's not going to be too happy when he finds out we've taken her away." His gaze locked with McBride's. "We've got to finish this fast. He's already a couple of steps ahead of us. If he comes back here before we find Agent Worth you know how this will end."

Like I need anyone to remind me. McBride turned to Grace. "Search the rest of the house with Arnold. Pierce and I are going back to that office to see if we can find anything that will help locate Worth." McBride shifted his attention back to Pierce. "Fincher will stay hidden somewhere near the scene where he's holding Worth until Grace and I come to rescue him. He likes to watch us do it. We can't do anything until we know where to go."

That was the hell of it . . . the clues sucked this time.

The manic ramblings of a *devoted fan.*

4:45 A.M.
Three hours, fifteen minutes remaining . . .

McBride found the cemetery map, the information regarding the sealing of tombs, the newspaper article related to the controversy with the Wellborne family. There was a schematic for Sloss Furnaces, created for the preservation board. A complete blueprint for the Sixteenth Street Baptist Church related to last year's restoration efforts. But nothing on where Worth might be now.

Grace and Arnold had come up empty-handed in their search of the rest of the house. The third room, at the end of the hall, was a kid's room. From the look of things, it was just as it had been the last time the Fincher boy had slept there.

Pierce had Agent Pratt on speakerphone.

"Any historic buildings recently abandoned for a new construction?" McBride inquired. Time was running out fast and they had nothing.

"We found three," Pratt reported. "An old military plane hanger that was deemed unsafe and beyond restoration. A piece of residential property that was supposedly used in the Underground Railroad during the Civil War. And the old *Birmingham News* building. But that last one is still up in the air. The Preservation Committee is lobbying hard to save the old *News* building."

"Which ones are brick and mortar?" McBride was reasonably sure he could count on that part of the e-mail as literal.

"The residence that might be part of the Underground Railroad and the *Birmingham News*."

"In the end, it is only the truth that really matters, not the story at all. Not even a century of stories."

"Wait." McBride mentally chewed on that a moment. "Is the *Birmingham News* still in operation?"

"Definitely," Pratt said. "They built a new building and want to demo the old one for a parking lot."

"But you say that's not scheduled," Pierce reiterated.

"No, the Preservation Committee is trying to save it."

"Amid a cloud of controversy the old sometimes falls . . ."

"How many floors is the old building?" McBride was itching to get moving. The tension was churning inside him. This had to be it.

"Five plus a mezzanine."

Definitely a lethal fall.

"They misspelled his son's name."

McBride's attention swiveled to Grace, who was reading another of the articles plastered on the wall. "Show me." He moved to her side, looked at the line in the *Birmingham News* article about the bodies found at the construction site. "Daniel Fitcher," he muttered as he shook his head. "Looks as if they focused more ink to showing how Byrne employed hundreds of Birmingham citizens in his construction companies than on covering the murder of two young boys."

McBride touched the misspelled name. "That's the place. He'll be waiting somewhere close by, watching for our arrival."

Grace nodded her agreement. "Just the two of us this time."

Pierce put his hands up in a hold-it gesture. "No way am I letting the two of you go into this without backup."

"Then we might as well all go back home," McBride warned, "because if we don't follow the rules, Worth is a dead man."

CHAPTER TWENTY-FOUR

"It's damned quiet." Vivian shivered as she stared out the window of her SUV. They had parked across the street, near the new *Birmingham News* building.

She could only imagine how Worth felt. Fear for his life had banished her worries over having her past revealed. She would just have to live with it.

Worth could die . . . they had no idea what kind of challenge waited for them inside that five-story building. Whatever it was, it could very well be capable of bringing down the century-old brick-and-limestone structure. So far Devoted Fan hadn't made a single claim he hadn't backed up.

"Birmingham PD, Pierce, and the team are only three blocks away if we need them," McBride reminded her.

Yeah, and emergency personnel were close by as well. In case of a fire or explosion or whatever the hell this sicko had in mind. The memory of his dead wife made her shudder again. The chief tech from the forensics unit had called McBride five minutes ago to pass along preliminary details. They had found Mrs. Fincher's organs preserved in spice-filled jars in the crawl space beneath the house.

If, as the tech suspected, a quasi-Egyptian mummification method had been used, the body would have been cleansed, rubbed in salt, and then filled with spices. Instead of wrapping her with cloth, it appeared he had varnished her. Original, but truly sick.

The guy definitely had done his research. That went hand in hand with what they had learned about his occupation, an aerospace engineer retired from NASA. If the certificates and plaques hanging in his house were any indication, a brilliant engineer.

An APB had been put out on Martin Fincher and his blue Volvo wagon, the same vehicle he'd had since his son was born. He had probably researched just the kind of car to buy to keep his child safe. The Finchers had been in their early forties before having their first and only child. Losing him certainly would have pushed them toward the edge Martin had eventually fallen over, perhaps with the death of his wife.

"Grace."

She snapped out of the disturbing thoughts. "Sorry. What did you say?"

"Let's get in there and find out what the hell we're up against."

They had two hours, but there was no way to know what obstacles might stand between them and rescuing Worth. Scanning the building's dark windows, she emerged from her Explorer and then pushed the door shut. She reached into the back seat for her backpack. She had brought along flashlights, a box-cutter-style knife, screwdrivers, pry bar, scissors, and a hammer, just in case. The trip to Sloss Furnace had taught her a lesson about being prepared.

"We'll start with the top floor." McBride met her at the front of the vehicle and took the bag. "Work our way down."

"You're the boss."

His gaze met hers in the moonlight. "I'm not so sure trusting me that much is a good thing, Grace."

Maybe not, but it was too late. She already did. She just hoped she wouldn't regret it.

"Don't give yourself so much credit, McBride," she argued, lied actually. "Worth told us all to follow your orders. I'm just doing my job."

That one corner of McBride's mouth kicked up, telling her that she wasn't fooling him one bit.

"Let's get this done."

He crossed the street, his attention on the front entrance. She stayed a couple of steps behind, monitoring left and right to ensure nothing unexpected got the jump on them. Birmingham PD's SWAT unit had scouts prowling the alleys and side streets. They all knew that Fincher would be here somewhere.

She took a last look around. Lots of places to hide.

A slow walk around the building revealed that Worth wasn't hanging from the rooftop or any of the windows. Since there was no roof access, they could assume he wasn't up there.

Pierce had suggested the use of wireless communications since they were going inside without any backup, but McBride had declined. What was the point? If anyone else entered the premises the game was over. So far no one had died, but they couldn't take the risk. Martin Fincher was not playing with a full deck, which provided the ammo Pierce needed to push for a compromise. Vivian was to check in every half hour or Pierce would send in a tactical team. McBride didn't like it, but he had left it at that.

The *Birmingham News* CEO had been rousted from bed for the necessary keys. The man had insisted on staying close to the scene with Birmingham PD. Vivian couldn't blame him, he was responsible for the building. Considering the ongoing war with the Preservation Committee, he was probably hoping it would blow so he wouldn't have to fight them anymore.

"I guess we won't be needing the keys," McBride commented as he opened the door.

Anticipation sent goose bumps scattering across Grace's skin. Time to face the last challenge. After this it would be over. All they had to do was make it happen one more time.

Her attention settled on McBride. He could do it.

Whatever the challenge, he could handle it.

She didn't know all the details about his career, but the one thing she knew for certain was that the Bureau had been wrong to allow such a talented agent to get away.

Inside Vivian paused while he took care of the lights. For security and insurance purposes the building's utilities remained active. She checked her weapon, then they climbed the few steps to the lobby. The building's two elevators were at the top of those steps.

"You want the stairs or the elevator?" She was fine with either one.

McBride hefted the backpack onto his shoulder. "I'll take the stairs."

Vivian hit the elevator's call button as he walked away. When he was out of sight, she turned back to the elevator but the call button hadn't lit up as it should have. She pressed it again and waited just in case the problem was only a faulty light. The stairwell door closing behind McBride echoed in the deserted lobby. She rested her right hand on the butt of her weapon as she waited another minute for the elevator to respond.

She pressed the button a third time. What was wrong with this thing?

Still no light and no bump and slide sound in the shaft.

Okay, that was it. She wasn't waiting any longer. Taking separate routes to ensure Fincher didn't come down one way while they went up another had been a good plan, but time was wasting.

Watching for the slightest movement anywhere in the lobby, she took the same route as McBride. The idea that Fincher could be in here somewhere watching his cracked plan play out had her just the slightest bit unnerved. So far there was every indication that this man didn't actually want to hurt anyone, but he was a nutcase—his motivation and goal could change any time without notice.

Once she was in the stairwell, McBride's footsteps overhead allowed her to breathe again. She hustled to catch up. It wouldn't have been possible if he hadn't heard her and slowed the pace of his climb to wait for her.

"Elevator isn't functioning," she said between gasps for air. She hadn't worked out in five days and her body was revolting against the abrupt extra exertion.

"Could be a safety precaution in case of a break-in," he offered.

Possibly. If vandals broke in there was no reason to make their work easier. But then it could be Fincher's doing.

"Top floor," he announced as they arrived on five.

Slowly, methodically, they searched each floor, turning on lights as they went. Every office. Every closet. That the rooms were empty helped speed up the process.

The room where the printing press had once produced the city's news still housed equipment that required additional time. Then there was the shipping area. Any place Worth might be hidden had to be examined. They didn't bother calling his name since the rest of the victims had been sedated. Chances were he had been as well.

They found zilch.

No planted explosives. No fire traps. No Worth.

"How much time do we have left?" McBride asked.

She checked her cell. "One hour twenty minutes."

"He's gotta be here. The door was open. The clues add

up." McBride walked around the lobby as they started back at square one. They surveyed the area, double-checked every nook and cranny.

"We'll have to call in soon or Pierce will be sending in the troops." She wasn't anywhere near ready to give up. Keeping Pierce and Birmingham PD out of here was essential. They didn't want Fincher making good on his promise.

McBride stopped in the middle of the lobby, dropped the backpack and bracketed his hands on his hips. "If we don't find him first, he's to take a fall," he said, repeating the threat in the e-mail. "He's not hanging by a thread anywhere outside. Not in the stairwell. Not from any of the ceilings."

His gaze landed on hers as the only other possibility took shape in her head.

"That's why the elevator isn't working," she said, giving voice to their shared epiphany.

"Back to the top." He grabbed the backpack and rushed toward the stairwell door.

By the time they reached five again, she was glad he was carrying the backpack. Her heart was racing. Her adrenaline was pumping hard, preparing her to face difficulty.

Once they reached the elevators on the top floor, McBride dug out the pry bar and dropped the bag onto the floor. "Make sure no one sneaks up on us, Grace."

He didn't have to worry, she wasn't taking her eyes off that corridor. If anything moved, she was drawing her weapon.

She did have to glance McBride's way a couple of times when it sounded like he was wrecking the elevator doors. When he got them pried apart he peered down into the shaft.

"Car's down on the first floor."

She nodded her understanding. Dead end. Dammit. Her stomach threatened to embarrass her. She swallowed, took a few deep breaths.

McBride moved to the second elevator. Pried, pulled, and pried some more until the doors slid apart. The elevator car waited as if they had summoned it for a ride down.

McBride stepped inside for a look while she kept up her surveillance on the corridor when what she really wanted to do was take a look for herself.

"Looks like the engineer has been at work." McBride motioned for her to join him. "Check this out."

The control panel had been removed from the wall and a black box had taken its place. On the black box was a timer, counting down from fifty-six minutes.

Their gazes collided. Oh Jesus. She suddenly understood what that timer meant. "The only reason he would have a timer on this elevator—"

"Was if he wanted it to start moving at a certain time," McBride finished. "We need to go down one floor."

He carried the pry bar but she snagged the backpack he'd forgotten as they rushed for the stairwell again. Every step down she reminded herself that they had time to get the job done. No need to worry yet. But the idea that the elevator could jolt into action in advance of the specified time had her stomach twisting into knots. McBride had told her how the timer on the Trenton explosive had reacted to his movements. And though the C-4 hadn't been real, there had been danger all the same.

On four, McBride began the same process of prying the doors apart. She served as lookout.

Her pulse started that frantic rhythm she had come to recognize as her ready-for-action mode. They had to find Worth. Had to get him to safety. And then the scary part would finally be over. Then they could focus on getting the bad guy. Considering what they had found in his house he would most likely be spending the rest of his life in an institution.

When the sound of straining metal signaled that the doors were opening, she abandoned her lookout post and moved in next to McBride.

The doors parted and there was Worth, his face pale. Like the other victims, he appeared asleep, sedated probably. The word HAUGHTY was written in black marker across his forehead. A harness had been secured around his upper torso, then attached to a line that hung from a pulley secured to the underside of the elevator, leaving him suspended in midair four stories—four and one half counting the mezzanine—above the lobby level.

Instinct had her reaching for him.

McBride held her back. "He's too far away from the door to reach. You could lose your balance and fall."

She stared into the deep, dark elevator shaft. Definitely a bad way to go.

"We have to call Pierce," she urged, her mouth going so dry her tongue would hardly push out the syllables. "We need help."

"If anyone else comes close to this building he might remotely set the elevator in motion. We can't take that ris'."

Worth would be squashed. She shuddered.

Vivian put her trembling hand over her mouth to hold back the sound that rose in her throat. McBride was right. What the hell were they going to do? That damned line holding him up looked too flimsy. He hung out of their reach from here. Fincher had evidently secured Worth in this manner while the elevator was stopped on the second floor. Attaching the cable would have been simple with a ladder. Then, one press of a button and Worth was hoisted upward.

Vivian shuddered. She was suddenly glad that Worth was unconscious. If he was awake he would only be trying to get loose, moving, fighting his bindings, and that would make matters worse. Other cables and wires dangled around him from the underside of the car. If there was only an access from the floor of the elevator car . . . but there wasn't—only from the top.

"Here are our options."

Did they have any? She searched McBride's face,

hoped he had a plan that would work. Even he couldn't do magic. Or fly.

"Since we can't risk trying to override the control, one of us will have to climb around to the back side of the shaft." He gestured to the various points around the inner walls where a foot or hand could find support. More cables lined the walls, offering something—however precarious—to hang on to.

"Once on that ladder"—he pointed to the back wall of the shaft where narrow metal rungs were attached about two feet apart in a path that appeared to go all the way down and all the way up—"Worth would be well within arm's reach. Whoever goes that route will give him a push, swinging him in this direction so the person on this side can grab hold and cut him loose."

Vivian wasn't stupid or slow. She understood that she couldn't possibly hope to grab Worth and hold him in position long enough to cut him loose and then drag him to safety. They would both end up swinging back out over the open shaft.

She would have to be the one to climb around to the ladder. No question about it.

"Or we could try to find a rope or something long enough for the person on the ladder to loop around him. Then one end could be tossed to the person over here or hung on to during the climb back around to this side," he suggested.

"The building is empty except for a few pieces of ancient equipment." She stated the obvious, mostly to let him know she understood there was no other way to do this. "There's nothing to use except the stuff we brought with us."

"So, which side do you want?"

"Like I have an option." Since when had McBride turned into such a gentleman? Maybe he was afraid she was going to fall and he wanted to be nice for a change.

She kicked off her pumps and peeled off her burgundy jacket. As an afterthought she shouldered out of her holster and passed her weapon to him.

"Listen to me, Grace."

"I know, I know," she mumbled. "You've been waiting all this time to have me strip in front of you."

He grabbed her chin and forced her to look him in the eye. That usual wicked gleam was missing, replaced by an intensity that made her heart stumble. "Hang on tight with your fingers and your toes. And whatever you do, don't look down."

"Okay." She wet her dry lips. "No problem."

With one last bracing inhale, she reached for the closest extrusion inside the shaft, settled one foot on the narrow concrete ledge that went all the way around to the ladder on both sides and prepared to push off.

Keep your attention on Worth. You're his only chance.

"Wait, Grace."

She froze.

"Your legs are shaking."

Well, duh. She was scared shitless.

"Take a breath," he ordered. "Try to relax your muscles."

Easy for him to say.

"Do it, Grace!"

"Okay, okay." Vivian closed her eyes and focused on relaxing her muscles, calming her nerves. *Concentrate.* One muscle at a time . . . *relax.*

"Good," McBride praised. "Just take it slow and easy. We're not out of time yet."

But, the truth hit her, if they ran out of time, she and Worth would both be killed.

No more wasting time. *Get moving!*

Slow but steady, she inched away from the safety of the door . . . of McBride.

The dust settled in her nostrils and she sneezed. The cables she grabbed onto felt greasy. But she kept moving. Along the side wall, then across the back.

When she got within reach of the vertical row of rungs,

she scrubbed her palm on her skirt then grabbed hold of
one. She swung her left foot onto a lower rung, then the
right. Thank God. She made it. Hanging on to the rungs
was a whole lot easier.

"Hook your left arm around a rung so you'll have a better hold," McBride suggested. "Then push Worth this way
with your right hand."

Easier said than done. She had to turn her body facing
the opening where McBride stood. No wonder he wanted
her to hook her left arm around the rung. Though she had
wiped her hand, her fingers still felt slippery.

With some precarious maneuvering she got into position.
Worth was still out cold. "Sorry about this, SAC," she
muttered as she grabbed the harness and drew his limp
body toward her then prepared to push.

The line went abruptly slack . . . Worth dropped . . . Vivian didn't let go.

His weight snapped to a stop as the line tightened and
her feet slipped.

She fell . . . dangled in the air . . . barely holding on to
the rung with one hand and Worth's harness with the other.

The unconscious man's body weight was pulling her
away from the rung . . . her fingers were slipping. Her
heart stalled.

"Don't you let go of that rung, Grace!" McBride
shouted. He was moving around the shaft, trying to get
closer.

"I . . . can't . . . hang . . . on . . ."

Her hand fell away from the rung.

Her stomach rushed into her throat.

Her grip on the harness was all that separated her from
a high-speed encounter with the ground floor.

The horrified scream echoing in the shaft as she looked
down was her own.

She grappled for something else to hang on to. Worth's
jacket. Her fingers wadded into the fabric. "God, oh God!"

Her face was plastered against his back. Her right leg stretched back toward the ladder but she couldn't reach it.

"Hang on, Grace," McBride called to her. "I'm almost there."

"Grace?"

Worth? She angled her head so that she could see his profile. He blinked repeatedly as if trying to clear his vision.

"SAC?"

His arms flopped uselessly as if he were trying to grab onto something but couldn't make his limbs work.

"Take it easy, Worth," McBride urged. "We've got you. Just stay calm."

Worth cried out . . . the sound pure terror.

"Don't look down," Grace pleaded. "Don't look down. McBride's coming to help us."

Her heart jolted against her ribs, floundering into a frantic rhythm. Dragging in air was impossible. All she could do was hang on. If that pulley gave way . . . she forced the thought away.

"What the . . . hell?" Worth looked from Grace to McBride. He swallowed with difficulty, gave his head a shake. "It's Fincher," he said to McBride, his voice hoarse. "Martin Fincher."

"We know," McBride assured. He had reached the rungs now. "We're gonna get him. Right now let's just focus on getting you and Grace to safety."

Worth's attention shifted back to Vivian. "He wanted me to call McBride . . ." Worth's next breath hitched like a sob. "I thought we had it under control. The kid died."

"We know what happened." Vivian gave him the most reassuring look she could under the circumstances. "You did all you could."

"No," Worth argued. "I should've listened." He looked to McBride again. "But you couldn't have saved them all."

"Listen up, Worth," McBride ordered, "we'll talk about this later. Right now, I need you to reach out to me."

Worth closed his eyes. "This is my fault . . ."

"Sir, you—"

"Grace!"

Her attention jerked back to McBride.

"We don't have time for this shit." He extended his hand. "If he won't listen, I need you to. Take hold of my hand."

One by one, the fingers of Vivian's left hand unknotted from Worth's trousers. Trembling, she reached toward McBride. She concentrated hard at keeping the fingers of her right hand gripped tightly around the harness. *Don't let go.*

Her fingers tangled with McBride's for an instant then he reached past her hand and got a grip on her wrist.

"Wrap your fingers around my arm," he told her. "I'm going to pull you toward me. Once I've got you back on the ledge, I'll get Worth."

McBride pulled her toward him, Worth swayed in that direction with her.

"All right now," McBride said when her face was only inches from his chest. "Get a hold on the waistband of my jeans with your other hand."

She shook her head. "I can't let go of him."

"You have to if—"

"Do what he says, Grace," Worth ordered.

"But what if—"

The sensation of falling sucked the air out of her lungs.

Her body jerked to a stop . . . Worth's weight tore at her shoulder. The fingers clamped around the harness started to sweat.

The only thing preventing her from falling was McBride's hold on her wrist.

The only thing preventing Worth from falling was her hold on the harness.

The line had fallen free of the pulley. It dangled from the harness . . . plunging straight down.

It took every molecule of determination she possessed to hold on.

"Don't you let go of me," McBride commanded. "Look at me, Grace."

She blinked, fixed her gaze on his.

That was when she knew just how bad the situation was. Fear glittered in his eyes.

"Okay," he said, his voice ragged. "I want you to grab onto my waistband with your left hand."

Since he was clutching her left wrist, she didn't see a problem with that. She only needed to be close enough.

"When you've got a good hold on me, I'm going to let go of your wrist and get a grip on Worth's harness. Then I want you to let go of him and climb your way around me and over to the ledge."

She nodded. She wasn't exactly sure she could do it, but she would try like hell.

"Here we go."

McBride's arm trembled as he pulled her upward the few inches necessary for her to grab onto his waistband.

"Got it?"

She moistened her lips. "Got it."

"Now, try to find a rung with your feet."

He held on to her wrist while she did so. She nodded to let him know mission accomplished. She couldn't speak now. All her energy was focused on holding on to Worth. Her arm felt numb and tingly. The nylon strap had burned into her fingers.

"Hang on while I reach for Worth."

McBride reached out, leaning over her as best he could. "Take my hand, Worth."

When Worth moved even slightly the strain on her fingers increased. She cried out.

McBride leaned farther away from the rung that he held on to with his other hand. "Come on, Worth. You gotta reach higher."

"I can't," he said, dropping his arm. The shift in his weight made Vivian's body quake. Though her arm was numb, pain radiated from her shoulder across her back.

"I don't know how much longer I can hold on," she warned McBride.

His fingers went back around her wrist. "I've got you."

A moment of dead silence passed while McBride considered the situation. "Can you swing him toward the rungs?"

"I can try."

"Worth," McBride shouted past her. "When she swings you toward the wall, try and grab onto a rung."

"I'll . . . try," Worth mumbled.

McBride locked his gaze with hers. "Easy does it, just a little swing."

Vivian squeezed her eyes shut, gritted her teeth, and commanded her throbbing arm to react.

Her fingers started to slip.

Her eyes snapped open. She tried to tighten her grip. Couldn't.

"I can't hang on!" Fear exploded inside her.

"Concentrate on holding on," McBride urged, his tone frantic.

"Just let go, Grace," Worth said softly. *"Just let go."*

"Grab on to my legs," she screamed at him. "Do something!"

"I . . . can't. My arms won't work . . . they're . . . they're numb."

"Dammit, McBride," she shouted at him now. "Help him!"

"Let go, Agent Grace!" Worth ordered.

She looked past her shoulder and downward, could just see his face. "I can't do that, sir."

"Let me go," he begged, "or we'll both end up dead."

She tried to manipulate her fingers . . . tried to get a firmer grip.

"Let go, Grace," he repeated.

"I . . . can't."

Then her fingers failed her.

The harness strap slipped out of her hold.

Worth's weight ripped from her grasp.

She watched him fall into the darkness. Heard him hit bottom.

He didn't even scream.

She hadn't been strong enough . . . hadn't been able to hang on.

"Reach for me with your other hand, Grace!"

She couldn't. Couldn't move.

"Reach for me, dammit! How the hell are we going to catch the son of a bitch who did this if we're both dead?"

Somehow her trembling hand moved upward . . . she watched in morbid fascination as his fingers grabbed onto hers.

He pulled her upward. Her feet found a perch on a rung beneath his.

"Let's just hold still a moment," he whispered against her hair. He held her tight against him with one arm. "Catch our breath."

She started to tremble . . . couldn't stop.

Worth was dead.

Oh God.

She hadn't been able to hang on to him.

"Pull it together, Grace," he urged. "This wasn't your fault. Right now we have to concentrate on getting out of this shaft before that car starts moving."

Fury whipped through her. He was right. She couldn't get Fincher if she didn't get out of here alive. And she wanted to nail that sick scumbag.

She nodded. "Okay."

"No looking down," McBride reminded as he helped her onto that narrow, narrow ledge.

Slowly, she made her way back to the door. He stayed

right next to her. Ready to go down trying to save her if she slipped.

He had saved her life.

But Worth was dead.

She had failed.

8:30 A.M.

Worth's body had been taken away.

Vivian felt numb.

SAC was dead.

As soon as she and McBride had gotten out of that shaft, he had rushed down to the first floor and pulled Worth's body out of the shaft in case the elevator moved before forensics arrived. Vivian couldn't bear to look.

How could this have happened?

Why did some sick son of a bitch have to do this?

For his dead son? His dead wife?

Was Worth's death going to bring either one of them back?

No!!!

Raised voices dragged her attention to the far side of the lobby. McBride and Pierce were going at each other like two slobbering dogs.

McBride had done all he could.

Even if they had risked calling in back-up there had been a problem with the rope that held Worth. Even before her weight had been added to his, the rope had given somehow. There was nothing else they could have done. It wasn't like either of them had had a free hand to phone a friend.

But, God, she wished there had been.

McBride stormed out, a Marlboro landing between his lips as he hit the door.

She should go after him. She could only imagine how he was feeling. He would see this as his failure.

But it wasn't . . . it was hers.

"Grace, we need to talk."

She turned to Pierce. She was too exhausted physically and emotionally to deal with him right now. "Later," she said wearily.

"Now. We've put this off long enough."

Before she could put up a fuss, he ushered her to one of the offices on that floor. The light was already on from where she and McBride had searched the place. Pierce closed the door.

"We have to get McBride off this case," he warned. "We're going to get this guy my way now. The line has been crossed. Randall Worth should not have had to die."

She shook her head, held up her hands in a back-off gesture. "McBride did everything he could. I'm the one who couldn't hold on." Frustration bolted through her. "Besides, why are we even having this conversation? You don't think I have what it takes to do the job. What just happened only confirms what you already thought. Why would what I think matter to you?" He just wanted her to take his side against McBride. She got it.

"You're wrong."

What the hell did that mean? She searched his eyes, tried to read that pained look on his face.

"I didn't ask you to be assigned here because I didn't think you could hack the pressure. That was an excuse," he confessed. "I did it . . ."—he exhaled a mighty breath—"because I needed you off the East Coast. Away from me."

That couldn't be right. "I don't know what you're talking about."

He nodded, closed his eyes for a beat. "I know you don't. To you, I was your mentor, your friend."

She started to inform him that that was before he had butted into her assignment, but he went on before she could string the words together with the necessary oomph.

"That wasn't the case for me. I wanted more. I was

wrong to feel that way. Not only was I your teacher, but I was married. Still am."

He couldn't be saying . . . impossible. Surely she would have noticed. "You wanted me away from you . . . because you were *attracted* to me?"

"I'm sorry, Grace. I didn't want you to ever know the truth but I couldn't let you keep believing that this was about your ability to be a damned good agent. I'm proud of the agent you are."

She couldn't deal with this right now.

"I have to go."

McBride would need her.

She would need him.

It was going to take the very best of both of them to get this son of a bitch Martin Fincher.

CHAPTER TWENTY-FIVE

McBride had failed.

Martin sat in the generic Chevy belonging to one of his neighbors who never bothered locking the old heap.

He couldn't go home.

The police were there.

Deirdre.

His heart squeezed with agony.

If they touched her . . .

It was McBride's fault.

Fury pounded in Martin's temples.

How could McBride have let him down like this?

Martin's attention was drawn to his home where a gurney was being maneuvered out his front door.

A long bag was strapped to the gurney.

A body bag.

Deirdre!

Dear God, they were taking her away.

No!

He reached for the door handle but hesitated.

If he showed himself now they would take him away as well.

Martin drew his hand away from the door.

He would wait.

Deirdre would need him and he could not help her if he was in custody.

Special Agent-in-Charge Worth was dead.

His death made Martin a murderer.

A murderer.

The realization twisted inside him like the blade of a knife. He could not allow this.

His hero had let him down. Had let Deirdre down. And Daniel.

How could that happen?

McBride never made a mistake. Never.

Or had he?

Had Kevin Braden's death been his fault? Martin had always believed McBride's side of the story, just as Deirdre had. Always. That story Nadine Goodman had done seemed to indicate so as well . . . but she was a bad person. How could he believe anything she said?

Could he have been so wrong?

It was true that McBride had risen to meet the first three challenges, but they had been simple. Martin had given plenty of time. And then, the first halfway difficult challenge he issues and McBride fails.

Worth is dead.

All those years Martin had hated the man. Had wished him ill so many times for refusing to bring McBride in on the case when Daniel went missing.

Now he was dead. He had paid for his sins. Found that atonement he needed.

But now Martin was the sinner . . . a man's blood was on his hands.

And it was all McBride's fault. If he had been good enough, he would not have failed.

The drinking and smoking and sex. McBride had given himself over to the sins of the flesh and now he was nothing.

He wasn't a hero.

Deirdre would be so disappointed. Peace would never be hers.

They had all let Daniel down.

If Katherine Jones had been monitoring her department properly, Daniel would never have been taken by that devil. If Allen Byrne hadn't hired all those illegal aliens who failed to keep the construction sites properly secured, Daniel would never have been taken there and been so brutally murdered. If only Worth had listened when Martin begged him to call in McBride to find his boy, Daniel might have been found in time. Martin and Deirdre had known all about Agent McBride.

But that was before he had succumbed to the evils of alcohol and such. He had been the very best. They had followed his every case. When their boy had gone missing, they had known he was the man to call . . . but Worth had played off their request and then it was too late.

Daniel was dead.

And if Dr. Kurt Trenton had not been so arrogant, putting his wealthy, powerful patients ahead of the ordinary ones, the first night home from the hospital after surgery, Deirdre would never have passed in her sleep.

Martin watched the ambulance carrying his wife drive away.

Now he was all alone. He would never be her hero.

Because of Ryan McBride.

Martin removed his glasses, pulled his handkerchief from his pocket and carefully cleaned each lens.

There was only one thing to do.

Now McBride had to pay, just as the others had.

Martin would ensure that he was properly humbled. Oh, and he most certainly had to be left completely alone. Just as he had left Martin alone.

A knowing smile touched Martin's lips. He knew what to do. McBride had no family to speak of . . . none that truly mattered. But he had grown rather fond of Agent Grace. Making sure she was taken away from him was the only way to ensure he learned his lesson.

Yes.

That was what he would do.

Proper preparation was essential. He would need to plan carefully and then lie in wait. Agent Grace would not be so easy to lure in. Martin would need means and opportunity.

This would not be a problem. Martin knew lots of ways to trap victims. Lots and lots of ways to execute an abduction. He probably knew far more than Agent McBride.

Perhaps he would show him so.

He would present McBride with one more challenge.

Only this time there would be no way for him to win.

Agent Grace would die . . . screaming McBride's name.

And Martin's former hero would never forgive himself.

CHAPTER TWENTY-SIX

5:30 P.M.
1000 Eighteenth Street

"Go home," Pierce announced.

Every agent in the conference room absorbed the order. No one wanted to go home. They wanted to find Martin Fincher and see that he paid for causing the death of the SAC.

It didn't seem possible that Agent Worth was gone.

ASAC Talley had given over complete control to Pierce. He felt too close to this to be objective.

Vivian settled her attention on McBride. He had drawn that "don't give a shit" shield around himself. His expression was blank, his posture indifferent. If he got the chance, he would drink the last twelve hours right out of his head. Maybe that wasn't such a bad idea.

But they needed to be doing something to find Fincher.

When she would have said as much, Pierce added, "There's an APB out on Fincher. Birmingham PD has roadblocks on all the main thoroughfares leaving the city . . . at the airport . . . bus terminals. There's nothing else we can do this evening. We need sleep, so we'll all be fresh in the morning. Be back here at eight sharp. You'll get a call if anything comes up before then."

Vivian pushed up from the conference table, grabbed her purse and holster, and headed for the door. Pratt, Aldridge, and Arnold filed out ahead of her. Schaffer had returned and was assisting Talley with the updating of the timeline board. Her lime-green cowboy boots were about the only thing Vivian had seen this crappy day that made her want to smile . . . reminded her in spite of the worst man could do to man life went on.

"Hold up, McBride," Pierce said.

Vivian turned back to see what Pierce wanted with McBride. If he planned to rake him over the coals again, she was going to call Pierce on it. If her statement of the way things had gone down in that elevator shaft wasn't clarification enough, then he would just have to do what he would. But he wasn't going to beat McBride down about it.

McBride hadn't asked for this.

He wasn't the one to let Worth go.

She was.

"What do you want, Pierce?"

The silent standoff lasted long enough for her to visually weigh the differences between the two. It went way beyond the physical. There was a kind of movement about Pierce even when he was perfectly still . . . as if he were constantly analyzing or roving around whatever subject his attention latched onto. His words were chosen carefully. McBride, on the other hand, said exactly what he thought when he bothered to interact verbally. Unlike Pierce, McBride gave off a sense of utter stillness that even now scared her to death and attracted her like a potent magnet.

She pushed away Pierce's confession. How could she have missed that? Maybe she had been so focused on her training that she just hadn't noticed.

Or maybe because of what had happened to her, she had been in denial.

"Talley has requested added security for your room as

well as Grace's town house just in case Fincher tries to have his revenge."

"Anything else?" McBride wanted out of there. The tension was evident in those wide shoulders and the set of his square jaw.

Pierce didn't answer right away, he glanced at Grace as if he wanted to be sure she heard this. "I realize your options were limited today. Both you and Agent Grace did all you could to save Worth. That's all anyone could ask."

McBride didn't say thank you but he didn't tell Pierce where to get off either. He just walked away.

Vivian strode past Pierce without a word, then hastened her step to catch up with McBride in the corridor. "Just so you know, I'm taking you home with me. You're not staying in that hotel alone tonight."

McBride glanced at the others waiting for the elevator and made a turn for the stairwell. Vivian was with him—she wasn't sure she would ever take another elevator. Maybe in a decade or two.

"I don't need a babysitter." McBride shot her a look before starting down the stairs.

She had to hustle to keep up with him. "Good. Because I wasn't planning on babysitting."

Another of those suspicious glances cut her way as he rounded the landing for the next flight down.

What was she planning?

She hadn't exactly gotten that far. She had just a minute ago made the decision about not allowing him to be alone.

Or maybe she didn't want to be alone. Every time she closed her eyes, she could see Worth slipping from her fingers . . . *falling*.

Being alone wouldn't be good.

The instant she and McBride hit the asphalt he lit up, walked to the far side of her SUV, the side the press couldn't see, and then leaned against it.

She took a spot next to him. "We should eat," she said,

though she wasn't hungry. But eating was necessary to survival. Going through the motions would keep her from ruminating about those moments in that elevator shaft. "Maybe have some wine to . . . help us relax." Yeah, that would work. Wine usually helped her to relax.

His interest locked on her but it was more suspicious than curious. "What're you angling for, Grace?"

Time to confess. Today was, apparently, the day for confessions. Pierce had confessed to her, had even complimented McBride—in an offhand way.

"I don't want to be alone tonight, McBride." She couldn't bear the idea of going home by herself. Dammit. She just couldn't be alone.

Since he was the last one to drive her SUV, he pulled her keys from his pocket and hit the remote to unlock the doors then pitched the keys to her. "I guess I'm going home with you then."

The drive across town took an eternity. McBride didn't say a word. But then, neither did she. Her entire body and soul felt drained . . . empty. As wiped as she was, those final seconds in that damned elevator shaft started playing again . . . like a scratched DVD that kept bouncing back and going over the same track time after time.

She'd held on as tight and as long as she could. Dropping Worth was the last thing she had wanted to do. An ache tore through her chest.

"Just let go, Grace . . . Just let go."

She bit her lips together, fought the urge to cry. All those times she had been so damned mad at Worth. And all he had wanted was to protect her. She was a damned rookie and she should have respected his concerns about her ability to take on cases . . . Instead she had fought him at every turn. She had wanted more. Had a goddamned point to make.

He had still been protecting her in the end. " . . . *or we'll both end up dead."*

Pierce had been right. She had been running away from the past, pretending it hadn't happened. Her determination to prove she was as good or better than any other agent had been foolhardy and an unnecessary pain in the ass for Worth.

Now he was dead.

Fury tightened her jaw. She was going to find Fincher. He would not get away with this.

The guard at the gate of her secure neighborhood waved her through. She drove the short distance to her place. Birmingham PD was already parked at the curb in front of her house. She took the turn into the alley behind the row of town houses and headed for her garage.

A poke to the button on the overhead console sent her garage door into the open position. Each town house had its own garage tucked beneath the deck that overlooked the security fence and woods. With her beefy SUV, it was a tight angle, but she had done it so many times that maneuvering between the support pillars and in through the door wasn't so bad. She pushed the gearshift into park and shut off the engine. Another stab of the button and the door lowered once more.

She thought about getting out, but moving suddenly seemed too monumental a task.

Food would help. Maybe have something delivered. The clutter on the shelf-lined wall directly in front of her had her trying to recall the last time she had cleaned up out here. Just one of those things she never took the time to notice.

There were a lot of things she ignored. Her parents. Her personal life. It was easier to remain focused on her career. Less complicated. Less painful.

And in the blink of an eye it could all be gone. Just like that . . . she mentally snapped her fingers . . . over. As if to prove the point, the resignation on Worth's face as he fell out of her reach flashed in front of her eyes.

She blinked it away. "I think I'll order in Chinese."

"I hate Chinese."

The lack of enthusiasm in McBride's voice matched her own.

"What about Japanese?"

"Same thing."

Well, hell. "Pizza?"

"Don't have the taste for it this evening."

Okay, he was being a shit. She turned her head so she could look at him. "So what do you have a taste for?" She had to make some effort to move past this place.

"What're we doing here, Grace?" He pointed his assessing gaze at her. "I don't think this is about food."

Frustration jammed into her chest. Of course it was about food. "We have to keep up our strength. Be prepared . . ." She looked away, felt that weight of frustration and fatigue pressing harder against her sternum. "How else are we supposed to catch Fincher?"

"What do you want from me, Grace?" McBride choked out an abrupt sound disguised as a laugh. It wasn't pleasant or amusing. "I told you the legend was dead. *This* is as good as it gets."

Fury knocked the frustration out of first place. "You're an asshole, McBride." He was right. The legend *was* dead. But, by God, he was all she had.

"That should come as no surprise to you, Grace. A guy who'd fuck you in a public bathroom can't be counted on for much."

As if the resurfacing of that dark attitude had been a cue the light in the garage door opener timed out, leaving them in total darkness.

She reached for the door handle, opened her mouth to tell him where he could take his smart-ass disposition, and a realization dawned. Watching McBride in action these past five days had taught her something about him. He wasn't the jerk he pretended to be. That screw-you attitude was about self-preservation. He wanted to keep his distance. Wanted everyone to believe he could never be that legend again. That way nobody could get hurt because of him.

Too late.

She was already hurting.

Agent Worth was dead and three people, including a child, had been terrorized.

She needed that fucking legend and she wasn't taking no for an answer.

"You will eat, McBride. You'll eat and then you will get some sleep because we've got a job to do. If you can't muster up any semblance of the man you used to be, then *fake* it."

He grabbed her by the hair, pulled her face to his and kissed her hard. She clenched her fingers in his shirt and kissed him back just as brutally.

Without breaking the contact of their lips, he tugged her closer . . . she scrambled across the console. Her knees settled on either side of him and her fingers threaded into his silky hair. She loved his hair . . . that beard-shadowed face . . . the broad shoulders . . . the lean waist . . . all of him . . . every damned inch.

His hands claimed her thighs, worked her skirt up around her hips and cupped her bottom, then squeezed. She cried out, the sound lost in his open mouth.

He hesitated.

"What's wrong?" she demanded breathlessly. He couldn't stop now. She wanted this, dammit. She needed it.

"This is a real shame, Grace."

His rumpled bedroom voice reached through the darkness, caressed her in spite of her need to be furious that he'd suddenly stopped doing what she needed him to do. How the hell did he make that surly arrogance so damned sexy?

"You see," he continued, turning her on all the more by

merely speaking, "I used my only condom the last time. No condom, no sex. That's my one rule. I never break it."

She practiced safe sex. He practiced safe sex. She didn't see the problem.

She reached for his fly, wrenched it open. "Then I'd suggest you don't look."

Her fingers closed around him and he groaned. Hard, hot, smooth, she slid her fingers down then back up that rigid length. His fingers tangled in her panties, pulled them aside, and she eased downward, taking him . . . all of him in one deliberate push.

For ten, hot frantic seconds they both held perfectly still. The filled-up sensation was incredible.

His hands bracketed her waist and he shifted his hips just enough to send himself deeper. She gasped, reached up to brace herself against the roof and started to rock back and forth, each movement plunging her closer and closer to release. With him this deep she wasn't going to last long.

The waves started. She cried out . . . didn't try to stifle the sounds. Her movements grew more frantic . . . his pelvis lifted, tilted, grinding against hers and driving him even deeper.

And then she went over the edge . . . couldn't wait another second. His hips lifted off the seat, down, up, down, up, until he came too.

She collapsed against his chest. Didn't want to move.

"Grace," he murmured against her hair.

"Hmmm?"

"At some point we're going to have to change our strategy and try this with our clothes off."

She smiled against his chin, liked very much the feel of his whiskers tickling her lips. "The only thing I want to change is positions."

He powered the seat into a deeper recline, rolled her onto her back, and took her again . . . hard and fast.

There were no guarantees in life. She had allowed

tragedy to rob her of her youth . . . of her ability to trust . . . to feel.

No more pretending.

She was going to start living again and feeling every moment of it.

But first, one way or another, she was going to get Fincher.

CHAPTER TWENTY-SEVEN

His eyes had long ago adjusted to the darkness. The vague impressions of their profiles were visible. The sounds of their animallike mating arousing.

It was the first time he had been aroused in seven long years.

Since *she* had murdered his true other half.

Number Thirteen. He was so close.

Her cries grew frantic now . . . she was coming.

He touched his crotch . . . wondered at how simply watching her again could make him hard this way. His gratification in the past had come from watching his other half, not the women he chose. The watching had been enough. He was never allowed to touch. Never allowed to do anything except take what remained. That, too, had been enough.

But it was different now. Now there was no one but him. Still, he had to be very careful . . . *very careful*. Getting caught would be bad. His other half had told him what happened to those, like them, who were caught. Bad, bad things. He would be tortured in prison . . . perhaps to death.

He would never be caught alive.

Death would be far more accommodating.

So, he was always careful. *This* was a risk. But he had to take it. He could not allow her to continue living. It wasn't right . . . not after what she had done.

Finding her home had been so easy.

Her parents had both been at work today. They would never know he had been inside their attractive home. He never, ever left evidence. He faithfully shaved his head, his arms, his legs . . . any place where there was hair he removed it. And his skin was meticulously exfoliated and moisturized. His fingerprints had been obscured by a laser technique years before. Nothing was left to chance. His entire existence had been as a shadow . . . a complement to his real self.

The grunting of the man's climax drew his attention back to the SUV.

Perhaps he would recall these sounds and images later for his own pleasure. When he was safe and alone in his own private dwelling where there was no fear of being caught.

Maybe he would take Number Thirteen home with him and use her the way his other half had. His car was parked on a street just beyond the woods. Why not take her? He was prepared, had taken all the necessary precautions. He was smarter than anyone knew.

That was how he had survived alone, without anyone to give him instructions.

Perhaps it was time he took charge and enjoyed some of the things he desired.

Number Thirteen and the man stumbled out of the vehicle and moved toward the door leading into the house, their bodies still entwined . . . their mouths devouring each other.

He hovered deeper into his corner in case the lights were turned on again. He wanted her to know he was here . . . just not yet. He would wait until there was an opportunity with her alone. And then he would finish what his other half had started.

No one had ever been as good as *they* had been when both halves had worked as one. No one had known who they were . . . nothing.

Nameless.

Brilliant and beautiful.

Perhaps that fear-inspiring name would rise again.

This time there would be only one. *Him.*

The door into the house closed, leaving him in the darkness once more. He would wait to see if the man left. There was no need to hurry. He had plenty of time.

He eased from his cramped corner and stretched. He opened the car door and sniffed, savoring the smell of sex. His cock twitched. Yes, perhaps he would take her home with him and keep her for a while before forcing her to face her destiny.

If he disposed of her properly no one would ever find her.

Just before he killed her he would eat those lips right off her face. She would scream . . . her blood would be hot with adrenaline.

He felt alive for the first time in years.

Perhaps his life could begin anew once he had settled his score with Number Thirteen.

A hand clamped over his mouth. He grabbed at it, struggled to pull it away. A needle stabbed into his neck. He tried to fight but his muscles went limp.

The darkness closed in around him.

He had made a mistake coming here . . . now he was caught.

The funny thing was, he was sure it wasn't the police.

CHAPTER TWENTY-EIGHT

10:00 p.m.

McBride reached for a slice of pizza and tore off a bite with his teeth.

He was still starving after three pieces.

The pizza box sat in the middle of the kitchen floor. Next to it was a half-empty two-liter bottle of cola. They had both been drinking straight from the bottle. For once it wasn't alcohol taking the edge off for him.

It was *her.*

He leaned against the fridge and devoured the rest of the slice. Sprawled on the floor next to him, Grace reached into the box for another piece, and rested her head in his lap. His lips slid into a grin as his gaze roved over her nearly naked body. She'd dragged on a T-shirt and panties to meet the delivery guy at the door.

McBride wished she were naked now. He liked looking at her. Every part of her was perfect. Great tits, great ass, amazing curves. And that mouth . . . holy hell. Since she'd straddled him in the garage, he'd stayed hard.

They hadn't come into the kitchen to have sex. They had come for glasses and napkins and whatever else they might need and had ended up going at it on the floor.

That was after doing it in her shower . . . on her bed and on her sofa.

"We should get some sleep, you know," she said after polishing off that last piece.

"First we need to talk about what happened today."

She got up, took another swallow from the bottle of cola, then wiped her mouth with the back of her hand. "I don't want to talk about it. Not yet."

He figured as much. "Pierce was right. We did all we could to save Worth."

Grace pulled her knees to her chest and wrapped her arms around her legs. "Are you trying to convince me or you?"

He didn't want her carrying this around for years like he had the Braden boy's death. She deserved better.

"I just know how that kind of story ends and it's not a happily ever after. Admit you did all you could and move forward. The only thing you can do for Worth now is to find the man responsible for his death. Martin Fincher put him in that position. *He* is the reason Worth is dead."

"But he did this for you," she countered, evidently deciding to play devil's advocate. "And if you'd had one of the guys with you instead of me, the two of you might have been able to save Worth. I was a liability."

McBride had sensed she was holding herself responsible that way. And maybe she had a point. But the one thing he knew with complete certainty was that you couldn't redo the past. It was done. Worth was dead. It happened.

Somehow needing to protect Grace enabled McBride to face the tragedy differently than he expected. Considerably differently than he had confronted those in the past.

"How are you dealing with Goodman's outing your secret?" That was another thing he worried about. For a guy who didn't give a shit about much, he'd done a hell of a lot of worrying the last couple of days.

He doubted she'd had time to think much about Goodman and her story. This case had kept them moving from one challenge to another without a lot of breathing room. Talking about the story now might distract her from blaming herself for Worth's death.

"Are you sure Worth didn't send me to get you so you could play my shrink?" she asked, instead of answering his question.

McBride pushed forward onto all fours and moved over to where she sat. He kissed her nose, kissed her temple. "There's only one kind of doctor I want to play with you and it has nothing to do with your head."

"You know." She avoided his mouth when he would have kissed her on the lips. "This happens every time. We talk about me and never get around to talking about you."

He stretched out on the floor on his side, parked his elbow and propped his head in his hand. "You know what happened. What's to talk about?"

"Do you have any siblings? Parents? Children? Former wives?"

The lady didn't ask much. "No siblings. Father lives in Detroit. Mother in Boston. The divorce happened a long time ago. And according to my former shrink, it's the reason I can't commit to anything but work. My parents and I don't do holidays but we do talk on the phone once in a great while. Every couple of years or so, anyway. I don't have any kids that I know of. And no former wives."

"What happened with Kevin Braden?"

The question—the one without a definitive answer. He'd worked hard for three years to drink all the theories out of his head. He thought it had worked. Until he'd come back here and faced the realization that it would always be with him.

"Worth was right about the evaluation report on me," he admitted. Might as well; she'd bared her soul to him. "I wanted to save them all. I worked day and night, seven days a week. My success record was unparalleled. But it was never enough. I needed to solve them all. Putting in that many hours and focusing on that many cases, at some point I was bound to make a mistake."

He thought about that, turned the idea over in his mind. Obsession had driven him . . . the same way it did Fincher. Not a pretty story. "I knew I was skating close to the edge, but I couldn't stop. Which child did I ignore and which one did I go after?" McBride remembered those moments all too well. "It was a nightmare, a vicious cycle I couldn't escape."

"That had to be tough on you. I can see how you would've wanted to save them all."

"But that night I was right. Quinn's assessments were wrong. I was ready to move in on the location where the boy was being held. A covert retrieval was the only way to go, but Quinn insisted on going the negotiation route. He said I was wrong. That I was burned out, hadn't had enough sleep."

"The operation went sour and you got blamed," she finished.

He toyed with a strand of her hair. "I guess it's possible the same thing could have happened if the operation had been executed my way, but I don't think it would have." He relished the soft lines of her face, hadn't let himself enjoy a moment like this in a long, long time. "We'll never know," he said, finishing the story. "Kevin Braden died. There's no bringing him back."

She looked at him as if she wished she could make it all better, could make it somehow go away. Now there was something he didn't see often.

"They took everything from you." She shook her head at the idea. "Your career, your reputation."

"They did." That he'd let Worth die today wasn't exactly making him feel like the Bureau had made a mistake. Yet, this time he understood that he'd done the only thing he could. Even if he could have reached Worth, which he couldn't have, and had tried to save him, Grace would have fallen. He'd made the only choice he could. Even Worth had recognized it was time to call it quits.

"You still have a lot to offer, McBride. You should think about teaching at Quantico. A lot of agents could benefit from your expertise."

He tugged her mouth down to his. "That's sweet, Grace, but I'm not interested." He kissed her, decided maybe he was up to another round . . . maybe on the deck . . . in the dark.

Cell phones vibrated. Hers on the counter, his on the coffee table.

She got to hers first.

"Grace."

McBride didn't bother going for his. The message would be the same. He put the empty pizza box and cola on the counter and walked over to where she leaned against the bar that separated the kitchen from the living room.

"Yes, sir."

She closed the phone. "There's an e-mail from Fincher. We have to go in."

Tension snaked through him. "Do we have a victim?"

"No victim." Her gaze locked with his. "Yet."

They dressed, stealing kisses between buttoning buttons and zipping zippers.

McBride didn't ever remember feeling exactly like this. *Content.*

The strangest part was, he felt it in spite of looming disaster.

11:35 P.M.
1000 Eighteenth Street

The street was oddly deserted. Most of the reporters had flocked to Fincher's and Worth's homes, though a few still circled the morgue, hoping to learn more about Fincher's mummified wife. Coming back here would have been a waste of time in any case, since Birmingham PD wouldn't let the media anywhere near the building.

Pierce and Talley had called an all-hands staff meeting.

Inside the conference room, the first thing McBride noticed was Agent Schaffer's bright yellow boots. When this was over, he was going to ask her about the boot fetish.

"Before we move into the next phase of this operation," Pierce said, "there's a matter that needs to be cleared up."

McBride tried to pay attention but the man just got under his skin. Mainly because of the way he looked at Grace. McBride didn't like it one little bit.

"Forensics has gotten back to us on the pulley and cable line used to suspend Agent Worth inside the elevator shaft." His gaze settled on Grace, and then he added, "The pulley was defective. That defect caused Agent Worth's death."

McBride saw Grace flinch. She wasn't going to let herself off the hook so easily.

Time to move on. McBride asked Pierce, "What does Fincher have to say?" Might as well get to the point of why they were all here.

"He's not happy with you, McBride."

McBride didn't take the satisfaction he heard in Pierce's voice personally even though it was meant exactly that way.

Pierce picked up a stack of pages and passed one to each agent in the room. "This, ladies and gentlemen," he said, "is trouble we need to head off. The state, county, and city police are providing assistance. Our top priority at this moment is finding Fincher and getting him into custody."

"Or on a slab," Schaffer added, setting off a rumble of agreement from her colleagues.

McBride would have added his concurrence but he was focused on the e-mail.

McBride,
   It is clear that you are no better than the others. I am completely disappointed in you. We believed in you despite

the fact that no one else did and you let us down. You pretended to be a hero when you were no such thing. I tried to save you as my Deirdre wanted and you could not be saved.

Now you will regret your actions. Allowing Worth to die was unspeakable. Taking my dear sweet Deirdre was a despicable, unpardonable betrayal. I am not a murderer and your failure has made the world believe I am. I have nothing now . . . because of you. No son, no wife, no honor.

The next communication you receive from me will be your worst nightmare. And this time, there will be no clues. The rules have changed. You think you have suffered, but you have not suffered at all. Not yet. Though you are about to learn what true suffering feels like.

Pray for death, McBride . . . it will be your only escape from the pain.

Martin Fincher

"He's out for revenge now, McBride," Pierce said, stating the obvious. "We're going to need to keep you in protective custody until we nail this guy."

"You know he's not going to play with anyone but me," McBride countered. "So let's not even go there. This started because of me, it'll end the same way."

Pierce looked frustrated but he kept any additional comments on the matter to himself. "Okay, let's get on with this then. Birmingham PD's providing surveillance on Fincher's home and at the morgue where his wife and her various parts are being held for an autopsy. Pratt, you and Davis go back to Fincher's home and see what you can find. We're looking for someone he knows or a relative—someone that he might be staying with. He has to be hanging out somewhere. Does he own any other property?

"Talley, you and Aldridge keep things moving with

local law enforcement. We don't need any bottlenecks. Grace, you and McBride dig deeper into Fincher's son's death. Make sure there isn't anyone else connected to that tragedy that he could use as a victim." Pierce's full attention moved to McBride then. "I want a list of anyone close to you he might try to hurt to cause you pain.

"Schaffer," Pierce said lastly, "stay on top of the ME's office about reports. We need to know anything and everything as it's available."

The roomful of agents jumped to action the second the final order was issued. Every last one of them wanted Fincher badly.

Grace pushed back her chair. "Why don't you get started on that list and I'll get coffee. I've got a feeling it's going to be a long night."

McBride rubbed the back of his neck. "Yeah. I could use a cup."

No sooner had Grace walked away, than he'd forgotten the list. His mind had shifted to the timeline board. Schaffer had updated it thoroughly.

What did this bastard have up his sleeve now? He wanted to hurt McBride. That part was clear. But how did he plan to do it? He was damned original in his scheming. That worried McBride the most. As fairly simple as most of his challenges had been, McBride was certain he could be a master at this if he wanted.

That list Pierce suggested, and Grace had reminded him about, nudged its way into his thoughts. It would be damned short. There was his mother and father, whom he barely knew anymore. And there was Grace. Fincher had mentioned her in a couple of his e-mails. Fear coiled in McBride's gut, constricted his chest. That was where Fincher would strike. Even the idea of it made McBride sick to his stomach.

"Agent McBride."

Hearing the title attached to his name startled him. "Yeah, Schaffer. What've you got?"

"Agent Pierce wanted me to give you Worth's collection of files on the Devoted Fan investigation."

"Great." He accepted the folders. "Thanks."

He dropped the stack onto the table and went in search of Grace. How long did it take to get coffee? Even if she'd had to make it, it should be done by now. He didn't want her out of his sight.

She wasn't in the lounge. No coffee had been brewed. He checked the ladies' room and the men's room. Then every office on the floor.

The unthinkable possibility that something had already gone wrong started to leach into his bones. He fought it back; refused to even consider it. They were in the FBI field office, surrounded by an iron fence with an armed guard at the gate. It took a key card to get inside and a dozen armed agents were milling about in here.

"Have you seen Grace?" McBride asked Aldridge when he passed him in the corridor.

"Not since I was in the conference room."

McBride started to run then. He barreled into Worth's office where Pierce had taken up residence. "Have you seen Grace?"

Pierce's expression turned as anxious as McBride's had to be. "No. She was with you in the conference room . . . what, ten minutes ago?"

"Something's wrong." McBride pulled out his cell phone and entered her number. A ragged breath whooshed out of him. "She's not on the floor."

"Maybe she went to her vehicle to get something she forgot," Pierce offered.

McBride hoped he was right. Five rings and her phone went to voice mail. His gaze locked with Pierce's. "You'd better lock this place down."

Pierce rocketed to his feet, reached for the phone on the desk. "We'll find her."

If she was even still there . . .

"The next communication you receive from me will be your worst nightmare."

CHAPTER TWENTY-NINE

Wednesday, September 13, 12:30 A.M.

McBride stood in the slot where Grace's Explorer had been parked. Pierce loitered nearby, pacing around as if he could somehow make Grace reappear by sheer power of will.

"Motherfucker," McBride muttered. The lobby video cameras had captured Fincher escorting Grace from the building. The parking lot cameras had shown them getting into her Explorer and going left out of the parking lot. He'd had a handgun. Possibly Worth's. Since no guard was on duty in the lobby after 6 P.M., Fincher had only needed to get past the guard at the gate.

Lila Grimes, Worth's secretary, was at the ER recovering from a knock on the head. Fincher had used her to lure Grace to the lobby with a phone call. Grimes had been forced to say she was on her way to the hospital where Worth's wife had been admitted with chest pains—also a fabrication—and needed to drop off Worth's files from home related to the Devoted Fan case. Grimes hadn't wanted to take the time to come upstairs to the office.

If Grace had taken a moment to think she would have recognized that something was wrong about the request.

But she hadn't been thinking . . . she was still reeling over Worth's death . . . his final words to her. It probably never entered her mind that Fincher was in the building or that he would use kind, harmless Lila Grimes in such a way.

McBride reached into his shirt pocket and pulled out the pack of Marlboros, tapped one out and stuck it in the corner of his mouth. He flicked his Zippo and inhaled long and deep.

"I don't see how this happened," Pierce argued with no one in particular. "We were all in the building. A god-damned guard is manning the gate, for Christ's sake!" He gestured to the guard shack. "How the hell did Fincher get in here?"

McBride hated to say out loud what he knew had to be the answer. "He had to have been at her house. Rode in here with us." The idea that the son of a bitch had most likely been in the back of the Explorer while they drove from Grace's house to here made him want to howl with rage. "After we'd gone inside and the coast was clear, he came inside."

"What about the guard?" Pierce flung his hand toward the guard shack again.

"His job is to watch the street, not the entrance to the building."

Pierce marched a circle around McBride as if he couldn't figure out what to do with all the pent-up rage he no doubt felt. "He couldn't have gotten inside without—"

"Worth's ID card," McBride finished for him. "One swipe and he was in."

"Shit." Pierce rubbed a hand over his face. "He'll kill her."

McBride threw the cigarette butt on the ground and pulverized it with his heel. "No. He'll make me do it."

Pierce's gaze collided with his. "You're right. He'll make this another of those fucking challenges. Only this time there won't be any way to win."

"That's the way I figure it'll play out."

Pierce went toe-to-toe with McBride. "This is your fault," he snarled. "If something happens to her—"

"You'll what?" McBride growled back. "Kick yourself for making sure she got assigned to this field office?"

Pierce blinked, backed off. "Yes." The word was barely a hiss of breath . . . a regret of monumental magnitude uttered in three innocuous letters.

McBride left him standing there and headed for the door. He had to start narrowing down places where this bastard may have taken her. Without any parameters to go on, it would be pretty goddamned pointless. But he had to do something.

The front entrance flew open, Pratt stuck his head out. "You gotta get in here. Fincher's sending us something. We think it's a streaming video feed."

"Pierce!" McBride looked back to make sure he was coming, then he followed Pratt.

The run up the stairs took two lifetimes. In the conference room the whole team was gathered around the computer screen. ASAC Talley manned the keyboard.

"It's loading," Davis told McBride as he moved in next to him. "Been doing that for about three minutes now."

Pierce claimed a spot next to McBride. "This came in an e-mail?"

"Yeah," Davis said. "When Talley opened it, something started downloading."

A box appeared with an option to open the file.

"Open it," Pierce ordered.

Talley selected the open file option. The screen flickered and went black. As if coming into focus, vague images faded in and out. Then the screen cleared.

McBride's heart stumbled.

Grace.

A thud in his chest sent fear and adrenaline roaring through his veins. He leaned forward, studied what he could see. The lighting was too dim—no, not dim, a low-light recording made in a room with no light. The room appeared to be small and square. Empty except for Grace. The white blouse she wore contrasted sharply with her surroundings. No audio. She kept moving, didn't appear to be injured. When she looked long enough in the direction of the camera the word INNOCENT was visible on her forehead.

The need to do something detonated inside McBride.

"Where's that coming from?" Pierce wanted to know. "Can you track that feed?"

"Systems is working on it," Talley said. "If it's encoded, they'll have to break down the code." Talley shrugged. "Could be jumping around from data center to data center to avoid being pinpointed. It'll take time to locate the source."

"Do whatever you have to," Pierce ordered. "Get Atlanta in on it. I want to know where this is coming from."

"Yes, sir," Talley acknowledged.

The screen flickered, went black again.

"What the hell happened?" McBride demanded. "Did we lose the feed?"

The screen brightened, then focused into a split view. The same one with Grace now standing in the middle of that tiny room looking helpless. Then the second view went from static to clear. A man paced another small room. He was tall, thin, with a bald head.

"Who is that?" Pierce tapped the blurred image next to Grace.

A rhetorical question, obviously, since no one in the room had a fucking idea.

McBride squinted in an effort to make out the guy's face as he came nearer the camera. The way he was looking around it was fairly clear that he didn't have a clue the camera was there.

No eyebrows. Weird. Letters written across his forehead,

in the same manner as with Grace and the other victims, snagged McBride's attention, but the man moved too quickly for him to read the word.

"Can you switch to your recorded version and run that back?" Pierce asked before McBride could.

"Yeah." Talley shifted screens and did a back search on the recording.

"Right there," McBride said.

The image froze on the screen.

N . . . A . . . M . . . E . . . L . . . E . . . S . . . S

McBride's gut plummeted to the floor. "Jesus Christ."

"That can't be right," Pierce argued. "No way. Name-less is dead. Grace killed him."

Fury coalesced with the fear. McBride pushed away from the screen, got in Pierce's face. "She tried to tell you there were two of them."

Pierce shook his head in denial. "Forensics said—"

"Fuck forensics." McBride jabbed a finger at the screen. "The victim said there were two, goddammit! And nobody listened."

"She was seventeen. She was traumatized—"

"And she was right," McBride said grimly. "Goodman's exposé must have brought him out from under whatever rock he's been hiding under."

The silence lasted until Schaffer cleared her throat and said, "Are we going to do something about this, fellas?"

Without breaking the stare-down, Pierce said, "Davis, Talley, find out where that's coming from. Also, find out if Grace's Explorer drove past any cameras in the city when it left this location. Check with every patrol unit cruising the streets. Maybe somebody saw something."

Doubt surfaced in Pierce's expression and he visibly swallowed hard, his pride probably. "Pratt, I still want you to go to Fincher's house to see what you can find. Arnold, you dig into the Nameless investigation. Call Kyle Cummings at Quantico, tell him I want him to look at the forensics evidence in that case again. If there's any chance this accomplice is for real, I want to know it."

Pierce continued to look at McBride as if he expected him to have something to add. But he didn't. They would know where Grace was when Fincher was ready to tell them.

Unless McBride could bargain with him.

Inspiration fueling his stride, he rushed to another of the computers and opened a link to the Internet. He typed quickly, anticipation building with the possibility of making a deal with the bastard.

Fincher,
    The fact is, if you hadn't used a faulty pulley, then
Worth wouldn't be dead. So, let's not pretend you're
innocent in all this.

"That could be a mistake, McBride." Pierce stood next to him now. "The last thing we want to do is piss him off." McBride ignored him, kept typing.

    Release Grace and I'll deliver Deirdre back to you. I'll
sweeten the deal by making it a two for one, you can have
me to boot.
    If you don't want the world to believe you're a murderer,
then release Grace. She hasn't hurt you. It was me, and only
me.

                                 McBride

He hit send.

More of that choking silence hovered in the room.

By the time the signal that he had mail sounded, the others, one by one, had gathered around him and Pierce. McBride opened the e-mail and read the response.

McBride,

Your offer was touching. But I'm afraid nothing I could do to you would trump knowing how you will suffer as an innocent takes your punishment.

I am not a fool. I know that you cannot deliver Deirdre back to me. I will see that we are together soon. Our family will not remain torn apart.

And as for the other one, I found him lurking in Grace's garage tonight. So you see, I've already gotten two for one. A pleasant surprise that will provide an opportunity for a truly exciting finale. I'll have to thank Ms. Goodman for sending Grace's old friend Nameless an invitation. You'll get an invitation as well, McBride, and when you do, you'll understand exactly what you must do.

You are right, though. This is entirely your fault. You let Deirdre and me down and you let Grace down . . . too bad she trusted you.

You have two hours, starting now.

Fincher

Two hours.

Defeat sucked at McBride.

"Nice try," Pierce said before stepping back. "Let's get the source of that feed triangulated," he announced. "It's coming from somewhere close by. There wasn't enough of a time lapse between when Grace disappeared and now for Fincher to have gotten far. A twenty- or thirty-mile radius, tops. Pinpoint it so we can get this bastard. Time is short."

McBride got up slowly. No clues, an impossible deadline. This wasn't going to be about finding her . . . this was going to be about a fight to the death—live and uninterrupted. That video feed hadn't been initiated for nothing. This sick son of a bitch had every intention of putting Grace in the room with that twisted fuck.

"Wait . . ." Talley shook his head. "We've got . . . the images are still now. No more live feed."

McBride rushed to Talley's station and took a look at the screen where the two images remained frozen. "He knows we'll try to triangulate his position," McBride said, hope funneling out of him. "He's too smart to let that happen."

Expecting any less was a strategic error. They wouldn't have nailed this guy's identity at all if he hadn't written those fan letters back before he planned any of this. That he hadn't considered the possibility that the letters would be found was testament to how far into the abyss of insanity he'd obviously gone.

McBride walked out of the room. He needed to think. He couldn't do it in here.

"Where're you going, McBride?" Pierce shouted after him.

When he didn't answer, Pierce double-timed to catch up with him. "I asked you a question."

McBride stopped, faced the persistent prick. "I'm going to the can. You want to join me?"

Pierce leveled a warning glare on him. "Don't you leave this building. We're going to need you. Grace is going to need you. You be back here in five."

McBride raised his hand as if he intended to salute but he gave him the finger instead. "I know what I have to do." He left Pierce standing there with his mouth gaping and headed for the stairwell.

Taking the stairs as fast as he could, McBride burst into the lobby and headed for the men's room. Instead of lighting up as he went in the way he usually did, he stalked straight over to the counter and braced his hands there. He closed his eyes and took a moment to fend off the panic clawing at him.

When he could breathe normally again, he opened his eyes and stared at the man in the mirror.

He looked like hell. His clothes were wrinkled. A lack of sleep and his indifference to shaving had contributed to his overall rode-hard-and-hung-up-wet appearance. That

Grace had wanted him at all was a miracle. One he didn't deserve.

He was a burned-out has-been. A nobody who had tried to pretend to be someone again. And now Grace was going to pay for that lapse in reality.

He had to find a way to help her.

The shaking started deep inside him. He told himself it was the fact that he hadn't had a drink in . . . he couldn't remember how long. Twenty-four hours? Forty-eight? But that was a lie. It wasn't about the alcohol. He didn't give a damn about the alcohol. He used it because it was easy. No one expected anything from you when you were nothing. The fastest way to give that impression was with alcohol.

He was afraid.

No, he wasn't afraid. He was fucking terrified. Terrified that she would die and he couldn't stop it.

He'd stopped believing in God a long time ago, about his fourth case, as he recalled. To his way of thinking, what kind of God would allow a person to do to children what some of the sick bastards he hunted down did? Just didn't make sense.

But right now he wanted to believe in a higher power more than he wanted to have his next breath.

"I've never asked you for one damned thing."

He took a beat, steadied his voice. Could hardly believe he would bother with prayer.

"Just let me do this right. Don't let her pay for my mistakes."

He swiped the wetness from his eyes and barked out a laugh. This had to be some kind of cosmic joke. After all he'd seen and done, who the hell would have thought he was capable of emotions this deep?

"You're fucked up, McBride." He stared at the pathetic reflection. "Majorly fucked up."

Then he pulled his shit together and walked out.

He had a bottom-feeder to find.

CHAPTER THIRTY

Time and place unknown . . .

Vivian still felt groggy. Fincher had given her a shot of something to sedate her once they had gotten into her Explorer. She couldn't be sure how long ago that had happened. He had taken her cell phone . . . her weapon . . . everything but the clothes on her back.

But how had he gotten her keys? She'd left her purse upstairs. The only other set of keys were in her kitchen . . . at home.

She felt her way around the walls of the pitch-black room. Ten by ten feet, she calculated. Walking around it so many times she was fairly sure of the measurements. The walls felt like metal. Cool, ribbed. Corrugated metal maybe. No windows. No door. Wait. She backed up a step. There was something else attached to the wall. A metal . . . track that went from the floor to a point above her head and then curved horizontally.

An overhead door? She dropped to her knees and felt around the lower half of that section of wall that was in actuality a door. She found the handle. Her heart skipped a beat. She pulled at it with all her might. Wouldn't budge. But it was definitely a garage-type pull-up door.

What she would give for a flashlight or McBride's damned Zippo. She sat down on her butt, leaned against the door that wouldn't open, and closed her eyes.

She couldn't let this bastard win.

He was responsible for Worth's death, dammit. No matter how painful his own past, murder was murder.

Get up and think, Grace!

She scrambled back to her feet, swayed a little, then started feeling around the walls in case she had missed something else.

Overhead door.

Small space.

Smelled stuffy . . . like a used-furniture store.

Metal construction.

Storage unit?

Her pulse picked up its pace. Yeah. A storage unit. It was deadly quiet. Probably deserted. Could be security somewhere on the property.

She rushed back to the overhead door and banged her fists hard against it. "Hey! Is anybody out there?"

For ten or fifteen seconds she listened. Nothing.

"Hey!" She started banging again. "My name is Vivian Grace. Special Agent Vivian Grace of the FBI! If you can hear me, please call 911!"

There were a lot of storage facilities around Birmingham. Some were close to businesses, gas stations, and convenience stories. Someone could hear her . . . maybe.

"Hey!" She banged some more.

"Vivian Grace?"

She froze. Listened.

Where the hell had that come from?

"Is that you, Vivian?"

Cocking her head in that direction, she moved toward the wall that separated her cubicle from the next one. The voice was a little muffled but definitely real.

"Talk to me some more," he whispered.

Male. Vaguely familiar. Too low to tell for sure.

"Who's there?" She touched the metal wall standing between her and the voice. Leaned her ear close to it. "Is Fincher holding you too?"

"It's good to hear your voice," he said, loud enough for every single nuance to filter through the wall.

Vivian drew back sharply. "Who . . ." She moistened her lips. "Who are you?"

A quiet laugh. "Surely you haven't forgotten me already. I know it's been a long time, but we knew each other so well. Didn't we, *Number Thirteen*?"

Vivian stumbled away from the wall. Impossible! *Oh my God.* She fell back another step. Oh no. *Oh God, no.*

"Only in my head," she murmured, her body quaking. "Only in my head." *Not real. Not real.* Please, God. *Not real!*

"When I close my eyes I can still see your lips. Such perfect, beautiful lips," he murmured through the wall. "I want you to do to me all those things you did for him. Only this time, after I'm done, I'll kill *you*."

She shook her head. This had to be a sick joke. The story. Goodman. This was her fault. Fincher had gotten the idea from her story and he was playing a trick on her.

But the voice . . . oh God, the voice was the same.

"I know you're there," he singsonged in the breathy voice she remembered all too well. "Come closer to the wall so I can imagine touching you."

Her feet tripped over each other as she backed as far away as possible . . . all the way to the metal wall on the other side. Her chest verged on rupturing as the organ inside slammed against it mercilessly.

No. She knocked the fear away. Grabbed back her courage. She was not that same hopeless, helpless seventeen-year-old girl. She damned sure wasn't a victim. Not anymore.

"All we ever wanted was for you to make us happy, Number Thirteen. Was that too much to ask?"

Fury hurtled through her and she charged back to the thin metal wall that separated them. Yeah, she was in trouble here. But, by God, he would have to kill her first to keep her from killing him.

Vivian bit back her rage and forced a soft, calm voice. "Let me tell you what I'll do for you," she whispered.

"Tell me," he urged, his voice excited. "Please tell me. Just thinking about those lips has me hard."

Another eruption of rage roared through her. She gritted her teeth to hold back what she really wanted to say. "I'll suck you just like I did him. I'll make you come so fast your head will spin."

"Oh . . . yes . . . yes . . . that would be nice."

"And then I'll tear out your jugular with my teeth just like I did your fucking friend's."

CHAPTER THIRTY-ONE

"The feed has gone live again!"

McBride rushed to Talley's station. Every government office and private business known to utilize exterior surveillance devices had been canvassed. No sign of Grace's Explorer on any of their systems. They had reviewed that initial feed over and over and had come up with nothing.

As the images began to move again, McBride's heart, the same damned one he'd thought had turned to stone, shattered like glass. He hoped this was live and that she was safe. But time was running out. He didn't want to be standing here watching when that final minute came.

Nameless or whoever the fuck he was had his hands and the side of his face pressed against the wall. His mouth appeared to be moving as if he were speaking.

Grace was pacing. Every few seconds she glared at one wall and said something. Shouted something, judging by the furious expression on her face.

"The rooms are next to each other," McBride said, mostly to himself. His mind immediately started ticking off the possible scenarios.

"What's she doing?" Pierce shouldered in closer between McBride and Pratt.

Grace went to the wall farthest from the camera and bent down. She appeared to be pulling on something.

"There isn't a door there," Talley noted.

"Maybe there is," McBride argued. "Can you lighten that at all?"

"I can try," Talley said. "I'll freeze a frame to memory and then try lightening that frame."

"Do it," Pierce ordered.

Talley reduced the live screen and opened another to which he copied the frame. He clicked a few keys then said, "That's the best I can do."

McBride leaned closer. "Is that a track?" He pointed to one side of the wall where Grace appeared to be pulling at something. "And over here?" He pointed to the other side.

"A garage door?" Pierce suggested.

"An overhead door," McBride agreed, anticipation igniting inside him. "But not a garage. Look at the size of the room in both screens." Talley maximized the live views. "Same size. It's as if he's talking to her through an adjoining wall."

"Public storage," Pierce said as if the epiphany had just dawned.

"We need a list of every public storage facility in this town," McBride said to Schaffer. "Start with the ones closest to our location and work your way out."

McBride's gaze returned to the screen, where Grace had given up on the door and started pacing again. "Hang on, Grace," he murmured. "We're going to find you."

"Here we go," Schaffer called to him from a computer station. "I'm sending the first dozen locations to the printer now."

McBride headed for the printer. "Pierce, we're going to need Birmingham PD for this." There would be far too many for them to hope to cover in ninety minutes.

"Done." Pierce was on the phone as he said the word.

The cell in McBride's pocket vibrated. He pulled it out, didn't recognize the number. "McBride."

"Ah . . . sir, this is Aldridge."

That the agent sounded hesitant ratcheted up McBride's tension level. "Yeah, Aldridge, what've you got?"

"I don't know if this means anything and I almost ignored her considering what happened, but she says it's urgent that she speak with you."

"Who?" McBride's instincts went on point.

"Nadine Goodman. She says she has information about Agent Grace but she won't talk to anyone but you."

"What's her number?" Instinct revved up the tension a little higher. McBride grabbed the closest pen and wrote the number on his hand. He thanked Aldridge and ended the call then quickly entered Goodman's number. As soon as she answered, he said, "What do you want?"

"McBride?"

"Don't waste my time, lady," he snapped. If she hadn't dug up that story on Grace this might not be happening. He started looking through the map printouts of the nearest storage facilities even as the anticipation of what Goodman might have pumped up.

"When everyone else was covering Worth's home and Fincher's residence tonight," the reporter began hesitantly. "I was watching Grace's."

He didn't bother asking how she got into the gated community. Scavengers like her had their ways.

"I followed the two of you back to the field office."

McBride set aside the page he'd just picked up. "And?"

"I saw Grace leave with someone."

McBride closed his eyes, fought back the ache in his throat. "That was more than an hour ago, what did you do next?"

"I followed them."

Anticipation fired inside McBride. "Where are you?" This could be the break he was looking for.

"I'm over on Highway 31 across the street from Trusty Todd's storage facility." She exhaled a shaky breath. "He locked Grace into one of the units. And then . . ." Her voice faltered. "He forced me to make this call."

McBride absorbed the impact of that statement. "He's there with you now?"

"Yes."

McBride surveyed the room. For one split second felt unsure of what he should do. But there was no reason to hesitate. Fincher had said he would get his invitation. This was it. "What's the message?"

"Come alone. He'll be waiting."

"What's your position, Ms. Goodman?" Again McBride looked around, this time to ensure no one was listening.

"I'm in a blue Windstar minivan across the street at the Shop and Go. My cameraman is with me. As long as you come quickly and alone, he won't hurt us or Agent Grace."

"I'm on my way."

McBride closed his phone and slid it into his back pocket.

"You'll get an invitation as well, McBride, and when you do, you'll understand exactly what you must do."

The message was loud and clear. All he needed was a way out of here . . . and a weapon.

He grabbed one of the maps and walked over to where Schaffer worked. He leaned down and pretended to show her something on the map. "Schaffer, I need you to do me a favor."

She looked from the map to him. "Sure, what do ya need?"

"I need you to locate Trusty Todd's facility on Highway 31 and print me a map."

Schaffer hitched her thumb toward the printer. "I already printed that one."

McBride verified Pierce's location at the station with Talley. "And I need to borrow your vehicle."

Her gaze narrowed. "I suppose you want me to let you borrow it and then not tell anyone."

He hoped like hell the part of her that had praised him in that cemetery would show up about now. "Yeah."

She reached into the pocket of her jacket, pulled out a wad of keys and then placed them in his hand. "Black Mustang. Scratch it and you're dead."

Now for the hard part. "One last thing."

Reading his mind, she reached beneath her jacket and withdrew her weapon. He took it, holding it behind the map in his hand.

"I'm going to tell them you took it and the car," she said quietly. "Don't expect me to admit any of this ever happened this way."

He smiled. "I'll back you up."

She put her hand on his arm when he would have moved away. "Don't go getting yourself killed, McBride. You make this place interesting."

He snagged the needed map to Trusty Todd's from the printer and headed for the door.

"McBride?"

He froze. Dammit. He glanced over his shoulder. "I need a smoke."

Pierce's disapproval showed on his face but he didn't argue; he turned his attention back to the computer where Talley was still trying to track down the source of the video stream.

Four steps outside the conference room, McBride tucked the weapon into his waistband at the small of his back then broke into a run. He'd just hit the stairs when a voice stopped him.

"You'll need backup."

McBride swiveled. "What're you talking about, Pratt?"

If Schaffer had given him up already, he was going to have to change his opinion of her.

"I saw you running, McBride. I don't think it's related to a nicotine attack." He shrugged. "And there was the weapon. I knew you didn't have a weapon."

"All right." McBride motioned for him to follow. "Come on."

They took the stairs two at a time and hit the parking lot running. When they had dropped into the seats of Schaffer's Mustang, Pratt said, "I've always wanted to ride in this car."

McBride started the engine and rolled toward the gate. Pratt waved to the guard and the gate slid open.

"Keep me going in the right direction." McBride shoved the map at him.

Pratt took a look at the map. "Yeah, I know this place."

"Tell me the fastest route."

Pratt gave the directions and McBride drove as fast as he dared. Before he reached the storage facility he pulled into a gas station parking lot on the same side of the street. A Check Advance and a pawnshop stood between the gas station and Trusty Todd's.

"Here's the deal, Pratt." McBride surveyed the parking lot of the convenience store where Goodman and her cameraman were supposed to be waiting. "Fincher knows I'm coming. I don't know how he managed it, but he had Nadine Goodman call me. Supposedly she and her cameraman are in that blue minivan over there. I know there's more going on than what she told me. Fincher's too good to allow a reporter to tail him."

You didn't have to be a rocket scientist—and judging by his numerous degrees, Fincher was one—to figure out that Goodman had sent Nameless his invitation, so to speak, and now she'd issued one to McBride.

Pratt glanced at the minivan. "What's your plan?"

McBride surveyed the area again. "I'm going over to

the storage facility to see what I can find. If you see anyone heading that way, blow the horn twice."

"But shouldn't I go with you?"

"If you want to back me up, you've got to do what I tell you."

Pratt shrugged. "Okay. But if I hear any gunfire I'm calling Pierce and heading your way."

"That's just what I want you to do," McBride assured him.

He got out of the car, considered his options, then headed into the shadows of the buildings. There was a chain-link fence around the storage facility. He hoped it wasn't hot. He touched it. The fence wasn't electrified.

Continuously surveying the area around him, he climbed over the ten-foot fence. Dropping down onto the other side put him on the back side of a row of storage units.

He didn't have any idea where to start, so he palmed the weapon he had borrowed from Schaffer and started with the row of units closest to him.

When he eased around the corner of the next row, he spotted Grace's Explorer. Moving quickly now, he made his way there. Anticipation had his heart thundering in his chest.

The SUV was empty.

"I knew you'd come."

McBride pivoted and faced the voice.

Martin Fincher.

What was probably Grace's weapon or maybe Worth's was aimed at McBride.

"Place your weapon on the ground and kick it under the SUV," Fincher ordered.

Taking his time, McBride crouched down and laid his weapon on the ground.

"Now scoot it with your foot."

Slowly, his hands out to the side, McBride pushed back to his feet, then toed the weapon away as ordered.

"Now the cell phone."

McBride did the same with his cell. "You've got me now," he suggested. "Why not let Grace go?"

Fincher smiled. The glow from the overhead security lamp highlighted the amusement in his expression. "I can't. She's not here. And I am certain I will need her to keep you in control."

Fury whipped through McBride. "Where is she?" He was just about through playing the bastard's games.

"Behave yourself and I'll tell you." He motioned to his right. "But first we have to take a little ride."

"What about the reporter, Goodman?" McBride demanded. "You made her call me, where is she?"

"She's in her van with her cameraman. They're a little tied up right now. I doubt they'll make the morning news with this. I did find it rather convenient that she followed me to the decoy location. Prevented the need for making the call myself. This way was much more interesting."

McBride started walking in the direction Fincher had indicated. "I don't want Grace hurt, Fincher," he said. "She isn't the one you want to hurt."

"We've had this conversation already, McBride. Just keep walking."

When McBride reached the end of the row, Fincher said, "Left here."

McBride took the left. A white Impala was parked between the next two rows of storage units.

"Get into the driver's seat," Fincher ordered.

When McBride had dropped behind the wheel, Fincher got into the rear passenger seat. He tossed the keys into the front seat. "Take a right out of the parking lot."

"Where're we going?" McBride started the engine.

"You'll find out soon enough."

Turn by turn, Fincher gave the directions. McBride followed them verbatim. Anything to get Grace's location.

"Are you going to tell me where she is now?" He made

a final turn into Elmwood Cemetery on Martin Luther King Drive.

"Soon," Fincher promised.

A short distance onto cemetery property and Fincher ordered him to stop.

They got out simultaneously. Fincher held a medium-sized brown paper bag in his left hand, the weapon in the other. "Start walking straight ahead," he ordered.

"We here to visit someone you know?" McBride asked in an attempt to rattle him.

"Turn left here," Fincher told him.

"I hate to keep repeating myself," McBride said, "but I'd really like to know where Grace is." He could take this guy, he was reasonably sure. But he couldn't make a move and risk him ending up dead before he got Grace's location out of him. This round had to be played by his rules.

"Stop right there."

McBride stopped in front of a headstone. The moonlight provided enough illumination for him to make out the name.

DANIEL FINCHER
OUR ANGEL

"Ryan McBride, meet Daniel Fincher, my son."

When you got past all the other bullshit, for Martin Fincher, this was what the whole nightmare was about. This and the wife he'd kept at home long after her death.

McBride turned to face Fincher. He wagged the weapon to remind McBride not to forget.

"I'm sorry about your son, Fincher. But hurting Grace won't bring him back."

Fincher shook his head. "It was all their fault. They should have been more careful. Wal-Mart trains their employees to watch for things like that."

"What about you?" McBride asked, taking a risk. "Where were you when Daniel went missing?"

Fury contorted Fincher's face. "Daniel and his mother went to Wal-Mart. Deirdre fainted and the paramedics had to be called. Her heart," he said pointedly. "We didn't know then. Katherine Jones should have been watching out for Daniel but she wasn't. By the time I got there, he was gone.

"And that Allen Byrne," Fincher snarled, "he sacrificed security to make another dollar when he already had more than he could possibly ever hope to spend. Trenton, Worth . . . they were all responsible for the pain. They all found their atonement."

"Some more than others," McBride reminded him. "Worth is dead."

"That wasn't my doing." Fincher shook his head firmly. "That was your mistake."

"You're right," McBride agreed. Trying to cajole the guy since confrontation hadn't worked. "It was my fault."

"Sit down," Fincher ordered. "Lean against the headstone."

McBride held his ground. "I've done everything you asked. But this is as far as I'm going. If you don't give up Grace's location, you'll just have to shoot me now."

"I am not a murderer." Fincher inclined his head and studied McBride. "You must know I would never be so crass. Deirdre would never forgive me. I cannot let her down. She needs a hero, and since you have failed to live up to her expectations, I have no choice but to step up to the task. I'll be her hero now."

Sweat rose on McBride's skin. The fear expanding inside him closed his throat. Fincher was right. McBride knew better than to believe it would be this overt or easy.

Fincher glanced at his wristwatch. "In twenty minutes, unless help arrives, the lock on the door to the unit where Nameless is being held will be released with a nice little popping sound that will alert him to the change."

McBride gritted his teeth to hold back the anguish ripping him open inside.

"How long do you suppose it will take him to get to her?" Fincher shrugged. "There's a hammer and a crowbar lying outside her door. The handy backpack in the Explorer was full of wonderful tools. Oh," he added as if he'd only just remembered, "and the key to the lock on Agent Grace's door."

Sheer hatred lashing through him, McBride lowered to a crouch, then took a seat atop the blanket of earth covering Daniel Fincher. He leaned against the headstone when what he wanted to do was pounce on that son of a bitch. But he couldn't. Not until he knew Grace's location.

"Your blood is going to spill, McBride," Fincher warned, "in atonement for your sins." He set the brown bag on the ground at McBride's right hand. "Drink. It won't hurt so much if you numb yourself."

"Nice to know you're concerned about my comfort." McBride reached into the bag and brought out a fifth of Jack Daniel's. It was the first good thing that had happened all night. He opened it and took a healthy swig. "Now make the call," he told the bastard, his tone dead cold.

"More," Fincher ordered.

McBride chugged a few more swallows, his throat and gut seizing at the burn. "Make the fucking call," he repeated. He didn't need a watch to know the minutes were ticking down.

"In the bag," Fincher said then, "there is a blade from a box cutter. Take it out."

At least now he knew what Fincher had in mind. McBride reached into the bag and pulled out the blade.

"Cut your right wrist first, then your left. As soon as you've made the second cut, I'll call 911 and provide Grace's position. I'm certain the Bureau will be thrilled to have captured the other half of the accomplice killers known as Nameless in addition to finding Grace alive and well."

"You keep saying you're not a murderer," McBride reminded. "This is murder."

Fincher shook his head adamantly. "I won't be a murderer. You're going to take your own life, McBride."

"If you're not a murderer," McBride countered, "then I can just get up and walk out of here and you can't shoot me."

A smile spread across Fincher's lips. "That is correct. But then Agent Grace would die. And that would be your fault for failing to obey me."

"How can I be sure you'll do what you say you will?" McBride argued, barely, *barely* hanging on to his fury. "Let's face it, it's a lose-lose situation for me."

Fincher pressed the weapon's muzzle against McBride's forehead. "You don't have a choice, McBride, you're going to have to trust me."

"Can I at least have a smoke first?"

"Suit yourself," Fincher said impatiently. "Just remember that the longer I wait to give Grace's location, the less time help will have to get to her."

McBride tamped out a Marlboro, fished out his Zippo, and lit it. He took a long deep drag. "I cut one wrist, whichever I choose, and you make the call. Then I'll do the other one. No negotiation."

Fincher considered his offer. He reached into his pocket for his cell phone. "One cut, then the call."

That was probably the best deal he was going to get. Might as well get this over with. He positioned the blade but hesitated. "Put it on speaker."

"You're wasting time, McBride."

That was all too true. Might as well get this part over with. McBride could think of better ways to die, but he couldn't think of a better reason.

"Just one other thing," Fincher said.

McBride exhaled a lungful of smoke. "What's that?" If this bastard didn't hurry . . .

"Do it right the first time," Fincher warned. "If it's not

deep enough, I won't make the call. Seventeen minutes are remaining, McBride. How fast do you suppose the police will be able to respond?"

McBride made the swipe. Pain seared along his nerve endings despite the buzz the alcohol had provided.

Fincher watched in morbid fascination.

"Make the call, asshole," McBride demanded, resisting the impulse to stop the blood flowing from the gash on his left wrist.

Fincher entered the three digits, set the phone to speaker.

The first ring strummed the air.

McBride's heart started to pound. He ordered it to slow. Didn't work.

Second ring.

"911 operator, what is your emergency?"

Relief almost numbed the pain. *Almost.*

"This is Martin Fincher. Please inform the FBI that Agent Vivian Grace is being held at the U-Store-It facility downtown. They have fifteen minutes to save her."

Fincher closed the phone and smiled down at McBride. "Your many sins will be atoned with the second swipe, McBride," Fincher said as he closed the phone. "You will have made the ultimate sacrifice. Given your life for another. Now, make the other cut."

McBride set the blade to his right wrist, watched as Fincher's attention settled there. Then he made his move.

McBride swung his leg hard and wide, swept the man's feet from under him. Fincher hit the ground like a rock. The weapon flew across the grass.

Holding his cigarette tight between his teeth, McBride scrambled on top of Fincher. He was stronger than McBride had expected, or maybe he was just weak. They rolled, and it was all McBride could do to keep him pinned down. He jammed the fiery end of the Marlboro into Fincher's cheek. Fincher screamed.

McBride reached for the weapon with his free hand but he couldn't hold on to it with the damaged one. He released Fincher and grabbed the weapon with his right hand.

Fincher clutched at the weapon. McBride couldn't draw it away fast enough. They struggled. The weapon fired. McBride felt the hot lead sear through his flesh.

He couldn't let this bastard go free. He fought harder. Got his fingers back around the weapon. Fired once. Twice.

Surprise claimed Fincher's expression. He touched his abdomen where a hole leaked red, but it was the one in the center of his chest that would kill his sorry ass.

Fincher's gaze connected with McBride's one last time then he collapsed across his son's grave.

McBride shook his head to clear his vision. He was dizzy and weak from the booze and blood loss. Damn. He'd cut deeper than he meant to. The bullet had ent his gut. Couldn't tell if it was bad. Plenty of blood. Not much pain.

Had to stop the blood pouring from his wrist. He toed off one shoe and yanked loose a sock. He wrapped it around his wrist, had to use his teeth to help pull it tight.

He was cold. He shivered.

Nothing he could do about the gut wound. His movements stilted and shaky, he crawled on his elbows and knees to where Fincher's cell phone lay in the grass. He collapsed on the ground, managed to get it open, and then tried to focus on the keypad. His hands shook and his vision blurred. He pushed what he thought was the right numbers, but darkness . . .

Darkness closed in on him.

"What is the nature of your emergency?"

The voice dragged him back. "Elmwood Cemetery," he muttered. "Send paramedics and FBI. Agent down . . ." The world was spinning hard. He had to close his eyes.

His face flattened into the wet grass and he pictured Grace.

As long as she was safe, he had done this right.

He'd been looking for an excuse to die for about three years now. His eyes slowly closed. Looked like he'd finally found it.

Just when he'd discovered a reason to live.

Grace.

CHAPTER THIRTY-TWO

A camera?

Vivian tried to reach it but she couldn't.

Fincher was watching.

Bastard.

She glared at the camera, considered flipping him off but that wouldn't do any good.

It was hard to tell how long she had been in here.

The piece of shit in the unit next to her started talking again. He'd been going on and on for what felt like hours.

"Vivian," he called. "Talk to me, please."

She shuddered. She could only assume that Fincher had plans for her that involved . . . *him.*

Closing her eyes, she blocked the sound of his voice. Images from seven years ago whirled in her head. She tried her best to block them. Stay strong. Focused. She had to find a way out of here.

A pop or break outside jerked her attention forward.

What the hell was that?

She moved to the door. The sound had come from that direction. That the bastard next door had gone silent told her he had heard it too. No footsteps outside. No voices. Nothing.

Reaching down, she pulled at her door, just to see if anything had changed. Wouldn't budge.

Dammit.

A metal-against-metal grind brushed her senses. Her heart launched into her throat.

A door was opening.

Close by.

Very close.

Her gaze settled on the wall between her and *him*.

His door.

She put one foot behind the other and started backing up.

Footsteps.

At her door.

Fear exploded in her veins.

Metal rattled against metal.

The lock?

Her lock.

The grinding sound told her brain her door was moving upward before the visual image registered.

Her.

Door.

Opened.

The letters written in black across his forehead stole her attention for one second.

Nameless.

Terror ignited in her veins.

"That's why he picked you," he said in that soft whisper she remembered too well. "The lips. Such beautiful lips."

He charged her.

She sidestepped at the absolute last second.

His shoulder slammed into hers, setting him off balance.

She rammed the heel of her hand into his chin at the exact instant that she launched her knee into his balls.

Too late.

His fingers gripped her throat.

They hit the floor. He howled in agony from her blows, his fingers tightening with the pulse of his pain cutting off her airway.

She kicked. Punched at his throat. Stabbed at his eyes.

She would not be a compliant victim again.

He pinned her on her back. Straddled her waist.

She banged at his trunk. Snatched at his balls. Bucked her hips.

"Oooh . . . that feels good," he said.

She couldn't breathe but she didn't stop clawing for a vulnerable spot.

"First," he taunted, "I want a bite of those lips."

He leaned down, swiped his vile tongue around his lips. Then bared his teeth and leaned closer still.

She snapped her head up, banged forehead to forehead with all her might. Spots formed before her eyes. Her head pounded.

"Bitch!" One hand loosened from her neck as he reached for his forehead.

She gasped for air. Reared her hand back and jammed her fingers into his throat.

He gurgled.

Vivian struggled to throw him off but he was too heavy.

"Have it your way then," he screamed. "I'll kill you first!"

His demented eyes locked with hers. "I've waited a long time, Number Thirteen."

His hands clamped around her throat.

An explosion filled the room.

He froze . . . fingers loosened as he stared down at his chest.

Blood leaked from a round hole there . . . the crimson color soaking into his pale blue shirt.

He slumped forward.

Vivian shoved him off her and scrambled away.

People were suddenly all around her. Cops. Paramedics. Pierce. Pratt. Schaffer and her yellow boots.

Pierce helped Vivian to her feet.

She looked around, then at Pierce. "Where's McBride?"

He didn't have to answer.

She knew from the resignation in his eyes.

Fincher had gotten to McBride.

And he'd used her as bait.

10:30 A.M.
UAB Hospital

McBride's eyes opened slowly. He licked his dry lips. Hadn't felt like this since that first week-long post-FBI drinking binge.

He tried to raise his arm to wipe his mouth. Pain shot up his forearm.

"Don't move."

He turned slightly to the right. "Grace?"

"You almost got yourself killed going off on your own like that," she fussed. "Too many stitches to count in your wrist and major surgery to remove the bullet and your appendix since the slug lodged there." She exhaled a weary breath. "But you're alive."

He inventoried various aches and pains and the damned hellacious fog in his head. "You sure?"

"You scared me." Her big dark eyes glittered. "I could kick your ass for that, McBride."

"I'll hold you to it," he said with the best lecherous grin

he could produce under the circumstances. His grin slipped into a frown. "What about . . . Nameless?"

"He's dead." She gave him a knowing look. "All of him this time. He and the other one were accomplice killers. They'd been friends since grade school."

McBride's confusion deepened. "How'd you get all that?"

"This guy had their real names tattooed on his chest right above his heart. We're hoping that information might help solve any other murders they might have committed by giving us a starting point."

McBride wished his throat wasn't so dry. "I'm glad that's over for you." He searched her face. "He didn't hurt you?"

She shook her head. "I beat the hell out of him before Pierce shot him."

Pierce. Oh yeah. The anesthesia had almost succeeded in helping McBride to forget about him, but he was damned proud of Grace handling herself so well.

Grace sighed, fiddled with the edge of the sheet. "I'm not sure what to do now. Pierce offered me a position at Quantico."

Yeah, McBride would just bet he had. "I hope you told him no." He hadn't exactly meant for the statement to come out so forcefully. He was damned surprised he had the strength.

"I did. My parents like it that I'm here. I'm beginning to fit in with the others." She shrugged. "I guess I should stay. There's room for advancement here too."

"Good." He tried to moisten his lips again. It wasn't working too well.

"Here." She reached for the cup and straw on the table next to his bed. "You can have water now." She touched the straw to his lips and he drew in a much-needed drink.

"What about you?" She set the cup aside. "You heading back to the Keys as soon as they release you?"

He wondered if that was hope in her eyes. She wouldn't hold his gaze long enough for him to see. Sure sounded like it in her voice.

"Depends."

Her gaze slid back to his. "On what?"

"On you," he confessed.

"Does that mean if I ask you to say," she ventured non-committally, "that you will?"

"I'm certain I could be convinced."

She kissed his lips, smiled timidly, and murmured, "Will you stay?"

"You'd be getting a shitload of baggage," he reminded her.

"I have baggage too," she reminded him.

"I do like my sex kinky," he added.

"I think I can handle that," she tossed back.

"I guess the answer is yes, then. I'll stay."

"Just so you know," she began, "there's an offer on the table from the director for full, permanent reinstatement, if you're interested."

"The offer's flattering, Grace, but I'm not so sure I want that."

"Whatever you do, it doesn't matter." She gently swept the hair back from his brow. "As long as you're with me, the rest will fall into place."

She was right.

Her. Him. Together. The rest was just bullshit anyway.

"Have you ever had sex in a hospital bed, Grace?"

She laughed, then kissed him and whispered, "When you're well enough, we'll have sex anywhere you want. Within reason," she qualified.

McBride grunted. "Finally, a reason to wake up every morning."

Keep reading for a sneak peek at Debra Webb's next novel

FACELESS

Coming in August 2008 from St. Martin's Paperbacks

CHAPTER ONE

Numbers 32:23—Be sure that your sins will find you out . . .
Sunday, September 5th, 9:40 p.m.
Mountain Brook, Alabama

She clicked off the flashlight, then froze.

Didn't dare move.

Didn't even breathe.

She listened intently beyond the frantic pounding in her chest and the roar of blood in her ears. She'd heard something. Anticipation fired through her veins.

The rustling of leaves. An animal? Maybe. These woods were full of wildlife.

Ten . . . twenty seconds passed with the breeze whispering through the trees. Her heart rate slowed. Nothing. Not another distinguishable noise beyond the night sounds. The consuming darkness continued pressing in on her; engulfing her, and the unsavory business to which she had no choice but to attend.

She had to do this and get out of here.

Now!

Slowly, the panic drained away. Urgency took its place. She was still alone. Hadn't been caught. Thank God. But she had to hurry!

Reaching for the courage that had momentarily deserted her, she drew in a ragged breath and forced herself to return to the task. With a flex of her thumb, she slid the flashlight's switch back into the "on" position and put it on the ground to illuminate her efforts. The narrow beam sliced across her arms as she continued digging, clawing at the soft earth with the shovel. Deeper. A shiver rushed over her skin. She had to hurry. Getting caught would not be good.

Not good at all.

Her respiration grew labored as that reality shrouded her as surely as the darkness had. *Dig!* Harder. Deeper. Faster. Get done and get the hell out of there!

She had to hide this mess . . . *all of it*. This part, th most important part, had to be here, where no one wou think to look. Not now, after all these years. On the off chance someone did, the evidence would only do what it had done all along . . . point in the wrong direction.

Good enough. She stopped, lowered the shovel to the ground and sat back on her haunches to scrutinize the hole she'd carved out. Yes. This was sufficient.

Twisting her torso, careful not to make the slightest noise, she reached into the bag she'd carried from her borrowed car parked a half mile away. The plastic bag felt heavy, though the contents weighed hardly anything at all.

Two gold bands. Symbols of love and commitment, the precious circles stained with blood after being tugged from cold, lifeless fingers.

Goosebumps spilled across her skin as that scenario played out in her head. She banished the images, dropped the rings into the Beanee Weenee can, then crushed the opened end as tightly together as her strength would allow before placing it in the small grave she'd burrowed. If anyone happened to dig around in this spot they would merely ignore what they presumed to be trash. Campers and hikers buried their trash all the time.

Satisfied, she carefully returned the excavated soil into its rightful resting place. She smoothed and patted the surface, then spread fallen leaves across it.

There.

No one would ever suspect that barely a foot beneath that seemingly undisturbed spot lay the final pieces of a puzzle that to this day, fifteen years later, had not been solved. She shivered.

Grabbing the shovel and flashlight, she pushed to her feet. The past wasn't important right now. What mattered was the present. And the future. Protection, survival, those were the key elements.

She had learned from experience that survival was the only thing that really counted.

She intended to survive.

Cautiously retracing her steps through the trees and dense underbrush, she reached the side road where she'd left her car. After scanning cautiously for any sign of approaching headlights, she moved more quickly.

She was almost home free.

Just one last detail to take care of and this bothersome night would be behind her.

The tools grasped firmly under one arm, she dug the keys from the pocket of her jeans and opened the trunk. The accessory light flickered once then steadied, filling the trunk with a dim, eerie glow. She tossed the shovel and flashlight inside and should have closed the lid then. That would have been the smart thing to do. But she didn't.

Instead, she stared at the one remaining obstacle in this monumental mess that required her immediate attention.

The body.

She had to figure out what to do with the body.